ANNIE MURRAY

Soldier Girl

MACMILLAN

First published 2010 by Macmillan
an imprint of Pan Macmillan, a division of Macmillan Publishers Limited
Pan Macmillan, 20 New Wharf Road, London N1 9RR
Basingstoke and Oxford
Associated companies throughout the world
www.panmacmillan.com

ISBN 978-0-230-70947-8

1 3 5 7 9 8 6 4 2

A CIP catalogue record for this book is available from
the British Library.

Typeset by SetSystems Ltd, Saffron Walden, Essex
Printed in the UK by CPI Mackays, Chatham ME5 8TD

Soldier Girl

ALSO BY ANNIE MURRAY

Birmingham Rose

Birmingham Friends

Birmingham Blitz

Orphan of Angel Street

Poppy Day

The Narrowboat Girl

Chocolate Girls

Water Gypsies

Miss Purdy's Class

Family of Women

Where Earth Meets Sky

The Bells of Bournville Green

A Hopscotch Summer

Acknowledgements

This is the sort of story that requires a very large number of small pieces of information, so my sources have been varied. But I owe some particular thanks. First to Dorothy Brewer Kerr for her memoir *The Girls Behind the Guns*, to Margaret Dady for *A Woman's War*, and once again to Eric Taylor for *Women Who Went to War, 1938–1946*. Angus Calder's social history of the Second World War, *The People's War*, was of assistance, as was Donald Thomas's *An Underworld at War*. The BBC's large online archive of oral testimonies on World War II has also been invaluable.

My special thanks also to Eric Hill and the other lovely members of the Heartlands Local History Society, based at Nechells Green Community Centre in Birmingham.

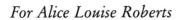

For Alice Louise Roberts

Reveille

One

December 1940

Molly was sitting on a bench at the back of the rowdy pub, squeezed in beside George, the bloke she was walking out with, and a bunch of others, nearly all men. She'd had so much to drink that all the faces were blurring into each other, like in a bad dream. Behind her, the windows were swathed in black. George was a pale, stringy man, his hair slicked back, eyes mean and glassy after all the drinking. His mood had turned ugly.

'You're not worth it. You're no good, you ain't,' he snarled. 'I want a proper woman, not a freak like you . . .'

Right, Molly thought. *I'm off!* She stubbed out her cigarette and pulled herself up from the table, making it rock, the way her head was rocking inside.

'Whoa – steady on, yer silly cow! You'll 'ave everything going over!'

'You off, Moll?' a kinder voice asked from among the crowd. 'Mind 'ow yer go. D'yer want someone to walk with yer?'

'No,' she managed to say. 'Ta, Fred.'

'You don't want to go with 'er,' George sneered. 'You don't know what yer might catch!'

Cursing under her breath, Molly pushed past George,

holding on to the backs of chairs, desperate to get out now. The mocking voices followed her.

'Look at the state of 'er!'

'D'yer think 'er'll make it 'ome?'

'Crying shame ain't it, with 'er looks? Could've been a beauty queen.'

Molly pushed the door too hard and almost fell outside, spilling light onto the pavement.

'Get that door shut – we'll 'ave that sodding warden round else! *Don't you know there's a war on . . . ?*'

'It's a miracle the siren ain't gone off yet tonight . . .'

The air was damp and shockingly cold after the sweaty fug of the pub. Molly rallied and kicked the door shut so that the frame shuddered.

'Bugger the lot of yer!' she tried to yell. She wanted to shout a whole lot of other things which boiled up inside her, but all that came out was a mumbled stream of rubbish.

She felt terrible suddenly, her insides heaving. Thinking she was about to be sick she leaned back against the pub wall groaning, breathing in gulps of air to try and stop it. After a few moments the nausea subsided, but the sickness in her belly was nothing compared with that in her heart. The mocking voices echoed in her head. *Course, you only 'ave to look at that mother of 'ers.* George's face, twisted with contempt. She closed her eyes, leaning into the pub wall. Loathing filled her: for all of them in there, for the mean, bomb-damaged Birmingham streets, the mizzling rain, and most of all for herself. Filthy, fast, ugly little Molly Fox. For she did feel small out there, all alone under the night sky. All alone with what Iris had said to her, what she'd blurted out that evening . . .

'Must get along . . . I'm *not drunk* . . .' she insisted to an invisible audience.

The street was deserted. The others in the pub were waiting for time to be called. Staggering, Molly felt her way along holding on to walls, rebounding off them as her legs took her in unexpected directions. A jittering finger of light passed by on the other side of the street and she realized it was a torch. For a second its light flickered over the white-painted edge of the pavement.

'Hey you!' she shouted. 'You cowing well stop and listen to me!' She wagged a finger furiously at the departing light. She didn't know exactly what she wanted from them except that they should do what she ordered. But they were gone, ignoring her. Rage bubbled up in her, then seeped away, leaving her desolate. Thoughts came and went, but she couldn't hold on to them.

It was too quiet. Houses were muffled in black. She caught the low sound of voices, the murmur of a wireless, then silence as she passed the deep darkness of the warehouses. More houses afterwards, where she grazed her knee on a jutting bit of wall, tearing her stocking. She yelped and cursed. Why was it so quiet? She'd better start singing, that was the thing. Forget. Forget everything.

'When you wish upon a sta-a-ar!' she bawled, lurchingly. 'Makes no . . .'

Her foot went down into nothingness and her body followed, overbalancing and crashing down into the road. Her shoulder, then her hip, hit the ground hard.

'Aaagh!' Molly cried furiously. 'What d'yer go and do that for?' She let out a string of curses.

Rolling on to her back she examined the situation from this new angle. The ground was hard and wet, and something was digging into her, but it felt like a rest

5

after trying to stay upright. She shifted, trying to get a bit more comfortable, and looked up into the gloom. Up there were the bloated barrage balloons to keep the evil black planes away. Bombs, bombs – but not tonight.

'But there'll be a raid – there will,' she informed the street loudly. 'Wipe us all out, punish us . . .'

Other stray thoughts popped out of her mouth and then more singing. There were things she had to say. Big things. Everyone had to know. She started singing 'I'm Gonna Lock My Heart and Throw Away the Key', loud and clear. She knew all the words, and put her heart and soul into it, broadcasting to the street at the top of her voice. It sounded fantastic – better than Ella Fitzgerald or Joe Loss's band. She sang her heart out, so much so that she didn't notice the shards of brick under her head and the hard road; she sang away the shadows, sang fit to burst!

Her performance drowned out the footsteps hurrying towards her along the road until suddenly a face loomed over her and she was so startled, she screamed.

'For goodness' sake – *shut up*, Molly!' a voice said heatedly. 'I could hear you a mile off. What the hell d'you think you're playing at?'

The face came into focus and Molly recognized her old school pal Emma Brown, who lived somewhere round here. The face was topped by a tin hat of the sort Molly was turning out in the factory where she worked.

'Hello, Em!' Molly cried amiably, at the top of her voice. She giggled. 'What're you doing 'ere? And why're you wearing one of them hats?'

'For heaven's sake, Molly, I'm a warden – you know that. I'm on duty! Now get up and stop making such an exhibition of yourself. You'll keep half the street awake making that racket!'

Molly felt her arm being tugged determinedly, and she resisted, stung by Em's commanding tone. Just because she was a stuck-up ARP warden these days, with her boring bloke and her perfect little life. Who did she think she was, bossing everyone around?

'Come on, Molly – I've got to get you home. Get up!'

'Don't want to.' Molly yanked on Em's arm and almost pulled her down with her. She was bigger and stronger than Em. 'I'm gunna stay here and sing. Can if I want to.'

'No, you can't!' Em panted, trying to stay on her feet. 'Just get up or I'll have to get a copper to help! D'you want to spend a night in the cells?'

'Oh, you mean nice, normal Norm, I suppose?' Molly sneered. The boy Em was courting was in the police. 'Gorgeous, dashing Norm.'

Em leaned down and snapped in Molly's face, 'Just get up, all right? Before I slap you one.'

'I'm getting up – see?' Molly tried to retain some dignity. She could sense that Em was not going to give up, and started staggering to her feet, mumbling resentfully. 'You've always thought you were better than me, haven't you? Always think you can look down your nose at me . . .'

'Oh don't be so *ridiculous*, Molly!' Em finally lost her temper. 'It's not to do with looking down on anyone. What d'you expect me to do when you're lying in the gutter drunk as a lord and caterwauling loud enough to wake up the whole neighbourhood? What the hell d'you think you're playing at getting in that state?'

'I dunno,' Molly said, suddenly tearful. 'Will you take my arm, Em? You've always been my best pal, you have. D'you know that? You were the only one I could ever turn to. You're golden, you are, not like me – I'm dirty, I am. I'm disgusting. Soiled goods. Not like you – you're golden . . .'

'Yes, all right – just take my arm,' Em said impatiently. 'Let's get you home. You can sleep it off and let's hope you've got a bit more sense in you by the morning.'

Though Molly had not realized it when she had stumbled to the ground, she had done so close to the end of Kenilworth Street, where Em lived and was a warden. It was only a short walk, across Great Lister Street, to her own house.

'Go on – get yourself to bed,' Em said, seeing her to the door with weary patience. 'You're going to feel bad tomorrow.'

'Thanks, Em,' Molly said, too loudly. She turned and tried to wave at Em and almost fell out through the door again. 'You're my best, best friend.'

'Get to bed,' Em said. 'And try not to wake up the whole flaming house while you're at it or you really will be for it.'

Em watched, intensely relieved as the door closed behind Molly. She straightened her hat – not the most comfortable of headgear – and set off, picking her way carefully along the road. With all the raids they'd had on Birmingham, everywhere was in such a state you had to watch your step. She tutted to herself. She'd only come along to have a word with the warden in the neighbouring street and ended up with all that pantomime of Molly's!

As usual, Molly aroused in her a sharp mixture of

emotions – fondness and sympathy mingled with impatience and a degree of revulsion. It had been that way ever since they were snotty-nosed kids together. Em was the popular one, the sensible one, while Molly was smelly and unkempt, always hovering on the edge of groups in the street or playground, struggling to be accepted. And was it surprising with a family like Molly's? Em shuddered at the very thought of Iris Fox, Molly's drunken, slovenly mother. As for that brother of hers, Bert, with his crooked, rat-eyed face. And the other men folk! Molly had never truly had a home, but had done moonlight flits from one bug-ridden back-to-back house to another to dodge the rent, scratching out a life somehow. When you thought about it, it was a wonder Molly wasn't far worse. She had a good heart despite it all. But if she'd only take a bit of pride in herself – learn to speak a bit better, for one thing. Em's mom had always nagged her to put her aitches on and watch her language. But what had Molly been on about tonight? *I'm dirty* ... Em put it down to the drink. After all, God knew, she thought, heavy-hearted, they'd all had their troubles! Troubles which never seemed to end, and which in her own family had fallen heavily on her, with Mom's mental state ever uncertain, always up and down, so that Em had grown up doubling as a mom to Sid and Joyce and Violet, trying to keep the family together, always having to be strong and adult before her time. It's not as if anything had been easy for her, either.

'That you, Em?' She heard Mr Radcliff's voice before she saw him. She felt very much the junior in the group of ARP wardens, not yet being quite eighteen, but of all of them, Mr Radcliff was the kindest to her in a fatherly way.

'Yes, it's me. You must have eyes like a cat – I never saw you!'

'Oh, that's me – eat plenty of carrots!' he chuckled. 'Doing all right are yer? A quiet night it looks like tonight, thank God. Jerry must be turning his attention somewhere else for once. We'll go and have a cuppa in a tick, shall we?'

'Yes, all right.'

'Did I hear a bit of a racket earlier? Pubs coming out? I s'pose they're getting into the Christmas spirit.'

'They're out now,' Em said, hearing voices at the other end of the street. A ragged rendering of 'Good King Wenceslas' drifted towards them then died in hasty shushing. 'It was just a bit of carry on – someone had a bit too much, you know.'

'Oh, ar. There's always one. So, shall us go and get the kettle on?'

Mr Radcliff liked to make tea and stand in the street drinking it, keeping an eye on everything. Em held the welcome warmth of the mug close to her chin and sipped the sweet brew. There was something very re-assuring about Mr Radcliff. They talked about the raids. They hadn't half had some nights – really frightening, with the sirens going, searchlights knifing across the sky, having to be out in it when the bombs were coming down, putting incendiaries out and trying to make sure everyone was under cover. It had started in August over Brum and there had been at least one really bad raid every month and others in between. Some nights the sirens were going on and off all night and the morning found them all exhausted, sick with nerves and tiredness and emerging fearfully to see what the damage was and whether there'd be any water to brew a cuppa. The centre of Birmingham was deeply scarred and many of the neighbourhoods too, especially the ones like theirs, the districts of Nechells, Vauxhall, Duddesdon, close to the centre. After the last lot the King himself had come and walked round nearby Aston, talking to people.

'Your young man coming to see yer tonight?' Mr Radcliff asked, taking Em's empty mug.

'Oh I s'pect so – he's doing a split shift tonight,' Em said shyly. For a year now she and Norm had been courting. He was a few months her senior. He usually came to find her and say hello whenever she was on duty, if he got the chance. It made her ever so proud when he did that, turning up in his police uniform.

'Nice lad,' Mr Radcliff remarked. 'You want to hold on to him.'

Em blushed in the darkness, though it was nice to hear someone praising Norm. She thought he was wonderful – certainly the best thing to happen to her in a long time – even if Joyce teased her and said Norm was like a clown with his two left feet and sticky-out ears. Em would get cross and upset with her until Mom said, 'That's just sisters – don't you take any notice.' He was sweet to her and he loved her and told her so earnestly, looking at her with his sincere hazel eyes, and that was all she needed to know.

'Better get back,' Mr Radcliff said.

'Ta for the tea – I needed that,' Em said.

She made her way back to Kenilworth Street, thinking about Molly again. Molly had a factory job, but she was in with a bad crowd, always off with some bloke, round the pubs. It had been sad, seeing how she was tonight. She couldn't go on the way she was.

With a sense of dread, Em thought, *What's going to become of you, Molly?*

Two

Molly woke the next morning with a thumping head-
ache, an urgently full bladder, and a sense of complete
despair. There were a few seconds before she remembered, and then it all came flooding back, what had
happened last night, Mom's vile words, her running out
to George, the pub. Of what she'd done after that, she
could only remember glimpses. Hadn't she ended up
lying in the street? And hadn't her old friend Em been
in it somewhere?

And what Mom had said. Molly turned on to her back,
the bedsprings squeaking loudly, and put her hands over
her face. Even the dim light from the window seemed to
knife into her eyes.

'Oh God,' she groaned. In that moment she truly
wanted to die, just be swallowed up in darkness for
ever, away from pain and shame. She felt too sick and
desperate even to cry.

But she was going to have to get up. It was either
that or wet the bed. Groggily, she hauled herself upright
until her magnificent frame was perched uneasily on the
side of the bed, and surveyed her options. Either she
could go and relieve herself in the shared privy, which
meant going out into the street and walking all the way
round the back – the way she was feeling this morning,
that seemed like walking to the ends of the earth – or
she could use the chamber pot by her mom's bed,

already half full of a bronze-coloured, stinking liquid. Her innards bucked at the thought.

The sight of the po, and the bare boards, and the crumbling walls of the room, and the even more depressing sight of the heaped mound of Iris, her mother, snoring intermittently on the other bed, did nothing to raise her spirits. Dear God, couldn't things ever get better? They'd always been rotten, ever since she could remember, and they were never going to improve with Iris and Joe pouring almost every penny that came into the house down their necks, that was for sure. When was she ever going to get out of here?

Anger drove her to her feet, and it only dawned on her then that she was still fully dressed. She stared down at herself bemused, trying to recall going to bed. She must have come in and flung herself straight down. Still, that settled it – all she had to put on was her shoes. Pushing her feet into them she winced, cursing. Looking down, she saw her lisle stockings were all torn and there was blood on her left heel. So she started shuffling along on the backs of them.

For a moment she stopped beside Iris. Her mother was forty-six years old and looked twenty years older. Molly stared down at her, seeing a big-boned woman who had once been statuesque, though she was now well past her finest. Her large frame, which Molly knew she had inherited, was upholstered with thick layers of fat. Iris lay on her back, one plump arm splayed over the side of the bed, her immense breasts only just contained by a torn camisole which had aged to a yellowish grey. As she shifted in the bed a rank and sweaty smell wafted up. Her head was turned to one side, pressing on the rolls of fat under her chin; her faded brown hair was still roughly pinned up in her distinctive topknot, though much of the hair had worked loose in her sleep and had gathered into a frizz. Iris's thick lips were parted, those lips which had spat out vile secrets to Molly last night. Snores rattled in the back of her throat.

She looks like a pig, she is *a pig . . .* Molly stared at Iris's rounded nose and pugnacious nostrils. But in the prominent cheekbones and long neck she could see her own inheritance of features. The main difference was her hair, which was thick and blonde. *Where did that come from?* she wondered bitterly. But heaven forbid she should end up like Mom with her coarse, broken-veined skin and liver spots already showing on her cheeks and red nose – like *him*. Molly clenched her fists. She felt like killing the great fat sow, breaking the chamber pot and its stinking contents over her head. She started to shake with anger and loathing.

Iris's eyes opened, narrow and piggy between dark lashes, the whites bloodshot from a life of drinking. That was all they did now, she and Joe, they drank and drank, courtesy of Molly's wages and Bert's.

Iris struggled to focus, frowning with confusion. 'Molly – that you? Make us a cuppa will yer? Don't feel too good.' The eyes closed, and in seconds she was snoring again.

A hand over her heaving stomach, Molly crept down the bare boards of the stairs. The house had one room downstairs with a tiny scullery at the back and two upstairs. Bert had the other room when he deigned to come home at all, and wild horses wouldn't drag her into sharing a room with him, the filthy bugger. She'd sleep in the coal hole rather than go anywhere near him. After all, he'd had the perfect grandfather to learn his dirty tricks from, hadn't he?

Downstairs, Joe was asleep in his chair by the dead fire and the room was very cold. He had an old blanket over his knees. Molly tiptoed past, seeing his almost hairless head tilted to one side, the scalp dotted with downy tufts of grey. She couldn't bear to look at his face, and not only because she knew how it would be: the drooping, toothless mouth, his defeated, old man's face even though he was only a year older than Iris. Unlike Iris, he had always been able to arouse tenderness in Molly. She couldn't remember him before the Great War, back in those innocent days when he was sprightly and fit and had even been able to play the piano. They'd actually owned a piano back then, she'd been told, though it'd been sold long since, after Joe had come back from France a wreck, his nerves and health shattered and his younger self buried in the mud with his dead comrades. Molly had often wondered what kind of man he would have been had he never gone to war, had married a different wife, had had a chance. Time after time she had been told of his decency as a young man, his intelligence, and she had clung to these stories. 'He were a good lad, yer father was,' those who remembered would say. 'A kind-hearted, decent fella, and he could sing and play lovely. Such a shame...' She had seldom seen anything of this, except for a kindly gleam in his more usually vacant eyes. But she had clung to that image in hope for the best she might have in herself. Maybe she was like him, not like Mom, she had often desperately hoped. *I don't have to end up like her*, she used to tell herself.

But today she would not look at Joe. Joe Fox – some man she lived with, but not Dad. A stranger, in terms of blood. She went to the mantelpiece for the privy key, tied to a cotton reel, and went outside, down the narrow entry and round to the yard on to which faced five back houses. Molly's own house was at the front of these. She slunk across the yard with her head down and her arms folded, not wanting to speak to anyone. Someone was in the brew house where the washing was done, steam curling out from the water heating in the copper. Two raggedy kids were playing outside, waiting for their mother. Normally Molly was friendly, and it was a nice yard, much better than some they'd lived on. It was clean and people were decent to her, felt sorry for her, most likely. But today she was too upset for friendliness.

All three toilets were occupied and she waited until a chain flushed and a woman came out of one, holding the door open.

'All right Molly? You ain't looking so good this morning. Bit of a night, was it?' She went off, chuckling.

Molly bolted herself inside the smelly privy, sinking on to the already warm wooden seat with a sigh – a combination of both physical relief and deep inner despair. The sight of the crudely built brick walls between which she was perched and the roughly cut squares of newspaper hanging from a nail on the back of the door dragged her down even further.

Surely to God there must be something better than this. There *had* to be ... She felt absolutely at rock bottom.

A thought came then, as if someone had shone a bright light in her head.

I'm not staying here any longer. I've got to get out if it's the last thing I do. I'll sink into the mud, else. And a second later, she had the answer. *I know – I'm going to join up!*

Three

What had set Molly off was what had happened the previous night.

She had always been restless about jobs, moving from firm to firm, easily bored. Her latest was in a factory in Vauxhall which had gone over to the war effort, making tin hats and jerry cans and other war needs that could be bashed out of metal.

Last night she'd worked on late to finish a batch and hurried home in the dark, tense, like everyone else, waiting in fear of the sirens going off. No one wanted to get stuck in a raid, having to get off the bus and find a shelter or risk it, depending whether the bus driver was prepared to go on or not. Some nights the raids began early and were on and off all night. You just never knew.

It had already been a dull grey day and the darkness was of a heavy, cloaking kind with a lid of cloud. No bomber's moon at least. It was hard to hurry in the blackout. Molly got off the bus with a weary heart and wended her way carefully along the dark Nechells streets. It was an old, poor neighbourhood, close to the heart of the city, which had suffered a lot of raids. So far, though, no one they knew had been bombed out. But the Buttons worried Molly to death. Stanley and Jenny Button lived a few streets away and were the kindest people Molly knew. Jenny Button had taken her in as a child, when Iris's behaviour to Molly had forced her to run away. Molly loved the two of them far more than she did her family. They had always been so kind to her, had shown her that life doesn't have to consist of cruelty and neglect. Stanley was an invalid and couldn't walk, but the two of them flatly refused to have anything to do with going into any sort of shelter.

'Stanley and me will take our chances where we are, in our own home,' Jenny Button said with dignity. 'We're not having those Jerries forcing us into some godforsaken cellar.'

There was no arguing with them. Molly knew that quite a few older people took this attitude. Every time there was a raid Molly rushed round to see if they were all right.

The walk home seemed to take ages. It had been a long day, her left shoe was rubbing her heel raw so that she was limping, and there was no telling what she'd find at home.

'I bet the fire won't even be lit,' she muttered resentfully, 'let alone anything on for tea.'

Practically everything in the house was now left to her. Iris could hardly bestir herself to get down to the shops for groceries these days. It was rationing that had finished her off.

'I can't do with all them stupid coupons and that,' she complained as soon as the system was introduced. 'You and Bert'll have to do it, Molly. You're the clever ones.'

Molly was enraged by this. Clever ones? Since when had Mom ever taken any notice of whether she was clever or not? It was just a marvellous excuse for Iris to sit on her backside and do even less than she did already except devote herself to her dearest friend, the bottle.

Molly could predict exactly how she'd find them tonight, Iris and Joe. (Never again would she call them Mom and Dad. When had either of them been a mother or father to her?) They'd be either side of the cold range, he half asleep, muttering to himself. Iris would be tanked up and aggressive, ready to pick a fight with the very draught under the door. Not a thing would have been done in the house, no shopping or cleaning up. As for Bert, they never knew from one day to the next whether he'd be there or not. Molly pulled her old brown-and-white-weave coat round her as if to shield herself from this squalid sight. She'd be so ashamed for anyone to come to the house. They never had callers: Iris had long ago frightened off anyone who might have set foot in there and no one knew what to say to Joe. His old cronies who had come years back to visit out of pity had long ago melted away. Fair enough, the number of moonlight flits the family had done to evade the rent meant it was hard for anyone to keep up. But now they were back in the district and settled, and still no one came. *What a shower*, Molly thought furiously. Why had she ended up in such a rotten, useless family? No wonder her older brother Tom had got out as soon as he could. It had been more than four years now since anyone had heard from him.

At least the house they were in now was a bit better. During the worst years, before she and Bert started work, they had lived in squalid, bug-ridden places, sometimes having the chance to move their few sticks of furniture with a handcart, sometimes, nothing. The worst time, they'd rented two rooms on the ground floor of a house, sleeping on straw mattresses on the floor, waking up a mass of flea bites. Since then things had come on a bit. With her and Bert out at work there were two lots of wages, and lately Bert had extra money about him, though she wasn't sure how he came by it. Probably they only saw a tiny fraction of it too, knowing him. But he had got hold of a wireless from somewhere, which graced the downstairs room, even though Iris mostly snored in front of it.

The front door was closed against the cold, but she could see the light was on inside. At least the street had electric lighting now, even though they still cooked on the old coal-fired range. She pushed the door open, letting out the usual odours of must and booze.

''Bout time you got 'ere.' Iris's voice assailed her before she was even inside the door. 'Where the 'ell've yer been?'

'Had to work over.' Molly shut the door, thankfully slipped off her shoes from her freezing feet and rubbed her sore left heel. 'There's a war on, in case you hadn't noticed.'

'Don't you be lippy with me,' Iris snarled. 'Bert's been in an hour and 'e brought some pigs' liver. You need to get on and get the tea.'

She never knew exactly what it was that had set Iris off that night, why then and not some other time. She was already spoiling for a fight though, that was clear. As Molly straightened up, she took a few moments to absorb the strange sight in front of her. Iris and Joe were, as expected, ensconced by the fire – nothing unusual in that – except that it was alight for once. The reason for this was also obvious: standing by the table in the crowded little room with his back to her was Bert, and Bert felt the cold.

He had not even turned to look at her. His skinny back, always slightly bowed – he never stood quite straight – was bent over the table. His shirtsleeves were rolled up and Molly noticed the sharp points of his elbows.

In front of him, covering the whole table, was a selection of objects which made the house look like a pawn shop.

'What's all this?'

Looking more closely, she saw a strange collection of things. There were ornaments, a china sheep, two clocks – one in a wooden case, one brass – a silver hand mirror, pretty and valuable looking ('What's this doing here? Where on earth did you get that?'), a hessian bag, wooden shoe trees, a rusty old biscuit tin and even a set of false teeth.

As she rifled through the things on the table, Bert's head turned sharply towards her, eyes narrowed. She thought how mean he looked, how unhealthy and cruel, with his mousy hair slicked back, his pasty face and extreme thinness which made him look sharp and pinched. There were angry pink spots on his chin and he smelt pungently of stale sweat.

Molly picked up the old biscuit tin, surprised by its weight. 'What's in here?'

Bert watched as she struggled to pull off the lid, a smug, calculating expression on his face.

'Ooh, see – she's interested now,' Iris said nastily.

A horrible suspicion was already forming in Molly's mind, confirmed when she managed to yank the lid off the tin, to find it more than half full of money. It was a mixture of change, mostly coppers, bitter smelling and green with age, shillings, and half crowns, but there were ten-bob notes in there too, and sitting crisply on the top, two pound notes. Molly gasped.

'What's this, Bert? Who the hell's is it?'

Iris raised her voice. 'Why don't you get the kettle on, and bloody hurry up. We want our tea!'

Molly knew there was something about this that was all wrong. Bombed-out houses made for rich pickings.

'This is someone's savings, isn't it?' she kept on. 'And this, I'll bet—' She picked up the old hessian bag, which gave off a sound of clinking coins. 'Where d'you get all this stuff?'

'Where d'yer think?' Bert sneered. He said most things with a sneer.

Molly looked wildly across the collection of possessions. 'You've never . . . Not . . . You *wouldn't* . . .'

'Wouldn't I? Why not? This stuff ain't gunna be any good to them where they've gone is it?'

Molly didn't notice Iris struggling to get out of her chair.

'You mean—' She tried to take this in. 'You've been sneaking into people's houses after they've been bombed out – pinching their things? How could you? What if – I mean, they could still have been in there, injured or anything, and you'd just go in and steal off them!'

'Hard cheese!' Bert gave his snickering laugh. 'Should've gone down the shelter then, shouldn't they?' he went on gleefully. 'It's all out there waiting. You go out, same night or the night after. Couple of sacks. Go somewhere where there's a bit of lolly about. Keep out the way of the fuzz, and those nosy bloody wardens. Early morning's the best – four or five. You can get more of a scout round without someone bothering yer. The dead 'uns don't take no notice!'

Molly was so appalled that it was a few seconds before she could say, 'I can't believe *you* could do anything so *wicked* . . . Even *you* . . .'

Iris shuffled over and stood holding the back of one of the chairs. She was wearing a big purple frock, her belly pushing it out at the front, with stains all down it. There was a strange, leering expression on her face.

'You're *vile*, Bert.' Molly felt like spitting, as if to get rid of the taste of him, far more bitter than the smell of old pennies. This was the worst yet. There was his bullying, sadistic nature, and then the gross maulings she'd suffered from him which he'd learned first-hand from their late grandfather, Old Man Rathbone, Iris's father. William Rathbone, who died when Molly was ten, had taken out his filthy masturbatory desires on her up until his final illness, and Bert had then set out to do the same – would have done worse in fact, had Molly not fought him off. Things had changed then. Jenny Button had taken her to see that doctor, and that had made Molly stronger. But she had hated Bert nearly all of her life, and at this moment she felt more contempt and loathing for him than ever before.

'You're just muck, you are, you're lower than a worm. I'm ashamed to be anywhere near you. I can't stand the fact that you're my brother.'

Iris, seeming excited by their fight, let out a blaring laugh. 'Oh, 'e's yer brother all right – make no mistake.' She leaned her hip against the chair, her weight on one foot, the other knee bent, in an oddly seductive pose. 'There's summat you've got in common at least. All three of us 'ave, come to think of it ... You both 'ad the same father, anyroad. Only shame was 'e ain't been alive to see the two of yer grow up.'

Molly and Bert were momentarily united then, if only in staring at her.

'What d'yer mean by that?' Bert snarled.

Iris laid her hand coquettishly on her thick waist. She

spoke with relish, as if delivering a juicy morsel of gossip.

'You didn't think you were the first one 'e ever messed with, did yer, Molly?'

Hearing her words felt like a blow. Molly could scarcely breathe. It was as if her body had shut down, was paralysed. To hear her shame tripped out so casually, and to realize Iris had known of it all that time, when she had never said a word about it before and never raised a finger to stop him, hadn't cared a jot in fact! But Iris hadn't finished. Swaying, she pointed towards Joe, who was sitting dumbly. It was hard to tell if he was listening.

'You don't think that wreck of a man could sire a child do yer? Didn't you ever wonder about that? The old man had been at me for years, even before my mother passed on. That's what 'e was like, see?' She made a sinuous movement with her hips that made Molly's lips curl in revulsion. ''E liked young girls, daint 'e, see?'

Neither Molly nor Bert could speak. But at last Bert said, choking, 'What – me an' all?'

'You an' all, Bertie. The old man was your father as well as your grandfather.' She delivered the words harshly, almost with pride. 'That makes us all brothers and sisters then, don't it?'

Molly leaned on the table. Her father – no, not her father! – *Joe* was making coughing noises as if trying to speak. 'I – I – I don't . . . don't . . .' he began. No one took any notice.

'But *why* . . .' In her outrage the words were hard to form. 'Why didn't you stop him? Why didn't you keep him off me? You made me share a room with him even though I begged you . . .' Her voice rose, but she swal-

24

lowed, determined not to weep. What sympathy would she ever get? 'You knew – you knew he was my *father*.'

'Well, there was no stopping 'im, that was the point.' Iris sounded indifferent now. This casualness was worst of all. 'And anyroad, it gave me a rest from 'im. I told yer – 'e liked young girls. And you 'ad it easy. By then he was beginning to get a bit past it – not like when he was young. 'E never gave you a bun in the oven, did 'e? You just had the fag end of it, that's all . . .'

Bert turned away suddenly, but as he did so, Molly caught a glimpse of his face. His movements were taut with revulsion, but she realized he was very close to tears, that her brother, for the first time since infancy, was showing signs of vulnerable emotion. He snatched up the hessian bag and pushed past Iris.

'Well, you 'ad to know sometime,' she yelled at him as the front door closed behind him. She tutted. 'What the 'ell's the matter with 'im? And look at all this junk. How're we s'posed to eat our tea? You get on with it, Molly.'

Molly seized the set of teeth from the table and hurled them as hard as she could at Iris.

'You can cook your own liver, you filthy old cow!'

Forcing her feet into the shoes again and seizing her coat, she slammed out into the street. In the distance she could just make out the shape of Bert, disappearing round the corner.

Four

'Molly – *Molly Fox!* We're going on our break – you coming or what?'

Molly was still stacking the tin helmets, lifting them down from the rack on which they'd been sprayed and piling them one upon another.

'Oh – sorry!' She looked up, dazed. 'I was miles away!'

'Yeah – we could see ... Come on. I don't know about you, but I'm starving.'

Molly followed the other two girls out for a cup of tea. Even now, though years had passed since a childhood of being singled out for exclusion, she was still surprised to be included, that the other girls seemed to like her. All her young life she had got used to being left out, being the butt of jokes and name-calling, smelly little Molly Fox with her raw eczema skin, her strange clothes and whiff of wee. It had got a bit better as she got older, and she and Em had stayed friends after all their childhood troubles. Once she got out to work in the factory she found they accepted her, with her pretty looks and obliging nature. She had learned not to fawn on others to gain their affection, and she found she had a sense of humour – it worked especially well if directed against herself. None of them knew anything about her home, her life outside the factory, and she kept it that way.

The girls took their mugs of tea and went and stood in the yard outside, where they could smoke as well, all of them dressed in thick navy dungarees, hair taken back in snoods. They all lit up, except Gladys, who patted her pockets, frowning.

'Can yer spare us one, Mol? I've gone and left mine on the kitchen table.'

Molly offered her packet of Silk Cut.

'Ta. I'll pay yer back.'

'No need,' Molly said easily.

They leaned up against the blackened bricks of the factory, eyes watering in the winter sun and cold breeze, smoke snatched from between their lips. The talk as ever was about raids. Gladys, who was a giggler, regaled them with more of her family's adventures with the Anderson shelter at the bottom of their handkerchief of a garden. Its construction had been an epic effort, her dad not being much on the practical side. The fact that they had a dog always seemed to be causing some trouble – it ate their tea when they dashed into the shelter, leaving the half-eaten meal on the table. And last night the dog – a manic terrier – got in the shelter with them and spent the night pouncing on their arms and legs, mistaking them for rats. Gladys, with her chesty laugh, was always full of stories and kept every-one cheerful.

Today, though, Molly was barely listening. She laughed when everyone else laughed, smoked, and drank the strong, sweet tea, but already she felt miles away from them all. As soon as she'd decided about joining up – the army, the ATS, that was the place for her – she felt different and strong, the strongest she'd ever been, as if she could do anything. What her mother had told her, the awful, revolting truth, was folded away in her mind, not forgotten, just pushed aside. Rather than wallowing in the shock and shame of it, instead she had picked out an escape route. She felt she was standing in a high place, way above them all, Iris and Joe, Bert, and William Rathbone, her dead grandfather, the whole foul bloody shower of them. But she was going to get out, oh yes she was! The way she felt now, she could stride across the world like a giant!

Em's family were still in the same house in Kenilworth Street where they had always lived, just down the road from the school Molly and Em had attended, and almost opposite the Buttons' place, where Jenny Button was still struggling to run a bakery from the front room, using the brew house to bake in.

When Molly stood on the Browns' front step, it always brought back to her being seven or eight years old again and going round to ask Em to play out, always steeling herself against being rejected. It brought back vivid memories of knocking during those dark times when Em's mom Cynthia was sent away to the asylum, when Em, a scared waif, would peer out through a crack in the door, terrified in case it was the School Board man. She'd been kept away from school to run the house for Bob and her brother and sisters when she was scarcely tall enough to see over the scullery sink. Molly wondered what state Cynthia was in now – she was up and down in cycles, had been ever since, poor woman. She never did anyone any harm though, just sunk into herself, and she was always all right to Molly.

It was Em who answered her knock. She had very straight, mousy hair which she tried to tease into waves and curls, but by this time of day they were always dropping out and her hair fell in straight hanks on her shoulders. She was slim, like a reed, always fragile-looking and pale in the face. It was Molly who had grown up taller, big and robust-looking like Iris, but without Iris's thuggish features.

Em gave a wary smile. 'Molly! All right are you? What're you doing here?'

'Just come to see you,' Molly said. 'I've got summat to tell yer.'

She could see Em sizing her up and deciding she was sober enough to be let in. Molly had only the vaguest memory of what had happened on Saturday night, though she knew Em had been in it somewhere. But she was too excited to get embarrassed about that now.

'You'd best come in,' Em said, standing back to open the door. 'I've not got long – I'm just getting my tea down me before I go on duty. It's Molly!' she added, calling through to the family. 'She's just popping in for a minute.'

They went through to the back, where the family were all round the table – plus Norm, Em's young man.

'Hello, Molly,' Cynthia greeted her kindly. 'How're you, love? We haven't seen you in a while.'

Cynthia was looking well, Molly saw, smiling back at her. She met Molly's gaze; there was a pinkness to her cheeks and her dark brown hair was pinned up, the fringe waved back from her forehead. Things were all right. Over the years they had all learned to read the signs. When she was feeling bad, Cynthia looked pale, her face twisted with inner pain, her hair usually un-kempt, and she would go silent, shut herself away, unable to look anyone in the eye.

'I'm all right,' Molly said, as Bob, Em's dad, nodded at her. Sid, now sixteen, kept on shovelling his tea down

29

him as if it were a race. Joyce, fourteen and always full of it, gave Molly a wink, and little Violet, the babby, aged nine, rather thin and like Em in looks, stared, fascinated by the sight of Molly.

'D'you wear them to work?' she asked, staring at Molly's dungarees.

'Yes—' Molly twirled round, in a mocking pose. 'Ever so flattering, eh?'

Bob Brown stood up. ''Ere, I've finished. You can 'ave my chair.'

'Oh – ta, if you're sure,' Molly said. Bob seemed thankful to be away. 'I'm just going out for a bit...' he said vaguely, and vanished pubwards.

Molly slid onto the chair beside Joyce, who grinned at her and moved her father's plate away with its smeared remains of gravy. Sid was wiping up the last of his with a piece of bread.

Em had sat down again next to Norm, who Molly thought was looking at her warily as well. I suppose he thinks I'm a bad lot, Molly thought. *Drunk and disorderly.* She didn't take to Norm. There was something so goody-goody and stuffy about him – and those ears! They were prominent and pink from the cold.

'All right, Norm?' she said teasingly. 'Caught any bank robbers today?'

'There aren't many out there robbing banks,' he said stiffly. He was only nineteen but seemed ten years older.

'Shame,' Molly said. 'Be a bit of excitement for yer wouldn't it?'

'D'you want a cuppa, Molly?' Cynthia asked. 'Rinse up yer dad's cup for her, will you Joyce, you're nearest.'

As Joyce sorted out Molly's tea, Cynthia asked, 'Your mom and dad all right, are they?'

30

Molly knew what everyone must think of Iris so it was kind of her to ask. She shrugged. 'Much as ever.'

'So – what've you got to tell us?' Em asked. 'I've got to go in a minute.' Molly could see she and Norm were holding hands under the table, all sweet like a pair of little lovebirds. She felt a stab of jealousy – even if it was Norm, old car-door ears. They seemed so sure of each other, as if they'd been married for years already. Not like George – or any of the other blokes she'd walked out with for that matter. The thought of George's face in the pub swam before her for a moment but she pushed that away as well. It had been full of loathing and disgust. That was the end of that then. Another one. They all seemed to go the same way in the end.

'Well—' Molly sipped her tea slowly for effect, then sat back. Violet was staring at her as if willing her to speak.

'I've decided – I'm going to join up!'

'What, *you*?' The words burst mockingly from Norm, Mr Superior, Norm the normal PC Plod.

Everyone was staring – even Sid had looked up and stopped chewing his last bit of bread.

'Yes, *me*,' Molly snapped back. 'I've decided. I'm going up the recruitment office, soon as I've got a minute.'

'Join up as what?' Em said, also sounding disbelieving, Molly thought savagely, as if they didn't think she was capable of anything at all. And Em moved her shoulder a bit closer to Norm's, as if to show she agreed with him.

'The army. I dunno as what yet, do I? I s'pose they'll tell me.'

'*I* wanna join the army,' Sid scowled. 'And they won't let me.'

'You're too young, Sid, don't talk daft,' Em said in her matronly way. 'And anyway, the firm needs you.' Sid scowled even more. 'You're Reserved Occ anyway.'

'I could lie,' he said. 'About my age. I'd *make* them let me go.'

'You gunna wear a uniform then, Molly?' Joyce asked, excited.

'I expect so.' She was grateful to Joyce for bringing the conversation back to her.

'Well,' Cynthia said, as if trying to take all this in. 'What's your mother said about this?'

'I ain't told her – yet.' She had no intention of telling Iris either, but she'd had to tell someone because she was excited, and it made it seem real. 'Don't say anything to her, will yer?'

Cynthia shook her head. 'Course not, love.'

They all knew what Iris would think about losing her lifelong skivvy.

'What about your dad?' Em asked.

The words *he's not my dad* rose to Molly's lips but she bit them back. Blood poured into her cheeks. And it was then she wondered if they all knew. If everyone had always known, if it was obvious to anyone who had eyes that Joe Fox could not have sired two children. Shame pumped through her veins. But she didn't see it in their eyes, saw only concern for a crippled man with a monstrous wife.

'Molly can't stay home for ever,' Cynthia said. 'She's go to make her own life. Good for you, Molly love.'

Molly glanced gratefully at her.

'It's Jenny and Stanley who're going to feel it.' Cynthia nodded towards the opposite side of the street. 'Have you told them?'

'Not yet.' The buoyancy and sense of triumph which

had filled Molly all day started to seep away. Iris and Joe were one thing, but Jenny and Stanley Button, who had never shown her anything but kindness, were quite another.

'Ooh Jenny'll miss yer,' Cynthia said. She saw Molly's troubled expression. 'But I tell yer summat else, Molly – she'll be ever so proud of you. I bet you anything she will.'

Five

Soon Molly was out of the Browns' and on the other side of the street, warmed by an unexpected embrace from Em. She had got up to see Molly out to the front door, prising herself away from Norm for a few moments.

'Oh Molly – I hope you'll be all right!' She was quite emotional suddenly.

'I'll be all right!' Molly laughed. 'Anyway – they might not 'ave me! Even if they do, I don't s'pose I'll be away from here 'til after Christmas now at this rate.'

'Well, I think you're brave,' Em said. 'Only, you'll have to behave, Molly – be careful with yourself.'

Molly blushed again. Lowering her voice, she said, 'Sorry about the other night. I don't remember much about it to be honest with yer, but sorry if I got you into trouble or anything.'

'No – I just took you home. You'd fallen over and were singing your flaming head off!'

Molly had only the dimmest of memories about this, even though she had the bruises to prove it had indeed happened. She shrugged, embarrassed. 'Dunno what comes over me sometimes.'

Em smiled then, properly, the sweet Em who wasn't a prim matron. 'I don't know,' she said. 'You're the end.' She was smiling as Molly left and crossed the street.

It took Jenny Button a few moments to answer

Molly's knock, though there came volleys of crazed barking from Wally, their wire-haired Jack Russell. When Molly first got to know the Buttons they had a gentle old dog called Bullseye, but he had long since passed away and a few years back they'd acquired Wally.

Jenny Button had always been very large and took time to move about. Food was her comfort in the face of a sad life, with a crippled husband and no children of her own. Now entering her fifties, she still had dark hair, scraped up into a little bun at the back, but she was very broad in the beam, and struggled to catch her breath. As it was evening, she was not wearing her huge white apron for once. She appeared in a navy blouse and skirt, the waistline of which disappeared deeply into the folds of her body, making her look like a tightly strung parcel. When she saw Molly, the fleshy little mounds of her face lifted in delight, bunching round her deep-set eyes. Every year she looked more like one of her own currant buns.

''Ello, bab! My Stanley said 'e thought it'd be you. "That'll be our Molly," 'e said when you knocked on the door. Come in – 'ave yer got a minute? Wally stop that – get in 'ere!'

'Yes, course. I've come to see yer,' Molly said, with a pang. She knew what store they set by her visits. Ever since Molly had run away from home as a child they had always offered her a haven away from Iris. If Iris hadn't insisted that Molly return home, and Molly hadn't felt that Jenny had enough problems already with an invalid husband, she would have happily stayed there.

Jenny Button waddled along the narrow passage to the sound of her own rasping breaths and Wally's nails tapping on the lino. They passed the little counter from where she sold her bread and buns on the way to the back room where she and Stanley lived, in one cramped room. The upper floor of the house was hardly used. Stanley had had his legs blown off by a shell in 1917 and could not move unassisted from bed or chair.

'Stanley!' Jenny announced at full volume. 'You were right, it's our Molly!'

Molly heard his exclamation of pleasure and felt even more wretched about what she had come to tell them.

They entered the back room, which was, as ever, stifling hot – 'I'm not having my Stanley catching cold' – with a fire in the grate and a single-bar electric fire pumping out heat as well. It was always very stuffy and rather smelly, but Molly was used to it. It felt like home. She immediately took off her coat, smiling at Stanley Button, who was sitting up in bed, bald as a baby now and beaming at her in delight.

''Ello, bab!' he chirruped, happily. 'Ooh, you've brought a cold wind in with yer, I can feel it billowing by! What're you up to, young lady?'

'I've come to see yer, that's all,' Molly said.

'You'll 'ave a cuppa tea won't yer?' Jenny said, disappearing out the back before Molly could say that she'd just had one at Em's. It would have done no good anyway. When Jenny was determined to feed you, being fed was what happened and no arguments.

'How's the big wide world out there?' Stanley wanted to know.

'Much as usual,' Molly said, as she always did. She perched on the chair opposite him, warming her hands at the fire.

'Ooh, not these days.' Stanley's pink, kindly face looked troubled. His loose denture clicked as he spoke.

'Never know what those Kraut bastards are going to've done for next. The Market Hall, the BSA . . .' He sucked in his lips for a moment. ' 'Scuse my lingo, bab. Terrible about that cinema though.' It had been playing on his mind ever since it had happened, a bomb landing on the Carlton cinema in Sparkbrook, while the show was on, at the end of October. 'Terrible. Imagine it . . .'

'But we still can't get you to go into a shelter.'

'I can't get down into no shelter, bab,' he said gently. Sometimes his watery blue eyes looked so little-boyish, he really touched Molly's heart. 'My Jenny says the same. We'll take our chances together, the pair of us – in our own bed.'

'There's no telling you two, is there?' Molly teased, gently.

'I'm lucky to be alive as it is, bab. Always living on borrowed time.'

Stanley gave her his sweetest of smiles and she knew not to say any more. Her heart lurched as his next question was usually what had she been up to, what was the news, and she didn't feel ready to talk about that – not until Jenny was here. But instead, he looked reflective.

'I don't know why – I've been thinking a lot about the past – how it used to be . . .' And he began to reminisce. Stanley was a local boy, had gone to another school in the area at Loxton Street. He loved to tell her about his childhood friends, many of whom had not survived the war, about their pranks and their games at the local playground known as Spion Kop. Before the Great War he had worked in a local metal-bashing company. Since the war maimed him, his working life – or much life at all, apart from Jenny pushing him along on rare outings in the wheelchair – had come to an end.

Molly liked to listen to him, even though she'd heard some of the stories countless times before.

He was chatting away happily when Jenny came puffing in with a tray of tea and buns.

'There yer go, bab – and there's a finger of Chelsea for yer to keep yer going.'

She sat down with a whoosh of exhaled breath.

'So, bab – how's everything?'

'All right,' Molly said lightly. *God*, she thought. Her mind recoiled again from Iris's words the other night, from the foul burden of knowledge she now carried. If they only knew. Or did they? Again, a dizzy feeling passed through her, as if the ground was moving under her feet. Perhaps they all knew everything? Perhaps her secret had never been secret after all? But if so, they showed no sign of it.

As she ate the cake, Wally the dog sat scrutinizing her every move, panting heavily with his pink tongue lolling to one side. Molly laughed.

'He's trying to mesmerize me!'

'He'll ignore yer, soon as you've finished,' Jenny said, and she was right – Wally did then lie down by the fire with a long-suffering sigh.

Molly chatted to them about work, recounting some of Gladys's funny stories, and about going to see the Browns.

'Cynthia seems quite good at the moment,' Jenny said. 'I saw Dot pop in to visit yesterday – that'll have cheered her up.'

'I'd've liked to see her,' Molly said. Dot Wiggin, Cynthia Brown's old friend, had been a tower of strength to her in her hardest times. Though Dot had been a war widow, she had now remarried, a widower called Lou Alberello who had three grown-up children. She'd moved over to the Italian quarter in Duddesdon to be with him, but she popped in from time to time.

'Oh, she's thriving on it by the looks of it. Filling out – must be all that spaghetti!'

Molly laughed. She was very fond of Dot. 'I'm glad she's all right then. She's a good sort.'

There was a lull in the conversation and Molly had almost finished her tea. She was also growing so hot and sweaty she could hardly stand it, her cheeks glowing pinker by the minute. It was time to get it over with. Putting her cup down, she took a deep breath, her heart pounding.

'I've come to tell you both summat.'

'Oh ar,' Stanley said. They were both staring expectantly at her.

'Thing is . . .' Molly stared down at her scuffed brown shoes. She had eased her left foot out at the back to relieve her sore heel. 'Well – I've come to a decision. I s'pose it may be a bit stupid . . .' The burning confidence which had come over her seemed to be leaking away.

'Oh I don't s'pose it is,' Stanley said encouragingly.

She glanced up at him with a grateful smile.

'Only – things at home . . . Well, it ain't just that – it's me an' all. Anyroad, I've decided – I'm going to join up.'

There, she'd said it! She looked up at them, ever so worried about what the reaction would be – disappointment? Ridicule?

Jenny Button was half way through a mouthful of cake, so it fell to Stanley to say, 'Join up? How d'yer mean?'

Molly drew herself up straighter. Sweat was trickling down her back. 'I'm going to go – you know – and join up. The army, I think. That's if they'll 'ave me.'

Jenny swallowed. 'Well I never,' she said.

The silence went on so long that Molly was beginning to feel really bad, until Jenny turned to her husband. Looking at him, Molly was overwhelmed to see that he had tears in his eyes.

'What d'you think about it, Stanley?'

'Well, bab—' Stanley wiped his eyes on a corner of the eiderdown. 'I think it's a terrible thing that a lovely wench like you should have to go and join up. But if you think that's what you should do – I think it's marvellous. They ought to be grateful to have you. I'm as proud of you as could be.'

Tears filled Molly's eyes and ran down her cheeks. No one in her life had ever said anything half as nice as that to her before.

'You don't mind, then?'

'Course we mind,' Jenny said gruffly. 'We mind like billy-oh. But I'll tell yer summat, bab – you're not to worry about us – 'cause I know you will. But we'll be with you every step of the way. Won't we, Stanley?'

'Ar, that we will,' Stanley said.

Everyone was rather watery-eyed by now.

'You're so kind,' Molly sniffed. 'I'm going to miss you both – I'll write. And I won't be going quite yet . . .'

'Told yer mother, 'ave yer?' Jenny asked.

Molly shook her head.

'Ah well,' Jenny said. 'There's some things some people don't need to know straight off. And I'd say this is one of them.'

Six

January 1941

'All right, take it easy,' the medical orderly said. 'I'm not going to amputate one of your limbs, you know!'

Molly had tried to smile and look less nervous. But all the way through the medical and the recruitment interview in the dingy offices in Birmingham, she couldn't stop shaking. While she sat waiting with the motley group of girls who were volunteering she had kept her gaze fixed on the floor, trying to look calm, but she could hardly stop her legs twitching up and down, she was so nervous. Supposing they rejected her! And what were they going to ask her? But it was the medical examination that made her shake the most.

When she finally emerged into the snowy evening street, her legs almost went from under her and she had to stop for a moment and catch her breath, leaning back against the building. But now she was full of triumph, her spirits soaring. She had done it! The Auxiliary Territorial Service had said yes to Molly Fox!

She had decided to wait until after Christmas to volunteer, mainly because she couldn't bring herself to leave the Buttons before that and she spent as much time with them as she possibly could. She knew neither Em nor Jenny Button would say anything to Iris. They all kept well out of her path anyway, and during those last weeks she never spoke to any of her family unless she had to, even with the raids going on. She held on to the warm knowledge that at least she had the blessing of Jenny and Stanley. It was as if she was walking on air, in a protective dream and full of a sense of possibility. She could put aside the person she was, all that she had come from. There would be a new Molly Fox, away from this squalid house and these confining streets. She was going to start again and make a new life.

There had been a lull in the raids before Christmas, almost long enough for them to believe it might have stopped, that the bombers had lost interest in Birmingham. But they started the new year with grim intent. The very first night of 1941, the sirens had gone off again. Iris was too drunk ever to take much notice or help Joe. Molly would sit under the stairs, hoping and praying. This time, in the cold, sleepless hours, she switched off to everything around her and dreamed only of escape. She pictured herself in full uniform, marching, giving orders, taking the army by storm. She just knew she could be good at something, that she had an important role to play!

It was a bitter winter. Making her way home from work, Molly huddled up in her old coat, pulling her hat further down over her ears as she trudged through the slush in her leaking shoes. But she wasn't thinking about the cold. On the way home she bought a second-hand suitcase. It was only small, as the army had instructed her not to bring more than the minimum with her. It was battered and brown with soft leather straps and buckles and she felt fond of it immediately. It felt like her partner in her secret mission.

Before going into the house, she went quietly round into the yard and stowed the case beside the copper in the brew house. Late in the evening, when Iris was snoring in her chair, too far gone to notice anything, Molly sneaked back out for the case and hid it under her bed, ready for her departure in a few days. In it were her travel warrant and other necessary papers.

All that remained now was to tell them – but she wasn't going to do that until the very last minute.

They were all there when she came down that morning, already wearing her hat and carrying the case. She put it down by the front door and took her coat from the hook.

The wireless was on and Bert, who was at the table, was squinting at yesterday's paper and sneezing every so often. Iris and Joe probably would not have even noticed her leave. Joe was in his usual seat by the fire, which Iris was kneeling beside, cursing as she rattled around in it with the poker, in her customary evil morning temper.

'Where d'yer think you're off to?' Bert asked. His tone was threatening.

'What d'you care?' Molly snapped, slipping into her coat. She'd been up before everyone else, made tea, had some bread and made sure everything was packed before Iris had even peeled back her eyelids.

Bert's lips curled back. 'Don't bloody talk to me like that, you—'

'I'll tell you where I'm going.' Molly leaned over the table. 'I'm off, that's what. I've joined up and I'm going away. And you can't do a bloody thing to stop me.'

She heard Iris start and say, 'Eh?' in the background.

Bert stared at her, then a nasty, calculating smile came over his face. 'You're 'aving me on.'

'No, big brother, I'm not.' She held up the case. 'I'm getting on a train this morning. I've got all my papers in 'ere, and all I can say is, good riddance to the whole filthy rotten lot of yer. I'm going where you should be, Bert – to fight for my country. Why ain't you in the army, eh? You're twenty-one. They called you up. What did you do to wriggle out of that one? Or 'ave you turned conchie or summat?'

'It's my chest,' Bert said, wheezing ostentatiously. 'Eh, Mom – did you 'ear that?'

Iris was looming over her now. 'What's all this, yer stupid little bitch? What're yer going on about now?'

Molly stared triumphantly into her mother's bloated face. How vile it was, how slatternly and low and disgusting she was! 'I'm going, Mom. I ain't going to be your skivvy no more. You're the woman of the house. You'll have to stop pouring so much booze down yer 'odge and start doing more work, won't yer?' She nodded at Joe. ''Cause he ain't gunna do it, is 'e? Or Bert 'ere maybe?'

'You can't leave – I won't let yer . . .' Iris stumbled for words.

'I'm going, Mom – you're too late.' Molly was trembling, her eyes gleaming with triumph and loathing as she moved towards the door. 'T'ra Joe,' she said. 'Good luck to yer with these two. Goodbye, *Mother*,' she finished with acid sarcasm.

As Molly stepped out along the street, her mother's

voice roared after her. 'Yer going to the right place then, wench – they're all just a load of whores, them lot!'

With these loving words ringing in her ears, Molly headed for the bus. Still shaky with emotion and lost in thought, she turned to cut along a side street to the nearest stop, when someone jumped on her. Before she could do anything she found herself being dragged into the gloomy entry which ran up to the back of a factory, and pinned against the wall. The case fell from her hand and toppled onto its side.

Bert's foul breath reached her nostrils, his snarling face close to hers.

'What d'yer think you're up to, sis?'

'Get off me, you vile little bastard!' Full of rage she tried to shove him off her, but though he was only an inch taller than her, he was full of wiry strength.

'I don't like this – you going off, without a by your leave . . .' He gave a nasty grin and she had a grim view of his yellow teeth. '*I* like to say what happens around at our place. After all – I'm the only real man of the house.'

'You're too late,' Molly said, grappling with him as he shoved her harder and harder against the slimy bricks. 'Just cowing well get off me – you're wrecking my coat. I'm going, and that's that. You can't bully me. You're a waster, Bert. You're just a lowlife . . .' She trailed off, unable to command words strong enough to express her disgust.

'Shut it, little sis.' His hand shot under her coat and grasped her right breast, squeezing it hard, and he pressed himself against her. To her horror she realized he was dangerously aroused. 'How about it, for old

45

times' sake, eh Moll?' he wheedled. 'You gunna let me have it this time – let me 'ave yer proper like, before yer go?'

His greasy hair was close to her face, his shiny, pitted skin, his body lunging at her.

'I said, *get off me.*' She pointed her finger and jabbed it as hard as she could into his left eye, and he backed off from her shrieking with pain. 'You bitch . . . you bloody bitch.'

'Get lost, Bert . . .'

She picked up her case and tore away from him, trying to straighten her hat with her free hand. Passers-by stared curiously as she ran along the road, until, looking back, she was sure that he was not following. Shaken, she slowed and walked with more composure to her stop, her breathing slowing gradually. But it was as if she could smell him on her, had his foulness in her nostrils. How long would it take to fade? How long before she could wash away from her the stench and stain of the whole lot of them?

Square-bashing

Seven

The burning excitement that had filled her ever since she had made her decision to join up, that had bubbled in her all through Christmas, had been seeping away all morning. It was the first time in her life that Molly had travelled more than a couple of miles away from her home streets, and now she was leaving all of Birmingham behind. For the first time she asked herself what the hell she was playing at. It was a day heavy with cloud and the promise of more snow as the train wound its way between the coal-blackened walls of factories and ranks of chimneys, offering brief glimpses of black canals with boats moving along them and slices of snow-covered parkland between the rows of cramped suburban houses with washing strung across their yards. Everything was in black and white. Then the buildings gave out and they were flanked each side by fields and hedges.

Sitting in a corner of the compartment, Molly kept her head turned to the window, listening to all the chatter around her. There were the two posh girls who had boarded with her, and opposite Molly, a middle-aged couple in black, who hunched close to each other with bereft expressions, talking in very quiet voices. They seemed to have a veil of grief around them, and everyone left them alone. At the first stop, a whoosh of cold air let some passengers off and a band of servicemen got on, three of them squeezing into the compartment. Molly, still facing the window, felt one of them sit down by her. Within moments, the three of them were in conversation with the two posh girls. After a while she heard one of the girls, she couldn't tell which, say, 'Yes, we've done our bit and joined up as well. We're off to our basic training somewhere in darkest Northampton!'

Molly shrank inside, all her optimism and certainty ebbing away. What on earth was she doing here, little Molly Fox, the one no one ever wanted to play with, among these posh, alien people? With every glance at the two girls, especially the one adorned with lipstick and fox furs, chatting peppily to the soldiers, Molly became acutely aware of the threadbare shabbiness of her brown and white coat, which had looked so promising in the rag market but now seemed hopelessly worn and dowdy. She feared there were green stains on the back, after Bert pushed her up against the wall like that. Her shoes were drab and scuffed. But she did have a hat she was proud of, even though that had also been a bargain from the rag market. It was a pertly shaped little number in chocolate brown with an upturned brim and a crimson band round it, into which was tucked a jaunty feather. She knew how to wear it at an angle on her wavy blonde hair and she knew it looked good, whatever the state of her shoes. But she did feel rough and ignorant set against these other girls, even though neither of them was what you'd call a looker, not by any means. The fox-fur girl had a narrow, shrewish face. But they were well-heeled and confident. It was frightening to discover that they were heading for the same place as she was.

She decided to try and avoid all conversation and

pretended to go to sleep. But the lad beside her was not to be put off. She sensed that he kept turning and looking curiously at her. Men always looked at her. Her striking appearance – tall, with a full figure and thick golden hair – brought her endless male attention. And she was used to responding. When she had reached a certain age, fifteen or sixteen, she had begun to discover that she was alluring to men. She had been tall for her age then, had a pretty face, and was past the worst of her physical problems. And her hair, so abundant and blonde, always drew stares. Suddenly, everywhere she went, blokes appeared at her side and chatted her up. It was a heady experience, confusing; she didn't know how to behave, but it was a revelation. For the first time in her life she knew she had power! And she liked to play with it.

'Where're you off to then?' the young man asked, when she risked opening her eyes for a few seconds.

She couldn't resist turning to glance at him. All right, she couldn't compete with those other girls, but she had something they didn't. And he seemed to be of her class. In a loud, arch voice she said, 'The army – joined up, ain't I?'

The lad grinned. He was definitely more like her, she could tell by his face, his slicked-back hair. 'You an' all, eh? 'Ere, girls' – he turned to the others – ''ere's another one going where you're going.'

'Oh – *really*?' Lipstick lips leaned forward enthusiastically. 'You're ATS, are you?'

Molly nodded. She felt insecure and prickly in the face of these foreign, superior creatures.

'Well how marvellous. Are you from Birmingham? That's where we've travelled from.'

Does she think I'm blind? Molly thought. *I saw them*

get on the train. 'Yeah – I'm from Brum, can't yer tell?' She laughed loudly and the lad joined in. 'What's yer name, soldier boy?' she asked. She wanted to shut the other girls out of the conversation, because she felt so uncomfortable with them.

'Billy – yours?'

'I'm Molly.'

'Nice to meet you, Molly,' Lipstick Lips said. Molly gave her a look which said, I wasn't talking to *you*. 'My name's Marguerite Dunne, and this is Ruth Chambers.'

'Oh,' Molly said. She knew she was being rude, but she couldn't think what else to say. Ruth, the other woman, was dressed more drably in an old camel coat, her black hair in a plait which snaked out from under her hat. She looked across haughtily and didn't smile. Molly turned back to Billy.

'So – how long've you been a soldier, Billy boy?'

'Only a few months,' he said. She could see it working already, feel herself reeling him in, by the way she looked at him, talked to him all intimately. God, it never took much.

The other two girls soon gave up and fell into conversation with the two lads closer to them. Molly spent the rest of the journey talking and flirting with Billy, who was a sweet-natured lad whose family lived in Winson Green. He seemed flattered by Molly's attention. She laughed loudly at his jokes and told him stories about the factories she'd worked in. Every so often, when she was loud, she saw the other girls glance at her as they might at some strange animal in a zoo and it made her want to laugh even louder. Billy, however, although looking a bit uncertain at first, as if he wasn't used to girls telling saucy stories, was soon laughing raucously along with her.

'Any chance of keeping the noise down a bit?' one of the other lads asked, not unkindly, but Molly was immediately riled.

'Sorry, Yer Honour,' she said with all the sarcasm she could muster, and she and Billy giggled again. 'Christ—' She leaned closer to him and brushed his thigh with her hand. 'I wish we had a drop of summat worth drinking in 'ere – and the place to ourselves.' She looked up at him through her lashes.

''Fraid I haven't got anything,' he said, blushing. 'But we'll be there soon. Fancy meeting up sometime, Molly?'

'Oh – I expect so,' she said, withdrawing again. Better not seem too keen. That was when they'd lose interest. 'We'll 'ave to see, won't we?'

The train slowed, as if running out of breath, and finally shuddered to a halt in the station.

'Northampton!' Voices took up the cry along the carriages.

The posh one, Marguerite, opened the compartment door, letting in a rush of cold air and flakes of snow. She poked her head out, then turned to inform the rest of them, 'Yes, it *is* Northampton, apparently – we're here!'

'I say – finally!' said Ruth in her odd, tight voice. She had unfortunate protruding teeth and a rather old-fashioned way with her.

'Could be anywhere really, couldn't we?' Marguerite said, yanking on her large case. 'Oh drat! I knew I shouldn't have brought this hulking great thing!'

All the signs had been taken down to flummox the enemy in the event of invasion, so Molly was grateful for all the shouting. There was a surge of movement all round her. The noisy group of servicemen who had been squatting in the corridor were now all hoiking kitbags on to their shoulders, and most of the other passengers in the compartment also got up, reached for cases and bags on the luggage rack, hauled packages out from between their legs and generally made plain their intention to get off.

Amid the hubbub of disembarkation, Molly called out loudly to Billy, feeling she somehow had to stay connected to him. 'Don't forget to come and see me, will yer Billy, there's a darlin'!' She gave him a wink.

As he called a cheerful reply, she saw Ruth and Marguerite roll their eyes at each other.

'Stupid bitches,' Molly murmured, and leaned down to pick up her case. She could see what they thought of her. She was already cast in the role of rough, mouthy Brummie, and the worst of it was, it was mostly her own fault.

She followed the throng of travellers from the platform out to the front of the station, which was a scene of great busyness. Small flakes of snow were falling slowly and there was plenty on the ground and rooftops. The crowd consisted mainly of servicemen and a number of young civilian women on their way to the training camp, and there were army vehicles coming and going. The women were ushered towards two army trucks, parked one behind the other, with open backs. There was no sign of any seats inside.

She longed to see a familiar face. If only Em was here and they'd joined up together! In the crowd she saw Marguerite and Ruth again, Marguerite nattering away, though Ruth looked cold and intimidated. The commanding voices of some of the other young women around her made her shrivel inside. They were going to the camp as well! Would they all be like that? How on earth was she, Molly, ever going to fit in? She cursed herself for being so loud and offish on the journey. What the hell must they have thought of her? Still, she rallied haughtily, holding her head up and looking round as if she had all the confidence in the world, what the hell did she care? It was her the blokes would go for, not some of those odd-looking toffs!

Holding her brown case, comforted by the soft feel of its handle, she took her place amid the group of young women. Some of the girls were chatting in animated voices, while others were silent and nervous. Molly felt small and very frightened, and at that moment she wished from the bottom of her heart that she could get on a return train and head straight home again

Eight

They worked up quite a fug in the truck, all crowded in together, clinging to the sides and to each other as the vehicle swerved round corners, making their insides lurch as well.

'I say,' a voice remarked, to scattered laughter, 'who-ever's driving must be keen to get back in time for lunch!'

Molly recognized the voice. She could see Lipstick Lips beside the more frumpy girl, Ruth, and although they were packed in quite close to Molly, neither of them turned to her or acknowledged her existence. The chatter was among the more confident ones. None of the girls close to Molly said much, all seeming shy and muted by cold and queasiness, and Molly stood silently, her feet so frozen she couldn't feel them.

It was not too long, though, before they piled out, to find themselves facing a bleak, snow-covered open space at the edge of the town, fenced off and laid out with rows of wooden huts. Between these, men and women in khaki uniform were hurrying purposefully, some saluting as they went. The wind was bitter, and the new recruits stood huddled and uncertain with their cases at their feet. Molly felt her nose beginning to run and reached into a pocket for her one, stained handkerchief.

'Is there no one to carry our luggage?' a high, nasal voice asked, among all the other mutterings of uncertainty. The tone was tentative, without the braying confidence of some of the others. Molly turned, intrigued, to see an unusual-looking girl with wisps of blonde hair blowing about her face. She was tall, thin and lanky, and had a wide mouth and a large, beak-like nose. She also looked pale and exhausted.

'You'll be lucky,' someone else retorted. 'This isn't a holiday camp, you know!'

'You're telling me,' another voice chipped in, and there was a brief ripple of laughter.

'Hello – who's this?'

A dumpy yet commanding-looking figure was striding towards the group. She planted her rather solid body before them, clicked her feet together in their shiny black shoes and looked them all over with darting brown eyes, not noticeably impressed by what was in front of her. Dark, wavy hair was visible under her ATS cap and Molly saw a tough, intelligent-looking face. Her heart beat faster. There was something about this alien creature that she found challenging; she also had a natural authority which invited respect. To Molly's surprise she realized that the woman was not very much older than the rest of them, but she looked completely in command, and tough as old boots.

In a booming voice the woman welcomed them and introduced herself as Lance Corporal Phoebe Morrison. 'Right – well, it's no good all of you standing here out in this weather. We've got to get you kitted out – but the first thing I'm going to do is show you your billets. Get into threes – that's how we do things around here – quickly now, no, threes, not fives, you numbskulls! In line, quick march!'

Molly found herself beside a small, wiry little person who she'd hardly noticed up until now. The girl was

57

very young-looking and the ancient carpet bag holding her possessions looked almost too big for her to carry. She had her hair plaited and coiled round her ears in a quaintly old-fashioned style and strange, bulging blue eyes. She reminded Molly of an insect. As they marched towards the huts, the girl turned to Molly, gave her a wink, and through adenoids, in broad Black Country, said, 'Well, I down't much like the look of 'er, do yow?'

For the first time that day Molly laughed with relief.

'She looks like summat you'd fire out of a cannon, don't 'er?' she replied, far too loudly. She heard the girl on her left, who had a head of wild red hair, splutter with laughter, and there were titters from among the others. Their corporal bawled, at astonishing volume, 'No talking back there!'

The girls made wry faces at each other.

'Where're yow from then – Brum?' the girl asked. She had a twitchy way of talking, as if someone was intermittently pricking her with a pin.

'Right first time – what about you?'

'Walsall. I thought anything'd be better than the factory. Our mom says I'll never stick it out. "They'll eat you up on toast," 'er said. But that's 'cus 'er down't want me to go.'

'Halt!' Corporal Morrison roared, causing them to come to a ragged standstill outside a hut. 'This is Hut F. Right – first twelve of you in there!'

Molly and the Walsall girl, who said her name was Lena, and the redhead were first in line for the second billet, Hut J, and found themselves leading the way right to the far end. Molly and Lena took the corner beds – or what passed as beds, because none of the black metal bedsteads even had mattresses or any bedding whatsoever. All the hut contained otherwise was grey lino on the floor and an unlit stove in the middle.

Molly put her case on the floor and perched on the edge of the metal frame, still in her coat. It felt even colder inside than out and their breath was visible on the air. If only she'd chosen a bed closer to the stove! Lena seemed to be muttering to herself, searching for something in her bag. Molly perched on the cold edge of the bed and blew her nose again, wondering what would happen next. The redhead, who had the bed next to hers, threw her bag onto the springs and grinned across at her.

'Dear God, they said it'd be basic! Would you not think they'd at least give us a little bit of straw or something to lie on? Even a cow in a barn'd expect that much!' The girl was Irish. She flumped down backwards and the springs screeched with surprise, making both of them laugh. She had dancing blue eyes and a healthy look to her cheeks that said she was someone who had spent her life in the open air. With that and her curling red hair and upturned nose, Molly saw that she was very pretty. 'Well, hello,' she continued, sitting up. 'Looks like we're going to be lying here side by side then.'

She said it with a measure of impishness that put Molly at her ease and made her smile.

'Looks like it,' Molly said, full of relief. At least Lena and this girl seemed more her type. The blonde beaky one seemed to be muttering and complaining in a distracted sort of way a couple of beds away. 'What's yer name?'

'Oh – I'm Cathleen Maguire – just call me Cath. And you?'

'Molly – Fox.'

'Lovely to meet you, Molly.'

'That's Lena over there.'

Lena looked up from rooting about in her bag and then came over, grinning. Molly was struck again by how tiny and frail she looked.

'D'you say yow're called Cath?'

'That's me,' Cath twinkled.

'Where yow from then?'

'Well, Ireland, as you can hear. Near Waterford, which is down in the south, in case you don't know. But I came over to Birmingham for work first. To be honest with you, factory work wasn't for me, not after growing up on the farm. So I've joined up instead.'

'Down't blame yer,' Lena said. 'Must be nice, living on a farm.'

'Ah, it's all right. But you want to get out, you know? Get away and see some life before it's all over! So I jumped on the boat.'

Molly watched her with admiration. It seemed a huge step to her, crossing the sea and being so far from home.

As they talked, Molly began to feel a bit better. There was a hubbub of chatter along the hut and they both looked around to take in who else was with them. In the next bed to Cath was the tall, beaky-nosed blonde. Over the other side, with a shock, she recognized Ruth, who had been on the train, but she was relieved to see that there was no sign of the overbearing Marguerite. Ruth was talking to a girl with her dark hair cut in a bob who had her back to them. Other girls were chattering along the rows of beds, everyone wondering what next and where on earth was the bedding and when were they going to get a cup of tea?

However, the blonde girl next to Cath was sitting bolt upright on the edge of her bed not joining in the hubbub. She looked very distracted and upset.

'She doesn't look too happy,' Cath said in her easy way. I'd better go and say hello.'

Walking round the bed, she went to the tall girl and held out her hand. 'Hello there – we're neighbours. My name's Cath.'

The girl looked up with stricken eyes, as if she'd been brought back from some faraway dream. Eventually it dawned on her to take Cath's hand.

'Oh – I'm Honor. Honor Carruthers.' Molly and Lena exchanged smirks at the sound of her posh, peculiar voice. 'How d'you do?'

'I'm doing all right,' Cath said in her easy way.

'Really?' Honor said, seeming appalled by everything around her. 'I – I didn't know . . . I had no idea it would be so perfectly *awful* . . .'

'Ah well,' Lena called across to her. 'Bit late now, ain't it? We're here and we're all gunna 'ave to get used to it.' She looked across at Molly and rolled her eyes.

'But I . . .' the girl started to say, but it was drowned out by Corporal Morrison's voice booming at the door, 'Right – outside in threes, quick sharp!'

As they milled out of the hut Molly found herself close to Ruth. Seeing who was beside her, Ruth glanced at her, then turned away, a thick blush rising in her cheeks, and moved right away from Molly as fast as she could. Stung, Molly stared after her.

Right, she thought, *I can see how it's going to be with you, you stuck-up little bitch!*

The occupants of Hut J were obviously a very mixed crew and Molly was grateful that her nearest neighbours were Lena and Cath. Imagine if she had to deal with one of those posh cows who had beds further along, with their bossy, cut-glass voices!

Outside, the snow had turned to a sleety rain, but this didn't seem to make any difference to proceedings. The twelve of them stood like lambs ready for the slaughter, hands raw in the cold, freezing droplets trickling down the backs of their necks, waiting to be told what to do.

'Squad! Move to the right in threes! Quick march – left, right, left, right . . . Right wheel . . .'

'Holy Mother!' Cath was already giggling at trying to set off on the right leg, or was it the left? The turn caused quite a few of them to bump into one another and there was much giggling and confusion. She and Molly seemed to set each other off and before they'd gone far, they were almost helpless with laughter.

'Quiet!' Corporal Morrison turned on them, glowering. She left the front and walked round to give Molly and Cath a particularly fierce scowl. 'We can take as long as you like over this. D'you want to stand out here all afternoon?'

Some of the others were shushing them, annoyed. Molly and Cath just managed to stifle their giggles. It was quite some time before there were two orderly lines of six at the back of the hut.

'That hut to your left is where you will find the latrines. You first six – quick march – you have one minute each!'

Molly found herself marching full speed, with Lena, Cath, Honor, Ruth and another quiet girl, to the latrines. Honor, who was detailed to go into the primitive toilet next to hers, made a gagging sound of horror. Molly thought it didn't look too bad compared with some in the yards where she'd lived, and she was used to people banging impatiently on the door demanding that she come out. Even so, one minute was a bit steep. She did her business as fast as she could and pulled the door open.

'Ah – at least someone can obey orders!' Corporal Morrison barked. Molly blushed, surprisingly gratified at having done something right for once in her life. Other doors were yanked open by the nervous, eager-to-please ATS recruits – all except one, next to the toilet where Molly had been.

'Right – come along!' The corporal barged her way into the cubicle. 'Out you come – you've gone over the minute.'

From inside they heard the girl's high voice protesting miserably, 'But I can't go any faster! I'm not feeling well. I've got my . . .' Her voice lowered to an embarrassed murmur. If she was hoping for any fellow feeling from Corporal Morrison, it was not forthcoming.

'I said one minute, not three! Get yourself out there! You're in the army now, not your boudoir!'

Molly felt sorry for her, but also scornful. She was going to have to harden up, that one was.

'Blimey,' Lena tutted lugubriously. Molly wasn't sure if she was expressing sympathy or scorn for Honor.

They waited for what seemed another agonizingly long minute and at last Honor left the latrine, shoulders hunched, her face red with mortification. She was obviously very close to tears.

'I haven't washed my hands,' she wailed.

'This is latrine parade, not ablutions parade! When it's ablutions parade, I'll tell you! Is that clear? Now – left wheel, quick march!'

The first stop was for bedding – three 'biscuits', or

straw sections, of mattress. They were ordered to carry these to their beds and return for the rest of the bedding allocation: three blankets, two pillows, two sheets, two pillowslips.

Next, it was clothing. Some of the girls had lapsed into silence out of pure exhaustion at the newness of it all. Others were full of ribald comments, often to cover their awkwardness. When they were issued with thick sanitary towels and a belt, Molly and Lena stared at them in embarrassed confusion, not liking to admit they'd never seen any before. Old, washed-out rags were all Molly had ever known. They both got the giggles.

'I've always wanted summat big between my legs,' Molly remarked loudly, which made some of the others tut at them.

Then, in the clothing store, to stash into their kitbag they were issued with every bit of clothing they could have imagined and more, down to bras and suspender belts, gloves and overalls, and as well as everyday army clothing, there were gym shoes and a hairbrush, cutlery and a mending kit called a housewife, or 'hussif'.

'Blimey – how big do they think I am?' Lena held up a dreadnought of a brassiere against her bony little chest. She and Molly laughed raucously, trying the suspender belts against themselves and holding up the massive pairs of khaki underpants.

'God, you'll both be irresistible in those,' Cath said.

'They'll take some getting off!' Molly cackled loudly. Out of the corner of her eye she saw Ruth and the other dark-haired girl staring at her in horror. Oh, so disapproving! She waved the underpants in their direction. 'Don't worry, ladies – no one'll get at you in these!'

Lena and Cath laughed, but once again Ruth and the other girl turned away, disgusted.

'Ooh, look at them,' Lena whispered. 'Poker-faced pair they are, ain't they?'

The group of girls was already breaking up into factions, and the more Molly, Lena and a couple of allies – Cath and another two girls called Doris and Mary – poked fun and came out with increasingly ribald remarks, the more frosty their reception became from the rest of the girls in their hut. The sense of their disapproval and superiority made Molly feel all the more like being loud and showing them she didn't care what they thought.

When at last they did get something to eat that evening, they learned that the place where they would eat was called the 'mess' and that they were to use their 'irons' – the army issue of cutlery – and their cup. In the mess, they were faced with plates piled with gluey heaps of macaroni cheese. Molly ate hers ravenously, thinking it tasted quite good. Lena and Cath did the same, but they could see Honor, across the long table, picking at hers with an expression of real disgust.

'She ain't gunna last long in this lot,' Lena decreed, loading her fork with more of the pale stodge. 'She hardly looks strong enough to pick up 'er own clothes off the floor.'

'Probably ain't never 'ad to,' Molly said. But there was something about Honor that also made her feel sorry for her. She looked so pitifully out of place, and even the more middle-class girls seemed to have given up attempts at conversation with her and were chatting instead with each other at the far end of the table. Honor's obvious loneliness and desperation pricked through all Molly's defences. But she couldn't think of a thing to say to her. She seemed to come from another world. She turned her attention back to Cath, who was telling a revoltingly graphic story about cows giving birth, and joined in the loud laughter.

The hut was warmer when they got back to it, with the coal stove lit in the middle. The girls undressed with careful modesty, wriggling out of one set of clothes and pulling on another without showing much bare flesh. Molly put her striped army-issue pyjamas on, finding them a bit scratchy, but lovely and warm, and they fitted all right, as she was tall. She had never had any proper nightwear before, other than the one nightdress which Jenny Button had given her during her stay with them. Otherwise she'd had to make do with sleeping in her underwear.

'You could fit three of me in these!' Cath said, pulling out the waistband. Lena had had to roll the legs and sleeves of hers up. She was already sitting cross-legged on her bed, writing on a pad in her lap.

A few of the others also put on the army issue, but some girls had brought nightdresses from home. Honor, who was already lying in bed with her eyes closed as if she never wanted to open them again, was clad in a pair of mauve silk pyjamas. Cath had rolled her eyes comically behind the girl's back as she was putting them on.

'Right girls – lights out!' The dark-haired girl in the bed next to Ruth was called Win, and she seemed to be self-appointed head of the hut. She was standing by the switch, overseeing them all. She had a pleasant, friendly face and a manner of natural authority that suggested she was used to being in charge. 'Everybody ready? Right – I'm putting them out now.'

Molly got into bed. It was one of the best beds she'd ever slept in, and with far more bedding. She found she was looking forward to snuggling up on the sagging mattress, with all those blankets and pillows!

'Night, you two,' Cath said, and they called back to her. There was something so good-natured about Cath that Molly had warmed to her immediately. She seemed to accept everyone just as they were, not like those other snobby Misses along the hut!

Molly lay between the stiff sheets. Her temples were throbbing, the bedclothes were heavy and everything felt strange. The hut had a dank, musty atmosphere and the blankets had their own, slightly rubbery store-room smell. There was a faint glow from the coals in the stove. She was overcome suddenly by astonishment that she had actually left home – was it only this morning she had told Iris and Bert, had caught that train? She and the others had all been given an army-issue postcard to send home, 'to let your people know you've arrived safely'. Hah – your people! What people did she have? None of them cared a straw for her. She wouldn't bother to send it off.

But her high spirits had sunk as the day went by, despite her loudness. Fear was taking over, along with her usual sense of not measuring up, ever, wherever she went. All this newness, and these alien, toffee-nosed girls around her: how was she ever going to manage? Doom-laden thoughts filled her mind. Would she just be little Molly Fox again, the one no one ever wanted? Those other girls had obviously already formed a very low opinion of her, the stuck-up cows!

The thought of Billy, the lad on the train, came to her again, as it had done several times in the afternoon. He'd been nice to her all right. He fancied her, that much was obvious. She thanked God there were men in the camp as well. Girls were an unknown quantity – she didn't know how to impress them. Blokes were a different matter. She'd kept an eye out for Billy that afternoon as they had gone from hut to hut, but there'd been no sign of him. Perhaps she'd come across him tomorrow? He'd been interested, that was for sure. She was lying picturing his blond hair, and his eager pink face, knowing she could hook him in. It gave her back a sense of herself.

Someone was sobbing quietly in the darkness near her and she knew it was Honor. Lena seemed to be already asleep, breathing lustily from across the way, and there was whispering coming from the other end of the room.

Suddenly, out of the darkness, a clear soprano voice started to sing. Molly didn't know the song and her first reaction was to laugh at the green forests and lovers' towers that cropped up in the words. But she heard several of the others join in. Some of the girls must have learned the song at their posh schools. She wanted to sneer, but there was something comforting about the sweet voices and she was taken over by the loveliness of the tune which finally lulled them all to sleep.

Nine

'The purpose of this three weeks of basic training is to lick you all into shape – and that'll be no mean task by the look of you,' Corporal Morrison informed them at the top of her voice.

The new recruits were gathered in one of the instruction huts at what still felt a very early hour, despite the fact that the morning PT – a run through the rain and slush – and breakfast of thick porridge were already done. Blisters burned on Molly's feet, her lungs felt stretched and she was tingling all over. PT felt very good – once it was over!

There were now snowflakes whirling in the air again outside. Corporal Morrison still seemed to think it necessary to address them as loudly as if she were outside bawling into a high wind.

'You will be drilled to learn the discipline of the soldier's life, and by the time you leave here you will know how to participate in the running of a military camp. Believe it or not,' she yelled witheringly, 'you will learn how to be a credit to His Majesty's uniform. You will then be assigned either to general duties or to a trade, depending on your capabilities.'

The girls sat listening in their stiff, unfamiliar uniforms. Their hut that morning had been full of fumbling, curses and giggles after PT as they came to grips with the starched collars and alien buttons, the clunky suspender belts and thick lisle stockings.

'Make sure you double them over at the top,' the quartermaster had ordered. 'You'll soon get ladders if you fasten them on to the thin bit – and don't come crying to me if you do. You only get a new pair when those are worn out – so you darn any ladders with your hussif.'

Of course Honor had forgotten this advice, and for the first time of wearing, she plunged the metal suspender clip straight through the stocking, causing a ladder. There were more tears. With her calm, kind manner, Win came and comforted the distraught girl.

'I don't even know how to darn,' the girl sobbed. 'I don't know how to do anything!'

'Look, don't worry,' Win said heartily, her dark hair bent close to Honor's almost colourless blonde. 'I'll teach you later. It's not difficult. We'll all help each other. That's the way forward, eh?'

It had been Win, with her apparent good nature and natural authority, who had left her bed first and ordered and cajoled the others out into the 6.30 a.m. darkness for their first session of PT – a run round the field perimeter followed by physical jerks in the freezing dawn drizzle. It had all come as a shock to Molly. She had lolloped along beside Cath, their metal army identity tags with their name and religion stamped on – 'C of E' for Molly, 'RC' for Cath – bashing up and down against their chests, struggling for breath, her untaught muscles screaming protest after just a few yards. Cath didn't seem to have much idea about running either and they sank towards the back, only Honor whimpering somewhere behind them. It didn't occur to them to wait for her: she was from another world. Lena, to Molly's surprise, seemed to be able to keep up the running quite well with her light frame and surged away into the wet gloom.

'That's what comes of working in service,' she told Molly afterwards. 'I mean I down't do any running, but yower up and down stairs all ruddy day – and yow should see the steps to the coal cellar – like climbing a mountain!'

Most of the middle-class girls like Ruth and Win, still trim after years of drill in spartan boarding schools, chugged along stoically as if they'd been doing it all their lives. Molly, envying them, felt like a giant puppy that's not quite in control of its limbs.

Those girls also seemed more able to cope with the communal nature of the draughty ablutions hut. Molly had found it mortifying with so many others about, trying to wash with no privacy at all. Sensitive about keeping clean, she really wanted to strip off and have a good wash down, but that was out of the question. She sneaked a glance at Win, who was performing some cleverly intimate washing while half wrapped in her towel. Why did these girls seem to have the knack of everything? She felt stupid and clueless, and in her inadequacy responded in the only way she could think of – she became loud.

'Ah, that's better,' Win said, wringing out her flannel as they finished washing. 'Ready for anything now!'

'Ooh!' Molly quipped. 'Ready for anything, eh? Well – there's plenty of fellas round here'd be ready to oblige, I'm sure!'

Win didn't turn to face her and Molly could see she was blushing uncomfortably. 'That's not what I meant and you know it,' she muttered.

'O-ooh – sorry I'm sure, Miss La-di-dah,' Molly said.

'Oh, I say – how rude!' Ruth protested.

'She must have a dirty mind,' Lena sniggered, winking at Molly.

'Oh, I say!' Molly mimicked Ruth.

The two of them left the ablutions hut together, but not without seeing Ruth and Win exchanging eye-rolling glances in their direction. Molly knew they looked down on her and it wasn't a nice feeling. She just didn't know how to deal with these posh girls. She felt loud and crude and unsure of herself, but she wasn't bloody well showing them that!

All in all though, sitting here now, pink-cheeked and glowing, she knew she felt the better for the run and the early-morning fresh air. And she'd liked the porridge and was surprised by the others complaining. One or two had pushed it away with grimaces of disgust. But as far as Molly could see, army food was a good deal better than meals had ever been at home!

Corporal Morrison gave 'What Next' instructions. Kit inspection, followed by – no beating about the bush – nit parade, followed by free-from-infection parade. To follow, on other days, there would inoculations, intelligence tests, and on and on it went.

'Hah, well,' Win said to anyone who was listening as they all limped outside again, 'no rest for the wicked.'

Nit parade. They all lined up. As the orderly carrying out the inspection came closer along the line, Molly, to her consternation, felt herself start to get the shakes. It always seemed to happen, whenever she was subject to any sort of physical examination. She was overcome with panic. *For goodness' sake pull yourself together!* she told herself fiercely.

Those found to have nits were pulled out to form another line the other side of the room. 'You see – happens every time. The peroxide ones – always sure to be infested,' the orderly informed them.

Sure enough, several of the nit-sufferers in the 'disgrace' line were bottle-blondes. Doris was one of them.

Molly's hands broke out in a sweat. Thank God Lena and Cath were nearby! She nudged Cath and winked at her. ''Ere – I hope you ain't got 'em – you and me're sleeping a bit too close together for comfort.'

'Ah no – I don't think so,' Cath said, evidently not worried.

'Don't they get nits down on the farm then?'

Molly suddenly found herself looking into the annoyed and penetrating eyes of Corporal Phoebe Morrison. Molly could smell stale cigarette smoke on her breath.

'Whenever there's a racket it always seems to be coming from you, Fox! Now just *pipe down*, will you?'

As she moved away, to Molly's amazement, Honor leaned close to her and whispered, 'The Gorgon!'

Molly grinned and was about to reply when the medical orderly reached them.

'Ah,' he said, and with only the very briefest of glances into Honor's pale locks, he moved on to Molly. 'Another peroxide – sure to be alive. You get over there.'

'What? Me?' Molly protested, horrified. 'No – you've got it wrong. You ain't even bothered to check! There ain't no nits in my hair – I'd know if there were. And my hair's not out of a bottle neither – it's always been this colour!'

'Don't argue, Fox!' the corporal commanded.

But Molly's blood was up. 'I ain't going over there

without you checking it first. Just 'cause you all think you're better than me! There ain't nothing crawling about in my hair, I can tell yer that!'

She was so furiously resistant that the orderly, who was moving on to check Cath's hair, impatiently came back for another look.

'No point in wasting time if there's nothing in there, I suppose . . .' He pulled Molly's hair roughly this way and that. 'No, there's no sign. You can stay where you are.'

'See? Told yer, daint I?' Molly said loudly. Her legs were shaking so much she could hardly control them, but she wasn't going to let anyone see that.

'Private Fox!' the corporal stormed at her. 'Silence, or you'll be on a charge! This is your last warning!'

Molly stared at her feet, blushing mutinously. Her insides were churning with dread. This was even before the free-from-infection inspection. That was bound to be even worse.

When they got in for the free-from-infection they were told, 'Right – strip – down to your pants and brassiere!'

There were cries of consternation all round.

'Oh no – they don't mean it!'

'Surely they're not going to herd us in like cattle . . .'

'. . . and the doctor's a man!'

Fingers shaking, Molly unbuttoned her tunic, trying, this time, to do what the likes of Win were doing – to obey orders and suffer in silence. But there was a sick twisting in her stomach and her hands were cold and clammy. She felt very small and frightened, and was worried someone would notice. But as the recruits laid their items of clothing one by one on the wooden chairs, attention was diverted to a commotion going on further along: Honor had slithered to the floor in a faint. Win, Ruth and some of the others rushed to her aid. Molly quietly peeled off a stocking. She could smell sweat – hers and other people's. For a moment her legs gave way and she sat heavily on the chair.

'You all right, Moll?' Cath whispered.

'Yeah, ta – just getting my other stocking off.' She wrenched the corners of her mouth up. She didn't show weakness – not her, not Molly Fox!

In those moments she was back in the doctor's brown waiting room in Vauxhall, sitting beside Jenny Button, aged nine, terrified, but with the old dull ache deep in her guts. There and then she had wanted desperately to pee, and she had to go to great lengths to hold it in.

'You can't keep going on like this,' Jenny Button had said. It was during that brief, heavenly time when she had lived with Jenny and Stanley. Of course the wet sheets had shown Jenny there was something wrong, and she had taken her to see the doctor. Molly had stunk of urine for years – was known for it at school, where the other kids taunted her and didn't want her too near. Even now, she felt she wanted to scrub herself repeatedly, to banish that stink. But no one had ever asked what was wrong or what it felt like, not up until now. It had come and gone, the pain, the burning when she passed water, the urgency, so that often she couldn't hold on. Iris screamed at her for wetting the bed, but it had never occurred to her to ask the reason.

By the time they were called inside, Molly was hopping from one foot to the other, but she hadn't dared say anything. In the doctor's frightening room, with its big desk, his books and instruments, the rubber tube of the stethoscope winding down his chest like a creamy white snake, she hadn't been able to hold on any more. The warm, stinking liquid had coursed down her legs, gathering in a cloudy yellow puddle.

'Oh,' Jenny Button had exclaimed, mortified. 'I'm ever so sorry, Doctor. She's got a bit of a problem – that's why I've brought her.'

The doctor was a small, bristly-haired, sagging man in a tweed suit. He was also, as Molly was to discover, a miracle of kindness. He was one of the people who had given her faith in life.

Looking over his pince-nez at the mess on the floor, he cleared his throat and said, 'Yes, I see. Well, that's no good . . . Molly, is it?' And his crumpled face lifted into a smile. Seldom in her life had Molly ever seen such a kind face. Enchanted, despite her clothes turning cold on her, she smiled back. But it didn't stop the trembling which seemed to take over every part of her.

'Now, what I'm going to ask you to do, my dear, is to take off those wet things and hop up on this little bed behind here' – he indicated a drab curtain – 'and we'll see if we can sort out what's going on.'

Jenny Button made an encouraging face at her and Molly staggered off behind the curtain, her teeth chattering. As she struggled to tug her clothes off, she heard the surgery door open and the murmur of the doctor's voice. A moment later, he appeared beside her.

'That's good – that's very good,' he said softly. 'Now – if you could just hop up on here.'

Lying on her back, Molly was overcome by tremors. She felt confused. The doctor was being kind and she didn't believe he would hurt her, but her body was in the worst panic she had ever known. Her breath came in panting gasps. She saw the doctor frown as if in puzzlement.

'Now, there really is no need to be afraid,' he told her. 'I'm not going to do anything to hurt you, my dear. We just need to sort out this nasty infection you're carrying about with you.'

Molly tried to nod, shaking uncontrollably.

'Now there, it's all right.' He spoke so kindly, and to her astonishment, tears filled her eyes and coursed down her cheeks so fast she scarcely knew what was coming next; in a second, she was sobbing violently.

'There, there—' The doctor didn't ask her why she was crying, to her relief, as she had no idea herself. He laid a hand on her chest and patted her soothingly, while his other warm hand pressed on her lower belly. Molly gasped.

'That hurts, doesn't it? I thought so.' The feel of his hands was comforting. Her storm of crying began to calm. He asked her questions, about how often she had to pass water, how it felt. Then, calmly he asked her to open her legs. He looked down at her carefully, just for a moment.

'That's all – sit up.' From his pocket he took a clean cotton handkerchief. 'Now – wipe your face. You may keep the handkerchief.' His kind face looked down into her tear-blotched one. That was still, to this day, her one hanky. She had vowed to keep it for ever. 'You're going to get better,' he said. 'There's no need for you to be suffering like this. I'm going to prescribe some medicine, and your kind friend will look after you. But it's important that you keep clean down there – so make sure you wash, won't you? And . . .' He hesitated. In the gentlest, quietest of voices he added, 'No one else should *ever* be touching you down there, because that's not right. Do you understand?'

Molly gazed back at him, wide-eyed. What was he talking about? She didn't think about night-time things, about William Rathbone and his dirty, poking fingers in the daytime. She pushed them out of her mind. Was that what he meant? But how did he know? Could the doctor be God in disguise? She nodded obediently.

'Good girl.' He reached out and patted her head.

To her astonishment, when she walked round the curtain, there was no sign of the puddle on the floor and instead, on the chair, there was a little pile of dry clothes.

'Here are a few extras we found,' he said.

Jenny Button was effusive in her thanks. 'You're so very kind, Doctor.' There were tears in her eyes. In a tone which seemed to have added meaning, she went on, 'I'll try to keep her with us for as long as I can. But she isn't my daughter . . .'

That week was the most delicious Molly could ever remember. On the doctor's instructions, Jenny Button insisted that Molly go to bed while she was dosed with the powder the doctor had prescribed, and fed tasty broths with Jenny's fresh bread. All that week she lay as if in heaven, the smells from the bake house in the yard drifting up to her window, with a picture book Jenny had bought for her and two knitting needles and some scarlet wool to try out her fledgling knitting skills. Never had she known comfort or kindness like it. She had lain, staring dreamily at the light changing on the bedroom wall, in ecstasy, and it was the most acutely happy memory she had.

And when, at last feeling better, she had to go back to Iris and Joe, and Old Man Rathbone was in any case already heading into his last illness, she hissed at him when he shuffled over to her bed.

'No – you're not to. The doctor said! Keep away, or I'll tell!' And to her amazement, after staring down at her through the gloom, he turned away and climbed groaningly back into his bed.

Even though the Vauxhall doctor whose name she never knew had been her first kind touch, a touch and understanding which strengthened her like wire, the old shaking still got the better of her now.

The medical orderly was a man – also kindly – and straightforward, dark-haired, quite young. When she appeared, quivering, in the little examination room, he said, 'It's really all right you know. I'm sorry we have to put you through all this. Army regulations and all that.'

He put her at ease. She didn't feel prickly or angry, even though he was so well-spoken. She didn't even feel like flirting with him. He was a doctor and well-educated. It somehow put him in a different category.

'I know,' she said, hugging herself. 'S'all right. You've got to do your job.'

'Sorry about this—' He pulled on the front of her knicker elastic and accidently let it go with a snap which made them both laugh. 'Sorry!' he said again. 'I say, you really are trembling a lot. Is it that cold in here?'

'N-no,' she tried to say.

He tapped her back and chest, looked down her throat and made her hold out her arms, hands stretched open.

'Ah – now, what have we here? Had this long?' He stared into the crooks of her elbows, at the red, raw skin.

'Years.'

'Just eczema? I don't think it's anything infectious, luckily. Here's some cream for that. Otherwise you look in pretty good health.' He jotted notes. 'Where're you from?'

'Birmingham.'

'Ah.'

Molly wasn't sure what 'ah' meant.

'Right – that's all. Dismiss!'

She groped her way back to the chair where she'd left her clothes and sat shakily on it. Thank God he hadn't found anything awful! On the other side of the room, Honor was slowly dressing, facing away from Molly, showing a long, white back. Corporal Morrison stood at the edge of the room, pressing the end of a pen to her lips as if it was a cigarette.

Molly felt exhausted suddenly, and bewildered. The doctor had been as kind and nice as anything, but what was this quivering ghost within her that kept coming back to haunt her?

'You all right?' a voice asked, making her jump, so that she felt caught in the raw. Win's wholesome face was looking down at her.

'Course I'm all right,' Molly snapped. 'Why wouldn't I be?'

'I only asked,' Win said tartly. 'There's no need to take it as an insult.'

'Poking her nose in as usual,' Molly muttered as Win walked away. But she felt small and ashamed, because she knew that Win meant to be kind.

'Right – outside in threes!' Phoebe Morrison let out her usual cry, and they all jumped to obey.

As they got themselves organized amid the comings and goings of the camp all around them, Molly saw a figure she recognized coming towards them, carrying a shovel. Without thinking, she called out, 'Eh – Billy, it's me, Molly – over 'ere!' She waved frantically.

'Silence!' Swelling with fury, their Corporal left the front and strode round to the side of the gaggle of women. 'Private Fox – I might have known.' She came up close so that Molly could feel her hot ashy breath. Close up, her skin looked tired. 'You carry on like this and you'll be heading for a charge. D'you understand?'

'S'pose so, yeah.'

'DO YOU UNDERSTAND?'

'Yes, Madam!' Molly couldn't keep the sarcastic tone out of her voice.

'Yes, Corporal!

'Yes, Corporal!'

Phoebe Morrison stared forbiddingly into Molly's face for a few more seconds, then turned on her heel. Molly saw that Billy had stopped and was watching the whole event, grinning. She raised her thumb at him, just in time, before Gorgon Morrison turned round again.

Ten

The next days were full of activity, for which the new recruits were frogmarched from place to place. Daily square-bashing led by members of the male battalions was inevitably a shambles to begin with, which could only improve in the face of much yelling of commands and daily practice.

Molly didn't find the drill itself difficult to master, but she got strict tellings off for messing about and behaving flirtatiously towards the drill sergeants. On the second day, stationed in the second row of the squad, she called out, 'Ain't you got nice big muscles then?' to the solid young sergeant. This caused much tittering in the ranks.

'Silence on parade!' the young man bawled, scowling and trying to see who had shouted out. Molly offered him a wink as his eyes met hers. He gave her a contemptuous glare before continuing, 'Left wheel, quick march!'

As a number of them drilled the women, each of them had to learn who the troublemakers were. Cath, who enjoyed mischief, usually giggled along at Molly's antics, but somehow never got into trouble herself.

On the third day, Molly called out again, this time to a very tall fellow who was standing before them, ''Ere – you're a nice big one, ain't yer?'

There were scattered giggles as the man blushed, but he couldn't see who had actually shouted at him.

'Who said that?' he demanded, irritated.

There was silence. Molly stared innocently ahead of her.

'Are we going to stand here all morning, 'til I get an answer?'

Molly could hear some impatient mutterings behind her. 'For goodness' *sake* . . .' and 'Why doesn't she just grow up? Wasting everybody's time . . .'

Unpopular as ever, Molly kept quiet and the sergeant gave up. But afterwards, some of the others gave her snooty looks. Then she ran into Ruth, soon after, in the ablutions hut. Ruth stared stonily at her, her protruding teeth making her look rabbity, a blush seeping through her cheeks. *What the hell's she got to go all red about?* Molly wondered. 'Summat the matter?' she asked, hand on hips.

'Well if you must know,' Ruth spluttered in her strangulated voice, 'I really think it's a bit thick of you to keep causing trouble during drill. No one finds it amusing, you know. It's really rather childish of you.' Her face was ablaze. Ruth was clearly not used to having it out with people.

'D'you think I give a monkeys what you f***ing well think?' Molly sneered. Somehow when she was talking to these posh girls, more bad language seemed to crash out from between her lips than at any other time. And Ruth was just *odd*. 'Some of us can 'ave a bit of a laugh, even if you can't, yer po-faced cow!'

Ruth made a distasteful face and turned away. 'It's no good talking to you, I can see.'

'Why – ain't I good enough for yer then?'

Ruth turned again, as if stung by this remark. For a

moment she seemed at a loss, her basic politeness clashing with her anger. 'It's not that ... it's just ... why must you be so *coarse* all the time?'

'Maybe that's just the way I am,' Molly snapped sulkily.

'Well just...' Ruth shrugged uncomfortably. 'Some of us don't like it, that's all.'

'Well maybe "some of us" will just have to lump it.'

Molly stood watching as Ruth walked out of the ablutions hut. She'd had the last word, and that was the way she liked it. She stuck her tongue out at Ruth's back. In the quiet, amid dripping taps, she found herself longing for a drink, a lot of drink, to blot it all out.

There were dental examinations, kit inspections – Molly fared very well with this, and received surprised praise from the Gorgon – and gruesome lectures about venereal disease, through which, surprisingly, the wilting Honor – who had quickly become known as 'Beaky' – sat with unruffled calm, while Lena turned green and had to put her head between her knees.

That week, the only time they were to be allowed out was on the Sunday for church parade. Molly wasn't bothered by this. The camp contained more male servicemen than women, so as far as she was concerned there was plenty of scope for excitement. She knew Billy was interested, for a start – they just needed to find a way to meet up.

In the meantime she quickly learned more about the other girls in Hut J, either through conversations she had with her friends, or overheard among others. Win, as expected, had spent seven years in a girls' boarding school and had been about to embark on her teacher training when she joined up. Ruth had a place to read natural sciences at Cambridge which she planned to take up once the war was over. Of Honor they still knew very little except that she came from a wealthy farming family near Banbury. Lena was the third in a family of six children.

'Our Cissie – that's my big sister – 'as been wed for two years now. Our mom wanted me to stop home and look after all the others but I down't like all that – I wanted a job. I mean it's not that I'm not fond of the little bleeders but I'm not their mom. 'Er was always making me stop home from school; course we daint want our Paul, that's me elder brother, stopping home, him being the boy. And the way our dad was . . .' She didn't say more, but an expression of loathing passed over her face. 'Then our Paul went off into the Merchant Navy, I couldn't believe it when 'e said 'e was going. I never thought 'e'd go and leave me . . .' She sounded almost tearful saying this. 'And I thought, well I ain't stopping 'ere, not with 'im gone. Soon as I could I went off and got a job in a big house out at Darlaston – you know, in service. I s'pose I'd've done better in a factory. The money's better, 'specially now. But they were all right, it wasn't a bad place to work, but one day I'd just had enough skivvying – I gave in my notice and signed up with the army. I don't like stopping anywhere too long, me. And I worry about our Paul. I wish 'e 'adn't gone and left . . .'

Molly was disappointed in Lena. She had thought, being fellow Midlanders, that they'd be friends, but Lena was a cheerless person who spent an awful lot of time mooning over her brother. It was Cath who Molly found she spent more and more time with, and they laughed a lot together. Cath was the seventh of nine children from a farm near Waterford.

'Nothing was ever the same after Mammy died,' she told Molly sadly one evening, perched on the edge of Molly's bed. 'She took sick when I was fifteen. It all happened so fast, and then she was gone.' Her eyes filled with tears. 'I've only brothers – all the other eight – and of course the eldest ones had the farm. The rest of us, well . . .' She shrugged. 'Daddy was a lost soul without Mammy. She was the heart of the house and the farm. It was all so sad, everything about the farm just felt so deserted and haunted. Even the horses missed her – they used to call out for her at first! I just wanted to get out of there as fast as I could . . .'

Head on one side, she gave a wistful smile through her tears. 'I don't know as I could ever face going back there.'

Molly listened, astonished. How lucky some people were, having mothers who they were so fond of, who they could love and miss!

'I hope if I ever have children I can be like her,' Cath said in a soft voice. She stared ahead of her for a moment. 'The day they buried her – it was May time, just gorgeous the day before, and the apple blossom was out, just perfect. I picked an armful of blossom – oh, it was so lovely! I wanted to put it on her grave. And the next morning, when we went up to the church, which is on the side of the hill, it came on to rain. God, it was Irish rain all right, came across the side of the hill in sheets, and I can remember standing inside the wall of the church, by the big crucifix, holding my flowers and trying to keep them from spoiling. But it was hopeless

– the rain lashed them all to pieces . . .' She shook her head, the tears running down her cheeks. 'D'you know, since that day I've never believed in God or Jesus or anything else about it. We went in to Mass and I knew the priest would have told me to offer it up and everything. And I just knelt there looking at Mammy's little coffin up at the front there, with my crushed flowers on it, with Jesus looking down, and I thought, God, if you're even up there, you're a bastard and I hate you for letting Mammy die. I don't want anything else to do with you. I've never been back to Mass since. Daddy couldn't make me – he never went himself. Now and then he'd just stand out with the other men. It was Mammy who went.'

She wiped her eyes. 'So here I am.'

Molly was really touched. 'That sounds terrible,' she said, sincerely.

'I'm not even close to my brothers really. Except my youngest brother, Donal – I write him now and then. But the others . . . some of them were so much older. You'd think growing up in the same house you'd have more in common, wouldn't you?'

'Oh – I don't know,' Molly said.

'Are you close to your brothers and sisters, Molly?'

'No – I've only really got one brother – the other went off years back. No – I wouldn't say we're close – not at all.' How much could she say? she wondered. There wasn't much she wanted to say about her family. 'I wasn't close to any of 'em. That's why I was keen to get away.'

The two girls smiled fondly at each other. The smile from Cath's pretty face warmed Molly's heart more than she could have ever said.

Two beds away, both with their backs to them, sat Win and Honor. Win, in tones of eternal patience, was trying to teach Honor how to darn her stockings.

'What's up with the Beak?' Cath whispered. 'She's a bit of a sad case ain't she?' Honor cried herself to sleep every night. Win had come over a couple of times to try and comfort her, but was soon driven back to her own bed by the cold. Lena had had the odd weep as well, and said she was missing her brother. But so far, neither Molly nor Cath had shed a tear. However tough the army was, in many ways it was better than life at home.

'She's not bad really,' Molly said. She'd told them about Honor coining the nickname 'the Gorgon' for Corporal Morrison and it had gone round the whole unit. Everyone called her that now.

They watched Honor. Molly thought she had never met anyone so strange, so alien and different from herself.

'That's it,' Win was saying. 'It's really quite easy. Just weave the needle back and forth like that – then the other way and you'll have covered the hole – see?'

'Oh, thank you so much!' Honor intoned in her nasal voice. 'I do feel so very hopeless – we've always had servants to do everything. I never even went away to school like you.'

'Well you pick up a fair bit there, inevitably,' Win said, getting to her feet. 'Can you manage now, d'you think?'

'Oh yes, I think so. Thank you!'

As she moved away, Win half turned and saw Molly and Cath watching her. Being a naturally friendly girl, she seemed about to smile, but then, as if registering who they were, she just nodded and walked away. Cath grinned. 'That was a bit of a straight look. I don't think she knows what to make of us.'

'I don't s'pose she does,' Molly said. She imitated the cut-glass tones of some of the other girls further along the hut. 'I s'pose she's never met rough types like us before.' They saw Win glance back at her, frowning.

There was a growing atmosphere of tension in the hut, which at the moment ran along class lines. Molly felt as if the likes of Win and Ruth looked down on herself and some of the others for being rude and childish – and the more it went on, the more rebellious and childish she felt. But she told herself she didn't care. She'd made a friend, and that was the most wonderful feeling of all.

Eleven

The first week of training was already almost over, and Molly and Cath were firm friends. Lena kept to herself a lot in the evenings, writing letters to Paul, or lying hunched miserably on her bed, just not seeming to want to be sociable.

'She seems ever so caught up with that brother of hers,' Molly said, puzzled, as she and Cath walked to the NAAFI for a cup of tea one afternoon. 'She's a bit of a wet rag really.'

'I know – I mean, it must be a worry to her,' Cath said, 'but there are limits. There's nothing she can do. You've got to get on with your life.'

Molly was about to remark that she wouldn't lose any sleep over her own brother, when a cheerful voice called out, 'Hello there, stranger!'

'Billy! 'Bout time!' Now life might start to get a bit more interesting around here! 'Where the hell've you been? I've been looking out for you all over the place!' Apart from that time during drill, she hadn't seen him at all since they arrived.

'Well – I get about!' Billy grinned. He had a pink complexion and a face that looked as if it had taken a few punches. He nodded towards the NAAFI. 'Coming in for a cuppa?' The two women followed him in.

'This is Cath, my mate,' Molly said as they queued up at the counter. Billy and Cath nodded at each other.

'All right, Cath – how're you getting on?'

Molly was tingling with life suddenly. They bought their cups of tea and sat at one of the tables.

'Bet you got it in the neck for calling out to me the other morning,' Billy said, seeming amused. 'You're a case, you are.'

'Ah well,' Molly shrugged, offhand. 'It was worth it to see you, Billy boy.' It felt as if they'd known each other a long time, just because each was a familiar face. 'What was you up to with that big spade then?'

'Oh – I'm one of the coke shovellers,' he laughed. 'Us blokes have to do the heavy work around here. How d'you think you get any warm water first thing of a morning?'

'I thought I heard a racket first thing,' Cath said.

'Yeah, well that'll be us stoking up.'

Molly took a sip of her strong, sweet tea. 'Ah – I needed that.' She looked deep into Billy's eyes. That always worked well. She knew how to hook a man. 'It's ever so nice to see yer.'

They talked about camp life for a bit, and when Cath had finished her tea, she tactfully got up and left them to it. 'See you later, Molly!'

Soon after she'd gone, Billy asked casually, 'D'yer want to come out one night, Molly?'

'Yeah – you're on!'

'You're not allowed out of camp this week – first week and that.'

'Oh, I don't know as I'd let that stop me!' Molly laughed, leaning closer to Billy. 'D'you know of a good place to go? It'd just be nice to see yer. You know – spend a bit of time together, like.' She could feel herself working on him, as if she was programmed to do it.

'You're all right you are, Molly,' Billy laughed. 'What about tonight? We could come in here if yer want . . .'

Molly leaned even closer. 'What about we sneak out – just you and me? I'm sick of being stuck in 'ere.'

Billy sniggered. 'Like that is it? But what if we get caught . . . ? We'll get a roasting.'

'We won't. We'll work it out somehow.'

Molly told herself she couldn't care less about army authority – so what if she got caught for sneaking out? What was the worst they could do? This was not the whole truth though. Over her days so far working under Phoebe Morrison, the woman had begun to get under her skin. She found in herself a childlike desire to please her, to try and win her praise. When it came to kit inspections, she had been outstandingly successful. She found wearing uniform a relief – she didn't stand out because of her old make-do clothes, and she kept herself as smart and clean as possible. When Phoebe Morrison came round to inspect their hut one morning and said, obviously surprised, 'Very good, Fox, keep it up,' the glow of those words lasted all day, as well as the startled looks on Win and Ruth's faces. When she put her mind to it and didn't fool around, she was good at drill. And she thrived on praise, starting to look out for ways she could please Corporal Morrison especially.

But there was another side to Molly that railed childishly against the rules, that felt she'd never amount to anything so she might as well spoil it all now. By the time she met Billy in the evening she was in that sort of defiant mood, all ready for naughtiness and daring. God, she wanted to get out of there and get some drinks inside her!

They'd arranged to meet near the NAAFI canteen again. Molly made sure she was a bit late. She wanted Billy to be waiting, not her, wanted him to see her walking towards him. Even in the unbecoming ATS uniform she knew that with her figure, her belt pulled nice and tight, she could make quite an impression. She knew the moves, walking sinuously as if along a tightrope, swaying her hips; she'd seen her mother do it often enough, though many men were too scared of Iris to come near. But the two of them had the same curving figure.

The effect was marred somewhat by the fact that as well as being bitterly cold and slippery underfoot, it was already dark, and she was only able to be sure Billy was waiting for her once she got really close. She saw the tip of his cigarette glowing in the gloom.

'That you, Billy boy?' she called softly.

'Over 'ere, Molly.' Billy pushed himself off against the wall.

She came up close, smiling, breathing in the rough tobacco smoke. 'Umm, that's nice,' she said.

'Want one?' He patted his pocket.

'Ta—' She took one and he lit it for her. The smoke felt nice, rough in her throat, part of the excitement. 'Let's just get away from here,' she said. 'Somewhere we can be alone – just you and me, Billy?'

To her disappointment, Billy stalled. 'We'd best not, you know. You'll only end up spending half the night in the guard room. T'ain't worth it. It's only a day or two more and then you can go out anyway.'

'Oh but, Billy – it's Friday night! You chicken?'

'No – it just ain't worth it,' he said firmly, as if to a child. 'You're bound to get caught – take my word for it. Come on – we can go in 'ere and have a sit down together. I'll take you out next week.'

'Promise?' she wheedled. She wanted booze, excitement, and to show what she was made of.

'Course – come on.'

'Take my arm, Billy.'

He seemed a bit surprised by this, but Molly pushed her arm through his. She wanted to make sure everyone knew she'd made a killing as they walked into the canteen – the tea-sipping types like Win and Ruth if they were in there. After all, she might not be a goody-goody like them, but she knew how to get a man all right!

The air inside was heavy with smells of cabbage, stew and the singed jam in the roly-poly pudding, mixed with smoke and the fug from lots of warm young bodies in uniform – which had its own musty smell. The place was crowded with young people drinking from beer bottles and sipping mugs of tea and chatting together. Molly saw a couple of the new recruits from her hut, Doris and Lily from Nottingham, and she waved at them, but there was no sign of Win or Ruth.

'Most of our lot are in the hut darning their stockings,' she said scornfully, as she and Billy found a space at the end of a table where they could squeeze in.

'I see that one from on the train's here,' Billy said, nodding along the table. Molly saw Lipstick Lips Marguerite at the far end, in animated conversation with a young officer, and rolled her eyes at Billy. To her surprise, halfway along the table she spotted Honor, seated with two young men, one on each side of her, both of whom seemed to be paying her rapt attention.

'Blimey,' she said to Billy, 'there's old Blarting Beak – see the blonde there. Hardly knows her arse from 'er elbow, that one.' She felt a bit disloyal saying this. Honor was all right really. She just said it for effect.

Billy glanced along at Honor and to Molly's surprise said, 'Looks a bit of all right though. But a bit posh for me.'

'Yeah,' Molly said, affronted. What on earth was it about Honor that men found attractive? 'She's right out of your league, sunshine.'

'Want a cuppa tea?'

'No – get us a beer, will yer?'

Billy went over to the counter and brought back two bottles and glasses. There were screams of laughter coming from that end of the room. The cook, a male in this case, had an apparently endless supply of disgusting puns for almost every item of food, and some of the girls were enjoying this, including Doris and Mary. Others sat looking po-faced.

'So – how're you settling in?' Billy asked.

'Oh, it's all right, I s'pose,' Molly said. She couldn't describe her true mixed feelings, how much she wanted to please, to do well, and at the same time, every time she was given an order she immediately wanted to do the opposite. She felt as if she was possessed by a two-year-old infant who wanted to scream 'NO' each time she was asked to do anything, then resented being told off.

'I've had enough of all that polishing buttons and cap badges and that . . .' This was not true, either. She liked it. 'And you should see the state of my feet! All blisters!'

'Oh, those'll soon go,' Billy said easily.

'How long've you been in, Billy?'

'A few months. I was Reserved Occ – munitions factory – but I kept on until they let me go. I wanted a piece of the action. No good staying at home when it's all happening, is there?'

'No, that's brave of yer,' she flattered him.

'What about you then?'

'Beats being at home.' She took a long drink. The beer was already making her feel mellow.

'Oh I see,' he laughed. 'Like that is it? Tell me about yourself then, Molly. Where'd you grow up?'

'Round Ashted, Vauxhall . . . in a palace!' She gave her full-hearted chuckle.

'Course you would round there! Like the Green where I come from – from another palace!'

They had an understanding then. Molly suddenly realized she genuinely liked Billy. She gave him a limited outline of her childhood – two brothers, father shell-shocked, leaving school for a series of factory jobs. She mentioned the Buttons, the neighbours who'd been kind, and Em, her best friend. All in all, she thought, she'd made it sound not too bad really.

'I'd've liked Em to join up with me really,' she said. 'But her mom's not too good with her health and she's sweet on this bloke called Norman. Shame really because he's the most boring so-and-so you'll ever meet – great big ears—' She waggled her hands behind her ears, making Billy laugh. 'He's a copper and you can't even have a laugh with him. Takes everything all serious, as if 'e's about to have you arrested.'

'She must see summat in him.'

'Well – each to their own,' she said, smiling winningly at him. 'Now – you tell me about you.'

Billy talked about his widowed mother and sister Jean who he was evidently fond of. 'Jean's a bit like your friend Em – sticks with our mom. I sometimes wonder if any bloke'll be able to win her away from Mom.'

'Shame really,' Molly said. 'How old is she?'

'Twenty-six next birthday.'

'Shame,' Molly said again. Half her mind now was taken up with thinking how to get Billy outside. Sitting here talking was all well, but she wanted to move things along. It was as if something was driving her that she had no control over.

They had a second drink. While Billy was fetching it, Molly glanced along at Honor. Honor's tall back was slightly slouched, one of her long arms bent up languidly to her face, holding a cigarette. She was talking to one of the young soldiers, who seemed deeply fascinated by her. Honor gave him a lovely smile. Molly was truly taken aback. Honor obviously had hidden depths that she hadn't realized.

Molly and Billy talked longer, amid the loud conversation and bursts of laughter, about home and the things they had in common. Molly didn't swear in front of Billy. She realized that he was quite a straight, respectable lad. After a time she drank up and leaned closer to him again.

'Fancy getting some fresh air for a bit?'

'Yes, all right,' Billy said easily.

He led the way out of the thronging canteen and they were out in the bitter air. There was a half moon, smudged with cloud. Once more, Molly took his arm and they strolled slowly, not aiming for anywhere in particular, but ending up heading towards the far end where the catering company and food stores were.

'Out on the town next week then,' she said.

'If you like. Not everyone's friendly though, you know. They're not too happy to have their park taken over by the army!'

'I thought it was a racecourse?'

'Used to be. They used to hang people there at one time as well!'

'Ooh they daint, did they?' Molly pretended to shudder. 'You're scaring me now.'

She nuzzled close to Billy and he put his arm round her shoulders.

'Maybe we'll see a headless ghost!' he chuckled.

'Don't say that. I get scared easily!'

'You? I don't believe yer!'

Over in the deep shadows of the huts she turned to him, inviting him to put his arms round her.

'Blimey Molly – you're hot stuff, ain't yer?' He sounded taken aback.

'There's no need to be like that,' she said coyly. 'I just like a bit of a cuddle, that's all.' She felt the excitement of it, the need to conquer him, mixed with the knowledge that that was what he wanted, to reach this point, what they always wanted. Everything else was just a preparation, a step towards it.

She pressed herself against him and raised her face to his. Billy seemed thrown by this.

'C-can I kiss yer then?'

'What're you waiting for?' she said, sliding her hand up and down his back. He was solid and strong.

'I s'pose I'm used to taking things a bit more slow, like,' he said.

'What's the use in waiting?' she said. 'Give us a kiss, Billy.'

His lips reached down for hers and in moments they were kissing passionately, pressed up against the damp planks of the hut. Molly clung to him, pulling him tighter, pressing against him, all her instincts primed to excite him, to give him what was expected.

'Jesus,' he gasped, freeing his lips after a few minutes. There was, if she had been able to hear it, something in his tone which was not pleasure but alarm, revulsion even. But she did not choose to hear it.

'There,' she said. 'How's that then, Billy?'

She was so close up to him that she could tell he was very excited. While still just in command of himself, he said, 'D'yer want . . . ? I mean, I didn't expect . . .'

Molly said nothing, unsure what to say, but smiled back at him, which Billy took as a sign of permission.

'Jesus Christ,' he said, unable to help himself. And his hands were struggling with her then, the tough uniform making her like a parcel that was frustrating to unwrap. He wrestled with her buttons, breathing fast, hands fumbling for her breasts. He managed to free one breast from the restraining army brassiere and nuzzled her hungrily, his hands moving down, tugging her skirt up. And Molly up until that moment was with him, leading him on, even with the cold air on her skin, but then baulked when he started on the skirt, trying to fumble down there . . . *No one should be touching you* . . . It was as if a freezing wind rushed through her mind, chilling any sense of involvement with him. She froze, suddenly outside it all, seeing his blond head at her breast in the moonlight, his desperate fumbling . . .

'Stop it!' she hissed. 'Not that! Don't do that!'

She tugged her skirt back down so emphatically that she startled him.

'What?' It was as if she had slapped him. 'What d'yer mean? I thought you wanted . . . I mean, the way you was carrying on . . .'

'No – not that. Not all the way!' she said, closing her clothes, wanting now more than anything to get away from him. Chasing them was one thing, reeling them in. Cold, physical reality was another.

'Don't tell me you're a cowing virgin now, after all that come on!'

'What if I am? What's it to you?'

Billy laughed contemptuously. 'You're just another f***ing tease. Go on – get lost. I know your sort.'

'Oh Billy!' She was stung by his rejection of her. After all, she'd given him a good time, hadn't she? What the hell was the matter with him? 'Don't be like that,' she wheedled. 'I thought we was going to be friends?'

'*Friends?* Friends is one thing, Molly – you've got a pretty queer notion of just being friends is all I can say.' Billy started walking, fast, back across the dark field, Molly struggling to keep up.

'I'm sorry, Billy – I daint mean to upset yer . . .'

'Well you have – all right? I don't like being mucked about with.' He strode on, furiously. 'I'll walk you back to your hut, Molly – which one is it?'

'J,' she said.

'Right – but that's it then. You're a bit too fast for my liking.'

'But I told yer – I daint mean—' she panted after him. 'We can take it more slowly, Billy – whatever you want.'

He ignored her and soon they reached Hut J.

'Right,' he said, standing up very straight, on his dignity. 'I'll see yer then.'

'Ain't you going to give me a goodnight kiss?'

'No. Don't think so. Cheers, Molly.'

He turned to go. Molly pushed the door of the hut open and made sure to say in a loud but seductive voice, 'Goodnight, Billy – thanks for a lovely evening.'

He was striding away and didn't turn round again.

Molly went inside and walked jauntily along the middle of the rows of beds. Some of the others looked up at her. Win and Ruth were on Ruth's bed, looking through some book or other.

'Evening, ladies!' Molly said mockingly.

'Do you see what I see?' a voice said. Molly wasn't sure who it was – one of the snooty ones by the door. 'I think an officer's groundsheet just walked in.'

'More like lower rank's groundsheet,' another suggested, and there were giggles.

Molly turned round. 'Least I know one end of a fella from another – not like some of yer!'

Lena was sitting against the head of her bed, her knees drawn up, hair in plaits, glowering at Molly.

'What's up with you?' Molly asked.

'Nothing,' Lena said sulkily. Molly knew it was because she hadn't had her expected letter from Paul. Anyone'd think he was her flaming boyfriend, not her brother! Even Cath seemed tired and grumpy.

'Not you as well!' Molly fumed, unbuttoning her jacket. 'What the bleedin 'ell's got into everyone to-night?'

Twelve

Molly did not sleep well that night. She couldn't settle and had horrible dreams. In one, Phoebe Morrison was furiously ordering her to leave the army and go home. She jerked awake in the darkness, feeling desolate, as if she had betrayed herself. Then Billy's face floated into her mind's eye, his eyes full of disgust. She felt wretched and confused about what had happened last night. Why did she spoil everything? Nothing ever seemed to turn out well with men: she always made a mess of it. As often as she could she just shrugged it off, but this time she genuinely liked Billy – not like George and some of the others who were a bad lot anyway. Why had she forced things to go like that, to upset him so badly?

As she lay there, she began to hear the distant scraping, rattling sounds of coke being shovelled into the boiler for the ablutions hut. Her heart fluttered. An impulse seized her. Slipping out of bed, she hurried into her clothes and crept stocking-footed along between the beds. Everyone else seemed to be asleep. There was almost another hour to go before the reveille bugle which would set up groans along the rows of beds. Molly slipped her shoes on. It was still dark outside, clear and frosty, and the cold air stung her nostrils.

Stepping outside, she was startled to find another figure heading straight towards her, head down.

'Cath?' she hissed. She hadn't seen that Cath wasn't in her bed.

Cath jumped violently.

'God, Molly!'

'Where've yer been?' Molly's scrambled brain somehow thought Cath had been to find Billy.

'Well where d'you think?' Cath pointed back at the latrines.

'Oh yes, course! That's where I'm off to – had too much to drink last night!'

Cath nodded, barely seeming to hear her, and went back inside. She wasn't looking too well. Molly hurried across the stiff grass towards the sounds, hoping it was Billy there this morning and that he hadn't been replaced.

In the pre-dawn greyness she was relieved to find Billy, with a lamp, bent over his shovel and a pile of coke. He jumped, startled to find someone appearing beside him.

'Blimey, Molly!' He stopped digging, laying a hand on his heart. 'What the hell're you doing creeping about this early?'

'I came to see you, course, Billy.' She spoke softly, wanting to get back on the old footing with him. 'I just wanted to see yer. Say sorry – you know – if I upset yer last night.'

His expression was severe and not especially welcoming.

'Well,' he spoke sourly. 'It's in the past, I s'pose. But at least I know now.'

'Know what, Billy?' She leaned on the low, jutting piece of wall that separated them.

He looked nastily at her. 'Know what you're like. You're all right in yer way, Molly – to talk to and that.

103

You're a bit of a laugh, I won't say you aren't. But you're not my type in the end. It's left a bad taste, Molly, that it has.'

'Look, I'm sorry,' she said miserably. 'I never meant it to be like that. I really like you, Billy. What if . . .' She brightened, tried wheedling. 'How about we go out tonight? Give it another chance? Would you like that?'

He stood up and leaned on the handle of the shovel. 'No, to be frank, I wouldn't. Just leave it, Molly. Go and try your charms out on some other sucker. I'm the sort that likes my girl a bit less forward than that. Just leave me alone – all right?'

'But—'

'Go on, Molly.' He jerked his head disgustedly. 'Get lost.'

'You two-faced bastard!' Molly shrieked. Rage and shame swelled in her chest and she knew she was not far from tears. 'You act like you're my friend and then what do I get?'

Billy came urgently towards her, laying a heavy hand on her shoulder. 'Shut up the racket, for God's sake.'

'You're all the cowing same you men,' she snarled into his face.

'Are we?' Billy said bitterly.

'One thing on your bloody minds then you blame it all on us! You never know what you flaming well want!'

'Well I know what I want now,' he spoke in a loud, hoarse whisper. 'I want you to get out of my sight – got it?'

Molly flung away from him with a screech of frustration. 'You rotten bastard!'

'Yeah—' Billy picked went to work with the shovel again. 'Nice knowing yer, Molly.'

Molly stumbled back to Hut J, for want of anywhere else to go. She crept back to her bed and lay down, fully clothed. There was no point in undressing again. She was boiling inside at first, so angry she could have laid Billy out. How *dare* he say those things? She punched the mattress but it made the springs squeak so she didn't do it again. How could he, the rotten, hypocritical bastard? And then she felt ashamed and very alone, and for the first time since she had left home, sobs rose in her. She curled on her side, wrapped in one of the rough army blankets, and cried as silently as she could into its thick, scratchy folds.

But by the time everyone was up that morning, Molly was dry-eyed, perfectly ready for her kit inspection, which she passed with flying colours.

'Good work, Fox,' the Gorgon said in her clipped voice. Molly glowed inside. No one would ever have known there was anything wrong.

Bugger you, Billy, she thought. There's plenty more fish in the sea. What makes you think I'd come running after you?

Cath, though, seemed to be struggling. She wasn't feeling very well. 'I'll have to muddle through the day somehow,' she said. 'I don't want to turn in sick.'

'You don't look too good at all,' Molly said, looking at her pale face.

'Oh, my stomach's not the most reliable,' Cath said. 'I'll be all right soon enough.'

Training continued to be just as intense. They passed the magic first Sunday, and church parade, which Molly found a strange experience as she had never been to church before. After that they were officially allowed out in the evenings, and Molly was determined to make sure she found blokes to go with.

On the Monday, though, they were faced with the written intelligence test. When Corporal Morrison told them about this, Molly felt a stab of dread, but she kept her chin up and looked as if she was full of confidence. Inside she was anything but. What if she couldn't do it? What if she was really as stupid as everyone had said all her life? She was shaky with nerves as they filed into the hut. You're not that stupid, she tried to tell herself. After all, it was she who had helped Em with her arithmetic when Em kept missing school. Inside the hut were arranged rows of little individual desks and on each lay an examination paper and a pencil. As she squeezed in behind the desk, Molly saw Win and Ruth take up their pencils with an air of confidence, as did some of the others. Cath was somewhere behind her, but Lena, who was just in front on the neighbouring row, turned and grimaced at her. She didn't look any too happy either.

Molly turned over the paper, once they were told to start. There were picture questions – images you had to match as if you were looking in the mirror, and visual patterns that you had to continue. She frowned, working her way through them. The problems seemed suspiciously easy. These were followed by mathematical questions and series to complete. Molly worked steadily through them and was able to put down an answer for every question. She thought they made sense, but she was so unsure of herself that she was certain she must have got it all wrong. Soon it was too late to go back and she had to hand the paper in. By the time she got out of the room, seeing Win and Ruth looking smugly satisfied (or so it seemed to her), she was convinced that the whole test had been a disaster and she would be thrown out of the army immediately.

Some of the other girls were looking stricken.

'God, that was awful,' Cath said. She looked pale and strained again, not at all her usual vivacious self. 'I couldn't make head or tail of it – I left nearly half of them. I think my head's all scrambled inside!'

'You were writing away there, Molly,' Lena said.

'Doesn't mean I got them right though, does it?' Molly joked. 'I probably just got the wrong end of the stick – I usually do!' But she was surprised to hear how difficult some of the others had found the tests. Could it be that she had got some of them right?

'Hey, Cath – are you all right?' Lena was saying. Cath had peeled away from them and was leaning groggily against the wall of one of the huts.

'What's up?' Win, prone to take charge as ever, came over to them. 'Is something wrong, Cathleen?'

'No—' Cath struggled to recover, not really comfortable with Win. 'I just felt a bit faint there for a moment. It was so warm in that room. I'll be all right now, thanks.'

'We can manage to ask her if she's all right without your help yer know,' Molly said.

Win turned, looking really insulted. 'I know – but I . . .' She was baffled by all Molly's aggression. 'I just saw her looking pale. Why do you always have to be so harsh? I was only trying to help.' She walked off, affronted.

Cath, still leaning over, started to sing softly, 'I'll take you home again Kathleen . . .' and the three of them got the giggles.

*

As the days passed, Molly was full of a prickly, restless energy. At every opportunity she could in Hut J she was loud and rude to the girls who made it clear they looked down on her for her foul mouth. She joined in with the Nottingham girls and Lena, who all made dirty jokes and found double, smutty meanings in everything. And she soon found another soldier to go out with. With her looks, Molly knew there'd be no shortage. She went out with a different one every night, making sure not to get too close. She didn't want them all thinking she was too easy. And she saw some of the lads looking warily at her. Billy had been putting the word about, she was sure of it. So she was especially careful, having a drink with Ron, then Mickey and Sidney, not to drink too much and only to give them a chaste kiss goodnight once they were near the guardroom.

On Wednesday nights they were expected to stay in for a domestic night, to clean up and catch up with any mending or letter writing. Thrown together in each other's company even more than usual, they were all destined to get on one another's nerves. And Molly didn't want to stay in. Too much time with her hut mates rubbed her up the wrong way. She found herself looking to make trouble.

She had written a quick letter to Em, and as she sealed the envelope, she looked across at Cath. To her surprise, Cath, who had been resting on her bed, was already fast asleep. Molly smiled. She looked like a sweet little child with her curls round her cheeks. So she called across to Lena instead.

'Coming down for a chat with Doris and Mary?' The two girls from Nottingham slept further along the hut.

'In a bit.' Lena didn't look up. She was laboriously writing a long letter.

'Suit yerself.'

Soon, Molly and the Nottingham girls were cackling with deliberately loud laughter, fully engaged in their ribald humour. After a while Lena came to join them.

'Ooh my word!' Doris boomed with laughter at one of Molly's wisecracks about the sausages they'd had for tea. 'You're a case, Molly – yer really are! I dunno how you think 'em up!'

'All comes from having a filthy dirty mind!' Mary tittered.

After a time, having sighed pointedly several times, Ruth looked up from the book she was trying to read.

'I say—' she said irritably, blushing as ever. 'Do you think you could possibly quieten down a bit?'

Win, who spent ages every night dutifully writing her diary, was also frowning at them.

'Why? Ain't our conversation highbrow enough for yer then?' Molly sneered. She rolled her eyes at Doris and Mary. 'Some of us ain't as la-di-dah as you, noses stuck in a book all the time.'

'Actually' – Ruth slammed her book closed, her face flaming pink as she got to her feet; her already odd voice became all the more peculiar when she was tense – 'if you must know, no, I don't enjoy hearing your conversation. Why does everything you say have to be so dirty and sordid? Can't you find anything else to talk about for once?'

'O-ooh,' Molly mocked loudly, enjoying herself. 'Dirty and sordid to you! Maybe it's you that's got the dirty mind, hearing things when there's nothing in it!'

'Oh don't be so ridiculous,' Ruth snapped. 'Everything you all say is . . . is just so *disgusting*. I'm sick to death of listening to it.'

The Nottingham girls were laughing unkindly at

Ruth's pompous delivery of these words. She was a stolid, scholarly girl who was not used to this sort of exchange at all. Until ten days ago she had been steeped in little else but boarding-school life, and calculus and chemical equations.

'Oh *really*,' Molly mocked, feeling she was gaining the upper hand. A nasty triumph overcame her. She mimicked Ruth's posh but constricted-sounding voice which seemed to come from somewhere deep in the back of her throat. 'It's all just ever so sordid my dear – I really don't know how I put up with it all . . . I really must go and read a book . . .' The others laughed.

Win leapt off her bed suddenly as if something in her had snapped. She advanced on Molly so determinedly that for a moment Molly thought she was going to hit her, and raised her arm to protect herself. Seeing her reaction, a flicker of shock passed over Win's face. She had no intention of hitting Molly – she was in full control. She spoke very fast, hands on hips, her pleasant face creased with passionate earnestness.

'What I want to know is why you think it's acceptable to mock us, Ruth and me, and some of the others. You mock the way we speak, the things we're interested in, the way we've been brought up – when we wouldn't dream of being so rude and unkind as to make fun of you and the way you speak. I'm not used, personally, to hearing the Birmingham accent – or Nottingham for that matter. It's all new for me, and strange, and to be brutally truthful it sounds uncouth and not very nice to listen to. But I don't mock *you*, do I? And nor does Ruth. Because we have something called *good manners* and we know that it's not fair or kind to make fun of someone for being the way they are when they can't help it because that's the way they were brought up.

Would you like it if I started making fun of you, Molly?' Win's voice was lower now. It was not accusatory – she was appealing to Molly's better side, and Molly had the wind taken totally out of her sails. It was true – not once had Win or Ruth or any of the others made fun of her or Doris and Mary, however rude or provocative they'd been. She felt small and ashamed – and angry. Her fingers fiddled with the blanket on Doris's bed. Once again this posh cow was telling her what to do and belittling her. And the worst of it was, she was right!

'Look – we've all just got to get on somehow.' Win's voice was quieter now. 'We're in something bigger than all of us: the army, the war. It's not easy for any of us. So can't we all just – well, put aside some of our differences?'

There came a scattering of applause from some of the others along the hut.

'Well said, Win!'

'If you say so,' Doris said, but still with a twinkle of mockery in her eyes.

Molly couldn't think of anything to say: she wasn't climbing down and losing face. She got up grumpily and went back to her bed without looking at any of them.

'Not big enough to apologize then?' someone called after her.

'Oh shut it, yer stupid cow!' Molly snapped. That very second she regretted it. Why didn't she just say sorry to Win and make things better? She knew Win was right. None of them, whatever their class, enjoyed having feet burning with blisters, the endless square-bashing, the cold, draughty showers where there weren't even any curtains, and the fact that there was no privacy anywhere. It was a shock to all of them. And they *were* all in it together. She could see really that Win was a nice person, but something in her couldn't stand showing her own softer side or admitting she was wrong.

She could hear murmurings about her across the hut. She looked to her friends for support. Cath was still asleep and had missed the whole thing. Lena, who had followed her down, rolled her eyes before flinging herself on her bed. But when it came down to it, Lena never actually said much. It wasn't her that caused the trouble.

An impulse seized Molly. She got up and strode down to the door of the hut, slamming out into the darkness. They may not be allowed out of the camp, but at least she'd go off to the NAAFI and see if she could find some blokes to talk to – she was sick of all these bloody catty women!

Thirteen

A couple of nights later, Molly found herself stumbling her way across the camp to Hut J. Two evenings in a row she'd been out drinking in the local pubs. Somehow she'd managed to check in with the NCO in the guard-room without him noticing quite how drunk she was. Now, reeling across the muddy grass, she could barely walk in a straight line.

Last night, Billy had been there, the first pub she went into arm in arm with a moon-faced lad called Eric and with a group of other lads in tow. She'd made up to Eric in front of Billy, making sure he saw, wanting to make him feel bad.

'Steady on,' Eric had said. He wasn't used to girls like Molly. He came from a village in Hertfordshire and had coughed nervously as she pressed her leg sugges-tively against his and cuddled up close to him. The more she drank, the more uproariously she laughed at every-thing the boys said. Another ATS called Lois, whom she didn't know, joined in with them, and she was a giggler too. Not that Molly knew her any better by the end of the evening – she was too drunk to take anything much in, except that her throat was dry from smoking, the pub was full of uniforms and there were sing-songs going on with the piano. There was someone there very good at playing.

After a time she saw Billy and his mates leave to go elsewhere. Billy didn't even cast her a glance.

'Ungrateful little bastard,' she mumbled, leaning forward to pick up her glass of beer. 'Eric,' she wheedled, 'get us summat stronger will yer?'

'Oh, I think you've already had enough, Molly,' Eric said in a humouring voice which roused Molly's temper.

'What d'you mean? You a flaming vicar or summat, talking like that? You gunna get us a drink or not?'

'Well . . .'

'Go on, Eric, darlin' – get us a Dubonnet, eh?'

'But I . . .'

'Go on, love!' Lois cackled. She was a pale redhead. 'What you waiting for?'

So he'd had to go and fetch Molly a drink, and then another.

Molly reached the door of what she hoped was Hut J. Suddenly she was assailed by memories of Eric's face once she'd got him outside. They'd had a bit of bother with a few locals, not all of whom were delighted at the mass of servicemen and women taking over their watering holes. Molly had given them a good old mouthful on the way out and Eric had looked shocked.

'Blimey, that one's got a gob and half on 'er,' one of the other lads remarked as they stepped out into the cold darkness. 'You've got your hands full there, mate!'

The lads disappeared along the street. Lois had already vanished.

'Come 'ere then, gorgeous—' Molly took Eric's hand and dragged him off along a quiet side street. You couldn't see anything much. It didn't matter where they were.

'Give us a kiss then,' she said, suddenly getting the giggles, though she didn't know why.

'What's so funny?' Eric asked, sounding peeved.

'I dunno!' Tears of laughter were rolling down her cheeks. 'I really dunno. Hang on – I'll be right in a tick. Ooh, I think I need to pee . . .'

Still recovering, she turned to him. Even in the gloom she could see the terror in his expression. This struck her as wildly funny as well and she was off, tittering again.

'I ain't gunna eat yer, yer know!' she guffawed. 'Don't you like girls then, Eric darlin'?'

'Yes, but . . .'

'C'm'ere then . . .'

He had kissed her enthusiastically enough, once she'd got hold of him. And her need to relieve herself meant she'd had to disentangle herself before she pushed anything too far. But the memory of his goofy expression made her titter again now as she stumbled back to her hut. Fortunately she'd already visited the latrine block on the way over.

Laughter tight in her chest, she pushed open the door of Hut J. Flipping blimey – the lights were already out! It must be a lot later than she thought. How the hell was she supposed to get ready for bed in the pitch dark? Shutting the door as carefully as she could manage in her condition, she bent down and removed her shoes. The thought of herself stumbling about in there was already making the giggles pop out of her. Picturing Win and Ruth's disapproving faces made it all the worse. She felt like exploding with laughter.

She stopped and listened. All seemed to be quiet. Holding her shoes, she began to tiptoe along the lino. The stove had gone out so there was no glow from the coals to guide her. She stumbled past it, a landmark in the middle. Stopping, she heard the sound of even breathing around her. *All asleep*, she thought with an expected rush of fondness. All those heads on pillows, closed eyes, all breathing away. For a moment she felt like a mother looking at her children, except that of course she couldn't see a thing. This also was funny.

Nearly there. Still trying desperately not to titter and wake everyone up, she went to her bed and put her shoes down with exaggerated care, then sank down on to the bed.

Immediately something was wrong. The bed was lumpy. It was also screaming, a horrified shrieking from behind her. Molly leapt up.

'What in heaven's name is going on?' Win's voice.

The screaming bed was now gasping and sobbing. Molly, in her befuddled state, couldn't make sense of any of it. Other voices were full of questions and confusion.

'I say – put on the light someone!'

A second later all of them were squinting like moles in the shock of illumination. Molly had sat herself down heavily on Honor, who was now sitting up hugging her knees, her pale hair a curtain down her back, staring at her in horror.

'Sorry,' Molly said, sobering up enough to realize that the girl was really frightened. 'I came in in the dark and I thought it was my bed.'

'Oh my goodness,' Honor half whispered. 'Oh, yes, I see. I – I just thought you were Nanny.'

This was an odd thing to say, but Molly, having been used to invasions in her bed at night as a child, could understand her fright, being woken from sleep like that.

'What the hell're you doing, Molly?' Win was coming over, impatiently. 'You've woken the whole damn lot of us up!'

'Sorry, Honor,' Molly said, ignoring Win, and all the other discontented muttering round the hut. 'I never meant to frighten yer, honest.'

Honor stared at her, bewildered. Her eyes had dark rings round them. Honor was never horrible to anyone and Molly felt genuinely sorry.

'It's all right. I'm sure you didn't – only I . . . Golly.' She shook herself and gave a faint smile.

'Are you all right, Honor?' Win asked.

'Yes – quite all right, thank you. I'm so sorry everyone's awake now.'

'Hardly your fault, is it?' Win retorted dryly. 'Get to bed, Molly, for goodness' sake.'

Molly got through the next morning's drill session feeling as if a crowd of devils were banging hammers in her head. She felt queasy and slow-witted and kept trying to turn the wrong way.

'Keep up, Fox!' the drill sergeant bawled at her. 'We're not ballroom dancing here – this is the army!'

'Oh bugger off,' Molly muttered savagely.

Lena, beside her, let out a snort of laughter.

'Serves yer right,' she hissed.

A couple of good strong cups of tea helped to pull her round. In one break in the NAAFI, she saw Honor, sitting on her own. Honor smiled and beckoned her over. Molly sat down with a groan, nursing her cup of tea.

'Are you not feeling too good?' Honor asked sympathetically. 'Would one of these make you feel better?' She held out a packet of cigarettes. Molly attempted a smile and took one. There was something so sweet and other-worldly about Honor, and she didn't seem to

117

favour anyone particular; she just took people as they came.

'Ta,' Molly said as Honor lit it for her. 'My own fault I s'pose.' The smoke was comforting. Between them was a dirty white saucer for an ashtray, with several dead stubs in it. 'Listen, I'm sorry – for jumping on yer last night. Only I thought it was my bed.'

'Oh, it's quite all right. Easy mistake to make. I'm sure if I was tiptoeing about in the dark I'd be stubbing my toes and all sorts.' She smiled, and once again Molly thought what an interesting face she had, the wide mouth and huge beaky nose. Honor's long, thin fingers flickered nervously on the table almost as if it was a piano. 'You must have thought me very strange. What I said . . .'

'No – it's all right,' Molly said, even though she had found it strange.

'It's just that, you see . . .' Honor's eyes filled with tears and she looked away a moment, taking a long draw on her cigarette. Molly felt slightly panic stricken. What was she supposed to say?

'You see, Mrs Dukes, my nanny, died just a few weeks ago. She suffered terribly. And I'd been at home, helping to look after her. She stayed with us, of course – she had nowhere else to go, really. My mother is an artist and she never spent very much time with me. She has a studio at the side of the house and she takes in pupils as well. She's always so busy. So it was Mrs Dukes who brought me up. We spent nearly all our time together – I could tell her anything. She was a wonderful woman, so kind, and well-read, and she spoke French and a little German. I didn't go to school – she taught me herself, everything. She was marvellous at gardening as well . . . We were everything to each other really: she had no children of her own. She fell ill quite suddenly, and after a few months, when I just stayed beside her, she was gone.' Honor's mouth puckered with emotion. 'I couldn't stay, not just me at home with Mummy and Daddy. Mummy's so very difficult and the house felt desolate. So on impulse I joined up. At first' – she made a wry face – 'I didn't think I could stand it. It was so cold and squalid and awful after our lovely house. But in fact it's all right, I think. Everyone's so kind. And it's helped me to get away. I think Mrs Dukes would be proud of me.'

'I bet she would,' Molly said, thinking of Jenny Button. She didn't know what else to say but she did feel sympathetic and Honor could see that.

'We're very different I suppose, you and I,' Honor observed.

'Well – yeah.' Molly laughed. 'I'll say.'

'But I think you're nice. Nicer than you show you are.' One of Honor's naked, odd statements, but it almost brought Molly to tears.

'Well – ta.'

Honor was looking closely at her. 'And you're *so* pretty.'

'Don't be daft,' Molly said, blushing now. She turned her mug round and round on the stained table.

'No – you really are. But I realize I don't know anything about you. You're from Birmingham? I've never been there.'

'Don't s'pose you'd 'ave call to really.'

'What about your family?'

Molly gave a harsh laugh, grinding her cigarette stub into the saucer. 'What about them?'

'Well – what're they like? Are you close to your mother?

This was such an absurd notion that Molly burst out laughing. Her head felt better suddenly, as if pressure in it had been released. 'No! I can't say I am!'

'Why? What's she like?'

God, Honor was an innocent. How could she even begin?

'You don't want to know, you really don't.'

'Oh, I see.' Clearly she didn't.

'Look – I've got to go.' Molly got up. 'I'm really sorry to hear about your ... nanny, passing away though,' she added gruffly.

'Thank you,' Honor said sweetly. 'See you later, Molly.'

But Molly didn't see Honor later. She felt a desperate need to get as well-oiled as possible, and after a long, drunken evening, most of which she could barely re-member, she was checking in at the guardhouse, while singing, 'I'm gonna hang out the washing on the Sieg-fried Line!' at the top of her voice.

'Shush, Molly, for God's sake!' the others had said who were with her. Who the hell they were she couldn't remember after either.

But what she could remember was being put on a charge for drunk and disorderly behaviour. The next morning, she also recalled with a groan that the Gorgon had walked into the guardroom at the fatal moment she was being given a dressing down. Molly had looked up with a swimming head to find Phoebe Morrison's dark-browed, fearsome face glaring at her from under the brim of her ATS hat.

'Fox,' she ordered, in a tone which admitted no argu-ment. 'I want to talk to you. No good now – I can see you're not in a fit state. Report to me tomorrow – two o'clock sharp. Got it?'

'Yes, Corp,' Molly slurred back at her.

'Corporal, if you don't mind! You will have half your pay docked. Now get to bed!'

'Aye aye, captain – I mean, yes, Corporal!' Molly said, lurching off outside.

'What's the matter with you, Fox?'

Molly was back in the guardhouse, where Corporal Morrison was standing behind the table on which papers were neatly arranged. Despite having got so completely drunk last night, today Molly didn't feel as bad as she had the day before. Her head felt strangely clear, as if it had been washed clean.

'What d'yer mean?'

She expected Phoebe Morrison to echo 'What do you mean, *Corporal*?' But she didn't.

'I mean—' The woman leaned forward, resting the palms of her hands on the table. Her face, turned upwards to look at Molly, without its frown of command, looked softer, more vulnerable: certainly no Gorgon. She paused for a few seconds, weighing up carefully what to say, her dark eyes fixed on Molly's so that Molly was forced to look down.

'I mean . . .' she began again, pushing herself upright. She picked up a pen and toyed with it round her lips as if she wished it was a cigarette. 'You may not have had the most refined start in life or the best of education like some of these girls here. But I suspect, Private Fox, that you are no fool. So why do you persist in behaving like one?'

Molly was truly taken aback by this. She'd come

expecting a rollicking, perhaps further punishment. She had not expected an attempt to find out anything about her. It felt alarming, but she was flattered by not being thought a fool for once in her life.

'I dunno, Corporal.' She lowered her gaze again.

'You were very drunk last night.'

'Yes . . .'

'Does that happen often?'

'You mean . . . ?'

'I mean at home as well – not just here.'

'Now and again.'

'You could get yourself into a lot of trouble in that condition, you know that, don't you? It doesn't just make you rowdy, it makes you vulnerable.'

'Yes. Corporal.'

There was a silence, which went on so long that Molly looked up, and found Phoebe Morrison watching her carefully. She had lowered the pen and was turning it round between her fingers.

'Any problems at home?'

'No more than usual.'

'I see.' Corporal Morrison took a couple of paces to her left, then turned and came back the other way.

'You have one final week of basic training, Fox. Then you'll all be assigned a trade or position somewhere. What do you see yourself doing?'

'I want to do summat good!' Molly said, eagerly. 'You know – guns or driving or summat. That's what I joined up for.'

'I see.' She turned on the ball of her foot again, moving back and forth. 'And do you think, in the light of your conduct, that such ambitions are realistic?'

Foolishly, Molly said, 'I dunno.'

'Well' – Phoebe Morrison became brisk and dismissive – 'you've got a week to try and redeem yourself. You'd better try and behave, hadn't you? Your pay will be docked, as you were told last night. Just try not to get yourself into any more trouble. Dismiss.'

Phoebe Morrison watched Molly depart from the guardroom, the frown troubling her face again. Fumbling in her pocket, she brought out the cigarette she had been longing for and lit up, sucking in the smoke with eager relief.

Something about her meeting with this magnificent-looking girl troubled her. She was a proper honeypot, there was no doubt, with that figure and hair – no wonder the chaps were all buzzing round her! She was a splendidly big, barely educated, rough working-class girl. So what? So were plenty of the others. But as Molly passed through her training, one minute fawningly eager to please – and, it had to be said, showing signs of being quite capable – and the next, outrageously flouting not just army regulations but the basic laws of decent behaviour, she had got under Phoebe Morrison's skin. Fox was irritating – somehow all the more so when she was keen to please, so hungry for praise! – a delighted child's smile spreading across her face at a word of approval. She was awkward and maddening and gauche. Why did she bring out this protective feeling, of tenderness almost, of somehow wanting to save her, even when she was almost driving one mad?

'For heaven's sake, don't waste your energy,' Corporal Morrison told herself. 'They'll all be scattered to the four winds by this time next week anyway.'

Fourteen

18 Kenilworth Street
Jan '41

Dear Molly,

We haven't heard from you so I hope you're all right. I hope you're keeping out of mischief and doing what you're told. Drop me a line when you get the chance. It's not the same here without you.

We're all going along. There've not been any big raids since the beginning of the month thank goodness, but all the queuing for this and that takes up a lot of time. We'll be queuing to breathe next! Violet's been poorly with a bad throat but she's better now. Our Mom's quite good as well, for this time of year. But we're taking each day as it comes as no one thinks the raids are over yet. Still, we hope. Oh, I told Mrs Button I was writing and she said to send her love and thanks for your note but she's not one for writing letters. She and Stanley are going along all right. I've not seen your Mom and Dad but I've not heard of any trouble.

I've got a bit of news to tell you. Norm and me have got ourselves engaged. He's bought me a ring, nothing fancy. We're not setting a date yet, with the war on and everything so uncertain. I don't see how I could leave Mom, not with so much going on.

124

We'd have to find somewhere very near. But we're promised, anyway.

Write to me, won't you? Oh – guess who I saw the other day – Katie O'Neill. Remember her? She didn't see me. Must've had things on her mind because I walked right there in front of her. I didn't think she looked too good, but who does these days.

I'll have to go now, and get the tea on. I hope you're looking after yourself Molly.

Love for now, write back,

Em x

Molly put Em's letter away, happy to receive it. It had been a surprise somehow, and all the more that Em seemed to be missing her. In the past it had always been Molly who did all the running for Em's friendship.

She began on her final week's basic training fired with determination. The way Corporal Morrison had spoken to her – the fact that she had bothered to speak at all – had given her a completely different sense of herself. The Gorgon had seen something in her, that was how it felt. Those words of faint praise, *I suspect, Private Fox, that you are no fool*, had made her want to do anything to gain the woman's approval. She clung to them as a lamp in the darkness, giving her hope. Perhaps she could really make a go of the army if she tried! Could even be good at something? She'd heard people talk about the army as 'making a man of him' – why could the army not make something of her? She knew she'd got off to a terrible start with almost everyone. Lena and Cath were all right, though Cath had withdrawn into herself and didn't seem as bright and friendly as when they first arrived. Honor just accepted everyone as they were. But as for the rest of them in

Hut J, Molly knew they didn't think much of her – that was putting it mildly. She was the rough one, the loud one who couldn't be trusted and most of them steered clear of her. Why had she carried on like that? She felt really foolish now, and regretted it bitterly. But she told herself that soon they'd all be split up anyway and she could make a fresh start when they began training to do something interesting.

The final week passed quickly. Molly tried her very hardest, on the parade ground and in all the other training and lectures. They had to learn about military law, about documents and crime and punishment. And all about cooking, or, as the army called it, 'messing'. How to get the best results from the quartermaster's stores, how to avoid wasting fat. This last lecture was especially revolting.

'Glad I shan't be cooking,' Molly heard one of the girls say as they came out. 'Best not to know too much about what goes into what we're eating!' They were walking a little behind her, but she still heard the girl go on in a low voice, 'That blasted Fox girl seems to have quietened down a bit at last.'

'That's the army for you,' the other said. 'Knocks the stuffing out of everyone eventually.'

'I gather the Gorgon had words with her.'

'Ah – well that would knock the stuffing out of anyone!'

Molly didn't feel she'd had the stuffing knocked out of her; instead, she was full of a burning desire to please Corporal Morrison and to do better. She put all her effort into doing her best that week. She passed every inspection with flying colours, her buttons gleaming, earning herself a nod of approval and a 'Not bad, Fox' from Corporal Morrison one morning which lit up her day.

She tore round the park during the morning PT, and drilled as if her life depended on it, pulling her shoulders back and jumping to attention. None of the classes had been too difficult and she was looking forward now to the end of the week, to finding out to which trade she had been assigned, and to beginning again somewhere else. And God knows, she was going to be different! There'd be no more going out getting kalied, no more clowning her way through drill. She would show them she could be miles better than she had been so far.

She was even one of the first into Hut J that night, intending to get ready for bed, where she would write a letter to Em before Win instructed them to put out the lights. It was a cold, windy night, unpleasant to be out in, and as she stoked up the stove to keep the place halfway warm, several of the others drifted in, including Honor, who smiled dreamily at her. Molly was just about to settle down to write when Cath came in, walking fast between the beds. Something about the way she was walking caught Molly's attention. Cath looked as if she was holding herself in in case she exploded. Her face was grim and tense.

'All right, Cath?' Molly asked.

'Umm.' She kept her head down, not meeting Molly's eyes, and wouldn't say any more. She got herself ready for bed, climbed in and pulled the bedclothes up high so that only her rusty hair was visible. No one else seemed to have noticed. Then Lena came in and started talking to Molly. She pointed at Cath and mouthed, 'She all right?'

Molly shrugged and whispered, 'Not sure. She wouldn't say anything.'

It was only once the lights were out and Molly was half asleep that she became aware of Cath crying. Some of the others were already breathing steadily. At first she wasn't sure, the sniffs and sobs were so quiet. But after a time she climbed out into the cold and sat on Cath's bed.

The sobs stopped for a moment. Cath clearly didn't want to be heard.

'Cath – what's up?' Molly leaned close, whispering. 'This ain't like you.'

There was a long silence, then a little more of Cath's head appeared over the bedding. 'Nothing,' she said moistly. 'Don't worry about me. You go back to bed, Molly, thanks anyway.'

'Come on, Cath – it ain't like you to be upset like this.'

'Isn't it?' Cath whispered savagely. 'Well how would you know that for sure?' Then her aggression crumpled and she began crying again. 'Oh my God, Molly, I don't know what's going to happen to me. I'm done for.'

As Molly was wondering what on earth could have made her friend feel so desperate, she became aware then of a tiny finger of light and someone else moving towards them. Win tiptoed across, lighting her way with a blackout torch, and sat on the other side of the bed, where she looked questioningly at Molly in the feeble light from the torch. Molly shrugged. She was annoyed by Win's arrival. Cath was *her* friend. Why did Win always have to put herself in charge of everything?

'Cath—' Win touched Cath's shoulder, trying to pull back the bedclothes, but Cath clung to them fiercely. 'It's Win. Do let us help. What's the matter?' Her tone was friendly but brisk.

There was no reply.

Molly leaned closer and, speaking very gently, said, 'Look, love, if it's that bad, why don't you let us help yer? A trouble shared and all that. You never know, we might have some bright ideas.'

Cath sat up suddenly, as if surrendering, pulling her knees up to her chest. Hesitantly, Molly put her arm round Cath's shoulders. 'Whatever it is can't be that bad.'

'Oh yes it can. I thought you might have all guessed by now, the way I've been. I mean, it's no good – you'll all have to find out in the end.' She wept, weakly.

'Oh there now,' Molly said, feeling so sorry for Cath, who had been so bubbly and friendly when they all arrived. 'Why don't you tell us and we'll see if we can help?'

Cath wasn't at ease with Win so she spoke to Molly, shaking her head with disbelief. 'I'm so frightened, Molly. I don't know what's going to become of me. I . . .' Her voice cracking again, she said, 'I'm certain now – I'm going to have a baby.'

Molly heard Win give a slight gasp, but for once she couldn't think what to say. Molly was utterly shocked as well. It hadn't even crossed her mind that this might be the trouble.

'I've been feeling poorly, a bit sick and fainting and . . . I've missed now, twice . . . They'll throw me out and I've no idea where I'll go – I've nobody . . .'

Still trying to take this in, Molly said, 'But what about going home – your family?'

'I can't go home. What would Daddy be doing with another mouth to feed and all the disgrace of it? And there's nothing for me there. Oh God, I wish my mammy was still alive!' She wept broken-heartedly.

'Does anyone know? Any high-ups, I mean?' Win asked. The conversation was all conducted in a fierce whisper.

Cath shook her head, wiping her eyes. 'I don't know what to do, where to go. I've been going half mad thinking of it.'

'Poor love,' Molly said, hugging her. She was frightened for Cath, full of dread. There were such stories about girls having babies, bad enough to make your hair curl.

'I can't keep it up much longer, can I?' Cath said. 'I didn't know, not when I joined up, I honestly didn't. It was someone in Birmingham, a fella, only saw him twice and he sort of made me . . . He wasn't even very nice . . .' Her tears flowed again. 'Oh why did I let him? I just thought it'd be all right the once, you know, he was so pushy for it.'

'Ain't they all?' Molly said. 'You poor babby. That bastard wants seeing to good and proper, that 'e does.'

Win, seemingly unable to cope with the way the conversation was developing, cut in with, 'Look – is there no chance at all of you marrying this man?'

'No! I told you – I don't even know where he is and he's a creep. I'd not want to chain myself to him for life, I can tell you!'

'You can't go on like this. You'll have to tell someone – before you get your posting.'

'I know. I know!'

There was a pause. Molly could feel Cath's desperation.

'What'll happen to me?' Cath asked in a tiny voice.

'I'm afraid I don't know,' Win said. 'There must be some provision, some way of . . .' She trailed off, out of her depth.

'Look, I'll come with yer if you want,' Molly said. 'Go and speak to the Gorgon to start. So you don't have to do it on your own.'

'No – there's no need to drag you into it,' Cath said. 'Thanks anyway, Molly. But I'll have to face up to it.'

These last words were spoken with such desolation that Molly felt tears come to her eyes. How dreadful for Cath to be so alone in the world.

'I wish there was summat we could do to help.'

'It's not your fault, is it?'

'No, but I feel for yer, love.'

'I'm terribly sorry, Cath,' Win said awkwardly. 'You must feel awful. But you are going to have to own up.'

'I know. There's going to be no hiding it once I'm swelled up like a balloon, now is there?'

'Oh Cath.' Molly gave her a squeeze. She had no real idea what might happen to Cath, but she felt so sorry for her.

There was nothing else they could do except go back to bed. Molly didn't sleep well that night, full of sad turmoil about the girl lying next to her and fearing what would become of her. She could hear Win tossing and turning in bed too.

When she woke the next morning, Molly was disturbed to find Cath already gone. Win came over to her looking very worried, and sat down close to her. 'Did you see her leave?' she whispered. Molly saw a couple of the others glace curiously at them.

'No – I mean she was there 'til not long ago because I could hear her moving about,' Molly said. 'I must've dozed off because I never heard her get up or nothing.'

Win looked very uneasy.

'You don't think she's done anything . . .' Molly

trailed off, awful thoughts rushing into her mind. She pictured Cath lying on the railway track.

'I just hope not,' Win said. 'I think I'd better go and see the Gorgon, right away.'

Win went to see Phoebe Morrison and Molly waited outside for her, growing more and more uneasy. A few minutes later Win appeared, looking slightly relieved, if not exactly happy.

'It's all right,' she said. 'Cath's seen her. She must have got up very early, gone straight there.'

'Where is she?'

'On her way to the station, apparently. They're packing her off to some home where she can have the baby.'

'Well then what'll happen to them?'

It was Win's turn to shrug. 'I'm afraid I really don't know.' Molly saw how pale and strained Win looked in the morning light.

'You did yer best,' Molly said as they walked slowly towards their breakfast.

Win looked at her, surprised. The corners of her mouth twitched up for a moment, then she sighed. 'Thanks. But I feel awful. I suppose I feel I should've noticed – should have been able to do more for her.'

'No – none of it's your fault.' Molly shook her head. 'How were you to know? You can't go blaming yourself. Poor old Cath though. Some factory Jack up an alley I s'pose. Wants putting up against a wall himself and shooting, 'e does.'

To her surprise, Win laughed. 'You certainly have a way with words.' She looked at Molly, attentively. Seeming slightly puzzled, she said, 'And you're really a very kind-hearted soul, aren't you?'

Molly felt the blood flame in her cheeks. 'I don't

know about that. But I don't half feel sorry for the poor cow.'

'You were good to her last night. I was so shocked I didn't know what to say.'

'Well I was shocked an' all,' Molly admitted. Sadly, she added, 'I s'pose that's that. We'll never see 'er again.'

The words came to her like a slap in the face.

'*Catering Corps?*'

She was still saying it over and over again when she came out of the selection officer's office.

'They want me to be a ruddy cook!'

Molly was so hurt and disgusted she could hardly put it into words.

'But—' She had tried to argue with the crisp-voiced officer. 'Are you sure? I was hoping for summat else – anything. Ack-ack – anything like that.'

The officer glanced down at Molly's record, then piercingly up into her eyes. 'We need good cooks – no one wants a bad cook—' She tried to laugh to soften what was so evidently a blow to Molly. 'An army marches on its stomach, you know – consider it the most useful of war work. You will be sent for training as from Monday. Dismiss!'

Molly just about managed to remember to salute before plunging outside again in a rage of disappointment. She had hoped for something important and exciting, and what did she get? Cooking endless vats of rice pudding for ungrateful mouths! She didn't even want to tell the others what her trade was to be. Still, she told herself, as any hope she had of better things melted away, what did you expect? She knew her behaviour during basic training had been bad and now she bitterly regretted it. But *cooking*! She hadn't joined the army to bloody well cook!

'You wait,' she vowed furiously, storming back across the camp. 'They get burnt sodding custard every day until they're sick of me!'

Homefires

Fifteen

Somewhere in the south of England!
Feb 3rd 1941

Dear Em,

Sorry I haven't written before, I got your letter, thanks. Glad your Mom's all right. I hope Mr and Mrs Button are still going along well? Will you look in on them now and then? I'm dropping them a line too.

My writing's not very good, sorry. It's because I'm on the train – in a seat but crowded as a hen coop as usual. I'm on my way to a new camp as our three week's basic training is finished now. They've told me to train as a cook, *me*!! That's two weeks or so and then I'll be off somewhere new again. I quite miss the old camp already. We had our ups and downs but I'll miss some of them girls.

Fancy you seeing Katie O'Neill. Not that I ever knew her – I don't think she ever said a word to me at school. She was that stuck up! I wonder what she's doing now.

Say hello to your Mom and Dad, and to Joyce and the rest. No more news at the moment. Will write again soon. Hope everything's all right.

Love from Molly

Em smiled faintly, slid Molly's letter back in its envelope and laid it on the table, yawning so hard it brought tears to her eyes. She sat at the table in the back room nursing her cup of strong, sweet tea, trying to pull herself together, settle her queasy stomach and jangled nerves, and get ready for work. It was so cold she could see her breath in the house.

There'd been a bad raid last night – the first really heavy one in a while – and she'd been on ARP duty, only returning home an hour ago, after the All Clear, after the checks she and Mr Radcliffe had made on the neighbourhood. Waves of planes had come over during the night. She hadn't had a wink of sleep, but the family hadn't been much better off roughing it down in the cellar either, in this freezing cold. They'd finally crawled up to bed before dawn to catch a few scraps of slumber before the day began.

She heard slow treads on the stairs. Her father appeared, unshaven, yawning, his eyes bloodshot. He'd been in his clothes all night. Though he didn't say as much, he looked relieved to see her home safely.

'All right, Em?' was all he rumbled, indistinctly. 'What a night, eh?'

He disappeared out to the privy at the back, then came back in looking a little more awake.

'There's tea in the pot,' Em said.

'Ta.' Bob poured himself a cup. She watched him, thinking how old he looked, white hairs winning over the brown. He wandered over to the table. 'Who's that from?'

'Molly.'

'Oh ar. Where's 'er these days, then?' He rubbed his hand gratingly over his salt and pepper stubble, overcome by another huge yawn.

'Somewhere down south. Don't know exactly.'

138

He nodded through the yawn. 'I 'ope it's a bit bloody warmer for 'er than it is up 'ere.'

Em pushed her chair back. 'I'd better wake the others.'

'Yer a good wench.'

The morning routine: Bob off to work at the power station, Mom up to be ready for Frankie and Brenda to arrive, so that their mom, Irene Skelton, could get to the factory. Not that Irene showed any gratitude, but Cynthia felt sorry for her kids. Frankie was seven, so Violet walked down to the school with him. Brenda wasn't yet five, so she needed minding all day. Sid, sixteen and full of it, would come tearing down, seize hold of Frankie and upend him, shaking peals of laughter out of him, and then he'd be out the door still eating, to work at the radiator factory. Joyce, who was nearly fourteen, was just finishing off her time at school. And Em – she had her job with Mr Perry.

Bernard Perry had run his fruit and veg shop in Great Lister Street for years. Em could remember when his pink-faced wife Jean was still alive and they ran it together. She'd died when their one son, David, was thirteen and as soon as he was old enough, David ran it with his dad. But David was in the army now, and Em had taken over the job, glad of something near home, of not having to go into another factory, even though the pay wasn't as good. And Mr Perry was very understanding. He knew Cynthia Brown had been up and down for years and he'd give Em time off when necessary.

'You'd best get home for the afternoon, love,' he'd say. 'Family comes first. I can manage, now the rush is over.'

He was a gentle, burly man with a shiny bald pate and a wide, humorous mouth. He kept a good temper even though Em knew he was very lonely without Jean, who'd been a sweet-natured, cheerful soul. His wistfulness at Christmas time had brought tears to her eyes. And she found working for him reassuring. He was fatherly to her, and she liked the way he was always there with his big green apron over his clothes, had a habit of always saying the same old things as if they'd never wear out. 'Fine weather for ducks,' when it rained, or 'Cheer up, it may never happen.' Lately he'd taken to saying, 'We'll 'ave to take it as it comes' and occasionally, in a surprisingly steely voice, 'We ain't gunna let them buggers finish us off.'

Em helped him open up every day, arranging whatever there was to sell, the fast-dwindling array of fresh fruit and vegetables, then dealing with the queues of short-tempered customers who waited, after standing long in other queues with their ration books for their bacon or cheese or tea, to buy minute amounts of whatever was available. A tomato, a beetroot, stored since the summer. At least potatoes weren't on the ration, and there were still winter veg about.

'Heaven help us when we get to the hungry gap,' Mr Perry forecast gloomily. There was always a lean time, come April and May, when the winter produce was running out and the summer stuff had not yet come in.

Em liked working with Mr Perry. She liked the predictability of it, the arranging of the vegetables in their boxes outside, the way she could make things look nice. Before the war she had gone to great trouble every day building pyramids of oranges and turning the wrapped mandarins round so that their delicate printed wrappers were all facing the same way. She built cascades of bananas and hung bunches of them from hooks around Mr Perry's awning. It was a long time now, though, since she'd seen a banana. But she liked Mr Perry's habitual ways, and the easy chat of the customers, the faces she recognized, taking the money, wrapping things up tidily in their paper bags. Vegetables were good, easy friends. They stayed where you put them on the whole, except for the occasional breakaway potato, and they didn't do anything alarming. Em had found herself what she craved – a quiet, safe way of life.

And she had found Norm. She had run into Norm – literally – over a year ago in a bus queue one evening in town, during the blackout. Or rather he had run into her. He had been walking along, a bit too fast considering how hard it was to see, and calling, 'See yer later, mate!' to one of his fellow coppers over his shoulder.

'Watch it!' Em called out, but too late, as he slammed into her. She was right at the back of the queue and there were exclamations of annoyance from the others near her.

'Oh my word – I'm ever so sorry!' Norm cried, leaping back from her as if she was scalding hot. 'I never saw yer! Are you all right?'

'Yes,' Em said, deciding not to mention that he had also stamped on her toe. 'I'm all right. Doesn't matter.'

She couldn't see him very well in the gloom, but she smiled at what she saw – a tall, skinny outline topped by a policeman's helmet with great big ears sticking out from underneath.

Norm produced a little torch and held it high, pointing

its beam down between the two of them. He smiled at her endearingly and even with such a small amount to go on, they liked each other immediately.

'You off down Vauxhall?' he asked.

'Yes – that's where I live.'

Norm gasped as if this was the most amazing coincidence in the world. 'That's a funny thing – I live in Saltley! What road're you from?'

'Kenilworth Street. Off of Rupert Street – near the gas works.'

'Oh – I know, yeah!' He continued to beam at her.

'So,' Em said stupidly, thinking he was sweet, 'you're a policeman.'

Norm looked himself up and down. 'Yeah – yeah, that's me!' They both laughed.

The bus loomed up and stopped, its engine throbbing.

'I'd better go then,' Em said.

'All right then. What's yer name?' he asked hurriedly.

'Emma Brown. Em to most people.'

'That's like me – I'm Norm to most people. Or Staples. My proper name's Norman Stapleton.' He gave a quaint little bow and Em was enchanted. No one had ever bowed to her before.

'Well, it was nice knowing yer,' she said as the bus quickly swallowed up the queue.

'Can I come and see yer?

She already had her foot on the step. Did he mean it?

'If you like.' She spoke a bit teasingly in case he was having her on. 'Number eighteen, Kenilworth Street.'

'Lovely – ta-ra then!'

'Ta-ra.'

She saw him gazing adoringly at the bus as it pulled away.

He came, even though she didn't expect him to. And

142

he kept coming. In the daylight she saw that he was pale and very thin, and his ears seemed to stick out all the more, often glowing pink in the cold, but his hazel-brown eyes still gazed at her with adoring amazement.

'I knew you were the one for me from the minute I saw yer,' he told her later.

'Even though it was pitch dark!' she teased.

'Even though.'

Norm's dad was a railwayman, born in Vauxhall; his mother, Edna Stapleton, was a kindly birdlike woman who Em felt safe with. Norm had one younger brother, Richard. Bob and Cynthia liked Norm. He was polite and helpful, he obviously meant a great deal to Em, and soon he was like part of the family. Joyce made comical faces and waggled her ears with her hands behind his back, making Violet giggle, but no one could dislike Norm. He was too sweet-natured and so accident-prone that he provided a lot of laughs. Em couldn't believe her luck. She had met someone by chance who she could love, who had asked her to marry him. Norm was to be her safe rock in the storm of life, and the wind had blown him to her almost before she had had time to wish for it.

Em's childhood had not felt in the least safe. After giving birth to Violet, their mom, Cynthia, had gone to pieces and spent time in the Hollymoor asylum. Em had only been eight at the time, and was left to cope at home, looking after Sid and Joyce. Bob had not coped well, had turned to the bottle and to the comfort of another woman. Em, frightened and alone, had felt as if their life had fallen apart. It had been a dark, desolate period in their lives that Em tried not think about now.

Even though Cynthia was finally restored to them, it had not been the last time she had a breakdown. She had been back inside Hollymoor on a number of occasions, though now when it happened, they had faith that she would come back – not like that first, terrifying time. The last thing Em wanted after that was any undue excitements in life, or too many changes. The war was already more than enough. All she really wanted was a quiet, preferably predictable existence – and she hoped she could have it with Norm.

As she got ready for work that cold morning, though, her thoughts were uneasy. Norm was a decent man, and a patient one. But now she had agreed to become his wife at some date in the future, there were changes that Norm wanted. In fact, she had been surprised, rather shocked at him and his persistence. She washed her face in the scullery, peering into the little rectangle of mirror with the crack across one corner.

'You look a proper wreck,' she told her reflection. Her brown hair had gone limp, and her face was pinched with tiredness, mauve rings under her eyes. For a moment she imagined Norm's face appearing over her shoulder, looking into her eyes in the mirror.

'Go on – we're getting wed. It won't hurt will it? It's not as if we're religious or anything.'

She stared back at his imaginary reflection. *No – please don't make me . . .* Of course she knew that once they were actually married she'd have to do all the things that were expected of a wife. The sexual act itself was only the beginning of her worries. She had a basic idea of what would happen and it just seemed embarrassing and a bit disgusting, although when she and Norm managed rare private times together, she certainly had feelings for him, loved him kissing her and the way he held her as if she was so precious to him. She thought she could probably put up with the rest of it. But it was what would come after that . . . She shuddered. It meant children, it meant swelling up, those screams of pain, and it meant . . . She told herself that her mother had had four children before there was trouble. Other people didn't go the way her mom had. Look at Mom's friend Dot – she remembered Dot having her little girl Nancy soon after Mom had Violet. Dot hadn't sunk into herself as if the very drawing of breath was a hopeless task. She certainly hadn't been sent into the asylum. Lots of people had babies and were perfectly all right. *But their moms were not Cynthia* . . . Could it be that if your mom was like that, you would be as well? The thought filled her with a deep, sickening dread.

Drying her face, she became more determined about what she'd say to Norm. It wasn't right before marriage and that was that. She wasn't fast. She was a respectable person. Then Em found herself wondering about Molly. The two of them had never talked about things like this – they were far too shy about it. Had Molly been with a man – all the way? She wondered. Things seemed to be changing now the war was on. Morals were looser. Eat, drink and be merry, for tomorrow we may die. She thought Molly probably *had* by now. But she knew she wouldn't ask her.

And it doesn't mean I have to, Em thought, wincing as she combed the knots out of her hair. *Norm will have to understand. He's waited this long – it won't hurt him to be a gentleman and wait a bit longer.*

There was a knock at the front door. That'd be Frankie and Brenda arriving, poor little mites. Em dismissed her disturbing thoughts and went to open up.

'Here yer go, you two,' she said, as the tousled-haired children tumbled through the door. Of course Irene never came with them; she just turfed them out, each with a piece of stale bread clasped in one hand. 'Sit down while yer eating that.'

She poured Cynthia a cup of the stewed tea and took it upstairs.

'Mom? Frankie and Brenda're here. And I've got to go.'

Cynthia uncurled from under the bedclothes, her face puffy. Em waited, dreading the dead look in her eyes of her bad days, but today there was light in them. In fact, considering how bad the night had been, she looked quite lively. She was a rounded, fleshy woman with tumbling dark hair, and wore her age of forty-four well.

''Ello, love,' she said to Em, looking bewildered for a moment. 'Is it that time already?' She lifted herself up on one elbow, memory flooding back. 'What a night! You all right?'

'Yeah. Not a wink of sleep, but we got through it.' She never said much about the nights. In fact, last night hadn't been too bad, but there were horrors other nights. The night they'd pulled Mr and Mrs Jenkins out from the remains of their house. Mrs Jenkins' dust-embalmed face had been contorted, the mouth open as if in a scream, and his arm was locked round her. But she wouldn't say anything to Mom.

'Good for you,' Cynthia said. She pushed back the bedclothes. 'It's all right. No need to wait on me. I'm up now. I'll take the two of them up to the Baths with me.' Nechells Baths was the grand building where they handed out the ration books.

'See yer later, Mom,' Em said, spirits rising gratefully.

She picked up her things, her gas mask, which she still carried although others had long given up, and her bag, and opened the front door. Even though the worst of it had not been directed at their area last night, you could always see the signs there'd been a raid. A smokiness in the air which was different from the usual factory smoke, the musty smell of houses, seeping gas and soaked dust and plaster. Sometimes after a night of fires came the whiff of burned flesh mingled with the smoke. And then there were the exhausted, shocked faces of people. They had a look in their eyes, the release of tension, the bubbling relief at being among the ones left alive. Now and then she found herself laughing hysterically at the slightest thing.

'Morning, Em!' Jenny Button was out at the front, emptying a pail into the gutter. Lemon sunshine broke along the street and the colours emerged like flowers.

'Morning, Mrs B,' Em called. 'You and Mr B all right?'

'Right as rain,' Jenny Button called. 'No need to worry about us.'

Em crossed the street. 'I had a letter from Molly. She's going along well. They want her to be a cook.'

'A cook!' Mrs Button laughed until all her body wobbled. 'That's a good 'un. I 'ope she don't poison the whole lot of 'em! Still, I s'pect she'll do all right. Molly's a good girl if you treat her right.'

'Yes,' Em agreed. 'I s'pect she'll be OK.'

Full of admiration for Mrs Button, she walked on. It did worry her that they didn't go down into a shelter of any kind, but they were far from being the only ones, and it would have seemed cruel to move poor Stanley Button from his big bed and make him squat all night in some stinking, chilly cellar. A lot of older people didn't bother. The Foxes didn't either, she knew, but then it was hard to dredge up any protective feelings towards Iris Fox. But she always wondered if she could do more, find a place for the Buttons.

'Fancy seeing you, Emmy-Wems,' a voice said behind her. Em had been lost in thought, and she jumped, her heart pounding. The low voice held mockery, and threat, and the breath stank of alcohol.

'Hello, Bert,' she said coldly. Molly's brother was walking beside her, too close, his thin face turned to her with his usual horrible smirk. Close up she could see the stubble on his cheeks, like hundreds of tiny fleas. He had his hands in his pockets, walked with a sag, his clothes too loose on him.

'You're looking very nice,' he said. 'Where're you off to then?'

'Work – where d'yer think?' She loathed him and his slimy ways.

'No need to be sour with me, Emmy-Wems.'

'Well I don't s'pose you're off to work, are yer?' she said sarcastically. 'I hope they catch up with yer one day.'

Bert grinned, showing his unpleasant teeth. 'Not if I can 'elp it. My 'ealth's not good,' he whined, patting his chest and coughing theatrically. 'I can't be expected to do a full day's work.'

'Leave me alone, Bert.' He made her flesh creep, always had. A vile, sadistic little boy had grown into a man the same.

'What if I don't – you going to set rozzer Norm on me? Ooooh!' He pretended to be terrified. 'I'm off any-road' He peeled away abruptly at the corner, taking a different turning. 'See yer, Emmy-Wems.'

'Just get bloody lost,' Em murmured. 'And don't call me that stupid name.' The last glance she had of Bert, shambling along, made her shudder.

Sixteen

It was Sunday afternoon and everyone was at home in the Brown household except Sid, who was out and about with a girl called Connie he'd met at Midland Radiator and seemed unable to be parted from. The back room was crowded, but it was the warmest place, and they were all sitting round after dinner.

Em sat next to Norm, and Dot was there, their old neighbour who had come over to visit with her daughter Nancy. Joyce and Nancy were upstairs giggling. Violet sat looking bored while the grown-ups, except for Bob, who was lying back drowsily in the easy chair, talked and drank tea round the table. Cynthia was at her brightest, seeing her old friend again, and Bob looked relaxed. When Mom was all right, he was all right, Em knew.

Dot, a lean, energetic woman with dark eyes and hair which was now fading to grey, had lived next door until she married Lou Alberello. She had seen them through all sorts of times, both good and bad, and Em was very fond of her. It was good to see Dot looking so happy.

'Lou's gone with his girls to see his sister – their auntie Margarita. She'd talk yer hind leg off given the chance. Makes me feel weary, she does. So I thought I'd pop over 'ere – give the girls a chance to see each other for a change.'

'She must be summat if she tires you out, Dot,' Bob

observed sleepily. He prodded Violet. 'Give the fire a poke, Vi.'

'Eh, enough of your cheek!' Dot said good-naturedly. Em had seen her cast her eye over Mom when she came in. Dot knew all the signs – she'd seen Cynthia through thick and thin, and today she seemed reassured, but she didn't say anything.

'You got them Skelton babbies to look after still?' she asked Cynthia.

'Yes – in the week,' Cynthia said, squeezing more tea out of the pot. 'Brenda'll be ready for school soon. They're not too bad really, considering.'

'Poor little buggers're lucky to be alive I should think,' Dot said forcefully. 'That Irene wants 'er head examining. Lucky they've got you looking after 'em, Cynth – I'm surprised she ain't finished off the lot of 'em by now.'

Irene Skelton had insisted – against all advice – on putting condensed milk into her infants' baby bottles. Since this had given them chronic and agonizing constipation, any visit to the Skelton house had been against a background of the sounds of children straining on pots, their faces screwed up in misery. Her youngest had died of an impacted bowel and Mr Skelton left before they could have any more children on which to inflict this agony.

'They're not too bad,' Cynthia said. 'They just need a kind word or two.'

Dot started regaling them with tales of some of her Italian in-laws, then Bob complained he couldn't get any smokes because there was no tobacco to be had, and as the talk moved, as it always did these days, back to raids and bomb damage and shortages, Norm leaned over and whispered in Em's ear, 'Let's go out for a bit of a walk, shall we?'

Em gave a slight frown. 'It's chilly out, Norm!'

'But I want to be on my own with yer. I've got summat to tell yer.'

'We're just popping out for a bit, Mom,' Em said, getting up a bit reluctantly. She liked seeing Dot, who'd been like a second mother to her.

It was a cool, clear April afternoon, the sun already sinking low, a yellow glow in the distance. The barrage balloons sat tethered and still in a quiet sky. Norm pulled Em's arm through his.

'Peaceful, isn't it?' Em said.

'Thought I'd never get a minute with yer by ourselves,' Norm burst out. Then, as if worried he'd been ungrateful, he added, 'That was a nice dinner yer mom did.'

'Mr Perry slipped me some extra spuds,' Em said. They'd padded out the tiny amount of meat. 'He's nice like that.'

'Well she's a good cook – you are an' all.'

'Oh I don't know about that!' Em laughed, flattered. 'Anyway – what was it you wanted to tell me?'

'Ah, well . . . that's a hard one . . .' They passed along the edge of the gasworks, in silence for a few moments. Norm chewed on his lip in an agonized sort of way, then stopped suddenly and turned to her, gazing anxiously into her eyes. Em looked back, loving him, knowing how true he was.

'What's up, love?' she asked.

'I don't know how to say it,' Norm said. He looked

quite tearful for a moment and glanced away to one side, trying to find the words. Then he turned to her again, more decisively. He put his hands on her shoulders and drew her closer.

'Go on – give 'er a kiss!' some lad shouted, whizzing past on a bike, but they took no notice.

'Thing is, Em – I love yer. I don't ever want yer to think I don't . . .'

'Norm?' Her voice rose anxiously. 'What's the matter? What're you trying to say?'

'I'm a young man—'

Oh no, Em thought, *not this again!* Him going on about her giving herself to him and all that! Molly was right – men really did only have one thing on their minds! The pressure made her feel immediately resentful.

'But, Norm . . .'

'No, listen – I've got to do it. I've thought and thought. I know they need police, but now they're bringing in the older fellas for the Reserve, and some of the young 'uns are going off and joining up. And, Em, I've got to go. Thing is, I'm trying to tell yer, I'm going to leave the police force. I've decided, I'm going to volunteer in the RAF.'

Em stared at him, almost unable to take this in. It was like an earthquake, things as she had expected them to be all overturning.

'The RAF?' she said stupidly, pulling away from him at this betrayal. 'But, you've never said a word to me about it. And, that'd mean you going away.' She stared at him in complete bewilderment. Shocks and changes were always an ordeal for her.

'Yes – it would love. Em, come 'ere . . .' He came to

her again and tried to hold her but she couldn't stand it, not yet. 'I ain't done anything about it. I've been thinking and thinking, round and round, and I wanted to talk to you first, not just go and do it. But it feels right to me. I don't want to be one of them blokes who sits in the pub, once it's all over, and listens to all the others canting about it. I want to do my bit.'

Em started walking again, head down.

'Em?' He hurried beside her on his big, ploddy feet. 'Are you angry, love?'

'No.' She was shaking, but not with anger. 'I dunno.'

'What, then?'

In her whirling thoughts she knew she needed Norm to be her security. She knew Molly thought he was boring, that others found him staid, comical even, but with him she felt safe. Yet also, knowing he was having these thoughts, there was a welling sense of relief – the pressure off her to be married and with him, to do those other things he wanted – and of admiration for him for feeling this way.

'Scared,' she said. 'And proud of yer.'

'Oh love!' Norm was moved. 'Are yer really?'

She reached up and kissed his cheek, tearful now. 'I don't want you to go – course I don't . . .'

'Em—' In the gloaming his expression was very serious. 'Before I go – if they'll 'ave me – I want us to get wed. I want to make you mine.'

Something in her baulked. *I'm not ready!* her thoughts protested. *Don't make me – not yet.*

'Course we'll get wed,' she said lightly. 'But there's no mad rush, is there? You know what they say: "Marry in haste, repent at leisure."'

'Don't be daft, there won't be any repenting,' Norm

said, sounding a bit hurt. 'I just want you to be my wife, Em. It's all I really want in the world.'

It was the week before Easter and Norm promised he wouldn't do anything until it was over, giving her a few days to think. Em was grateful for his usual kindness. Norm could be a bit hapless but he certainly had a good heart. She felt ashamed of her hesitation but couldn't help her terror about all that marriage and motherhood might mean.

But before many days had passed, something else happened. She came home from work on the Wednesday, tired from standing all day, anxious to have a sit-down before her warden duty later that night. All day, working side by side with Mr Perry, she had been thinking, and she felt she had been mean and ungrateful towards Norm. It all kept going round and round in her head and the family chatter – Mom rejoicing because she'd managed to get hold of a tin of golden syrup, Joyce going on about getting a job and how much she might earn – all grated on her nerves.

'Huh – *you're* in a mood,' Joyce said grumpily, when Em had replied snappily to everything she said.

Em stood up, putting down her teacup. 'Gotta go.' Stepping out into the darkness in her ARP uniform, she thought of Norm, also on duty across the city. 'You keep safe,' she whispered. Suddenly she felt a powerful longing to see him, almost a superstitious feeling that something bad might happen. She worried that because he was so conscientious he might do something too heroic and get himself into danger.

She joined Mr Radcliff and they began their patrol of

the street, checking for any lights showing in breach of blackout regulations, or any other sort of trouble. It was quiet, eerie almost, hardly anyone about, the pencil-thin beam of their torches the only light. Mr Radcliff often talked about the last war, telling her stories about France, the trenches, about having to burn lice out of the seams of his shirt. He liked to have someone young to talk to, instead of the others who could remember too and didn't necessarily want to hear it.

The clocks had already struck nine when the sirens went off.

'Oh-oh, here we go,' Mr Radcliff said. The beams of the searchlights began to criss-cross the sky, looking for the incoming bombers. Soon Em could hear their droning engines, and the ack-ack guns started up, hammering reassuringly. It always made you feel better hearing them. Em's stomach clenched, her breath catching with fright as she and Mr Radcliff tried to keep calm. Already she had a sense of foreboding that this was going to be a bad one. She wondered if he was as frightened as she was.

'Where're those buggers going?' Mr Radcliff muttered, face tilted to the sky. Em caught a glimpse of his moustache in silhouette.

It wasn't long before the first one fell, and the next, and the next. They stood pressed against a wall, eyes and ears straining, trying to calculate where the bombs were coming down.

'Bordesley?' Mr Radcliff said hoarsely, then, 'That sounds like over Aston way . . .' It was close enough to feel a faint tremor. Moments later, he said, 'That was further south . . .'

'I've got a bad feeling about tonight,' Em said.

Mr Radcliff sighed heavily. 'You and me both, wench.'

They kept coming and coming. Em and Mr Radcliff continued their frightening patrol up and down the street. Mr Radcliff bawled at a couple of young lads to get under cover and knocked on someone's door to get them to let in their dog, which was whimpering on the step. The bombs thundered down, sometimes close enough for the ground to shake. Fires burned across the city and the night took on a coppery glow.

'Come into my house, just for a tick,' Mr Radcliff shouted, breaking into a run. 'We'll have a look out from the attic. Get our bearings.'

They scrambled up the dark, musty-smelling stairs. Mrs Radcliff was safe in a shelter at Maskell's Foundry Supplies. The attic window was high up, so to see out they each perched with one leg on a chair. There was not much of a view, beyond the other attics of houses across the street, but from this height, the ominous glow coming from the southwest was all the more obvious, and from all round: from Aston and Saltley, Bordesley and Deritend.

'Christ!' Mr Radcliff breathed, his language uncharacteristically colourful for a slightly religious man. 'Those Kraut *bastards*.'

Em held a hand up. 'Listen!'

Their eyes met at the sound of the planes moving closer. They each jumped from the chair and rushed downstairs, on the brink of stepping outside when a massive impact very close by knocked them off their feet. Something smashed to the floor in the darkness, the ground shook and the house rattled around them. Em's nose and mouth were clotted with dust and she was coughing and spitting it out as the shaking died away. A cloud of soot had been knocked down the chimney.

'Jesus Christ!' Mr Radcliff exclaimed between coughs, his voice high-pitched as he babbled with shock. 'That was us! That was bloody Cromwell Street, that was! It bloody was! Come on, Em – we've got to get out there!'

They moved to the door. Em was aware of her face coated with soot, and her mouth felt gritty and sour. The light seemed brighter outside. In seconds it was obvious why – there were fires burning further along the street, which was blocked with rubble. They could hear shouts, the crackle of flames, and further away, the guns, and the jangle of bells from fire engines and ambulances. There'd been a direct hit.

Em turned, looking wildly back towards Kenilworth Street. Hadn't she heard something near that sounded as if it came from there? The house – Mom! She longed to go and see if they were all right, but she steeled herself to stay in control. She must stay for now and do her duty. A fire engine turned into the street behind her and edged along as far as it could go. The driver climbed out, grim-faced.

'This is a bad 'un.' He shook his head, looking at the ruins of one of the houses that had taken the hit. 'I've 'ad a job getting here. You should see the middle of town. It's a hell hole over there.' He called orders to the crew. In seconds everyone was taken up with the sorry business of damping down the flames, seeing to the bombed wreckage and trying to establish if anyone had been inside the house. Em tried to put her own family out of her mind. If anything was wrong, someone would be helping, wouldn't they? She had to do her job here.

She mustn't dwell on Norm either, and whether he was safe.

Not long had passed before everyone realized there were not enough people for the job – not anywhere near enough. Em and Mr Radcliff got stuck in with the firemen and some neighbours who appeared, all digging and pulling at the rubble. As time passed it seemed that one of the houses had been empty. As they dug into the other they could hear a voice calling out, 'I'm under 'ere! Under the stairs!'

A toothless old lady was soon released from her cubbyhole, in great agitation.

'They're down in the coal cellar!' she cried in a cracked voice. 'My granddaughter and the babbies!'

Em gave the old lady a blanket. 'I'll go and give 'em a hand looking. You wait there a bit – I'm sure we'll get them out for you, missus.'

It wasn't long before the young woman, with a toddler and a baby in her arms, was released from below, black with coal dust. Em realized she must look much the same.

'Oh Nana!' the young woman cried, seeing the old lady waiting for them. 'You're safe – oh my God! Oh!' She took in the sight before her. 'Look at our house – what are we going to do?'

'For now,' Em said, 'get yourselves over to Thimble-mill Lane, to Johnny Wright's. They'll look after you.'

The family disappeared, stunned, into the gloom.

'Hope they'll be all right,' someone said. 'God knows where they'll go in the morning.'

There were still planes coming over, but now the houses seemed to have been cleared, Em was desperate to see if her own family were all right. 'Mr Radcliff, can I just run round the road a minute?'

'Go on, bab. Mind 'ow yer go.'

Em tore along to the end of Kenilworth Street. She felt sick with nerves and the strains of the night. With a jolt she saw that the street had been hit – rubble, confusion – and for a few seconds she could not take in the scene. Then she breathed more easily. Not number eighteen! Oh thank God, thank God!

Then she took in the rest of the scene. There were people at work, an ambulance.

'What's happened?' She tore up to the wreckage, trying to make sense of it. Everything seemed out of place. She stopped, appalled. A dreadful, sick feeling rose in her at the sight. It was the Buttons' house that had been hit, and the one next to it. She knew the warden, a Mr Birch, from down the street, and she hurried over to him. 'Are they in there? Are they all right?'

Mr Birch was a small, sad-faced man in his sixties. He was shaking his head. 'They was in bed,' he said. 'They've got him out all right.'

'What, Mr Button – he's alive?'

'He's in the ambulance – nowt much wrong with 'im – but her . . .' He shook his head.

'Mrs Button?' Em was trembling. Kind, jolly Mrs Button. She thought of Molly, that she'd have to tell her.

'Main beam came down, right onto 'er. You all right wench?'

Em brought her shaking hands up to her face to block out the sight of it.

By the time the All Clear went, it felt like the longest night Em could ever remember. Throughout that day, the reality of the night's wounds became increasingly clear: bombs all over the inner wards of the city; damage to St Martin's Church in the Bull Ring, which made Mr Radcliff gnash his teeth with fury; and the Midland Arcade in town had gone up in flames, as had several pubs and – a local disaster – the nuts and bolts factory, L.H. Newton's. There was talk of a river of blazing tar flowing down towards New Street Station, of devastation everywhere, of gas and water mains smashed and people having to be fed in halls and schools.

At last, going home, numb in the cold morning, Em saw a figure coming towards her out of the dawn gloom.

'Em?'

'Norm?' She found she was running along Kenilworth Street, jumping over bricks and hoses, glass crunching under her feet. She hadn't known how overwrought she was, tears streaming down her face, her chest bursting with emotion. All she wanted was his arms around her. They hugged each other as close as they could, arms pressing into each other's backs.

'You're all right,' he said into her hair. 'God, I've been so worried about yer. It's been that terrible . . .'

'I thought it was never going to end.' She was still trembling, clinging to him. Norm looked round at the street, taking in what had happened. 'Mrs Button?' More tears came, all the fear and destruction of the night seeming to overwhelm her. 'Oh Norm – I've been so stupid about everything.' Life seemed so fragile, so absolutely precious.

He gave a fond laugh. 'What're you talking about?'

'About getting married and everything.' She looked up at him with wet eyes. 'Of course I want to marry you. I love you, Norm – you mean the world to me. Let's do it as soon as we can.'

On the Cliffs

Seventeen

June 1941

Molly had caught the train soon after two o'clock. In the scramble to get aboard at Reading Station she had managed, with some determined use of her elbows, to get a seat by the window. She faced herself firmly towards it, lit a cigarette, then another, and watched their progress westward, while the weather alternated between brilliant sunshine, banking clouds and fast-falling rain. As they drew out of Bath, a rainbow straddled the sky as if trying to promise her that things were not as bad as she feared.

She could not bear the thought of talking to anyone today. Earlier, a civilian woman had tried asking her questions – 'Oh I do think you're all so *brave* – *do* tell us all about it!' – only to be silenced by Molly's monosyllabic replies. The conversations had washed over her from behind, the personal gossip, the usual moans about food and shortages and worries about elderly parents, and about the German attack on Russia. Hitler's troops had invaded just days ago and were advancing east.

Molly's mood was dark and disorientated. All day she had been unable to shake off the memory of her morning dream, which hung like a pall over her thoughts. It had contained an atmosphere of threat so powerful and repellent that she knew it had been about her grandfather. He had been waiting there at the edges of it, in the shadows where she couldn't see him, as he always had been waiting, in the dark of the attic in Kenilworth Street, or in any of their temporary lodgings.

'He's gone for good, the filthy old bastard,' she told herself bitterly, yet remembering the odd twist of her emotions when William Rathbone had died, away in hospital, gangrenous and stinking. She had wept when she heard. Why the hell had she done that? Mom had been crying, Mom who had been his victim too until she had handed him down a generation. She had sat by the grate with her apron over her face, howling with grief over him. And Molly cried because Mom was crying, because even though the old man had not an ounce of kindness or goodness in him that she had ever seen, he was familiar, had always been there, and now he was gone.

Back then she had not known the very worst of it, as she did now. Today, after the dream, all the things she had tried to forget, far away from home in the army, had come flooding in like foul water backing up from a blocked drain. *That was my father* . . . She had an acid taste in the back of her throat which even the cigarettes could not dispel. Was it really true? She still half doubted. Would Mom have invented something so vile just for the spite of it? She didn't think even Iris was capable of making up something like that. Everything about it had carried the horrible ring of truth.

Where her fair colouring came from was a mystery, but in every other way, she and Iris and the old man were all so alike – tall, big-boned, big-featured. A shudder passed through her. Was that her birthright – just the two of them, both so cruel, with so little in the way of redeeming features? Was that all she was? How could there be anything in her that was good or worth loving, when the only blood relations she knew were those two – and Bert? Her brother Tom had been all right, but he made himself scarce years ago. A dark self-loathing enveloped her, and the approaching dusk only made her mood deepen. Scrabbling in the packet, she drew out her last cigarette.

They pulled into another station and passengers got off and on. 'KILL THE BLACK MARKET WITH YOUR RATION STAMPS', read a black-and-white poster. This also made her think of Bert, his dodgy dealings. She could never remember a time when he had been sweet natured or kind either. The acrid taste in her mouth increased at the thought of her brother. She knew he'd fooled his way into failing his army medical somehow, convinced them he had poor health. He was like a stoat or a weasel, sharp-toothed, mean, and bent on nothing but his own survival.

As darkness fell she felt more and more as if she was hanging in limbo. A camp on the South Wales coast was her next destination. There had been changes already: leaving Northampton and having to say good-bye to Lena and the others, the ache that Cath was already gone and that she had no idea where. She left there disappointed with herself, but resigned. What more could she expect? She was no good – not compared with all those others. The likes of Win and Ruth weren't going to be cooks, were they? Or any sort of general duties staff. They would get the plum jobs while the likes of her did the drudgery of general duties, and what else could she expect? She should never have fooled herself into hoping for more.

She had spent a fortnight on the catering course, with lectures about supplies and cooking, learning the tricks of providing food for the huge numbers lining up before them. She experienced the joys of being up at five on a freezing February morning, trying to light a bloody-minded range with damp coal. She was not motivated and passed sulkily through the course, coming out graded as a B1 cook. From there she had been sent to cook at a training camp in the Berkshire countryside, and it was there, eventually, that she received Em's letter about Jenny Button. The letter had done the rounds before it arrived there, as Em had sent it to the training camp at Northampton.

Molly had the letter in her pocket now, but she didn't need to get it out to read it – she already knew it by heart.

18 Kenilworth Street
April 11th, 1941

Dear Molly,

I'm sorry to say I'm writing to tell you very sad news. You may have heard that we had a very bad raid here in Birmingham on Wednesday night. I was on duty and it was one of the worst nights I've ever known. Your Mom and Dad are OK but I'm very sorry to tell you that a bomb came down on the house next to Mr and Mrs Button and their house collapsed as well. It's a terrible sight. Mr Button is all right, despite it, but I'm very sorry to say that Mrs Button was seriously injured and has passed away. I know how much she meant to you Molly as she was such a kind lady. We don't know yet what will happen to Mr Button as he has no family. He was taken to a rest centre and some of the neighbours are looking after him for now but I'm afraid he may have to go into the workhouse. There'll be a funeral for Mrs B next week but I don't know if they'll let you out for it.

My other news is that Norm has decided to join up. He's going into the RAF. I'm proud of him though its taken me time to come to terms with it. I'll miss him and between you and me, I wish he hadn't decided to do it. We are hoping to have a wedding when he comes home on leave.

I hope you're all right Molly and I'm sorry to have to send such bad news. Write and let me know how you're getting on. We're all all right, keeping going.

With love, Em xx

By the time she received the letter she knew the funeral would have been long over, and as Jenny Button was not family she might not have got leave to go to it anyway. After she heard, Molly felt numb for days. She couldn't seem to face up to it. Jenny Button had been a mom to her like no one else. It was impossible at first to take in that she was no longer there.

Gradually, grief built up in her. One night she had been out drinking with a lad from the camp. They'd walked a couple of miles to the nearest village pub and as they wove their way back between the dark trees of one of the country lanes, Molly grew more and more silent, unable to keep up the larky, joking front she usually put on.

'What's up?' the lad kept saying, nudging her. 'Come

on, Molly – this ent like you. Have I said something that's given you the hump?'

'Tell yer what,' Molly said, stopping suddenly on the road. There was a thin moon but otherwise a deep, country darkness. 'You go on – I'm just going in there a minute.' She nodded towards the woods beside the road. Normally she would have been terrified, but tonight she was too drunk and too upset to care about anything but getting away from him.

'Oh – like that is it?' he said easily, thinking she wanted to relieve herself. 'Well you go – I'll wait for you along here.'

'No,' she insisted. 'You go on ahead. I'll catch you up.'

'Don't talk soft, I can't just leave you in the dark,' he protested, but she was already moving away into the woods, desperate to be shot of him and to allow her distressed feelings to have free rein.

The trees closed round her and she could see barely anything at all, just smell the earth and a hint of something sweet on the fresh air. She walked slowly, feeling her way into each step, arms outstretched. Tips of branches scratched her face. Something large fluttered away above her head, giving a shriek in the distance. She stumbled over a hard object in her path and just saved herself from falling. After a time she heard the lad shouting from the road and realized she had not gone very far though it seemed she was already in another world. He shouted a few more times, sounding angry now, and she kept moving away from him.

'Go away,' she whispered. 'Go away and leave me alone.' She realized vaguely that she couldn't think what his name was. Pat? Eric? Or was that the last one? A giggle escaped her. It occurred to her that she might just as well relieve herself while she was here, so she squatted down, hand on the mossy trunk of a tree.

Afterwards, she waited a long time and it went quiet so she took it that he had given up. She found a place among the trees where she could just see the little arc of moon, and turning her face up towards it, she felt the waiting tears begin to fall, her chest heaving. She imagined Jenny and Stanley in their little house with the bombs dropping from the flaring sky and Stanley lying there with Jenny silent beside him until they were rescued. And Wally the little dog – what had happened to him? She imagined him killed in the house as well. Her mouth opened and she screamed and yelled up to the moon, cried out with all her force until no more would come and then sank down on to the moist ground, sobbing and rocking herself.

Why? Why did it have to be Jenny? She was kind and nice. Why didn't you let it be someone else? She wished with all her heart that the bomb had fallen on Iris and Joe instead, and she didn't feel wicked for wishing it.

Only when she had had a good cry did she start to feel afraid, to know that she was in a wood in the pitch dark, alone at night. Some other creature gave a screech in the trees above her head. Picking herself up with a groan she stumbled back, confusedly, towards the road, half hoping that he, whatsisname, would still be there as now the night felt cold and sinister. She hit the road after not too long a time but it was deserted. No doubt he was another one who thought she was mad.

'Never mind,' she muttered, walking exhaustedly towards the camp. 'He was nothing much any'ow.'

What was it that other one had said, so bitterly, that sweet northern lad from the Arborfield Camp? 'You may be a looker, Molly, but you don't want a real man beside yer, to feel owt for, do yer? You just want to be seen on a man's arm – but you're hard as nails inside, that you are.'

This thought made more tears come just when she thought they were all finished. She had never cried that much in her life before.

Now, in her low state, she was dreading arriving at yet another new place with a sea of strange faces around her. There'd be no Phoebe Morrison to give her brusque encouragement. She was on her own. And she felt peculiar, as if she were behind a screen, so that she was cut off from everything around her. It was a strange, frightening feeling.

As dusk came on they all blacked out the train and sat on in the dim blue light. Molly pulled her coat over her and closed her eyes, wanting to shut out everything on this journey into the unknown. She felt terribly small and alone and full of grief.

Eighteen

She emerged from her hut the next morning to find herself in the wide open space of the camp where the grey, square buildings, the parade ground and gun park were all swept by a blustery wind. There was a sense of movement everywhere, squads of artillery people hurrying here and there, ATS and others saluting officers as everyone went about their business along neat, well-laid-out paths.

There was energetic weather that morning, with fast-moving clouds blocking the bright sunlight, which only managed to burst through intermittently. On and off all day came the sound of guns firing from the cliffs. Molly was busy finding her way about and being introduced into her job in the cookhouse, finding out all the things you can do to disguise tinned herrings, helping with the mass of spud-bashing and other menial tasks involved in feeding very large numbers of people every day. She found herself glad to be in her cap and apron, busy with the kitchen tasks which were now becoming familiar, if not particularly welcome.

One of the other cooks was a friendly, fresh-faced girl called Mavis, originally from a village near Swindon, and Molly was relieved to know that they would probably get along well enough. The others were all right as well, and Molly was learning to try and keep her mouth shut and approach things more quietly instead of throwing herself straight into trouble. Mavis was engaged to a soldier called Alfie, about whom she could talk endlessly, but at least she didn't ask Molly too many questions. They were working in the mess frequented by many of the newly recruited gunners of the Royal Artillery, who came to the camp for training periods of about three months.

She found all the newness tiring, but it was not long until, out of the mass of new faces, one suddenly emerged that was familiar. Molly was ladling out a potato-thickened soup at lunchtime, when someone caught her attention in the queue coming towards her. There were those high cheekbones, the wide eyes and pale straw hair tucked under an ATS cap. Was it . . . ? Yes, surely that was Honor! Her heart started to beat faster. She was more pleased than she would ever have imagined to see Honor, but would Honor even recognize her, or want to know her in return? She was so posh, and the other ATS women she was standing beside looked equally refined. Molly broke out in a sweat, feeling her own roughness, how hard and cracked her fingers were from the long winter of work, how she could never be like them. She kept her eyes cast down on the mess tins she was filling with pale green soup, feeling prickly and defiant, as if she had been rejected already.

Then she heard a voice, high and well-spoken: 'I say – Molly? It *is* Molly, isn't it?'

Blushing, she looked up as Honor came closer.

'I *thought* it was you – how lovely to see you!' Honor cried.

'Hello,' Molly said gruffly, but a smile broke across her face. She remembered Honor's sweet strangeness, her precious blindness to class difference, so odd in someone called Honor Carruthers, as if she had never been let out in the world to know quite how it all worked and the prejudices you were supposed to have.

'Gosh – so you're *cooking*,' Honor said, with apparent admiration.

'Yes. 'Fraid so. Gets us out of church parade, at least! What're you doing here?' Molly asked as they presented their mess tins. These tins were filled in groups of four. Honor and her companion were taking food to two other ATS. 'They ain't let you loose on the guns, have they?' Then she cursed herself for saying 'ain't', but Honor didn't seem to notice, and gave a laugh of genuine mirth.

'It does seem a little rash of them, doesn't it?' She spoke in her usual floaty way. 'Of course we girls are on the predictors – they won't turn us loose on the guns! I'd rather hoped they'd make me a driver or something. But this is what was decreed. It's not really too bad, as long as you can concentrate all right and you're not gun-shy.'

Molly ladled soup for her. 'Gun-shy?'

'Some people just can't stand it. They jump about like rabbits every time a gun goes off. Oh – this is Gina by the way?' Molly and Gina, a rather horsey-looking girl, smiled nervously at each other. 'And guess what – Ruth's here too!'

'Oh.' Molly's heart sank. Honor was one thing, but she wasn't so pleased at the idea of seeing snooty, academic Ruth again. 'She a gunner an' all?'

'No – something far more brainy. She's a Kinny! There's a bunch of them training here.'

'A what?'

Honor and Gina were having to move along the line – others behind were starting to mutter. 'They're Kiné-

Theodolite operators, she says. It's a more technical way of working out where the target is, apparently.'

'Oh,' Molly said. Trust Ruth.

'I'd best move on – we must get together for a chinwag, Molly! See you!'

'Er – see yer,' Molly said, pleased, but startled to hear Honor use a phrase like 'chinwag'. The army was changing her. She saw Gina lean in and ask something and Honor glance back in her direction. *What were they saying?* Molly wondered, digging out another ladleful. She burned with envy at their work. Here was she, stuck with a vat of flipping soup!

Though she had expected a lonely day populated by strangers, it turned out differently. There was so much work to do that Molly was kept very busy, baking football-pitch-sized trays of dry Madeira cake made with powdered egg and minimal sugar for the afternoon tea break. The kitchens were full of the waft of hot sponge and big urns of tea when Ruth turned up.

She was standing by the long serving counter. As their eyes met, Molly saw Ruth blush in confusion and look down for a moment. Sewn on her khaki uniform Molly saw the Royal Artillery gun badge above her left breast pocket. The other ack-ack girls in the mixed batteries wore the flaring bomb badge. There was also the white lanyard across her right shoulder. Kinnys were evidently something rather special. Molly took all this in enviously.

'Hello, Ruth,' she said forcefully, in case Ruth should try to pretend they didn't know each other.

'Oh!' Ruth looked up, giving a flustered, buck-toothed smile. 'Hello, Molly. I thought it was you, but

I wasn't sure.' Her tone was non-committal, neither friendly nor off-putting. Then, with forced jollity, she added, 'How're you getting along?'

'All right, thanks. With or without?' She pointed at the tea. Ruth held out her big bone china mug.

'Oh, without please. Though many more days out on the park and I'll be taking sugar as well!' She spoke fast, in her odd way. 'Nice cake, by the way. Glad you're getting along all right.' She moved away, saying, 'See you around.'

Watching Ruth's departing back, her small, curving figure swathed in battledress, Molly realized that if anything, Ruth was even more nervous than she was.

At last there was a little bit of spare time, once tea was cleared away.

'D'you want to come over to my hut – have another cuppa and a chat or anything?' Mavis asked kindly. But Molly replied that she was going to go and have a look round. She didn't tell Mavis that she had never seen the sea before, but now she had time to think about it, she was excited. The smell of it was in the air, and while she could see where the land gave out in the distance, she had not yet been over to have a look.

'All right then,' Mavis said easily. 'It's a nice after-noon for it now. See you back here later. No rest for the wicked, eh?'

Mavis was right: it was a beautiful afternoon. The buffeting winds of the morning had died, the rain had passed off, and it was warm with a gentle breeze. Molly felt the sun hot on her face and her spirits lifted. Last night's journey seemed a long time ago, and strange as this place was, she was beginning to be glad to be here, and was eager to explore. Saluting absent-mindedly, even at a junior ATS who giggled at her mistake, she made her way towards the cliffs, noticing that for the time being most of the guns seemed to be quiet. Though she was curious to see the gun park, she steered away from it, making for a place where she could walk and be alone.

Suddenly, on the high cliff, with its wind-ruffled grass, she was looking out over the sea. The sight made her gasp, though it was not just the sight of the jewelled blue, the great reach of it as far as the eye could see, it was the whole experience of standing in the breeze, gulls seeming to float in the sky above, with more open sky around her than she had ever known before in her hemmed-in life.

'The sea! The sea!' she squeaked to herself, delighted. She was bubbling with excitement, wanting to run about like a child. Everything about being there made her soar inside. 'It's lovely and I want to stay here for ever!'

She saw a movement out of the corner of her eye: a rabbit's white scut disappearing behind a wiry bush. No wonder the grass was so short, as if someone had mown it! Enchanted, she moved along the sward, seeing in it tiny pink, yellow and white flowers and clumps of ferns. Further along she noticed two figures sitting closer to the cliff edge, off-duty ATS, their hair, one chestnut, one ginger, blowing back behind them, and laughing together. She felt a pang. Where was Cath now? What was happening to her? Snatches of their voices came to her. Molly passed quietly along behind them, not wanting them to see her.

After walking further, to what seemed a more solitary spot, she found a perch on a grass-cushioned lip of ground which made a step, from where she could look out over the sea. She sat, astonished by the depth of colour brought out by the strong sunlight. She thought she had never seen the sky such a rich blue, the sea a dark, lovely line meeting it in the distance, the white waves forming little ruffles. And the grass: a vivid green that was completely new to her. Why had no one told her the world could be so beautiful? That there was so much to see outside the walls and alleys of the city? Turning her face towards the sun, she closed her eyes, feeling its warmth pressing on her lids. The dizzy wind whirled in her ears, and gulls screamed, their cries echoing against the cliffs, then wheeled overhead. The shadow of a pair of them passed over her, and she jumped, opening her eyes.

'Well you're some big buggers, ain't yer?' she said to them as they swooped out of sight over the cliff edge. For a moment she found herself wishing Em was here, to see all this too. But it was hard to imagine Em ever leaving home.

She lay back for a moment, drinking in the warmth, head resting on the grass, hearing bees in the flowers. She started to feel as if she was floating, weightless, her head spinning. Everything – home, the war, all troubles – felt so far away. She stretched luxuriously, then frowned. The sun had gone in. More of those piled clouds must have sneaked up without her seeing . . . But there had been no clouds . . . She opened one eye, and leapt into a sitting position.

'Oh my God – what the hell're yer doing creeping up on me like that?' she raged at the man standing over her. 'You've almost made me jump out of my bleeding skin!'

He laughed, even with Molly's fury directed at him. She felt as if her privacy had been destroyed. Shielding her eyes against the sun, she glowered up at him.

'You didn't 'ave to come sneaking up on me like that, did yer?'

'I suppose I could wear bells on my toes,' he said, laughingly. 'Sorry – I didn't see you there 'til the last minute. I come and sit in that spot myself sometimes.'

'Oh,' Molly said. She felt a bit ashamed of her reaction. And she liked his deep voice, with a bit of an accent she wasn't sure of, and even his half-mocking manner. 'Sorry. D'yer want to sit down then?'

'Well – if you don't mind.'

She budged up. There was enough room for two, quite easily.

'You a new one?' he asked, fishing out a packet of cigarettes from his breast pocket and holding it out to her. 'I've not seen you round here before.'

'I just got here yesterday.'

'Here?' He lit her cigarette skilfully, hands cupped round the match, and then his own, twisting his body away from the wind. Molly took the opportunity to look at him carefully. He had seemed tall standing over her, was broad-shouldered but slender. She saw army cropped hair of a middling brown, a large, beaky nose which, like Honor's, dominated his face, and hooded eyes. His smile had shown a wide, slightly lopsided mouth. The effect was not so much obviously handsome as intriguing. She wanted to keep looking at him, couldn't imagine getting bored by the sight of his face. She leaned close to him to light her cigarette, then back again, drawing on it.

'You in a mixed battery then?'

'No,' she admitted, tetchily. If only she could say yes to that! 'I'm a cook, worst luck.'

He laughed, leaning back on one elbow. Long, very

lean legs stretched out in front of him. Somehow, even reclining, he seemed to give off a restless energy.

'Nothing wrong with cooks – well, except the ones around here! Everyone's got to eat.'

'I'd rather be out doing something else. Cooking's like being at home, not like being a soldier.'

'Women shouldn't be soldiers.'

'But we are – nearly. They can court-martial us now.'

'So they can.' He looked round, studying her face. Then he couldn't seem to look away.

'What's that corking accent?'

'Birmingham,' she said defiantly. 'And what's your "corking accent"?'

'Norf London,' he joked. With mocking courtesy, he held out his hand, continuing in a very strong London accent, 'Pleased to meet you, ma'am. Allow me to introduce myself – my full nomenclature is Anthony John Belham. Known to my closer associates as Tony. Might I 'ave the privilege of knowing under what appellation you formally introduce yourself?'

'*What?*' Molly asked, unable to keep from laughing.

Deepening his voice to a roguish growl, he said, 'Your name, young lady – your name.'

'I'm Molly.'

'Molly. Molly . . .' He turned the name round. 'A Moll, eh? Molly what?'

'Fox.'

'No middle name?'

'Nope.' Molly blew out a mouthful of smoke as elegantly as she could manage. 'I'm surprised our mom even bothered giving me a first one.'

Tony looked concerned. 'Oh dear, like that is it?'

'Nah – just pulling your leg,' she said hastily, sorry she'd brought Iris anywhere near the conversation.

'Molly from Birmingham.' He grinned. 'Well, Molly from Birmingham. That's where all the best things come from – where my princess is from, in fact.'

'What're you on about now?' She squinted at him.

'My bike. A Norton, made in . . .'

'Aston – I lived near the works for a bit,' she said, excited. 'You got it here? I've always fancied a go on one, but I never knew anyone with one.'

'No – it's back home. I only get to see her on leave. I keep her in the shed, locked safely away.'

'Are you a gunner then?'

He told her he was Royal Artillery, had been there training getting on for two months already. 'We'll be here a while more, and then – well, anyone's guess where next.'

'It's lovely here. I'd never seen the sea before. Today's my first day ever.' She didn't know why she told him that either. Something about him made her find it easy to be truthful.

'Is that right? Yes well, I suppose Birmingham's about as far from the sea as you can get. You got much family?'

Molly stubbed out her cigarette on a bare patch of ground. 'No – well, a bit.'

'Brothers. Sisters?'

'Two brothers. What about you?'

'I've got a brother, Mick – he's in the Merchant Navy. Bit older than me. And two sisters – they're still at home. They're all right, and they're company for Mum. She says if she'd only had herself to see to in the bombing she'd have gone to pieces.' His cigarette was finished now. He threw the stub away, but sat on in silence for a moment. Molly liked sitting with him. He interested her. He seemed to know what he liked.

'Fancy a drink sometime?' he asked, easily.

'Yeah. Why not?'

'Good – I'll see you.' He scrambled to his feet. 'I'd better get back. See you soon, Molly.'

'Ta-ra,' she said, more casually than she felt.

He turned after a few energetic paces and waved to her, his uniform billowing round his thin frame. The wind was getting up again and he walked off, bending into it. Molly stared after him until she couldn't see him any more.

Nineteen

'I hope whatever's in there's better than the last lot – tasted as if it must have dead cat in it!'

Tony was at the counter, rattling his mess tins. He had that restless air she recognized from before, of someone on the verge of running, or dancing. He was smiling winningly.

'Cheeky bleeder!' she retorted, though she couldn't help a blush of pleasure at seeing him. 'I'll give you dead cat! It's mutton stew and it's ... well, not too bad ...' She had to laugh at herself for not being able to claim any better than that. The food at the camp did not have a good reputation and Molly had no ambition to improve on it. Even so, she was still eating better in the army than she ever had in her life before.

Standing there, he seemed even taller and thinner than before, as if he burned up every ounce the moment he'd eaten it. But he was also more handsome than she'd remembered, his eyes stony grey and alight with energy. She felt drawn in, excited at seeing him – and here she was hardly at her most glamorous in an overall, with her hair taken back under an unflattering hat!

'Hmm – looks just about edible,' he mused as she spooned stew into the mess tins. 'Give us plenty of spuds, eh?' He was more nervous than he was letting on, she saw. There was an edginess about him that made him seem more alive than other people. 'Coming out for a drink tonight then, Molly?'

'I might think about it,' she said archly. 'So long as you're not rude about my cooking.'

'For you, lady, I'll eat dead cat any day . . .' He backed away to join his mates. 'Meet you at eight by the guardroom?'

'I'll think about it.' She wouldn't have missed it for the world.

'He looks rather nice,' Mavis said, though with a note of doubt in her voice. From the sound of things, Mavis's bloke was a quiet, steady type, more like Norm. There was something much livelier and more exciting about Tony, and Molly bubbled inside at the thought of tonight.

Being stuck there as a cook seemed as nothing now. Suddenly she didn't care as long as she could be there, by the sea, where *he* was. This was a new start. All she could think of was him as she went about her chores of the day. But she was nervous at the same time. There had been so many blokes she'd walked out with, almost for the sake of it, as if life would have been empty without them. But she hadn't felt anything for them really. Sometimes she could barely even remember their names. And so often she made a mess of it, not knowing how to behave, or what was expected. She could hardly bear to admit to herself how confused she was about this, about what men wanted, or what *she* might want, or about what was right in any given situation. Instead she blundered from one to another, getting it all wrong. And she desperately didn't want to mess it up this time.

*

The village, like many situated near camps which had sprouted up all over the place, must have been wondering quite what had hit it, with the arrival of crowds of young people, all full of life and hungry for drink and fun to pass the time. There was a truck going there that night and Molly and Tony climbed aboard, anxious for something other than the NAAFI, and planning to crowd into the two village pubs.

On the way, someone started singing, and they all joined in: 'Run Adolf, Run Adolf, Run, Run, Run' and 'Boogie Woogie Bugle Boy' ... Molly saw Tony join in, heard that he had a good strong singing voice, and she joined in too. They smiled at each other and she felt immediately, soaringly happy.

Don't let me go wrong this time, she prayed inwardly. *Please, let it be OK. He's the nicest bloke I've ever met* ...

Most of the men she'd been with sat in groups and talked mainly to each other whenever they went to the pub, while she sat, bored and ignored. Tony was different. As soon as they'd managed to buy drinks in the crowded little village bar, he said, 'It's warm out still – let's take it out on the grass, shall we?'

So the two of them sat on a grass bank outside, a bit away from the other knots of joking, laughing drinkers, chatting the evening away while the sun went down and the midges came up. Molly felt herself relax. There was something about Tony that made him easy to be with. She realized there was something new in it, that she'd never really felt with anyone before – that for all his teasing, he respected her. And he was open and talked about his family. He talked with affection about his mother and father, Dymphna and Fred. Molly smiled at his mother's name.

'Does she 'ave dimples?'

Tony laughed. 'Yeah, she does, come to think of it. But that's a good old Irish name – you not heard it before?'

'No, can't say I have.'

'My dad's English – became a Catholic to marry Mum – she's very staunch that way.'

'What's 'e do – for a living, I mean?'

'Oh, he's got a little shop, off the Holloway Road – newsagents, all that, but he's got a chair in there, gives haircuts as well – for kids mainly.'

Molly sipped her beer, laughing. 'Are they the only ones'll risk it?'

'Yeah – too young to complain. Mum taught him – he only does one style, short back and sides, *very* short.'

'Your mom nice, is she?'

'Mum?' Tony seemed puzzled by the question. 'Yeah, course. Then there's Mick, the oldest – he's away at sea. They thought he was going to be a priest for years 'til he got a girlfriend and that was the end of it!'

'A priest? Why shouldn't he have a girlfriend?'

Tony lit two cigarettes and passed her one.

'Here – give us one, Tony!' another lad said, passing, and Tony threw one over, saying, 'Get your own you lazy blighter,' and the other lad laughed.

'You can't be a priest and have a girlfriend and get married or anything. Not Catholics – they're not allowed.'

'Oh,' Molly said. 'I daint know that.' Teasing, she added, 'So you don't want to be a priest then?'

Tony drew on his cigarette so that his cheeks sucked in. The evening light made his face glow golden, but his voice was suddenly bitter. 'I wouldn't go near those twisted bastards again if you paid me.'

'God, why?' she asked, startled at the angry change in him.

'Anything I know, that's in here?' He tapped his head. 'They beat every ounce of it in there, every crumb, every date in history, every word of Latin, every number of arithmetic . . . the sadistic—' He bit back an obscenity and got restlessly to his feet. 'Finished your drink? Let's walk a bit, shall we?'

Molly swigged the last of the beer and stood up, taken aback at his sudden change of mood. Slightly tipsily they left the pub, ignoring a couple of the others who called after them. Tony pushed his hands down into his pockets, seeming tense and ill at ease.

'What's up?' Molly asked, timidly. 'Was it summat I said?'

'Oh – no.' He seemed to shake himself out of it. 'Just thinking about it – that school, those blokes . . . *Christ*. Vicious bastards. Anyway. No good thinking about them. Tell me about your lot.'

'I told yer – not much to tell.'

'Come on – there must be something.'

He was nice, and she wanted to talk to him, but how could she begin on the truth of her family? So she gave him a part of it.

'My mom's . . . well, we don't get on. She's had a hard life. My dad was shell-shocked in the war and he's an invalid, can't do much for himself. And I've got two brothers but one's left home and we never see him.'

'What about the other?'

'Bert. He's two years older than me.'

'Has he joined up?'

'No.'

186

'There's a lot of Reserved Occs in Birmingham, I suppose.'

'There is, but Bert ain't Reserved Occ. He's a waster and pig. I hate him.'

Tony stopped in the lane, a tender expression on his face. The air was full of summer smells, the hedgerows, the damp earth and pungent flowers.

'That's a tough thing to say. You're a funny girl, Molly. You're so blinking beautiful, did you know that? And you come across all tough and mouthy, but...' He frowned. 'I'm not sure what to make of you.'

Don't make a mess of this, Molly admonished herself, biting back a smart-alec comment to hide her tender feelings. Tony was like Jenny Button: he tried to see you, see you properly, and it was touching and frightening at the same time. The fact that he was keen to talk about family was strange enough to her – most blokes rambled on about football or motorbikes or some other girl they wanted to see. She wanted to laugh it off, but instead she tried to be more gentle. She didn't want to lose this one.

'I s'pose I'm a bit of a mystery to myself,' she said lightly.

'What about your mother?'

'Look, I've told you – we don't see eye to eye.' Under his gaze, which seemed to embrace her, she felt disarmed. There was something in him that she recognized, and she sensed that he felt the same about her, though neither of them could have named what it was. 'Look – she's ... It's not summat to be proud of. She's a drinker ... Has been for years. She's a hard woman, not much kindness in her.'

Tony reached out and took her arm, pulling her close as they walked again.

'My uncle's a boozer. Wrecked his family with it.' She was glad of his words, but best of all was the warmth of his arm, wiry and strong. 'Mum ran round after him for years. It took her all that time to see it was useless. She thought there was something she could do – say the right thing, keep praying. She thought she could save him. In the end his wife left and he wrecked his health ... It's no good getting hooked on the stuff ...'

Though happily mellow from the beer, Molly was immediately glad she hadn't drunk any more. They'd had just enough to feel relaxed and playful.

Tony was silent for a moment, then said, 'Did you know there's a castle here?'

'No!' A castle, with Tony, sounded exciting. But then, a cardboard box with Tony would have felt exciting too.

'I'll show you. Quick, we've just got time before it gets dark.'

He walked her swiftly along the lane and soon the grey gatehouses and crenellated walls of a castle came into view.

'Oh!' Molly cried, full of wonder, like a little girl. 'I saw a picture of one once. Never seen a real one before! It's like summat out of a storybook!'

'It is,' Tony said. 'Blimey – you *have* led a sheltered life, haven't you? Up there – see that cottage? They call that the "Dak Bungalow" and the lady there'll do poached egg on toast for you if you ask her nicely. Her husband wears a panama hat, come rain, come shine!'

Molly laughed, still gazing at the castle. 'Can we go in?'

'Don't see why not.'

They went up the grass-lined path and through an

arched entrance, and once inside, they were suddenly enclosed by the old stones, pierced through by dark-eyed, pointed windows. They explored passageways and chill little rooms and the open green area inside. Molly was quite surprised to find there was no one else there. By the time they had gone part of the way round, in the cooling air of dusk, Tony had taken her hand and they were exploring like children on an adventure.

'D'you know,' Molly said, finding the words coming naturally, to her surprise, 'I've never had such a nice time as this before.'

'You kidding?' Tony asked.

'No! This is . . .' She shrugged, laughing – she couldn't even explain how she felt set free and full of the newness of it all. She wanted to tell him it was because she was there with him. But she was being careful, and held back from saying anything.

They left the castle building and climbed up to a rise where they could make out the sea in the distance with the pale shimmer of the sun's dying light on it. Darkness was creeping softly up from everywhere, bringing with it even stronger scents from the summer flowers. They sat down on the sloping grass. A bird was calling somewhere near, insistently. A thrush, Tony told her. His father was keen on birds, could name them all and even imitate some of their calls. Molly realized they were still holding hands, Tony's slim and warm in hers. She hoped her hands didn't feel too rough.

'It's so lovely,' she said softly, awed by how beautiful it all was, by the way she felt, seeing it all, and him beside her, his profile, as he looked out to sea.

Tony turned to look at her. Molly felt herself go weak, but she didn't move. Normally with blokes she liked to be in charge, to force things and make happen what she knew they really wanted from her, the things she was good for. But this time that felt wrong. Everything was different.

For a moment, the way Tony was looking at her, she thought he was going to turn and take her in his arms, kiss her, but instead he lay back, looking up at the sky. She did the same. Above was a pale grey vastness. It made her feel a bit dizzy. She breathed in deeply.

'I feel ever so small all of a sudden!' she said.

Tony gave a slight chuckle. 'Me too.'

'I like you being from London.'

He turned his head. 'Why?' He face was close to hers but she carried on looking up.

'It just seems – glamorous.'

Tony laughed. 'Does it?

'Yes – you know, *London*. It's special, ain't it – *isn't* it? – not like old Brum where I come from. Full of smoke and metal-bashing.'

'Well it's none too glamorous where I come from, I can tell you. Cramped streets. I have to get out when I'm there – the bike, that's my ticket to freedom.' There was always passion in his voice when he spoke about the bike. 'But it's got its good bits, I'll grant you.'

'Palaces and that.'

Tony seemed to find this very funny. Laughing loudly, he rolled over onto his front and looked at her.

'You're a caution. Have you any idea what state London's in? It's a mess! God – you should have seen when the docks went up!'

'Well it sounds lovely to me,' Molly said dreamily. 'I'd like to see it. The river and all the big buildings . . .'

Tony looked down at her, and she stared up at the darkening sky, almost pretending she didn't know he was looking. He reached out and chucked her gently under the chin. She turned to look then. He stared into her eyes, then smiled slowly.

'Best be getting back,' he said.

She nodded, glad and disappointed at the same time. She'd thought he might kiss her then. Didn't he want her? Was that it?

They walked back, hand in hand, to the pub. Before they got there Tony said, 'Molly? Will you come out again?'

'D'yer want to then?' It came out a bit harshly. She had begun to convince herself he was disappointed in some way. She was used to men being more basic and forward. It was usually the way she encouraged them to be.

He looked a bit puzzled, offended even. 'Yes – course I want to. You're a funny girl, Molly.' Awkwardly, he added, 'This has been the best night I've had in ages – ever – just in case you want to know.'

Twenty

Molly knew she had never felt like this before, not in any of her relations with men. At first, with all the lads she made up to, she had naively believed that they would really want her and care for her, but all of them had just tossed her aside. After that her attitude had been a mixture of need for their attention and contempt for them once she'd got it. It had been like an itch she had to scratch: she had to make men notice her, desire her, but even though she often ended up in their arms, there was nothing warm or close about it, and no respect on either side.

But Tony ... he's different – he's so lovely, she thought, getting ready for bed that night with a big smile on her face. The lights in their hut had still been on when she got back and Mavis was sitting on her bed, legs tucked under her, leafing through *Picture Post.*

'Well, *you* look happy,' she observed, seeming amused.

'I am,' Molly said, surprised at the feeling. It was a warm night and she hesitated before climbing into the thick army-issue pyjamas. But she had nothing else; she'd have to put them on and throw off the bedclothes.

'Is it that chap I saw you with? The one with the nice laugh? He looks a bit of fun.'

Molly nodded, pinning back her hair. ''E is. 'E's blooming gorgeous! Ooh – I feel like bouncing on the bed!'

'Go on then,' one of the others said. 'I dare you!'

'All right then.' Giggling, Molly clambered onto the bed, but the sagging springs made it so hard even to stand upright that soon she was staggering about in fits and the others laughed at the sight of her. 'I can't – I'll go straight through the thing!'

'Come on, Molly – bounce!'

'I can't . . .' She fell back, helpless with laughter. 'I'm too much of a lump!'

'Well you aren't wispy, I'll say that,' Mavis said, giggling. 'More of a Venus de Milo!'

'Only with arms,' someone else said.

'Who?' Molly tittered.

'Listen to that bed – it's complaining!'

Molly climbed into bed as things quietened, excited, and thinking how different things were now. She'd got off to such a bad start in her first billet, with Win and Ruth and the others. Now she was learning not to be quite so prickly and take things a bit more gently. For once she seemed to be getting on all right with the girls.

And Tony . . . She was brimful with happiness. He'd said it was the best night he'd ever had – and he sounded as though he meant it. She kept picturing his face, the way he looked at her, the way she had wondered if he would kiss her, and he didn't. She went over everything, treasuring it, but wondering and scared at the same time. Would he still feel the same tomorrow? And even if he did, wouldn't she go and make some awful mistake and spoil it all?

He was there at breakfast the next morning, as she stood in clouds of steam doling out ladles of porridge. She saw him the moment he came into the mess, that long, unmistakable face and with some energy about him that made him stand out.

'Mornin', girls,' he said roguishly, exaggerating his London accent. He gave Molly a wink which lit up her morning, but she saw Mavis blush. Mavis seemed to find Tony rather alarming. Lowering his voice, he said to Molly, 'See you later?'

'He's a one,' Mavis remarked as he went off with his breakfast.

'What d'yer mean?' Molly said, a bit put out.

'Oh, I don't mean no harm,' Mavis said hurriedly. 'He just looks ... I dunno – a bit of a handful, that's all.'

Molly shrugged. Mavis obviously liked her men very staid. Tony had a liveliness and sense of adventure that so many other blokes didn't.

After they had finished the midday meal, there was a break, and Tony showed Molly round the windy gun park, the ack-ack guns pointing out from the high cliffs towards the sky, and generators, height finders and predictors on their tripods to plot the planes' courses.

'See, the height finder tells the predictor where the plane is now?' Tony indicated the dusty electric cables joining the two instruments like an umbilical cord. 'You have to be able to see two images of the plane and line them up. Then the predictor tells you where it will be in a few seconds' time, so that the fuse setter can get ready for firing. It's all got a lot better. In the early days when they were bombing London, it was like clay-duck shooting in the dark. They were banging away at them and hardly hitting anything.'

Molly looked at the instruments, intrigued.

'I wish I could do that. I reckon I could.'

'Oh, I expect you could,' Tony said. He elbowed her playfully. 'It'd spare the rest of us your cooking.'

He ran off before she could thump him.

They spent every bit of time they could together, talking, joking, finding out more and more about each other. Both of them were full of energy and happiness, often walking hand in hand. Molly felt like a child again with him – this time, a happy, excited one. They explored the village, and the coastline. Walking along the cliffs in the opposite direction to where they first met, the going was more difficult. The Kinnys, who had a hut on the cliffs each side of the gun park, were beginning to wear a path along there, but other than them, there were not usually many people about. It was steeper, and involved scrambling between clumps of bracken and brambles, with foxgloves and honeysuckle beginning to flower among it all. Molly often got the giggles, losing her footing and clinging to clumps of broom or ferns.

'Wait for me!' she'd call, laughing helplessly. Tony would roll his eyes comically and turn back to give her a hand.

'Well you can tell you're a townie,' he'd say.

'I can't help it – I keep slipping over!'

And then, having stopped, they'd look out to sea and be struck by the sight all over again.

'God, it's lovely,' Molly kept saying.

It was here, two days after their first date, sitting on the sandstone cliffs in the scent of bracken, looking out over the bay, that Tony put his arm round her shoulders, drew her close and sat for a moment, their shoulders touching as they companionably looked out at the view. When he turned and looked at her, the expression she saw in his eyes almost brought tears to hers. Suddenly she felt shy. There had been so many men she had kissed, so many that didn't matter, but with Tony she felt like a complete beginner. He didn't say anything, just looked at her intently for a moment as if he was memorizing her, then leaned in close to kiss her.

It was the first of many kisses. In the July weather there were places to escape to once their shifts were over, and warm, balmy evenings to do it in, always with the scent of the flowers and bracken, the buzzing insects and the salt sea on the breeze. Molly loved the place, and she knew she loved Tony. He said he loved her, and the way he looked at her, she believed him. Being with him, she felt for the first time that something in her life made sense. She also understood that Tony was not just 'nice', though he was. There was something deeper which bonded them, though she could not have put it into words.

To her surprise, one evening when they were sitting side by side on the cliffs, shoulders touching, holding hands, he told her he loved fishing.

'Fishing? What, down the cut?' That was the only fishing she'd ever heard of, and any fish was lucky that managed to stay alive in that fetid canal water!

'Nah – the river. Or anywhere really. My dad'd take us, me and Mick, sometimes of a Sunday, get on the bus ... It was, well, a treat – sometimes when . . .' He trailed off, face darkening. She saw that happen to him sometimes, as if a memory had come over him like a cloud.

'When what?'

'Nothing. It was just something we did. Nothing like

it – sat there with your line, rain or shine, glare on the water . . .' He moved his arm as if it was all there in front of him. 'Or raindrops down the back of your neck. The old river going by, the quiet. No one bothering you. Mick used to fidget, but Dad said it was the only thing'd keep me still. We left Mick behind in the end. I always liked being out and away somewhere. Then when I got my bike, well, I could go off anywhere. That's heaven to me.' He looked at her. 'That and sitting here.'

Molly blushed in delight.

'Mind you, I wouldn't mind a go sitting out there on a boat. Never done sea fishing, but one day . . .' He gripped her hand. 'When it's all over, sunny days on a little boat, you there with me . . .'

'You're on,' she said. It sounded like heaven to her as well.

'Perhaps I'll be a fisherman – move to the seaside.'

'We could live up there.' She pointed at a little cottage, remote, in the distance. A life unfolded in her imagination – the little house on the cliff, Tony, children . . .

'I'd like to see where you live,' he said suddenly. 'I've never been to Birmingham.'

Molly looked ahead of her, towards the empty sea. An image flashed into her mind of the poky house, Mom sitting there, sozzled as usual. Joe. Bert. After her sweet fantasy, it was like being slapped.

'No yer don't,' she said tersely, patting her pocket in search of cigarettes. 'There's nothing much to see.' They both lit up, the breeze seeming to suck the smoke away from their lips.

'But love, I want to see where you were when you was growing up. It's natural to want to.'

She turned to him. He was sweet like that, the way he thought family was so important. 'No, yer don't, Tony. I'll tell yer summat, I can't think of anything worse than going back there again – to stay there, I mean. There's nothing there for me. It ain't home, or family, it's just where I was young, that's all. I had no choice then.'

'Molly?' He was startled by her bitterness, but she knew too, somehow, that it was something wounded in each of them that drew them together, something they shared. She laid a hand on his khaki thigh. Under the tough cloth, his leg felt lean and tough-muscled.

'Look, just take my word for it, will yer? Can I meet your family?'

'Course. They'd love you. There's only one thing . . .'

'What?'

'Well – them being Catholic . . .'

Molly frowned. 'Yeah – you said before. So *you're* Catholic then?' she asked uncertainly.

'Yes. Course. But Ma – she's very devout. Her faith means the world to her.'

'Well – that's all right.' She couldn't think what else to say on the subject. Religion was outside her experience. Half joking, she added, 'They're not too posh are they?'

'*Posh?* No – course not.' Tony chuckled. 'What gave you that idea, you silly?'

'Dunno.' She pulled the head off a piece of grass, scattering the seeds. 'When?'

Tony, in turn, picked a piece of bracken, shredding the leaves off it. 'When we've finished here, I'm due leave. Before the next posting. End of the month. I don't suppose there's any chance of you getting any?'

'P'raps. I haven't taken leave yet.'

'Didn't you get any after basic?'

'Didn't bother with it. Nowhere I wanted to go.'

He leaned close and kissed her cheek, taking a wisp of her hair between his fingers, looking at it in wonder. 'You're so lovely, d'you know that? Your hair's just – well, it's magnificent.'

'Magnificent?' Molly giggled, head back. It was so strange, someone saying nice things to her and meaning them.

'It is. You are. God, girl ... I've never seen anyone as fine as you before.' He stared longingly at her. 'Let me kiss you again.'

Laughingly she turned to him, pouting her lips to be kissed. Then she stopped him and said seriously, 'I've never been happy before – not like this. When you're young, life's ... a misery. Everyone pushes you around.'

That sour look on his face again. 'Yeah. You can say that again.'

'It's much better now – even in the army.' She wanted him to look happy, to chase away the cloud. And he did.

'Yeah.'

She wrapped her arms around him. 'I'd do anything for you, Tony – d'you know that?'

'And I would for you,' he said into her hair. 'You crazy Brummie girl. I love you to bits.'

Some of their free time coincided in the daytime, though more often they were together late in the evening, when the work was finished. Molly's days were full of food preparation and the endless cycle of cooking and clearing up. Tony spent much of every day practising out on the gun park, rain, wind or shine.

'I'm glad we've come over here in the summer,' he said. 'It must be bloody bitter in winter.'

His face was taking on a tan now, which Molly thought made him look more handsome than before. Her own nose and cheeks had caught the sun too. She had never felt so well and happy in her life, and her good spirits even extended to the work. She would still do her best in the army, even if she was a cook. It could still be her chance to better herself.

Having spotted the girls from the first billet on the camp, Molly had rather hoped she wouldn't bump into them often, other than sometimes serving their meals. She particularly didn't want to bump into Ruth. Unfortunately she soon realized that the General Duties ATS and the other women there training were all sharing the sanitary block. There wasn't much privacy in the primitive building – a row of washbasins with a door at each end and howling draughts passing through – where they were all expected to try and perform all their intimate washing. There were also bath cubicles, which were a bit less draughty.

The girls who were working in the gun park all day wanted nothing more than to soak in the bath for as long as possible, which made it difficult to get a bathroom. One evening Molly was in a tearing hurry to get out and be with Tony, but, ever particular about keeping clean, she wanted to make sure of bathing and washing her hair first. She hurried to the block only to find that all the baths were already occupied. After waiting for a while, she started to get impatient.

'Come on, you lot – isn't anyone finished in there

yet?' She knocked on a few of the doors to chivvy them out. 'You've all been in there flippin' ages!'

None of the occupants bothered to answer and after waiting a little longer, almost hopping from foot to foot with impatience, Molly rapped hard on one of the doors again.

'You nearly finished in there? Come on, for heaven's sake!'

A moment later the door flew open and a very irate Ruth appeared, hair tousled, her towel and washbag bundled up in her arms.

'I might have known it was you!' she said furiously, her cheeks all pink. 'You've got a damned sauce coming and shouting at us like that. It's all right for you general duties people – some of us are out there doing a proper job of work all day! But I don't suppose anything like that would occur to you, would it?'

She strode off without even giving Molly time to apologize – not that she was intending to. She stuck her tongue out at Ruth's departing back, just as one of the girls who worked in the stores came out from her bath. She grinned at Molly.

'That told you, didn't it? Madam's one of those Kinnys, isn't she? They think they're way above everyone else.'

'Oh well,' Molly said, rushing in to claim the bath. 'Sod her.'

She had more luck with Honor, who was always willing to have a chat if there was time. They got together for a tea break together one morning, sitting each side of the end of one of the long tables. Looking across at Honor, Molly thought her face had filled out a little and there were signs of colour in her cheeks.

'You're looking well on it,' she said.

201

Honour gave her tinkly laugh, lifting her cup to her lips. 'I feel well. All this fresh air and stalwart food! It's done me good to get away from home. It's so very sad without Nanny there. And Mummy and Daddy never really needed me anyway!' For a moment, her large eyes were full of sadness.

Molly was struck yet again by Honor's strange openness, especially when she added, 'I really don't know why some people have children. There should be a law against it!'

She looked at Molly. 'Sorry. I'm keeping on again. How are you, Molly? You look fighting fit as well.'

'I'm all right – very!' Molly said.

'Funny meeting up like this. We're all scattered about, the basic training lot. There's no telling where people might turn up.'

'I never heard from Lena – the girl from Walsall.' Molly had been rather hurt by this. She'd thought Lena was her friend, even though she'd found her a bit odd. 'There was some talk about her being a driver but I don't know if that's what she did.'

'Oh – didn't you know?' Honor said. 'Now who told me this? Maybe Win – I ran into her somewhere. Win's off in the Ministry of Information or something pukka like that now, but I met up with her a couple of months ago . . . Lena left the service, very early on. Her brother was killed – one of those poor boys in the Atlantic. And her mother went to pieces. She had to go home and be with her, so I gather.'

'No – I never heard,' Molly said, very shocked. 'God, that's terrible. She was ever so fond of him, as well.'

'She was,' Honor said thoughtfully. She put her head on one side. 'It's strange, rather an awful thing to say I suppose, but when you don't have any brothers or sisters, it's hard to imagine how you'd feel. Do you have brothers and sisters, Molly?'

'None to speak of, no.'

Honor gave a puzzled frown, then smiled. 'What on earth does that mean, Molly? You are a funny girl, you really are!'

Twenty-One

Through most of July the weather was fair, and even when it wasn't, Molly didn't notice. For her, it was a month lit up by sunshine and warmth in this beautiful place, and by the miracle of having Tony near, made all the more precious by knowing it was soon going to end when he was re-posted.

Most evenings, once they were free, they went out. The trip invariably took in the pub, beers quickly drunk down so that they could go out into the country lanes and be alone. Sometimes they bought an extra bottle to take away with them and spent the evening in a laughing, kissing haze. Though they held back from it, Molly knew that both of them could easily tilt over into drinking too much, that Tony was like her in that way.

One evening they had sneaked over the gate into a pasture and hidden themselves near the hedge, lying on Tony's jacket. The sun was going down fast and midges hung in a fidgeting cloud above their heads.

'We could go down to the sea one day,' Molly said muzzily. She felt warm, half-drunk and contented.

Tony, resting back on one elbow, tilted his head back, swigging from a bottle. He swallowed, then said, 'Can you swim?'

'No – course not. Why – can you?' She sat up,

excited. 'You could teach me! Some of the beaches are open round here – little coves . . .'

'No – I can't either.' He turned to look at her, and in their tipsy state this seemed so funny that they lay together cackling with laughter.

'We're 'opeless,' Molly laughed. 'We can't do anything, neither of us!'

'You can cook porridge – well, after a fashion!'

'Huh – you cheeky so-and-so!' She tickled him, giggling. 'And you can fire an ack-ack gun, Mr God Almighty, Royal Artillery!'

'That's me.' He pulled her closer. 'Give us a kiss.'

They lay twined together. It had been the same every night for a while now, each time longing for each other more and more.

'Tell you what else I wish I could do,' he said. 'And no mucking about.'

The laughter left Molly's face. She knew he was serious, and she knew she wanted him too, not like the others she had always pushed off once they'd got excited. But she was afraid all the same.

'Have you ever . . . ?' She could see he found it difficult to ask.

'No.' She looked down, shame washing through her in a blush she hoped he wouldn't notice in the half light. She hadn't, had she? She had never given herself fully to a man – course she hadn't! Even her grandfather's fumblings, messing with her, groping at himself, had never involved the full thing, not as she understood it. But she didn't feel like a virgin. She felt used, soiled.

'Have you?' She raised her eyes to him.

'Nah. Not – you know, all the way . . . Too risky. And Catholic girls – well, they won't, least, not the ones round our way.'

For a moment they heard voices in the lane the other side of the hedge – another couple, chatting and laughing – and they both froze. But the couple passed.

'Phew!' Molly said.

'I love you, Moll.' He pulled her close to him, his eyes imploring. 'And I'll be gone soon. I want you, girl.'

'I know,' she said. It was all easier when she'd been drinking, she knew – it always had been. And she knew her eyes had said yes.

The sky was already sunset pink when they set off that evening. Molly slipped out of the cookhouse, leaving the washing-up fatigues to finish off. She and Tony stopped to pick up bottles of beer, which they started on as they set off into the fields.

'Well, I'm glamorous as ever,' Molly observed, looking ruefully down at her ATS uniform and flat shoes. She was very nervous, her palms sweating, and hoped Tony couldn't tell.

He squeezed her round the waist. 'Stuff the clothes. You're gorgeous, girl.'

Molly giggled. 'Where are we going?'

'Up here – shhh.' A bit further along the country road he swung her up a lane. 'Up the end here there's a place . . . Look – quick – run!'

He snatched at her hand and they were tearing along the rutted track, Molly gasping with laughter.

'Stop, you mad sod, stop, I'm gunna trip up! Tony – where're we going – slow down!'

'Shhh, you noisy great thing – you'll have all the farmers on our tails!'

They came to a low building of blackened corrugated iron.

'Is it a barn?'

'I don't think so,' he said. 'More of a feed store for the cows. It should be all right.'

'How d'you know?'

'I don't – I'm hoping for the best. Come on – there's not much hay in here but we'll be all right if we go right to the back.'

The store was open along one side and there were some bales stacked just inside. Tony disappeared behind them.

'Where are yer?' Giggles were still fizzing out of her. 'It's *dark*.'

'Here – come on—' He popped his head out and held out his hand to lead her in. 'And I've got a torch – it's not really dark – not yet, anyhow.'

Molly stepped inside, smelling the sweet, musty hay. The giggles subsided. She shivered suddenly.

Tony busied himself lifting bales, making a nest at the back. Then he picked up one of the bottles and swigged. He offered it to her and she took it, gratefully, drinking down as much as she could. The time had come – she had promised him, sort of – and she felt cold and closed. Now her eyes had got used to it, it wasn't yet dark. Everything was black and grey, like an engraving. She could see him watching her. He took the bottle from her and set it down, then put his hands on her shoulders, looking into her eyes.

'Molly Fox, I love you and I want to be with you – for always. Will you be my wife?'

'What?' Molly was so startled she set off giggling again, and immediately regretted it because Tony was completely serious. 'You mean . . . get married?'

'Course that's what I mean. Make it proper. Will you?'

'Well . . . yes! Course I will – yes!' She jumped with excitement. 'D'you mean it? I love yer, Tony, I truly do. I want to be your wife. And I'll be a Catholic if you want.'

'God, yes – I should've said. You'd have to. I mean, my mum . . . We'll have to see a priest – that'd be the best thing.' He closed his eyes and leaned in to kiss her. 'It doesn't matter to me – I just want you.'

'Oh Tony – my Tony!' She was so happy that tears began to run down her cheeks. 'All I want is to be with you. I've never had anyone want me before!'

Startled, he drew back and looked at her eager face, moved. 'Oh girl,' he said tenderly. 'That can't be true – it can't. But *I* want you.'

Gently he unfastened her jacket, fumbling with the buttons. She watched his furrowed eyebrows as he tried to see in the dusk, loving the way he looked when he was serous like that. It made her feel very tender in return.

'We'll make a bed with our clothes,' he said. Soon the hay was a patchwork of garments. When he undressed she was afraid of the sight of him, his thin white body, taut and aroused, his maleness. A moment of panic filled her. How could she do this? It was all so strange, yet so horribly familiar. *Just keep calm*, she told herself. *This is Tony, your Tony. He loves you – he doesn't want to harm you.*

'My God, look at you—' He ran his hands down her arms, over her generous hips, gently touched her breasts. 'You're magnificent . . .'

Hysterical giggles rose in her again but she pushed them down. She couldn't seem to look at him, or speak, although she wanted to say something loving to him.

'Don't be scared.' He seemed moved by the timid

thing she had become. He held her close, hands gently moving down her back, stroking her buttocks. Molly closed her eyes, her head pressed against his shoulder. Moving her fingers up and down she explored the long, warm dip of his spine, the taut muscles on either side of it. The skin of his lower back felt marked with ridges. She frowned, tracing them with her fingertips. Tony's breathing was fast and excited. He kissed her hair, nuzzled for her lips. Sensations poured in, overwhelming her: the tense hardness of his body, his smell, sweat and salt, his man's thing pressed insistently against her stomach, the realization that he, too, was trembling.

'Come and lie down,' he said, his breathing short. Molly obeyed, lying back on the scratchy khaki clothes, and he, a lithe shadow, came down beside her. He caught her ribs with his elbow.

'Sorry . . . Oh girl—' She felt his tongue brush her left nipple. A mixture of desire and panic surged through her. *Stop*, she wanted to cry. *Please – just wait. Slow down!* She longed to love him, to give him everything, but as soon as he began touching her she knew it had all gone wrong. Already he was immersed in his need, could not hold back, but she froze and could not lose herself in it. Every touch brought back that poking, black-fingernailed touch from before. She could even smell William Rathbone, the unwashed mix of sweat, of urine-soiled clothes, her foul grandfather – *father!* She could not stay here, not in her head, being touched like that, like *he* touched her, even though Tony explored her gently and with love. *No one should touch you there* . . . She could not tolerate it. It was as if in her head she had disappeared somewhere else entirely.

'You all right, darlin'?' he asked, gasping. He was aware of her withdrawal, but was too excited to make

209

sense of it. He gave a moan, moving over her. 'Oh God, just let me, will you? You're too much for me . . . Lift your legs . . .'

She held him as he lost himself urgently inside her, reaching his release in seconds with a strained cry. All she could think was what a strange business, and how detached she was, not being able to feel any emotion, or enter into it. She didn't hold it against him. His own pleasure pleased her, the sight of his urgent frame moving over her, his sinking into her arms afterwards.

He nuzzled her neck as he came to, his warm breath on her skin.

'Oh Molly – my Molly.' He raised himself on one elbow, and was looking down at her. Her face was hidden in shadow, and she was glad. 'You're a marvel . . .' He hesitated. 'But you . . . ? Was it . . . ?' He stopped, looking puzzled.

'It was lovely,' she reassured him, stroking his back. It wasn't his fault, that much she knew. 'First time and everything. I love you – you were lovely.'

When he had withdrawn from her he reached round, looking for the bottles.

'Damn – dunno where I've put them. I'll get the torch.' There was a cone of light for a moment. 'Ah – down here.'

Switching the torch off, he passed her a bottle and Molly drank, then they lay cuddled up in the hay, the last light of day dwindling outside. Tony gave a contented sigh, and Molly was happy now. This warm cuddling and closeness was what she needed. She lay with her head on his chest, her hand stroking his belly, with its thin line of hairs.

'That's the only soft bit of you,' she said.

She felt laughter ripple through him. 'I should hope so.'

'When it's all over . . .' he began a moment later. So many conversations these days began like that, with dreams of the future, of a normal life.

'What if we don't win?' she interrupted. 'What if the country's full of Germans?'

'Maybe they'll still need fishermen. Anyway, Churchill won't let us lose, that's what my mum says. She think's Churchill's up there with St Anthony and the Holy Family.'

'We don't seem to be winning much at the moment,' Molly said. It was always bad news, warships being sunk like the *Hood* and the *Bismarck*, losing Crete and Tobruk.

'But we'll still be together, won't we? Man and wife. We'll rent us a house down here, and I'll go fishing, and we'll have . . . how many kids, eh?'

'Four,' Molly said firmly, thinking of Em's family. When things were good in the Brown household, it was where Molly wished she had grown up. Then a terrifying thought forced her up. 'You don't think I could have a babby now – after what we . . . ?'

'Nah – shouldn't think so. Takes a while, doesn't it?'

'I s'pose . . .' She had no idea, but lay down, choosing to be comforted. Of course she wasn't going to have a baby.

They lay talking for a time, about the Blitz, how it had been for each of their families.

'I still worry about them,' Tony said. 'London still gets it off and on. It was bloody terrible, the worst of it. One of those incendiaries came through our roof one night – thank God Mum had got a sand bucket ready.

And at least we've got a cellar, not like some, all in public shelters and down the Underground. The pits. We could just be family even if it was cramped. Feels very quiet out here in the wilds, doesn't it, another world? As if it's not really happening. Where did your family go?'

'They never bother. Dad can't walk, see.' 'Dad' – what else could she call Joe?

'What – they just chanced it?'

'Yeah. Think so.' She didn't want to talk about them. 'And they weren't the only ones . . .' Instead, she told him about Mr and Mrs Button, how kind they had been to her, what had happened, until she was sobbing.

'She was like a mom to me – she kept an eye on me. My mother's cruel, she's no good. But Mrs Button took me in and looked after me.'

Tony held her tightly, stroking her. 'Blimey.' She could tell he was shocked, moved. He kissed the top of her head. 'I'll look after you, babe. Promise.'

'I know you will.' She kissed his chest, then shivered. Her head was beginning to ache. She wiped her face on her tunic, which she had discarded nearby. 'It's getting cold. I s'pose we'll have to go.'

'We'll come back here though. It'll be our place, won't it?'

He reached round for the torch so that they could find their clothes, and planted it in one of the bales of hay, at an angle, so they could dress easily. As he stood up, the light fell across him.

'Tony!' Molly said, staring. She knew she'd felt something strange. 'What's that – on your back?'

He turned to face her.

'No – turn round again.'

'Oh,' he said airily, his back to her. 'That.'

'Who in the *hell* did that to yer?'

His buttocks and lower back were streaked with the scars of deep welts.

Tony rubbed his hand over them. 'Oh – my slug trails. I told you.' His tone was light, sardonic. 'Those religious paragons at that school.'

'Bloody hell, Tony – I thought they were, well, priests and that?'

'Some were, not all of them. But most of 'em were twisted perverts, I can tell you.'

He pulled his clothes on. '*Sod 'em*, that's all. Past history.'

'I mean, we all got knocked about, but *that* . . . !'

'Yeah – well that's how we learned about our loving Jesus.'

'*Christ.*'

'Yes, that's him. Ten out of ten.'

'But your mom and dad – did they know?'

He looked at her as if she was mad. 'No – of course not. Look, I don't think you understand. My mother thinks priests are gods almost. You don't criticize them – not to her. They know all the answers and that's that. And Dad – well, he just follows her lead. I told you – they're good Catholics. If the Church says black is white, you say it too.'

'Oh, sweetheart . . .' He stood stiffly as she held him, full of fierce sorrow at his bitterness. For a moment he was rigid, angry, then he relented and kissed her back.

'We've got each other now,' he said. 'You and me, Molly. That's what counts.'

'Yes—' She hugged him, fierce with love. 'You and me.'

Twenty-Two

Molly wanted to slow down time. The end of July meant that Tony would be leaving the camp, his battery would be re-posted – they did not know where. Although she was longing for that time to come because they were hoping to have some leave together, after that, when would she ever see him? The thought was almost un-bearable.

Ruth's three-week Kiné training course in Wales had ended and she had gone. Molly was relieved. Ruth despised her, she knew, and she was a snooty reminder of her early ATS days, when she had found it so hard to fit in. Honor was still there, but she was a different kettle of fish altogether.

One lunchtime she came into the mess to collect her food, chatting to one of the other ATS girls in the line. It was a scrag-end stew that day, and Molly had to admit, it didn't look inviting. She was very unfussy about food, but even she didn't fancy eating it! There were groans and disparaging comments when everyone caught sight of the greyish bony mess and the grey boiled potatoes to go with it.

'I say,' one of the new Kinnys quipped, 'perhaps we've all been sent off to a prisoner of war camp by mistake?'

'Ha, ha,' Molly said dryly. Along the line she saw Honor coming towards her, laughing. She seemed so different these days, so much stronger, more definite in herself.

'Hello, Molly!' she greeted her. Even her voice was firmer. 'Hey—' She leaned over the counter, talking almost in a whisper. 'Guess who's turned up?'

Enjoying this, Molly hissed back, 'Who, then?'

'The Gorgon!'

Molly drew back. 'You're having me on!'

'No – she's here all right. And she's been promoted. Sergeant in charge of General Duties ATS – you, in other words!'

'Flipping 'eck,' Molly grimaced. 'That's a turn up for the books!'

'Yes, well, quite!' Honor laughed at her expression. 'I knew you'd be pleased!'

'Oh well – I don't s'pose she'll remember me, any'ow.'

Smiling, Honor picked up her mess tins of grey gloop without complaint. 'Oh, I shouldn't count on it, Molly!'

Molly felt a mixture of excitement and nervousness at the thought that Phoebe Morrison was around somewhere in the camp. It wasn't long before she ran into her. Later that afternoon, in the distance she caught sight of the unmistakable dumpy, determined figure of her new sergeant stumping along one of the paths. Molly's heart started to beat faster. She had a strong, childish longing to be noticed. The two of them coincided at one of the corners, which were marked with large, whitewashed stones. Nervously, Molly glanced at her. *Don't be stupid*, she told herself. *She's trained hundreds of new ATS in her time. You're nothing special. Why would she remember you?*

As they met, Molly gave the required salute and went to walk past.

'Fox? Is that you?' The dark eyes scrutinized her.

'Yes, Sergeant,' Molly said, blushing.

'Thought so.' Her tone was abrupt, as usual, but almost friendly. 'How're you getting along?'

'All right, Sergeant. Thank you.'

'Good – what're you doing here – cook?'

'Yes, Sergeant.'

'Well the messing here is dreadful. I'm sure some pigs are faring better. Not that I can blame you single-handedly for that, since you're not even cooking for me.'

'No, Sergeant.'

A hint of a smile twitched at Phoebe Morrison's lips. 'Jolly good. Dismiss.'

Molly departed, relieved not to be in trouble for anything.

'Pigs,' she grumbled. The pig bins behind the kitchen contained the slop of all the leftovers. Nothing was to go to waste. 'Bet they show a bit more gratitude an' all.'

She soon saw Phoebe Morrison again, to request leave.

'You don't seem to have any leave on record that's been taken,' the sergeant said. 'No leave after basic training?'

'No, Sergeant.'

Molly stood bolt upright in front of the desk in the gloomy hut, her heart beating hard. She had to have leave – just *had* to! What if the Gorgon turned her down?

'Did you not want to go home, Fox?'

'No.'

Sergeant Morrison waited, staring up piercingly at her as if expecting an explanation for this aberrant behaviour, but none was forthcoming. 'I see,' she said at last, looking down at the ledger in front of her. 'Well, we can spare you for three days, I'm sure. The cooking couldn't possibly be any worse in your absence . . .'

'Thank you, Sergeant.'

'That was not a compliment.'

'I know, Sergeant.'

A twinkle came into Phoebe Morrison's eyes. 'I'm beginning to think you have a sense of humour, Fox.'

'Yes, Sergeant.' *For goodness' sake*, Molly thought, *stop beating about the bush and tell me if I've got leave or not!*

'Right – well, you can have three days, beginning on the thirty-first. Back by the end of the weekend. Come to me for a travel warrant before you go.'

Molly's heart soared, her face breaking into a grin.

'Oh *ta*, Sergeant – I mean – thank you ever so much!'

Phoebe Morrison watched Molly's exuberant figure almost skipping out of the hut, no doubt to go and tell some young beau that she could join him. Her amusement was tinged with considerable envy. How nice to be the sort of girl who ever had a young beau! Phoebe Morrison was not, and had never been, that sort of girl. Even man she seemed to get along with never asked her out or showed interest in any other way. They treated her more like one of them, which she knew was her own fault, but she couldn't seem to do any different. She was too gruff and off-putting with them.

Standing up, she closed the ledger in front of her and got ready to busy herself with the mind-boggling muddle that the quartermaster seemed to have got into. Thank heavens for the army, she thought. Molly Fox wasn't the only one who didn't want to pay visits home. And the army had got her out of that dead-end clerical job that she had seen herself stuck in for the rest of her miserable life – marriage not a likely rescue. It had given her something to do, something with a purpose. And thank goodness again that they'd sent her out here, away from London, or anywhere within easy reach of home, with its invalid smells, Father's silences, and Uncle Horace.

She tidied a few things – pens, blotter, ink – putting off the next job. The girls under her command often unsettled her, but none more so than Molly Fox. There was something about the girl that was – *naked*, that was it! The way she was large, exuberant, astonishingly handsome (more than just sweet and pretty, the girl was handsome), sexual in a raw way, but also an intensely vulnerable person, was deeply unsettling to Phoebe Morrison. The girl made her feel powerfully envious and protective all at once. She must keep an eye out and see who the chap was that she was seeing – check what type he was. She tutted at herself. If he was unsuitable, what exactly did she think she was going to do about it? Molly Fox was evidently far more worldly than she was in that department.

Leaning against the desk, she mused for a moment, seeing a cluster of lads in uniforms running past, packs on their backs. They were undergoing punishment for something. Her mouth twisted sardonically. She hoped it hurt them.

She thought about Molly, rushing off eagerly to her chap, somewhere in the camp. Men. Men. The staircase up to Uncle Horace's attic – 'We'll have our game of

218

chess now, Phoebe' – the fusty green travel rug on his bed, its tassels tickling her nose as he pressed her down, shuddering, on her front. She still didn't know how to play chess. If only Mother hadn't been so ill, everything would have been different. That was the only attention from men she was ever likely to get.

Twenty-Three

'You have told them, you promise me?'

Tony chuckled, reaching up to her as she climbed out of the carriage at Paddington. 'How many times've you asked me that already?' He took her hand, squeezing it, swinging his canvas bag over his other shoulder. 'Of course I've told them. I'm coming home *with my fiancée*. I sent them a wire.'

'Well that doesn't mean they're happy about it,' Molly said uneasily. She clutched her bag tightly to her. 'It's a bit sudden for them. They might not like me. They'll think I'm rough . . .'

Tony stopped abruptly, causing a man behind him to curse at him, and pulled Molly close, an intense expression in his eyes.

'Look – they're not like that. They're nice – they like people and they'll like you, honest! If you tell our ma that you're prepared to "go over to Rome", as they say' – this was said in a satirical tone – 'they'll love you for ever.'

Molly's butterflies calmed a little. 'You sure?'

'*Yes*. Now come on!'

She started to relax, looking round her to take in the busy spectacle of the station, with its elegant arched roof. Among the crowds, a large number were wearing khaki like them, and everyone seemed to be in a hurry.

She drew in a deep breath, coal dust and cigarettes mingled with the summer air.

'I'm so glad I joined up!' she said, with sudden passion. Tony looked round at her. 'If I hadn't, I'd still be stuck in that factory, those same old streets. And now I've seen so many other things, the sea and all these places, and I'd never've met you, would I?'

Again, his arm pressed hers and he smiled. 'No – thank God you did.'

Everything felt exciting. Next came the new experience of the Underground, the mysterious, rumbling journey, then flowing out with the crowd, back up the steps and into the sunlit street. Tony laughed at her shocked expression.

'See – it's not that glamorous, is it?'

She had still had a dream in her mind, a city made of pearl. Instead, all around her were blackened buildings, their profiles broken by bombsites, and a sense of squalor and neglect. Very like home, in fact. Except the scale of it was bigger, and grander.

'God,' she said, dismayed.

Tony squeezed her arm. 'See – told you we aren't posh.'

In a side street, he led her towards a dark little shop with newspapers on racks outside and so many advertisements for Tizer, Oxo, Woodbines, Cadburys and Players Weights in the windows that it was surprising any light got in at all.

'Here we are – come and say hello to my dad. We live just round the corner.'

The newspaper headlines were all about Russia, Molly noticed. The door was wide open, and inside the shop was very cramped, shelves lined with packets and tins, candles and scrubbing brushes, and racks with all sorts of useful things – string, pins, hooks and eyes, brown paper – and a counter all squeezed in. The shop smelled musty, with a strong whiff of camphor.

Somehow, in a cramped space at the front of the shop, they had found room for a chair, its seat and back covered in aged leather, sagging like an elephant's skin. Bending over the chair, Molly saw a burly man, and perched on the seat, a boy of about nine. The woman watching from the other side was clearly his mother, since the wisps of hair showing at the edges of her scarf were of the same pale auburn as his.

'That's it, Mr Belham,' she was saying. 'Nice and short – I don't wanna 'ave to come back too soon.' The boy's views on the subject were unknown as he was facing the other wall, where a small rectangular mirror was perched lopsidedly. All Molly could see in it was his chin.

'Hello, Dad,' Tony said.

The two adults turned. 'Ooh!' the woman exclaimed. She was a pasty, underfed-looking person, with anxious blue eyes. 'Look who's 'ere – is that your Tony? Ain't 'e grown up?'

'Tony!' Mr Belham held out his arms, the scissors waving about alarmingly. A smile spread across his fleshy face, showing a set of teeth with noticeable gaps. It was an appealing, happy-looking face, the skin swarthy and a jolly, upcurling moustache. 'You're back, lad! Your mother said you was on the way!'

'Hello, Dad – this is Molly.'

Mr Belham suddenly became very courtly. 'Oh yes, yes – I'd best put these down to greet a lovely lady,' he said, dislodging the scissors with some difficulty from his thick fingers. He held out his hand and shook Molly's. 'A tonic to meet you, love – a tonic, that's what. Well' – he turned to the boy's mother with a soppy grin – 'ain't she lovely, eh? What's your name then?'

'Molly, Dad – I've just told you!'

'Oh sorry, sorry – Molly. This is Tony's intended, or so he tells us.'

'Ooh, fancy,' said the woman.

'I'm afraid you've put me in a bit of a dither,' Mr Belham said.

'That's all right.' Molly blushed but couldn't help laughing as well. Tony's dad seemed quite bowled over at the sight of her.

'Nice to meet yer,' she said shyly, conscious that all of them were staring at her, even the little boy, who had turned a freckly face to her and was gawping with his mouth open.

'It's a pleasure to meet you, Molly—' Mr Belham bowed over her hand, showing her a head of bristly black hair. 'You all right, son? You're looking fighting fit!' He patted Tony's arm. 'Well, you'd better get over and see your mother, or she'll never forgive me! She'll've been waiting. I'll be over later. You're looking fine, son, fine . . .' He picked up his scissors in some confusion and put his beefy hand on top of the small boy's head. 'Face the front now, son.'

Tony and Molly did as they were told, looking laughingly at each other as they went back into the street.

'See,' Tony said, 'the old man's all right!'

'He's nice,' Molly said. She was more than relieved, she was astonished by the warmth of the welcome. 'Oh Tony, I'm so glad – you're so lucky to have a dad like that!'

'Come and meet Ma now.'

223

Nerves assailed her again. Supposing his mom was the fly in the ointment?

There was already a face peering out from behind the nets in the front room of the Belhams' little terrace. As they drew closer, the curtains gave an uncertain twitch and then were pulled back wider. A hand waved.

'There's my ma,' Tony said. 'She's got second sight.'

'What – really?'

'I dunno. She always seems to know what's going on before anyone else!'

The curtain was hanging back in place now and the door opened to reveal a curvaceous middle-aged woman in a green skirt and tan blouse, each half concealed by an apron with pink flowers on it, her hair the same brown as Tony's, jaw length and arranged in gentle waves each side of her face. Molly was impressed. She looked very gracious and dignified.

'Tony!' She stood waving on the step, beaming with pleasure. There was a hint of lipstick on her lips. She reached up to kiss Tony's cheek, gazing at him fondly and clinging to his arm. 'I knew you'd be coming about now.' Her voice was deep, Irish and smooth as syrup. 'Ah, now is this must be Molly then – how are you dear? Did you both have a good journey then? Come on in now – what are we doing standing out here on the step all day? You must come in and have a cup of tea!'

She ushered them along the dark hall, still talking. 'You've seen your father then, I suppose? Geraldine's at work of course, but Josephine's here waiting for you – oh, she'll be so pleased, now. *Josephine!*' she called up the stairs. 'Our Tony's home! Now let me get the water boiling. I hope you don't mind coming through to the back, Molly, but that's where we are and we get the warmth there in the winter. Are you hungry? You've been travelling a long time, I suppose – where've you come from now? . . .'

Tony smiled at Molly and shrugged. She grinned back. So far neither of them had had to say a word. Led into the back room, she was overcome by the sense that she was in a different sort of home from any she'd visited before. Around the walls, on top of the leafy wallpaper, were a great many pictures which she recognized as religious, even if she wasn't sure who they were. A crucifix about a foot high hung on one side wall, with a string of white rosary beads draped over it. Molly recognized the Virgin Mary because she wore blue robes. After that, she was stumped. In one corner, on a small table, stood a statue in brown robes, holding a baby in his arms. It was all rather strange, but she liked the room, which felt cosy and welcoming, with two chairs flanking the fireplace and a table and chairs squeezed in at the side. A large aspidistra stood on a pot on a stand behind the net curtains.

'Now then.' Dymphna Belham stopped to draw breath once she had put the kettle on to boil. She came back in and stood before then, her darting blue eyes looking them both over. Molly felt herself smile. Never before had she met a family that gave off such a sense of warmth and acceptance so immediately. She was rather in awe of Tony's mom though.

'I haven't even said hello to you properly yet, Molly,' Mrs Belham said. Molly thought she would hold out her hand, but she leaned close and kissed Molly's cheek. Her touch was gently firm and she gave off a scent of rose water. She did not let go of Molly's hand straight away, but pressed it between hers and looked piercingly into Molly's face. 'You're very welcome, dear.'

'Oh, thank you,' Molly was saying, feeling intimidated, when there came a frantic drumming of feet down the stairs and a girl with long, flame-red hair tore into the room.

'Tony!' She propelled herself at him and Tony just about managed to lift her from the floor. 'You're back – where've you been? You didn't write to me, you stupid!' she was pummelling his chest furiously. 'You said you would – just to me, and you never!' She was cross and delighted all at once.

'I'm sorry, Jo – I am. I didn't get round to it, that's all.'

'Not even a mingy post card, you meanie!'

'Jo – this is Molly.' He put the girl down and she grew more serious, taking in the stranger in the room.

'Hello,' she said, looking curious. 'Are you the one he's going to marry?'

'Um . . . well . . .' Molly said, smiling.

'Josephine!' her mother scolded. 'You don't just jump in with a question like that.'

'I like your hair.' She peered at Molly with great interest. 'How d'you put it up like that?'

'I'll do it for yer if you like, later,' Molly said, enjoying the thirteen-year-old's frank ways.

'Don't be bothering her when she's only after coming through the door!' Dymphna chided. 'Now come along – we're all going to have that cup of tea.'

They drank from delicate china cups with little wreaths of ivy painted on them, and Molly was given the best chair in the room, leather, with a perilously slippery seat. She planted her feet firmly on the floor in order not to slide around. Dymphna Belham fussed

226

around them constantly, hardly ever sitting still for long herself. Did Molly wish for sugar, or something to eat, and was the chair comfortable? She kept getting up and down, and only settled, in the chair opposite Molly, by the fire, when Tony said, 'Come on, Ma – stay with us. We're perfectly all right.'

Josephine, a pale, intelligent-looking girl, plonked herself on Tony's lap and sat listening to every word that was said. His mother wanted to know all about where they had been and what they were doing.

'Will you have a hot drop in your cup there?' Dymphna asked when Molly put her cup down. 'I know it's weak these days, but at least it's warm and wet.

'It's the nicest cup of tea I've ever had,' Molly said truthfully, holding her cup out. There was something about Dymphna that made you want to do anything she suggested. It was the force of her personality, combined with her embracing warmth and welcome.

Dymphna gave a rich, bubbling laugh at Molly's enthusiasm. 'Well now, there's a thing!' she said.

They told her all about the camp, and the work, and how beautiful it was there, and then Tony said, 'Come on, Jo, shift – I need to get up a minute.'

Josephine twisted round, tweaking her brother's nose. 'Where're you going?'

'Out the back – you know, for a tinkle.'

'You're not going for that – you're going to see your princess!' She scrambled off him. 'I'm coming too!'

'No I'm not – well, maybe . . .' he admitted sheepishly. 'But for a bit of the other too! Back in a tick.'

Dymphna watched her children fondly as they left the room. Then she turned to Molly, who felt the full force of her powerful attention fixed on her.

'The girls miss their brothers such a lot,' she said.

'Mickey's our biggest worry – he's in our prayers all the time, God love and protect him. Did Tony tell you? He's serving in the Merchant Navy. Oh, I'll bless the day when he's back here with us. No home is the same these sad days. I'm sure your mother feels the same.'

Molly smiled politely, not sure what to say. Would Iris even have noticed she wasn't there?

'Do you have brothers, Molly?'

'Yes, two.'

'And I suppose they've joined up as well?' Dymphna released a sigh. 'God help us, I'll be so glad when it's all over.'

She looked appraisingly at Molly. 'So strange you know, seeing you girls in uniforms like that. It seems all wrong really, a bit on the unnatural side, even now. It's quite becoming though – especially on a girl with a nice figure like yours.' She leaned across and put her hand on Molly's arm. Molly felt warmed, and slightly intimidated. 'I'm so pleased that our Tony's met someone nice like you,' she said. 'You know, I don't like my boys being away, but Tony joining up has been good for him. He was starting to run wild a bit you know, before the war. He's a restless sort of boy, with a spark of anger in him, but he's got a heart of gold.'

'Yes,' Molly agreed, startled. It was so strange, being treated like one of the family, talked to like this, by someone she'd never met before.

'Now, my dear – I know we've all got to get to know one another, but there's something important you need to know about this family.' Again she looked deeply into Molly's eyes. Her own were a mottled blue. 'We are Roman Catholics, and our faith is of the greatest importance to us.'

'Yes, I know. Tony told me.'

'You're a Protestant?'

'I'm not really an anything,' Molly admitted, blushing under this close scrutiny. She already felt as if she would do anything that Dymphna Belham asked, such was the force of her.

'Good. Perhaps that's better,' Dymphna said. 'You can come and join us without prejudice – and you know dear, you'll be discovering an enormous treasure in your life, the comfort of God and the Church.'

Tony came back in then, grinning, Josephine still shadowing his steps.

'So your princess is still all right,' Molly teased.

'Don't you be spending all your time on that thing so that we never see you, now,' Dymphna warned, getting up. 'That's what he was like before, Molly. Out all hours, no idea where he was or what he was doing . . .'

'I wasn't doing anything! Just riding.'

'Yes, well don't you be doing that now – we want to see something of you.'

'I've got to have a bit of a ride, Ma – keep her working. And I promised Molly.'

Dymphna turned to Molly, rolling her eyes. 'You see? You'll have to put your foot down. He's not just got himself to please now.

'I will,' Molly said, smiling happily at the way Tony's mother had instantly recruited her as a member of the family. She felt she loved Tony's mother already.

'Molly and I were just having a little chat,' Dymphna said, meaningfully. 'But we can carry on later. I'm sure Molly will soon be very much one of us.'

Twenty-Four

By the time they had finished their tea the light was beginning to fade, and soon the rest of the family were home from work.

Molly found herself sitting round the table with them all that evening, eating a tasty stew – 'It's mostly potatoes, I'm afraid,' Dymphna apologized – and getting to know Tony's family. His father arrived home from the shop, whistling cheerfully as he came through the door, then calling out, 'Where's that boy of mine then?' Geraldine, a lively sixteen-year-old who seemed older than her years and favoured her father's dark colouring, came back from her job where she was being trained with the telephone exchange. She was polite and friendly to Molly, though less forward than Josephine, who fired questions at her whenever they popped into her head.

'Why d'you talk like that?' the younger girl asked as they were eating their stew and potatoes. Molly had been telling them where she was working before the war. Josephine's face had puckered up with puzzlement.

'Molly's from Birmingham, cheeky chops,' Tony told her. 'That's how people speak up there. She probably thinks *you* talk funny.'

'Do you?' Josephine demanded earnestly.

'Er, no!' Molly said. 'I s'pose being in the army you meet all sorts, from all over the place. So I've got used to it now.'

'Molly's a cook, in the army,' Dymphna informed her husband, from her queenly seat at one end of the table.

'A cook? Well now. Big buckets of slop?'

Molly laughed. 'Summat like that, yeah. I'm not very good at it. They complain all the time!'

'I expect you *are* good at it,' Dymphna said. 'And there's you, Tony love, on the back end of those big guns. Oh, it makes me tremble to think about it.'

'Well, it's better than being on the front end of them,' he said. Both his sisters giggled.

'Don't you be laughing,' Dymphna protested. 'That's not funny, girls. It's serious – life and death.'

'Bet you're always in trouble,' Geraldine observed of her brother. 'He's always been in trouble. At school he was the naughtiest in the class.'

'He was Trouble itself,' Josephine said, big-eyed.

'Ah, he's got over that now,' Dymphna said fondly. She looked at Molly. 'They were a little bit strict, you know. Great believers in discipline. Anyway, Tony – being married'll make a responsible man out of you.'

'I was in the last lot, you know,' Fred Belham said, chewing energetically. He shook his head sadly. 'We never thought we'd all be at it again so soon. War to end all wars – huh! What about your father, Molly?'

'Oh, my father?' Startled, she had to think quickly. She told them he was an invalid.

'The poor soul,' Dymphna said, her eyes blue pools of sympathy. 'Poor man. It's a wicked thing.'

'Yes.' To Molly's consternation, tears welled unexpectedly in her eyes. Seeing Joe's state through the eyes of others made her feel the tragedy of him.

'Oh, you poor girl, what a sadness for a family,' Dymphna went on, and Fred was nodding and the others were all staring at her and Molly had to struggle not to weep in the face of all this sympathy. In Tony's expression was also surprise, hurt: *You never told me that* . . .

'We're making the poor child fill up now,' Dymphna said. 'So let's stop that and be talking about something else.' She asked Molly and Tony questions about the camp, and they told her some of the day-to-day routines, the jokes, and about the beauty of the place.

'It sounds like where I grew up in Ireland,' she said, wistfully. She looked round the table. 'We're all finished. Now, Geraldine – will you and Jo be clearing the dishes, please?'

As they sat on over a cup of tea, Dymphna said, 'Now, these two have stated their intention to marry – and you've told your family, Molly?' Molly nodded, uneasily. 'Now, there are some important preparations you'll need to be making, won't they, Fred?'

Fred Belham, sitting back to rest his round tummy, nodded sagely through a cloud of cigarette smoke, but let his wife do all the talking. Dymphna sat with her white hands on the cloth, fingers locked loosely together, looking solemn and in command.

'You must go and see Father Callaghan while you're home, Tony. Molly here will be needing to take instruction from him.'

Tony nodded, seeming to take for granted that they do this.

'I'll see him after Mass on Sunday.'

'Well you make sure you do. Of course I can have a word as well. Molly will need to be received into the Church before you go getting married.'

Molly was intrigued by the seriousness of all this. She didn't really understand what it was all about, but it felt as if she had been invited to join a very special club, and if Tony and his mom were in it, it was good enough for her.

Before they turned in for the night, Dymphna led the family in saying the rosary around the statue of Mary in the corner of the room. She handed Molly a set of pearly white rosary beads and said, 'We'll just be saying one decade. That's this set of ten, dear. Just follow on the rest of us.'

Molly followed as the family said their Hail Marys and Our Father, in a serious, but matter-of-fact way.

'Who's that one?' Molly asked afterwards, pointing at the brown-robed statue.

'Oh, d'you not know that?' Dymphna laughed. 'That's St Anthony, heaven bless him. And that—' She pointed at a small black-and-white profile on the wall beside him, of a thin-faced, austere-looking man. 'That's our Holy Father in Rome, Pope Pius the twelfth.'

'Oh,' Molly said, glancing at Tony, who, to her surprise, winked at her. 'That's nice.'

'Our priests are very special to us,' Dymphna said, passionately. 'You'll come to understand that when you're a Catholic. It's a marvellous blessing, what those holy men do for the faith. Our Father Callaghan now – he's a pure, holy man.'

Tony was staring past her, out at the darkening sky.

Later, she insisted that Molly sleep in the small room Tony had always shared with Mickey.

'Tony can bunk up downstairs like a gentleman,' she said. 'Here we are now, dear, I'll show you where to go.'

Molly lay cosily tucked up behind the blackout curtains which shut out the summer night. This had been

Tony's boyhood bed and she enjoyed the thought of it. He had come up and given her a long, tender kiss goodnight, and then, to her surprise, he had whispered, 'I'll see you later!'

Sure enough, a long time later when the house was really quiet, he was at the door, so silently that she had not heard him climb the stairs. He tiptoed across the room, to pull back the edge of the curtain, letting in the thin moonlight, then he was beside her, his breath on her cheek.

'Budge up, wench!'

'You shouldn't be here! What if your mom finds out?'

'She won't. Don't fret.'

Very quietly so as not to make a single spring squeak, he eased himself in beside her as Molly inched up by the wall. Both of them giggled quietly, settling themselves cuddled up close together.

'Your family are so nice,' she whispered. 'Is your mom always like that? So friendly before she even knows people.'

'She is like that, yes. But she likes you – I can tell. She took to you straight away.'

'Really? D'you think so?'

'Course.' He cuddled her, kissing her back. 'You're lovely, Molly. Only you don't seem to know it!'

She was squirming with pleasure.

'I think she thinks you're going to settle me down. She thought I was going off the rails before. And so long as you'll be a Catholic – that's what matters to her – being in the fold.'

'Course I will – I said I would.'

He gave her a squeeze. 'Everything'll be all right

then.' He kissed her neck, then whispered, his tone a little hurt, 'You never said – about your dad.'

She stared into the darkness. 'Daint I tell yer? He's in a poor state really. And there's nothing much you can do. I s'pose I try not to think about it.'

'Poor man.' He kissed her. After a silence, he said, 'What about your ma, love?'

'I've told you.' She turned her head; anger and resentment swelled in her just thinking about Iris. How could she explain to Tony – especially after meeting his warmhearted mother? 'I'm not proud of what I've come from. I don't really want to tell you about her – or you to meet her.'

There was a hurt silence. 'Seems a bit bad that. We're supposed to be getting married and you won't even tell me about her. I love *you*. It won't make any difference.'

Oh, won't it? Molly thought, bitterly. Should she pour it all out, the full horrible truth – well, my granddad used to molest me several nights a week and as it turns out he's my father as well because he bedded my mother, his own daughter? No – she couldn't tell him everything – not even Tony, who she loved most in all the world. Harshly, she whispered, 'She's a boozer, OK? All she cares about is staring into the bottom of a bottle. She's never been a mom to me and I don't want anything to do with her. And Joe – my dad – well, he's done for.' She twisted round to him, emotionally. 'I swear to you, when we get wed, I want your mom to be my mother – you can forget about mine.'

In the very faint light she could see him watching her intently. He brought his hand out from under the covers and smoothed back her hair. 'All right – if that's really how it is.'

'It is,' she said firmly. 'My family're nothing like yours. Yours are wonderful.'

'Yes,' he agreed. 'I know.' But there was a dry sadness to the way he said it, in which she could hear his sense of betrayal. And Molly could see what he meant: the impossibility of telling his mother the truth about the saintly priests, the lash of their canes and leather straps. It was as if Dymphna could not have believed it even if it was happening in front of her very eyes. Molly cuddled him tightly.

'I just want to be part of yours. They're a proper family, not like mine. When can we get married and make it all right?'

'Soon,' he said passionately. 'We'll get leave – next time. We'll do it then.'

'Oh love! D'yer mean it?'

'Course I do. The sooner the better.'

Ecstatic, she turned to the wall, snuggling back against him. 'I love you *so* much,' she said. For a second she tried to imagine life without him, a future without his love, now she knew what it was like with it, and the thought was so dizzyingly awful she banished it immediately.

'I love you too, my girl. And tomorrow,' she heard in her ear, 'I'm taking you for a ride.'

She clung to him, arms wrapped tight round his waist, the sun on her face and the wind buffeting it as they raced away, first from his cramped, sooty-faced neighbourhood, then out past the villas of north London, further and further until the barrage balloons shrank to tiny dots in the distance behind, then vanished, and the houses spread further apart, and soon there were no factories or chimneys in sight, nothing but farmhouses and barns. It was a warm, sultry August and they had the whole weekend ahead of them. Molly didn't think it could be possible to be happier.

'I want to show you my favourite place,' he said, before they set off. Dymphna had given them a packet of sandwiches, urging them not to be back too late – 'Because I know what he's like,' she twinkled at Molly. 'There's no knowing where you'll get to – it's a mystery tour you're going on! Now you just be careful, Tony,' she added seriously.

After miles of country road, Tony turned into an obscure lane leading to a wood, heading gently down-hill, through dappled light, until they reached a stream at the bottom among the trees. The water caught the sunlight through the leaves.

Molly exclaimed at seeing the soft grass and flowers edging the water and feeling the gentle atmosphere of the place. 'How did you know it was here?'

'I didn't. I just came here by accident one day, nosing about. It's the most peaceful place I've ever been. I've been wanting to bring you here ever since we first started.'

Molly climbed down from the bike. 'I'm going to dip my feet in!' She was still in uniform as she had nothing else with her, but her legs were bare. She slipped off her shoes and sat on the edge of the bank, squeaking as the cold water slid over her feet. Tony came and sat beside her, put his arm round her and kissed her neck.

'You're getting tanned.'

She put her hands to her cheeks. 'They feel as if the wind's been slapping them all morning!'

'You look lovely – like a big strong farm girl!' Then he nuzzled her. 'My Molly. My wife-to-be.'

She laughed, seemed to be forever laughing these days, despite the war, despite everything. He laughed with her, for no reason, and she thought how handsome he looked, boyish and happy.

'Mr and Mrs Belham. Like your mom and dad. You've made everything so good – I'm so, so happy.' She beamed into his face, and they moved in closer for a long kiss.

'Come here,' he said, and she knew what that meant, could hear how much he wanted her.

'Here? Surely we can't?'

'It's all right – I've never seen another soul anywhere near. Oh love, let's – please.'

He laid her back on the soft grass and made love to her urgently. Molly did her best to respond, to not go off to the faraway place that these sensations sent her to. She so much wanted it to be right for him, for both of them. *This is Tony*, she kept saying in her mind. *Lovely Tony*, not him. Not him. *Tony who you love* . . . And then he was lying, spent, in her arms and she kissed his face again and again.

They spent the afternoon there, eating the sandwiches, lolling, playing in the stream like children and talking and cuddling in the green quiet and the heaven of a long, lazy afternoon. The war seemed far away, even here, quite close to London. They did not talk about it, didn't even want to think about it. Today was enough – tomorrow they would deal with when it came.

Twenty-Five

The next day Tony took her into London town. They walked round looking at the sights – the Houses of Parliament, Westminster Abbey – and strolled across the parks. Despite the sandbags, gun emplacements, shelters and rubble from which it was impossible to escape completely, the London parks were full of people, many managing to find some weekend relaxation in deckchairs and sprawled on the dry grass with handkerchiefs or newspapers shielding their eyes.

Dymphna had asked Molly if she would like to borrow a frock for the day, so that she didn't have to stay in uniform. Hesitantly Molly agreed, not liking to offend her, though after the odd hand-me-downs Iris had dressed her in, she wondered what she was in for. At least her ATS uniform didn't make her stand out as strange, and it often commanded respect. But to her surprise, Tony's mother came to her with a very pretty pink-and-white floral dress.

'I can't fit into it any more,' she said wistfully. 'Geraldine says it's old-fashioned, but I can't quite bear to part with it.'

'Oh, it's ever so pretty!' Molly exclaimed, fingering the soft folds of the skirt. She felt honoured to be offered such a lovely thing. 'But I don't know if I'll fit into it either.'

'I should think you will,' Dymphna said, looking her

up and down. 'It might be a shade short on you, that's all. But that's more the fashion these days.'

Molly, who had never had the luxury of being able to take any notice of what the fashion was, slipped into the cotton frock in the bedroom and found that it not only fitted her, but it showed off her curving figure beautifully. She turned this way and that in front of the mirror, excited at how nice it looked. After brushing out her hair and pinning it back, she went self-consciously downstairs. Tony whistled appreciatively and Dymphna beamed with pleasure.

'You're a picture,' she said softly. 'Oh, I don't think I ever did look as lovely as you in it!'

'I s'pect you did,' Molly said, overwhelmed by all this attention. She could see the pride in Tony's eyes.

'You can wear it to Mass tomorrow as well, dear – in fact, you can keep it. It's no good to me any more and it's a joy to see you in it. Oh now – you can't go out in those great army shoes, can you? Here – you and I are much of a size. Would these fit now?' She held out a pair of white sandals.

Molly was delighted. 'What – you'd really lend them to me?'

'Go on with you – you'll look a picture.'

They were a little bit tight, but Molly wasn't going to let that stand in her way. She thanked Dymphna, overwhelmed by her kindness.

After their lovely day in town, Molly's feet were blistered with the heat and all the walking, but it had been worth it, to feel prettily dressed. She soaked her feet luxuriously in a bucket of cold water. Then they settled down for a cosy evening in with the family. Everyone sat round talking and drinking tea, the girls nagging Tony and Molly to play cards and hangman with them, Fred teasing them, all laughing, and someone remarking several times, as they did every evening, how strange and marvellous it was not to have air raids.

'Those buggers can stay in Russia,' Fred said.

'Fred, language now!' Dymphna said, tutting. Fred lit a cigarette and sat back, blowing smoke to the ceiling with a mischievous grin. 'Good bloody riddance to 'em. You all right there, Molly? Another drop of tea?'

She woke the next morning, aware of Tony slipping away to his bed on the floor downstairs before his mother came down. They were to go to Mass early, keeping to the Sunday fast, and soon everyone was ready and walking out, past the rubble of bombed-out houses at the end of the road and round the corner to the parish church. The morning was hazy with cloud that would burn off later.

Molly found Dymphna beside her and realized she had come up next to her because she wanted to talk. She felt extremely smart and proud in the dress Dymphna had given her and Dymphna looked very fresh and nice in a pale blue shirtwaister. Geraldine and Josephine were ahead in their frocks and socks and Tony had fallen into conversation with his father. Molly heard them laughing. She thought for a moment of Bert, and for the first time, felt sorry for him. When had Bert ever had a decent bloke in his life who he could laugh with, a father figure to show him a decent way to be a man?

'I'm glad you've come to be with us,' Dymphna said, kindly. 'You've made our Tony very happy – it's written all over him. He hasn't always been a happy soul. You've done wonders for him.'

'Well, he's made me very happy,' Molly replied. 'And

'. . . and all of you. I don't really know what to say. It's lovely – my family's not, well, not up to much really, to tell yer the truth.'

Dymphna reached out and took Molly's hand between both of hers, holding it gently.

'Well, you're welcome in ours, dear. I can see you've a good heart.' There was a pause, and then she said, 'Now, today we can have a little talk with Father Callaghan.'

'Yes, all right,' Molly agreed, though the thought made her a little nervous.

'Did your family really not give you any religious instruction?'

'No, not at all.' *Nor any other sort much either*, Molly thought bitterly. 'But I'd like to' – she struggled for the right words – 'to go into being a Catholic – I mean, if that's all right.'

'Of course it's all right,' Dymphna said. 'Bless you dear, it's more than all right, it's what we'd expect.'

'I'd want to be the same as him. It seems the right thing.' Molly was so eager to please, to be part of this family, that being a Catholic now seemed a rather glamorous thing and certainly the least she could do, especially if it meant gaining their approval.

'Well, I'm glad to hear it.' Dymphna patted her hand, seeming reassured. 'You're a good girl. We'll speak to Father after Mass.'

Molly sat between Tony and Josephine in the dark church with its musky smell of polish and incense, seeing the dark-suited men, the lace veils shrouding the women, including herself, as Dymphna had provided her with one. All of it was mysterious to her, the priest's robes, the Latin, which everyone but her knew as second nature, the strange ritual going on in the far distance at the altar, with the altar boys flanking the priest, none of which she could see very much, but which seemed to move everyone.

She followed what everyone else did, as well as she could, trying to make out the way to cross herself. Now and then, Tony took her hand and squeezed it. His face was solemn throughout. Molly felt a little foolish and shut out. She had such a lot to learn! But sitting there in a row with all the Belhams, as if she was already part of the family, was satisfaction in itself. *This will be my family*, she thought, and a warm feeling filled her. This was the greatest prize of all. She dared to imagine herself in the future, married to Tony, already a Catholic, perhaps with their first baby, sitting there among them. What more could she ever want?

Afterwards, a lot of people were pleased to see Tony, and the family was evidently very well known. Molly found a lot of curious looks directed at her. Tony proudly introduced her as his fiancée and Molly basked in being welcomed and congratulated with him. One elderly lady, called Mrs O'Malley, with a very crinkly face, beckoned her close.

'Come down here, darlin', and give me a kiss. I've known this young fella since the day he was born. I was a midwife, see – in fact Tony here was one of the last babies I ever helped bring into the world before I retired from it, so he has a special place in my heart.'

Molly bent to kiss her soft skin while Tony grinned rather sheepishly.

'Perhaps you can help us one day,' he said cheekily.

'Ah, go on with you – I'm well past all that now,' she said, giving a cracked but delighted chuckle. She gripped both their hands with her cold, bony ones and asked all sorts of questions about the army and what they were doing and how they had met. Molly basked in all this attention, proud to see how much affection everyone had for Tony.

Dymphna was hovering close to them. 'Father Callaghan will have a word with you now,' she said, ushering them towards the priest, a small, sharp-eyed man. The matter was soon settled.

'As your time's so limited, perhaps you could come and see me later – let's say four o'clock?' he suggested. 'We are having to do things a little differently in these unsettled times.'

Molly agreed gladly, wondering what she was supposed to see him for.

'He'll take you through the basics, I expect,' Tony said. 'Nothing to worry about.'

'Come on now, son,' Fred Belham said, appearing to lay his hand on Tony's shoulder. 'Time for a quick one.'

Tony looked apologetically at Molly. 'I usually go with the old man for a quick one after Mass.'

'They won't be long,' Dymphna said, appearing beside them. 'Molly, you can come back with me and the girls and help with the dinner.'

Tony made a comical face. 'Careful what you let her loose on,' he said.

Dymphna tutted. 'You cheeky boy – I'm sure Molly can cook very well. Now you won't mind will you, Molly?'

'No – it's OK,' Molly said. She didn't mind at all. In fact, almost as much as being with Tony, she loved the warm, all-embracing company of his mother. The thought of being with her and cooking together was blissful.

'They'll not be long,' Dymphna assured her as they

turned back towards the house. 'The pub's only at the end of the road. We'll go back and have a nice cup of tea and a biscuit to break our fast – we'll not be doing it on ale, like them!'

Molly suddenly realized she was extremely hungry. She'd forgotten they hadn't had any breakfast!

'Everyone was delighted to meet you,' Dymphna said, as they strolled along, the sun just beginning to ease through the clouds. 'That lady you met, Mrs O'Malley – she brought Tony into the world – not the girls, mind, but she's been like a grandmother to them all, so she has. She's a marvellous lady, you know. Her husband was . . .'

An immense, crumpling explosion stopped her and they felt the vibration of it pass all through them. Everyone turned to see a thick pall of dust rise lazily into the air from the next street, from where they'd just come. There were shouts, screams, sounds of falling masonry.

'Holy Mother . . .' Dymphna's hand went to her mouth, her face instantly pale. 'That's down . . . Oh dear God, what's happened?'

'Mam, Mam!' Geraldine shouted. 'That's down the end of Stanley Street.'

'Oh please God . . .' Dymphna started to run back towards the church and they all followed. Molly, catching the acute sense of dread from Tony's mother, tore along with her. *Whatever it was, not Tony, please God, not him . . .*

Round the corner, a terrible sight met them. Further on, past the church, the road was a mass of smoke and dust and rubble. Someone was crying hysterically and there were people rushing about in confusion.

'What is it, what's happened?' Dymphna shouted at a boy who came running towards them, his eyes wide with fear.

'Dunno – think it was a bomb, got lodged somewhere. Mrs Flynn's house blew up . . .' He tore on past.

All Molly could think was, *Tony, where are you, where are you?* She waited for him to appear out of the whorls of dust, the wreckage, the confusion.

And then Dymphna screamed, 'Fred, Fred!'

A familiar burly shape, shoulders hunched, was silhouetted against the chaos, the smoke and licking flames. They reached him in seconds. For the first time Molly saw his face without a smile. His hair and moustache were grey with dust, which had caked the lines of his face. He seemed too stunned to speak.

'Fred, oh my God, you're all right!' Dymphna and the girls flung themselves at him.

'Daddy, Daddy!' Josephine was crying.

'Where's Tony?' Dymphna was shouting in his face. She shook him by the shoulders, seeing how shocked he was. 'Where is he? You were together, remember?'

'I dunno. He was here, right beside me . . .' Fred held out his arm, completely bewildered.

In the distance they could hear the sound of bells, fire engines, ambulances. Through the dust and smoke, Molly caught sight of the pub a few houses up, people spilling out, talking, shouting. Now there was a jagged gap in the row of houses, its wreckage blocking the street.

'Tony!' She leapt into life suddenly, running closer to look. He had to be here. He'd be helping, dashing about in his usual energetic way. 'Tony – where are you?' she cried, then stopped. Dread, disbelief took over. All they could do was stand and stare, and wait.

246

Fire engines revved up, unravelling hoses, damping down the flames. Lifting crews arrived, and the neighbours pitched in and helped as the dust gradually settled. As the air cleared of smoke, everything became starkly visible. Two houses had come down, exploding out into the street, leaving the jagged arms of the supporting ones beside them, their walls covered in visible stripes of green and raspberry pink, a brass bedstead hanging as if it might topple down any moment. Everyone fell silent.

It didn't take long. Not long enough. They brought out two bodies – Mrs Flynn, in whose attic, it seemed, the unexploded bomb had nestled unnoticed, and Tony. Though Molly recognized him instantly, achingly familiar with every tiny part of him, he looked strange to her. He was pumice-coloured, except for the blood on his face. He seemed longer, thinner. After the cries of recognition, the sobs of horror, the five of them, too numb for words, silently linked hands and stood round his crumpled body.

Twenty-Six

Molly could scarcely remember anything about those days later on. The army had to be informed, compassionate leave applied for, a funeral arranged. Somehow these things were done, somehow they lived, breathed, ate – did they? Somehow.

Dymphna's sister came from across London to comfort the distraught family. Ann, who was kindly and of a practical nature, took in the whole situation and insisted that Molly stay until after the funeral.

'The poor girl's got nowhere to go,' Molly heard her say to Dymphna, 'and the state of her, she looks half mad.'

'Well he was her future husband,' Dymphna said, in a tear-thickened voice. 'Now it's all taken away from her – from us all.' Sometimes she'd say, 'When they join up you're always afraid for them. But it shouldn't have happened like that, not like that.'

They all kept inside, the curtains half drawn, Fred smoking silently, Dymphna with rosary beads in her hands, lips moving constantly, the hours swimming by somehow. Molly was too lost and bewildered by the shock of her grief to take in how kind they were – Ann kept them all fed and supplied with cups of tea, and she and the two girls tried to help, but then one would start crying and they'd all set each other off. At night, it was an agony for Molly to lie in the bed where Tony had slipped in to join her so few nights ago; the time seemed so close that she could almost feel him, yet it was also an eternity away. She hugged the pillow against her body, which ached inconsolably, wondering whether she should try to go with him. Was it worth carrying on living after this? And she would picture him again and again as she had seen him being brought out from under Mrs Flynn's ruined house, ashen with dust, the blood, so still, all his electric life drained from him. Then she would see him as he had been on the cliffs, lying back, his whole body shaking with laughter, or pulling her close for a kiss, and this made her weep until her whole body hurt from weeping.

And none of it could bring him back. Ever.

The church was packed. The family was well known and liked in the district and many of those attending the funeral had watched Tony grow up. Molly was utterly dreading it. It was a warm day and she wore Dymphna's dress, which she had washed carefully, remembering the look of admiration she had seen in Tony's eyes when he first saw her wear it.

She filed into the church with the family, aware of everyone's pitying looks. Fred and Dymphna leaned on each other, distraught. A number of people were already weeping. The shock of his dying so close by and in such a way had been terrible for everyone. The contrast with the last time she was there, when her hopes were full of marriage and family and belonging, was too much to bear. Tony's coffin was waiting for them at the front of the church, and at the sight of it, Molly, rather than letting out more of the ocean of tears inside her, seized on her old habit of making herself numb. By the time they were all seated in their pews, she beside Josephine, who was already crying quietly, she had a floaty, detached feeling that none of this was real. She could not hold her attention steady on what was going on. It was like all those times in her bed, as a child, when Old Man Rathbone had shuffled over her, and she had heard his breathing coming closer, closer. She had not been able to get away from him, not in her body, but she had drifted away in her head, separated herself, her eyes making shapes out of the shadows in the room, floating above what was happening, escaping him the only way she could. And now she could not stand to be here, to face the truth that Tony's body was in that coffin, so close – his hands, his laughing face – yet gone for ever, wrapped round in the only love they could offer now: Latin words and the sound of muffled weeping. Instead she went into a kind of trance, that lasted until they were outside again, and people were speaking to her, offering sympathy, she hearing it suddenly loud, as if she had come up from under water.

She could not stay after that. Tony, her love, was gone. Being with his family was now an agony, and especially now the funeral was over, she felt in the way. There was nothing for her there.

'I'll have to get back,' she told Dymphna. 'They gave me a few days' leave, but I've got to go tomorrow.'

'My poor darlin',' Dymphna said. She seemed at a loss and physically shrunken. There was nothing she could offer Molly, no enduring link they could have with each other now. After all, she and Tony had not even been married and they had not known each other long enough. She would not be a Catholic, or part of the family. She could not belong there now.

Molly dressed in her uniform the next day, leaving the pink-and-white dress folded on the bed. She could not bear to wear it again. With desperate sadness she said goodbye to all of them and made her way to Paddington, carrying all the ache of grief inside her. As the underground train rumbled across London, she sat staring at her reflection in the blackness of the window. The journey ahead of her spun through her mind. There would be the long ride all across the south, to the Welsh coast, the transport from the station, arriving back at the camp, the mess, the kitchens, guns firing off the cliffs, the ATS girls, the gunners, the lovely sea, and cliffs, all haunted now with taunting happiness. But not her love, her future. Not him.

She climbed out at Paddington and in the bustle of the station she found her way to the army transport, to which she was automatically entitled.

'I need to go the Euston Station please,' she said.

She could not go back there, not to Wales, not to the army, or anywhere near it. Not now. The memories would be too much for her. She had to go anywhere but there.

Within just over an hour, she was on a train to Birmingham.

Homefires

Twenty-Seven

Edna Stapleton, Norm's mom, was quite a religious woman, and since Bob and Cynthia scarcely ever darkened the doors of a church, Em agreed to be married in her church, St Saviour's in Saltley. The question then arose of where they were to live. With Norm about to join up and houses in short supply, the obvious thing was for Em to remain at home while he was away.

'In the meantime, before I go, you can come and stop with us,' Norm told her enthusiastically. 'We've got more room with Rich gone and everything.' He was determined that they were going away after the wedding too, at least for a night.

'Where d'yer want to go?' he asked Em, when he was round at the Browns' house one night. It was late and everyone else had gone to bed. Norm seemed to have endless energy.

'I don't know,' Em said, swallowing down a yawn. She'd never been anywhere in her life beyond the borders of Birmingham and wasn't even sure if she wanted to.

'Tell yer what' – Norm looked very pleased with himself – 'I'll surprise you.'

'Well we can't go too far,' Em said, nervous enough about leaving home at all.

'I'll think of summat, love – you leave it to me.'

*

Em wore a much prettier and more elaborate white wedding dress than she had expected to, satin trimmed with lace, which Dot had been given by her Italian sister-in-law, Margarita.

'No point in leaving it hanging in the cupboard for the moths when that lovely girl can use it!' she said kindly. 'Where's she going to get a decent dress these days? No – you let her have it. We'll alter it for her so that it fits her perfect.'

It had a long, flowing skirt and Em wore a lacy headband and veil. Cynthia was overcome by emotion when she saw her all dressed up, ready to leave for the church.

'Oh Em – you look so beautiful,' she wept. 'And so grown-up. Oh I hope you'll be happy, love!'

They embraced up in the bedroom and Em nearly cried as well. She was so excited and so apprehensive all at once and she knew that within her mother's emotion lay anxiety and mixed feelings. But she couldn't say anything. Forcing a smile, she said, 'I s'pect I will be. Norm's a good sort. And I'll be back here soon, once he goes off, anyway.'

Entering the dark, rather grand church felt very strange to Em, and as she processed along the aisle on her father's arm, she was suddenly full of nerves and found her legs trembling so much that she could hardly stand. Bob, hair trimmed specially and squeezed into his Sunday best suit, was taking short, wheezing breaths and she felt very affectionate towards him. Her dear old dad wasn't used to this sort of thing – she was the oldest and first to get married!

Norm turned as she approached, and she saw his face change from nervousness to wonder, to the makings of a grin of utter delight, which he quelled immediately since this was a solemn occasion. Even she had been taken aback by her own transformation when she looked in the mirror. Of course her same old face had looked back at her – young-looking for her eighteen years, a few freckles still scattered across her nose – but with her hair pinned back, curled under at the ends, and the lacy veil, she looked suddenly grown-up and dramatic.

'You look lovely Em. Really beautiful!' Joyce had said, sweetly, once she was dressed that morning, and it was a rare thing for Joyce to pay compliments.

Norm stood beside her, tall and proud in his policeman's uniform which he had yet to exchange for an RAF one, and took her arm in his. He spoke his vows with the confidence of a man without a shred of doubt about what he was doing.

Later, when they caught the train, Em still didn't know where they were going. The two families had gone back to the Stapletons' house and eaten the food they had pooled. Em was relieved to see that her mom and dad got on all right with Norm's. When all the eating and drinking had been done, and the last cups of tea were being drained, Em went up and changed into a simpler dress, regretful that her moments of magic in the white satin one were over so quickly.

'Back to being Cinders,' she said wryly to herself. But she was very grateful to Dot that she had been able to dress up so beautifully, at least for a short while.

She had enjoyed the day, basking in the attention, with Joyce, Violet and even Sid being good-natured to her, and Mom and Dad looking proud. But once she was alone with Norm in the compartment of the train, the brass ring on her finger, and he slipping his arm under hers and taking her hand, she was seized with panic. *What the hell've I* done? she kept thinking. *I'm married* – married*!*

'So – where d'yer think we're going then?' Norm said. Em had no idea – she'd boarded the train in a trance.

I don't care, she thought, trying to take deep breaths to calm herself. *I want to go home. Why on earth did I get myself into this?* The thought of the evening to come, of being alone with Norm in a strange room somewhere, was making her increasingly uneasy.

'I dunno.' She forced herself to speak amiably, looking down at Norm's long, spindly fingers wrapped round hers. After all, Norm was being so kind – it wasn't his fault she was in a state, was it? She just felt unprepared, too young, as if she wanted to wind time back and let herself be a child again, when now she had to be a woman. She didn't seem to have been a child for long enough. She was glad that the compartment was crowded, because she knew that otherwise Norm would want to kiss her. She could sense his excitement, that at last he would soon be getting what he wanted from her, what it was her duty to give him, and this made her even more nervous.

They arrived in Worcester, and Norm took her to a pretty guest house a mile from the station. He was excited, and full of chat.

'It's a nice place – I thought you'd like it. I came here once with our mom, to see the cathedral. She likes old places; she says she gets a nice feeling off them. When the war's over, we'll go to the seaside, eh? Go on the beach?'

In their little room with a sloping roof, looking over the street, Em busied herself settling in, talking lightly about where she should put this and that as if to keep him at bay with chatter. But Norm came up behind her and took her by the shoulders.

'Come 'ere, love – I haven't even had a proper kiss yet.'

Seeing his ardent expression, Em felt ashamed of her hesitation and smiled shyly at him.

'So – Mrs Stapleton.' He wrapped his arms round her and kissed her enthusiastically. Em, touched by how much he wanted her, did her best to respond, and she felt better. Best not dwell on what might happen later, she thought. This was her Norm, her sweet, kindly husband. (*Husband!!*) She told herself not to be so silly.

'It's nice here,' she said, when he drew back to look at her. Their room was simple, but clean and cosy, with a couple of old rugs on the bare boards, a big, solid wooden bed, a cupboard and two chairs. 'Thanks, Norm,' she said, then giggled. 'Your ears have gone all pink.'

Norm grinned sheepishly. 'They're like blinking traffic lights, aren't they?'

She put her hands behind them and waggled them affectionately. 'I can always tell it's you coming along, anyhow.'

They ate the filling evening meal provided by the guest house, a tasty rabbit stew and potatoes followed by Miss Muffet junket, and then strolled round the sedate old city in the dying light. The streets were very quiet and it felt as if they had the whole place to themselves.

They walked beside the river Severn and looked up at the old façade of the cathedral as the first stars were appearing.

'Let's go back now,' Norm murmured, his arm round Em's shoulder. His lips brushed her ear.

As soon as they were back in their room shrouded by blackout curtains, the dim light on, Norm could not contain his excitement any longer. He took her eagerly in his arms.

'Let me undress yer,' he begged. 'I've thought about it so many times – seeing yer, love.'

With rapt concentration, he removed her cardigan, then began undoing the buttons down the front of her frock.

'What's the matter?' He looked into her eyes. 'You're all of a quiver. Oh Em, love – I ain't going to hurt yer!'

'I know – only, you know, it's . . . I've never . . .'

Very tenderly he put his arms round her again. 'I'd never hurt yer. You're everything to me – yer know that. I just want to love yer, that's all.'

'I know – just be gentle, won't you?'

'You're my goddess. Course I will.'

He lifted her frock over her head so that she was down to her camiknickers, feeling chilly and also shy, since he was still fully clothed and gazing longingly at her.

'You get undressed as well,' she said.

'Oh – OK then!'

Em got into bed, wondering whether she should take the rest of her clothes off. Already covered with goose pimples, she pulled the covers up, fumbling with the fastening on her brassiere, conscious of Norm's urgent movements which were shaking the end of the bed.

'I'm coming love,' he said, bending down to unlace

260

his shoes. Each was dropped with a thud on the floor and the clothes followed. Em braced herself for the sight of her naked husband as he quickly turned to her, but then just as suddenly, stepping towards her, he disappeared with a crash. She felt the bed jar.

'Norm?' She kneeled up, holding the sheet over her bare breasts. 'What're you doing – are you all right?'

There was silence from the floor, then a groan. Em crawled along the bed to see him sitting up, hand over one eye.

'I slipped on the flaming rug, didn't I?' he groaned. Cautiously, he removed his hand and squinted up at her.

At the sight of him sitting there starkers on the floor, ears sticking out and with the makings of what tomorrow would be a huge shiner on his left eye, Em put her hand over her mouth and tried to choke back her giggles.

Norm, still groaning with pain, managed a chuckle as well. 'You can laugh – it blooming well hurts!'

'I'm sorry, love...' The laughter burst out of her. 'You just look so funny...' She lay back, cackling hysterically.

Norm got groggily to his feet and came and lay beside her, and the fact that he laughed as well made her love him all the more. He leaned up on one elbow then, his face suddenly rapt and serious.

'Well *you* look lovely,' he said. 'You're the loveliest thing I've ever seen.

Twenty-Eight

Norm set off to begin his basic training a few days later. Em did not go to the station to see him off as she had to be at work that morning. As they lay cuddled up in bed together in his mom and dad's house in Saltley very early that day, knowing that soon he must go, she felt as if she was being torn apart.

'I don't know why you had to go and do it,' she wept, lying curled up next to him. 'You could've stayed here where you were and we'd have been together.'

'I know,' Norm said, his hand moving across her soft hair. He sounded wretched, full of second thoughts about the wisdom of joining up too. 'I wish I'd never done it now. It was all a bit spur of the moment. Only – I dunno, I s'pose I'd feel less respect for myself. Our mom's proud of me for it, even though I know she'll worry.'

Em sobbed for a while, sad and a touch angry with him, then quietened, and lay treasuring the luxury of being there warm together, before it was snatched away.

Norm turned to her and kissed her damp cheek, then her lips.

'Oh, love . . .' His arms wrapped round her. 'Can we – you know – once more? Before I go?'

'*Again?*' Em teased. 'Blimey, you're a one!'

'No, *you* are.' He kissed the end of her nose. 'I can't resist yer.'

'Oh, go on then.'

But she was happy. Ever since their wedding night, when they had started to learn lovemaking together – one consequence of which being the dramatic black eye Norm was sporting the morning after – it had been a happy, loving thing. She had lost her fear of it and got past the strangeness of it, and she felt loved and wanted. They had spent a happy few days in the Stapletons' house, where his mom and dad were kind and welcoming to her, and all she really wanted was for it to go on like this for ever.

After Norm's enthusiastic lovemaking, cold reality returned like a slap. He had to get up, and then leave on a train to Aberystwyth, and when she would see him again and for how long, none of them knew. And when she did see him, he would be different, with cropped hair and a uniform on.

She clung to him before he left, not wanting to let go, until Norm almost had to prise himself away. He held her shoulders and looked solemnly at her.

'Don't cry, bab. I love yer – I'll be back, and I'll write to yer, often as I can.'

He kissed her once more, parted fondly from his mother, and then Em and Mrs Stapleton stood at the door, each wiping their eyes, watching Norm's loping, big-footed frame recede along the street, then vanish with a final cheery wave.

'Ah well, bab,' Mrs Stapleton said, rallying, 'we mustn't keep on. He's a good lad and it's got to be done.'

But Em felt cold inside. *At least he's only training for the moment*, she told herself. Even though he had only just gone, she ached for him to come back. That day she thanked Mrs Stapleton and said she would move her things back to Kenilworth Street after work. All day she felt on the edge of tears, trying to be brave and not cry in front of Mr Perry or the customers. The moment she set foot back home and saw her mom, she burst into sobs.

'Oh I wish he hadn't gone and joined up!' she wept. 'He didn't have to – and he's gone and left me, when we've only just got married!'

Norm wrote faithfully, brief but affectionate letters, telling her a little about what he was doing and saying how much he missed her. Em soon felt better and got used to things. Life went back to how it had been before, though the absence of people who had always been there before did make her think.

Perhaps I should have joined up? she mused one morning, absent-mindedly putting onions in a bag for one of their customers. Suddenly she was full of a restless sense of anti-climax. Things had quietened down, so that her warden duties were a routine thing now, with no raids. Life had gone back to normal, back home with Mom, while others had gone off for a new kind of life. Molly had done it, and now Norm. She found herself wondering about Katie O'Neill, who had once been a friend at school, though she had proved two-faced and turned her back on her when Em's family ran into troubles. She hadn't seen Katie or her mother in the area for some time. Maybe Katie had joined up as well? Anyway, it was too late for Em herself now, she realized – she was a married woman – even if it didn't feel much like it at the moment.

'Em, are you with us?' Mr Perry called. 'Mrs Clothier's still waiting for her onions over 'ere!'

*

And then she started being sick. The first couple of days she thought she was ill. She got up feeling very poorly, though the sickness cleared up as the day went on. When it had been going on for a few days, Cynthia noticed. She was washing up in a bowl on the table one morning when Em came in from the privy, her face a ghastly white.

'You all right?' she asked, guardedly.

'I don't feel too good,' Em admitted, sinking onto a chair in the back room. 'I keep being sick.'

Cynthia paused. She rested her hands, pink from the hot water, on the side of the bowl.

'How many days?'

Em shrugged, resting her head wearily on her hand. 'Dunno. A few.'

'You know what it is, don't yer?' She moved over to the teapot, which was wrapped in a green and yellow crocheted cosy, and poured a cup, bringing it over to Em. ''Ere – get that down yer.'

Em looked up into her eyes.

'It means you're expecting.'

Em's eyebrows shot up. 'Does it?'

Cynthia nodded, an odd, mixed expression on her face.

Em's heart was thudding hard. She suddenly felt hot, slightly faint. 'Does it – I mean, I might just be poorly . . .'

Cynthia sat down beside her. 'You're just sick in the mornings, bab, aren't yer?' she said gently.

'Yes – well, I feel a bit sick of an evening too.'

'Anything else?'

'Standing in the shop – I just feel so tired, dizzy sometimes. And I keep forgetting things.'

'D'you feel, sort of – different?'

Em considered. 'Yes, I s'pose I do.'

Cynthia leaned forward emotionally and touched Em's arm. 'Oh love – I think you've got a babby on the way.' Her face crumpled and she burst into fearful crying, one hand clasped over her mouth. 'Oh I'm sorry, love,' she sobbed.

'Don't, Mom,' Em said, disturbed by seeing her like that. 'Please don't cry like that. It'll be all right – I'm sure it will be!'

The sickness, and Cynthia's reaction, sent Em into a panic. Here she was, expecting a child – she knew Cynthia was right, all her instincts told her so – with no Norm here to make her feel safe, and with all her mother's fears and suffering laid upon her. There were moments when she felt angry with Norm. Fancy going off at a time like this! She knew it wasn't his fault really, and that there were women all over the country without their men at home. But her mother's reaction had made all her old fears come crowding back and there was no Norm to reassure her. That first day her mind rushed back and forth like a rat in a trap. Why had she let this happen? Should she try and do away with the child? It was a wicked thought, she knew, but it came anyway. What if she was like Mom after the babby and lost her mind, what if she had to be taken away, what if . . . ? The thoughts churned round and round all day until she felt exhausted.

After work she was desperate for someone to talk to. She went to call on Mrs Stapleton and give her the news of a grandchild on the way. Edna Stapleton welcomed her joyfully, which made Em feel a bit better.

'Aren't you a clever girl!' she said enthusiastically,

sitting Em down and giving her tea and a slice of dry cake. 'Well, we must take good care of you, bab. That's our first grandchild! What lovely news! Oh, Bill'll be over the moon! Let's see now – it'll arrive ...' She counted on her fingers. 'January or so. Well, you've made me a very happy woman, bless yer.'

Em was cheered by her mother-in-law's kindness, but she didn't feel she could discuss her real fears with Mrs Stapleton. It would have felt wrong and disloyal talking about Mom and what had happened to her and how she was sometimes. But she longed to pour out her heart to someone, and when she'd left the house in Saltley, tired as she was, she made her way to Duddesdon, to see the one person who she knew would understand – Dot.

As she knocked on the door of the tall terraced house she realized she had not come at the best time. Dot would be cooking tea and the family would be there, but she was so desperate and she'd come all this way and didn't want to turn back now.

The door was opened by Dot's youngest, Nancy, who was thirteen, dark-haired and dark-eyed, with a jaunty prettiness. Nancy's father had been an Italian, a musician passing through the area whom Dot, then a widow with twin sons, had fallen for. She had had to bring up Nancy on her own, the itinerant father never knowing of his child's existence. But now Dot had remarried, and she and Nancy had changed their names from Wiggins to Alberello, a surname that suited Nancy's Neapolitan looks. Em saw she was growing up into a beauty.

'Hello, Em!' Nancy said, surprised. 'What're you doing here?'

A smell of frying onions was wafting out from the

back, which Em would normally have found delicious, but today it turned her stomach.

'I just want a word with your mom. Is she there?'

Dot's tall, wiry figure came along the dark hall; she was wiping her hands on her pinner and looking concerned.

'What's up, Em? Is it Cynthia?'

'No, she's all right,' Em said, feeling the tears prickling in her eyes. She was aware of Nancy hovering curiously in the background. 'I'm ever so sorry to come when you're cooking, but could I have a quick word, in private, like?'

'Nancy – go and watch the stove,' Dot ordered. 'Come in, love, it's no trouble.'

Dot led Em into the front room, which was shrouded by net curtains. Em was in too much of a state to notice much, but she took in the atmosphere of formality, the heavy furniture and framed photographs on a table: Dot and Lou's wedding and old First Communion pictures of his daughters. It was a much more comfortable house than Dot had had when she lived next to them in Kenilworth Street.

'Sit down, bab,' Dot said kindly. 'You look in a bit of a state – what's the trouble?'

'I'm so worried!' Em sank into a chair, the words pouring out confusedly. 'I think I'm expecting a babby and I feel sick all the time and Mom cried and I'm so frightened! I don't want to end up like her! D'you think I will?'

'Oh bab!' Dot came and sat on the arm of the chair, her strong arm round Em's shoulders. 'What's all this to-do about? You think you've a babby on the way already! Bless yer – ain't that lovely!'

She sounded so pleased and not frightened and in a panic like Cynthia, and Em felt a bit better already.

'Well, you and Norm haven't wasted any time, have yer?' Dot chuckled.

Em was glad her blushes would not be visible in the shadowy room.

'But I'm scared I'll go like Mom – have to go to the asylum and . . . Oh Dot!' She turned, frantically, to face her. 'What if I get like that? The thought of it terrifies the life out of me!'

Dot gently rubbed her back, her face serious, and Em was grateful to see that she was not going to dismiss her fears and tell her not to be silly.

'I don't s'pose you will, love. I don't know what happened to your mom exactly. But remember she'd had three babbies and been all right before. I don't know if it was anything to do with the shock of Joycie going missing so soon after. I don't s'pose we'll ever know. But I don't know as it runs in families. Best thing is not to worry too much. You know – hope for the best and don't get all down and gloomy. Keep cheerful for the babby's sake! You've always been a happy little soul, despite it all – I'm sure you'll be all right.'

Em went home a little comforted, especially taking with her Dot's reminder that she was always there, and to come and see her if she ever wanted a natter.

Over the summer months, the sickness gradually wore off and Em adjusted to the idea that she was going to be a mother. Sometimes she felt completely unprepared, like a child herself, but mostly it was an exciting, awesome thought. Norm greeted the news with huge enthusiasm and at last, at the end of July, when his basic training was over, he was allowed home on leave. Once more they stayed for those few days in Saltley. Norm, Em realized with amusement, would have been happy to spend his entire leave in bed with her.

'God, I've missed you,' he kept saying, before snuggling up to her and pressing her to make love all over again. Em wondered if it was safe, but it seemed to feel all right.

'I thought you'd have a bit of a belly on you by now,' he said the first time he saw her naked. She was lying beside him and he examined her carefully as if she was a precious piece of china and he was checking for chips and cracks.

'No – I'm only three months gone,' she said. 'It's at the end you get big.'

He stroked his hand over her tummy. 'Well, I wonder who's in there. Oh love – it's so ... Well, it's a miracle, ain't it?'

Norm seemed stronger, a little older somehow, with his service haircut and his blue uniform. Naked, he seemed to have filled out a little. He talked a lot, telling her all about it, the other lads he had trained with, from all over the place, about the planes and routines. She could see that, much as he missed her, in some ways he was having the time of his life, and she was both glad and a little jealous.

'Don't forget me, will you?' she said, wistfully.

'Forget you?' Norm said, appalled. 'How could I forget you? You're my missus. You're the most precious thing in the world!'

The blissful days of his leave tore past. He saved the news that upset her until the end: he was going to Canada next, to complete his training as a fighter pilot.

'*Canada?*' she said, bewildered. He might as well have said Timbuktu. It was so strange and far away.

'It won't be for ever,' he said. 'Then I'll most likely get a posting back here.'

And he was gone. While holding fast to the knowledge of how much he loved her and she him, she resigned herself to adjusting to being without him and going back to her old routine once again.

But things had a way of not settling down for long. A couple of weeks later, Em was walking back from work, her feet aching from standing in the shop, but appreciating no longer feeling sick, and enjoying the feel of the warm air on her bare arms and legs. She turned her face up to the sun, squinting. She was carrying a few vegetables that Mr Perry had given her which she knew Mom would be glad of for tea, and she stopped to donate a few of them to one of the elderly ladies along the street.

The front doors of most of the houses were open and she heard the sound of music from several wireless sets floating out to her, then the music cut off and a man's voice was talking. Their door was open too, but to her surprise, Cynthia was not listening to the wireless as she often did while she cooked. Em felt an immediate sense of foreboding. Had something happened? Was she going to find that Cynthia had taken to her bed upstairs?

'Mom? I've got some stuff for you from Mr Per—'

She stopped in amazement in the doorway through to the back. Cynthia was sitting at the table looking perfectly all right and a familiar figure was sitting opposite her with her back to Em, unmistakable at a glance, with her striking figure and thick blonde hair. But the face that then turned to greet her was pink and puffy with tears.

'Molly?'

''Ello, Em,' she said dully.

Em's first thought was that Molly had seen the Buttons' ravaged house across the street. She knew how upset Molly would be about Jenny and Stanley and thought this the reason for the strange, tragic expression in both Cynthia's and Molly's eyes.

'It's terrible, isn't it?' Em said sympathetically. 'We just couldn't believe it when it happened.' She put her hand on Molly's shoulder. 'It's ever so nice to see you, Molly. Have you got a bit of leave?'

'No,' Molly said, fresh tears running down her cheeks. 'I've left the army. I was engaged, Em, to a lovely fella, and he was killed – last week. I can't stay in the army, not after that. I'm home now – for good.'

Absent Without Leave

Twenty-Nine

Turning into Kenilworth Street that afternoon, Molly had thought her heart could not weigh any heavier, until she saw the smashed wreckage of the place she had long thought of as her refuge and home – Jenny and Stanley Button's house.

'Oh my God,' she breathed, the sight of it jolting her to a standstill.

She'd known about it, of course, but seeing was another matter. The front of the house had collapsed, leaving black, gaping holes. Most of the rubble had been cleared away to make the street passable, and much of the smashed brick and other mess had been piled into the shell of the ruined house.

Slowly, Molly moved closer, trying to come to terms with the reality of it – that the Buttons were gone for ever. She could see the white walls of the room she had slept in upstairs, the door frame leading off the postcard-sized landing. It was one of the worst things she'd ever seen. And it all brought back the explosion that had killed Tony only a few heartbreaking days ago. She looked down to shut out the desolate sight, feeling herself start to shake again. Already immersed in the wrenching awfulness of losing him, this was too much. Everyone she had ever truly loved in the world was gone, and being back here, instead of being any sort of comfort, made it all feel starkly worse.

Why had she even come back? She had panicked, turned on the spur of the moment towards something familiar, to get away from anywhere that could remind her of Tony. But of course it did remind her. It pressed her further into the pain. And what comfort could she find here? Here there was nothing that could be called a home. There was Em, of course, but she was married now, had her own family and future. But for Molly now, there was nothing anywhere. What did it matter where she went?

Standing in the street on that warm afternoon, for a few moments her anguish grew until it was unbearable. She squeezed her eyes tightly closed, desperately craving a drink to blot out the pain, to blur the edges of everything and let her sink into black unconsciousness. But no. NO! She mustn't start down that road. No now: not ever. *I'm not ending up like my bloody mother!* she raged inwardly. *If I only do one good thing in my life it will be not ending up like that sodden old cow.*

A tiny sound snagged her attention. It was someone coughing further along the road, but it was instantly familiar. Opening her eyes, she saw a figure in the distance: skinny, slightly bent, walking in a furtive manner, head turning from side to side, glancing behind as if uneasy about being followed. Yet there was something different. She watched, rooted to the spot, as her brother came towards her from the far end of the street.

Realizing that the last thing on earth she wanted to do was run into Bert, she dashed to number eighteen, rapped urgently on the Browns' half-open door and stepped inside.

'Who's that?' Cynthia came through from the back.

It took her seconds to recognize her. '*Molly?* What on *earth* are you doing here?'

'Shhh!' Molly put her finger urgently to her lips. She'd nipped in quickly and hidden behind the door, pretty sure Bert hadn't seen her. 'Sorry, Mrs Brown, only Bert's coming along . . .'

'Huh,' Cynthia said contemptuously. She folded her arms and the two of them peered out from behind the nets as Bert went slouching past. His greasy hair was parted in the middle and slicked back either side.

'Look at that suit – those lapels!' Molly whispered. 'He daint get that down the pawn shop – he looks a proper dandy! Those shoes! How did he get hold of all that?'

'Not by a hard day's work, you can bet,' Cynthia said.

Bert disappeared and the two women turned to each other. Molly was struck by some change in Cynthia. She had always been a lovely-looking woman, strong and curvaceous, with her dark eyes and dark wavy hair. She was wearing a loose frock under which could be seen clearly the outline of her generous breasts. She looked suddenly older, slacker in the body. But she appeared steady: she was not going through one of her bad patches, by the looks of things.

Molly saw Cynthia take in the sight of her in her uniform, of her hair taken up smartly under her hat. Even in the fog of her grief, Molly had automatically dressed as if for an inspection.

'You look so different! Very grown-up.' Cynthia smiled, then took in Molly's hollow-eyed, desolate expression and closed the front door. 'Come through, bab – I'll get you a cup of tea. What's happened?'

It all came pouring out as Molly sat at the table. Cynthia busied herself making the tea, until Molly got to the bit about being in London with Tony, and then the bomb, and she came and sat close, her dark eyes seeming to reflect the horror she was hearing.

'Oh love – what a terrible thing to happen – and on top of Mr and Mrs Button!' She rested her hand on Molly's arm as she talked, weeping wretchedly. 'You poor, poor thing. No wonder you can't go back there. That's right, you have a good cry and let some of it out.'

Once Em had come home and heard the news, they'd told Molly to go up on Em's bed and have a rest.

'You look all in, love,' Cynthia said.

And though she did not think she would be able to, as soon as she lay down sleep overcame her.

She woke in the late-afternoon light to find Em sitting on the edge of the bed and the low sun slanting through the window.

'Brought you another cup of tea,' Em said.

Molly sat up, disorientated, her hair rumpled round her face. 'I couldn't think where I was.'

'I'm not surprised.' Em still looked stricken. 'I'm ever so sorry, Molly.'

Molly took the cup of tea, her eyes filling with tears again at the sight of Em's sympathetic face. Sipping her tea, she looked around her. She was in the bigger bed that Em shared with Joyce, and by the wall was Violet's single one.

'What're you going to do?' Em asked.

Molly shrugged. 'I haven't thought. Go back to the factory, I s'pose.'

Em was frowning. 'Won't they come and look for you? Surely they will?'

'Will they?' Molly looked unconcerned by this thought. 'Oh I don't s'pose so.' Looking over the rim of her teacup, she said, 'How're you, Em? Norm all right?'

'I think so.' Em smiled. 'He's in Canada. Can you believe it? All that way.' She blushed prettily. 'Did Mom tell you?'

'What?'

'I'm expecting.'

A terrible pang went through Molly, seeing Em's face, which she now noticed was different, radiant in a way she'd never seen before. Em looked happy and excited, with a husband and future, whereas she . . . But she dragged her features into a smile.

'Oh I am pleased for yer! That's lovely, Em! When's it due to arrive?'

'January,' Em said. 'I've got my special ration book, it's a green one they give you if you're having a babby, and Mr Perry's being ever so kind when I haven't been feeling too well . . .' She stopped, seeing the sadness in Molly's face. 'Sorry – not very nice of me.' She touched her friend's shoulder. 'Rattling on after all that's happened to you.'

'No – I'm happy for yer,' Molly said, wiping away the tears which wouldn't stop running down her cheeks. 'Em – d'you know what happened to Stanley?'

'No.' Em thought for a moment. 'It was a terrible night. I was on duty round the corner. I came round and saw it, after . . . They'd gone by then. They took both of 'em away – I s'pose he went to the hospital. D'you want to go and see him?'

'They were ever so kind to me. And he must be lost

without Mrs B. She was the life and soul, did everything for him.'

'We'll have to find out,' Em said. 'I'll ask around.'

'And what about Wally?'

'Who's Wally?'

'The little dog – don't you remember?'

Em looked vague. 'I don't know. He must've got killed – or run off.' She got up from the bed. 'Look Molly, I don't know what you want to do, but you can bunk up with us here if you like. If you don't want to go home? Have you even seen their new place?' Em saw Molly's blank look. 'You *did* know they've moved?'

'No! Where to?'

'Only up the road. To a bigger house. One of those ones up the end.'

'Oh, *have* they?' Molly said grimly. 'They seem to be in the money all of a sudden.' She ran a hand over her face. She hadn't thought anything through. 'I don't want to be over there – I'll stop 'ere with you, if that's all right?'

Em leaned down and squeezed her hand. 'Course it is.'

Thirty

'I s'pose I'd better look in on Mom,' Molly said when they'd all had their tea. 'See how they're getting along in their new palace!'

She was a bit curious about the new house in Lupin Street, but as she left number eighteen, she was also anxious not to get in the Brown family's way. She'd promised Cynthia she'd go and apply for a civilian ration book the next day, so that she was not a burden on them. She was still wearing her uniform, the only clothes she had with her, and she wanted to retrieve a few old things she had in the house to make do with for now. After that she was going to have to get back on her feet, get a job and pay her way.

It was only thanks to Em that she knew the number of the house. It was in a terrace, two up, two down – hardly a palace, but an improvement on the old back-to-back they were in before. Like all the other houses in the neighbourhood, its brickwork wore a thick powdering of grime, and the window frames were rotting, but the front door, which was dark green, had recently been given a lick of paint. Molly stood on the step for a few seconds, bracing herself. As well as the usual musty smell that emanated from these houses, there was a whiff of something else seeping out round the door, a pungent, sickly smell.

Molly pushed at the door, but to her surprise it was

bolted from the inside. She tutted. It was very rare for anyone to bother locking their door round here. There was nothing much to steal anyway. What the hell was going on? Impatient, she rapped on the door.

Immediately she heard someone running downstairs and then Bert's muffled voice: 'Who's that?'

'It's Molly. Remember me – your sister? For God's sake, let me in.'

An elaborate performance of undoing locks and bolts went on behind the door, and then Bert's rat-like face appeared in the gloom. He gave a disparaging laugh.

'Oh. It's only you! What're you doing back 'ere?'

'Just passing through,' Molly said as he stepped back to let her in. She could see the shapes of furniture in the dark room. 'What's that horrible pong?'

''Oo's that down there with yer?' she heard Iris bawl from upstairs.

'It's Molly,' he said indifferently.

'Oh-ho – *is* it?' Iris shouted nastily. 'What's *she* want?'

'I've come to pick up the last of my clothes,' Molly said, moving towards the stairs. 'I s'pose you've brought my things here with yer?' She was already longing to get away. She'd known better than to think she might find a welcome.

Bert was barring the way upstairs, a nasty, taunting expression on his face.

'Just let me get my clothes and go,' Molly said wearily. Hearing a cough from the back room, she realized it was Joe, and pushed her way in past Bert. Startled, she looked round. There was a dim light bulb hanging in the middle of the room over a table she had never seen before, with four chairs pushed in under it. It wasn't new, but it was better than any furniture they'd ever

282

had before. Against one wall stood an old Welsh dresser, arranged with pink flowery crocks, all of which were new, and in the back corner of the kitchen was a gas stove. Joe was parked in his chair by the grate, as he had usually been in the last house, though the evening was too warm for a fire, even if anyone had been prepared to light one.

'Hello, Joe,' Molly said once he noticed her in the room. She wasn't even sure if he knew who she was, in her ATS uniform. 'It's Molly.'

Joe nodded. 'All right?' he said. He moved a trembling hand up to his face and fussed at his cheek as if some insect had landed on it. Molly couldn't see anything.

'I've just come to get my things,' she said. 'I've got to go away again for a bit.'

'Have yer?' He lowered his quivering hand onto the arm of the chair. It continued to shake.

'Is there anything I can get yer?'

He shook his head, then closed his eyes and put his head back as if to shut everyone out. Molly pitied him having to live with this stink. She pitied him altogether, but there was nothing she could do. And in his odd, twisted way, it did seem as if Bert was looking after the family, at least in terms of bringing in the money.

Turning, she saw that Bert was watching her, leaning on the door frame and barring her way.

'It's a good job you ain't coming to stop 'ere,' he said, and there was a note of pride in his voice. ''Cos there ain't no room for yer now. You'd better come up and see what we're doing, little sis.'

She followed Bert's shiny shoes and the pungent smell up the stairs. These, she noticed in the light of another dim bulb, had deep red carpet running up them, an unheard-of luxury in any of the other houses. At the top, a tiny landing separated the back room from the front, and Bert turned into the back one. Molly stopped at the door, trying to make sense of the startling sight in front of her. There was a narrow bed against the back wall away from the window, across which had been laid a flat board, covered in newspaper to make a makeshift table. On it, arranged methodically, were a number of large metal cans and several rows of small glass bottles, and in front of it, Iris was sitting on a chair, clothed in a satin confection of a dress in a harsh shade of peacock blue, all pleats and flounces and plunging neckline. Her legs were braced wide apart, the skirt hoicked up indecently high, and she was pouring liquid from one of the cans through a funnel into one of the little bottles. Beside her, on the bed, rested a half-empty bottle of Johnny Walker. Iris finished pouring, took a swig from the bottle, and, staring aggressively at Molly with bleary eyes, said, 'Oh – so *you're* back, are yer? I thought you was too good for us.'

It was only then that Molly noticed a movement from behind the door and realized there was someone else there. A young woman walked towards the bed holding another of the cans, which she put down near the others. She turned to look at Molly, who saw a thin, sallow face with a poor complexion, dark eyebrows plucked to a thin line, the eyes heavily laden with make-up. Her hair, blonde, unlike her eyebrows, was obviously dyed, and was scraped back from her face in tight, lacquered waves. She had a pert little mouth which seemed to express a sneering scorn at the sight of Molly. She too was wearing a fancy little frock, pink and too short for her.

'This is my little sister, Molly,' Bert said to the girl.

She made a sour movement with her mouth and turned away. He didn't bother to tell Molly who she was and Molly couldn't have cared less anyway. *Just another of Bert's nasty little bits*, she thought.

She stared round the room. Against all the other walls were stacked cartons. Some were open and she could see that they contained empty bottles like the one Iris was filling, but the others held other booty. She went over to look and Bert didn't stop her. He stood with his arms folded, a scheming, satisfied grin on his face. She opened one box and tapped at the smaller boxes inside, shocked to realize that it was crammed full of packets of cigarettes. In another, under the window, she prodded blue wrapped packages.

'Sugar?' She turned to Bert.

'Bingo. And here—' He rifled in another smaller box behind the door and brought out a sheaf of papers. Petrol coupons – hundreds of them.

'Are they . . . ?' Molly looked at him, only gradually taking in the magnitude of what he was involved in.

'Straight up?' Bert gave a sneering laugh. 'What do you think?'

'And what's . . . ?' She gestured towards the bed, the bottles.

'Perfume – straight from the boulevards of Paris!' He pronounced it Paree. 'The ladies love it – it's the scent of love!'

'Smells lovely,' Iris murmured. 'D'yer like my frock, Moll? Bert got it for me.'

Molly stared at the grotesque sight of her mother in the silky dress, fit for a glamorous night out, yet so tight on her that she looked more like a stringed ham, the silky folds pulled about in all directions. Her hair was scraped up chaotically, and she was wearing daubs of rouge and bright red lipstick, no doubt all courtesy of Bert. She and the girl were most likely drenched in perfume too, though the sickly smell was so generally overpowering in here that there was no way of telling.

Bert became expansive, seemingly enjoying showing off his prowess. He went to a box in the corner and brought out another bottle of Johnny Walker. Molly's gaze fastened hungrily on the bottle, a look which Bert didn't miss.

'That's it, sis – come down and have a drink. I know you like a drop. There's plenty more where this came from. Hilda – you stay here and help our mom for a bit. I need a conflab with my sister.'

Hilda stared balefully as Molly followed Bert from the room.

'Our mom dozes off on the job,' Bert said as they went downstairs. 'I like to 'ave Hilda up there to keep 'er going as long as 'er can. Help earn some of the money for all 'er finery! Right – go and sit in the front – the old man's in the back.'

When Bert turned on the light, Molly looked round in amazement. Everything in the room was new to her – a settee and two chairs, all in a matching brown, a wooden dresser by the wall with plates arranged on it, a rug on the floor, bright blue and gold vases on the mantel either side of a clock in a curving wooden case, and all sorts of other knick-knacks. There were even two pictures on the walls – sentimental portraits of little children, girls with long golden hair tucked into bonnets.

''Ere – get yerself tucked round that.' Bert handed her the bottle he'd brought with him from upstairs and went to the dresser cupboard, reaching in for glasses – *glasses!* He handed her one, then flung himself down in one of the chairs, lying back like a king surveying his empire. He lit a cigarette – the first of many that evening – and passed one to Molly as well. Molly, sitting opposite him on the strange brown chair, didn't exactly relish the thought of time spent with her brother, but the offer of free whiskey was too big a lure. And she was curious about it all. Bert was looking so flaming pleased with himself. She took a big slurp of the liquor, feeling it burn warm down inside her, beginning to soften the edges of the pain which lay so heavily, like a rock inside her. She was still trying to come to terms with what she had seen upstairs, with the new state of the house. It was no surprise to her that Bert was a criminal, but she was startled by the scale of it.

'What the hell are you playing at?' she asked. 'Where did all that stuff come from?'

'It ain't a game.' Bert sat forward, tensely resting his arms on his thighs. 'D'you think I got all this stuff just from some stupid game?' He sounded really affronted.

'How did you *get* it all here?'

'Ah well – that's down to Wal. Wal Spence. We call 'im "The Mole". His old man's an undertaker, over Kings Heath way. Now he ain't gunna notice if his wheels do a few night trips, is 'e?'

'You mean – in a *hearse*?'

Bert nodded gleefully, his shrewish face creasing with amusement. 'Plenty of room in a hearse.'

'But what about the petrol?'

'You saw – I've got all the coupons you could want. We've got a fella prints 'em up for us. Once you got your wheels – I mean there's a gang of us – Wal and me, and there's Horrid Harry, Soapy Joe – oh, and Fred.'

For a moment Molly felt as if she was in conversation with a twelve-year-old, the brother she remembered shinning over the rooftops of the yard to get away from

287

trouble; his little gang of bullies and pilferers, always up to something, always mean and sadistic at the same time and Bert always the meanest of the lot. She felt herself recoil from him, an urge to get up and slam out of the house. But the generous amounts of whiskey she was gulping down were making her feel warm and muzzy. In fact she hadn't felt so at ease in a long time. She picked up the bottle and hugged it to her.

'That's it, sis, you have a good go at it,' Bert said indulgently. 'Plenty more where that came from.'

She realized he was enjoying lavishing the drink on her, playing the big man. She sat back drinking steadily while, proudly and ramblingly, Bert outlined the under-hand plots and heists that were bringing his and Iris's standard of living up no end, not to mention being a draw for the girls who now seemed to swarm round him. Hilda was apparently the latest in a queue. Molly listened to a list of lootings at the railway yards and wharfs, of robberies from warehouses – one where they had crowbarred a whole section of wall away to get at the stocks of sugar now occupying the upstairs room, and one consisting of consignments of butter and meat – the last of which had proved a nightmare to get rid of, crawling with maggots when they finally despatched it into the cut.

'The stuff we managed to sell must've given a few of them buggers a tummy ache!' Bert chortled, then took another swig, straight from the bottle now. The whiskey fumes mixed with the strong stench of the perfume were beginning to make Molly feel quite peculiar. She couldn't seem to care whether what Bert was doing was criminal. She took big mouthfuls of whiskey.

'And all that in Wal's old man's hearse!' Bert slapped his leg with mirth. ''E's no idea of the trips it goes on of a night! We've shifted tea, lipstick, razor blades – and once we get that lot up there finished ... What shall we call it d'you reckon, Moll? You're a girl. I reckon Parisian Mist, summat classy like that?'

'I thought it wash called Shent of Love?' Molly slurred.

'Nah – that's just what I call it. D'yer like that? Shall us call it that?'

Molly shook her head and the room swam. 'No – call it Parishian Misht ...'

Bert leaned forward, deadly earnest suddenly. 'D'you know 'ow much we'll get next week, shifting that lot? Do yer?'

Molly shook her head more cautiously this time.

'Six hundred quid – when we've shifted 'em all. *Six hundred*. Now – don't tell me you wouldn't like a slice of that, eh, sis? Stuff the army! Why don't you stick around? I could do with a lady, a looker like you to help shift it. You could be very useful to me and the boys. I'd cut you in.'

Molly stared at him, glazed. She'd drunk an awful lot, fast.

'What're you talking about?' she mumbled. 'D'you think I wanna be in your silly little gang?'

Bert's face darkened. 'Silly? Silly eh, Moll? D'you even know what six hundred quid would look like, altogether in one place? Do yer? That's gunna be mine and some of it could be yours if you're not gunna be a stupid cow about it.'

For some reason the phrase 'stupid cow' made her giggle. 'Cows,' she said, and giggled again.

'D'yer want to come in with me or not?' His voice was sharp now. 'This is a serious business proposition, Moll – no messing around.'

'No!' She was giggling uncontrollably now. 'You and Mom and your silly little bottles – business ploposal . . .' She was losing the ability to talk properly now as well.

Bert stared at her, eyes narrowed, a half-burned cigarette jutting from the side of his mouth. Suddenly he said, 'Right then,' and got up and disappeared out the back.

Molly, with no sense of what was going on, or of time passing, closed her eyes. She was not sure afterwards whether she had drifted off to sleep, but she woke with a jolt to find something hard and cold jutting into the right side of her neck, under her jaw. There was a click. She could hear Bert breathing loudly. Her confused senses couldn't work out what was going on at first, but instinct made her sit still.

'Silly, is it?' His breath puffed at her ear as he spoke. 'Silly little business, eh? Keeps our mom all right though, doesn't it? The fat old cow's got more than she's ever had in her life before. And I done that for 'er – 'er son, see. Not Tom, or you – me. 'Er favourite – that's what I am. The only one that's stood by 'er.'

Bert reached round and to her horror Molly felt him fondle her breast, pinching painfully at the nipple, but she didn't dare move. Was that – that thing in her neck – was it a gun? Could it be . . . ?

'No one pushes Bert Fox around – no one.' He jabbed her harder in the neck. 'You breathe a word about this to anyone and you'll get this right 'ere. Right in the 'ead. If you don't want in, yer can clear off back to old tight-arsed Emmy-Wemmy.'Cause if you breathe a word, one of us'll get yer, army or no army. Wherever you are. So yer can keep yer gob shut, right?'

Molly's head had cleared, at least enough to make sense of this. 'Yes,' she whispered.

'Louder!'

'YES!'

'Well go on – bugger off out of 'ere – and don't bother coming back.'

He let her get to the door, then came at her, ramming the gun into her cheek again, his face stretched and vicious.

'Not a word – right?'

And she was out in the dark street, reeling, as if from a nightmare. The air felt remarkably fresh, free from the heady, cloying smell of the perfume. She struggled to walk along the street. She was shaking all over.

Thirty-One

They came for her the next morning. Cynthia answered a hammering on the door to find two redcaps on the step. Molly, feeling very rough, her head pounding, had to hurry into her uniform, to be escorted back on the train to Wales. Cynthia persuaded them all to drink a cup of tea to give Molly time to pack her things. One of the redcaps was local and seemed sulky; the other, talkative one, had a London accent and thick, hairy hands.

'You've been a naughty girl then,' the hairy one said when they set out from Kenilworth Street.

'Who told you where to find me?' she asked, struggling along with her bag, which neither of them offered to carry. Her stomach, her head and everything else felt horrible.

'We asked around – found your brother,' said the Brummie one, contemptuously. 'Proper wide boy that one, ain't 'e?'

For a moment she considered telling them about Bert, getting them to set the Birmingham police force on him. But she didn't trust these blokes either, even if they were military police. And what happened last night now felt so strange and unreal that she wondered if she'd dreamt it. Had Bert really pressed a gun to her neck? She knew, really, that he had. The thought of the cold steel made her shudder. But had he meant it – even

292

threatening his own sister? Would he really stoop to anything? Although she knew he was vile, it was hard to take that in. *Best keep quiet and bide my time*, she thought. With any luck he and his little gang would all get caught anyway and banged up for as long as possible, without it being laid at her door.

Sitting on the rumbling train between the two redcaps, Molly rested her head and closed her eyes to make them think she was asleep as she tried to still her pounding head. But she couldn't stop her mind flashing between competing images, each worse than the last. The previous evening came back to her in nightmarish flashes – the sight of her mother sitting in the squalid, dimly lit room, dolled up her in her gaudy black-market flounces as if for a ball, Bert's gleeful expression telling her about all his dodgy dealings, the hard-faced girl who'd been there, the cold snout of the gun – *'you'll get this right 'ere, right in the 'ead'* – and all the time, the reeking perfume . . . Drunk as she'd been, she knew it was not a dream. Bert had always been heading for this. And after all that, she never did pick up her clothes. Well, she thought grimly, I'm not going to need them now anyway. How could she have thought you could just walk away from the army? It had reached out and grabbed her again. And even though she was in trouble, she found she was pleased to have been caught. At least it got her far away from her so-called family again.

But the memories wouldn't leave her alone, the past flooding in. All the horrible things their grandfather – *father* – had done to her, and most likely to Bert as well. And to Iris in her turn. But she felt no pity for her mother. When, in all her life, had Iris ever been soft and

293

kind or protective? When had she ever smiled on Molly with love or given her anything that she needed? Molly thought of her childhood, cold, always itching with eczema and impetigo and nits, and the worst thing, the terrible burning pains down below, the accidents. She had grown up surrounded by the aura of urine, unable to control herself when the infections – as she now understood they were – reached their worst. Always sore, in pain, humiliated. *No wonder*, she thought, bitterly. When had anything ever been clean? Iris had never been any sort of housewife – she was too devoted to her first love, the bottle, after which children, cleaning, everything else came second, third and fourth, if anywhere at all. The army, with its rough and ready free-from-infection inspections every Friday, had treated her with more care than her mom ever had.

Pushing these thoughts away, she found they were replaced by worse ones. Grief over Tony crashed in waves over her, until she wanted to cry out with the pain of it and had to contain herself. She had never felt more wretched. If only she could have another drink! Wrenching her eyes open, keeping them screwed up against the light, she peered cautiously around her. To her relief the redcaps had both fallen asleep. The Brummie one was snoring lightly, mouth agape. Moving very carefully so as not to wake them, she fished in her bag for a cigarette, lit up and sat staring out through the grubby window. She let the green fields pass before her eyes, trying to force her mind to go blank.

Once she was back at the camp, the repercussions of her absence turned out to be quite minor. There were compassionate grounds for her absence – they all knew by now about Tony's death – and she suspected that Phoebe Morrison had also put in a word for her. Molly was put on a charge, confined to barracks for a week and her pay docked. No more was said. She soon returned to the early-morning toiling in the cookhouse.

Ruth and her group of Kinnys had long moved on to a posting along the coast, and now Honor had gone as well. There was a whole new set of unfamiliar faces, though Mavis was still with her in the kitchen. Molly had no spirit for getting to know anyone, though. Even when her hangover had cleared, her dark, grieving mood remained. It was a torment being back in the camp, every familiar path and stone, the scent of bracken on the cliffs, and the sight of the shifting sea reminding her of Tony and all that they had had. For a few days she lived in a dream, walking with him in her head, thinking only of him and all the times they'd shared, his face smiling at her as they sat side by side out in the salty breeze, and grieving at how all her future had been stolen from her.

Then, in the depths of her grief, she even began to doubt how things had really been with him. She'd loved Tony, of that she was certain, but more uneasy memories began to filter through. She could see now that all had not been well. She thought of their lovemaking, the way she froze and drifted off when he touched her and couldn't relax and give herself to him. She knew he had noticed, had stopped more than once and said, 'Is everything all right?' She had assured him it was and he must have put it down to nerves. But she knew it was something else, that through all the molestation she had suffered from Old Man Rathbone, she had cut off, mind and body, and now she could do nothing else. The thought made her feel dirty and despairing. If Tony had lived, would she have spoiled it in the end? Wasn't it that there was something rotten in her that would always turn everything bad? Look at the family she came from, after all! They were all vile and disgusting, and they were the flesh from which she had sprung. How could she ever have fitted into the family where Dymphna ruled the roost and she was expected to fill the role of devout Catholic wife? Dymphna had been so kind to her, of course, but she sensed that the kindness would have lasted only as long as she did things Dymphna's way. She had been in love with the idea of becoming a new person – different, far away from her family – a wife and mother. But would she have been able to keep it up? Wouldn't the old ways have come back to haunt her somehow? She had moments when she was almost glad Tony had died, so that he and his family would not find out about her and what she was really like. She could preserve their love intact, as it was.

The days passed agonizingly. Being back at the camp, with all the feelings it stirred up of loss and self-disgust, made it unbearable. Sensing her misery, Mavis tried to be kind and draw her out of herself.

'There's a group of us going into the village later,' she said to Molly, the second day she was back. 'Why don't you come along, pet – take your mind off things?'

Molly attempted a smile, but her face felt like a piece of rusty machinery that had forgotten how to move. 'Ta, Mavis, that's nice of yer – but I think I'll stay here. I'm not much company these days.'

'Well, it's not surprising,' Mavis said kindly. 'You've had a terrible sad time of it. I just thought it might lift you out of yourself.'

'I just can't,' Molly said, her eyes filling. 'But thanks anyway. You have a nice evening, all of yer.'

Instead, she went out to the cliffs and sat in the wind, cooling now, at the waning end of summer, watching the eternal movements of the sea and talking to Tony, crying for him. It was the one thing that could soothe the ache in her for a while.

'There's nothing here for me without you,' she said to the buffeting air. 'I hate it here now. Oh God, Tony, why did it have to happen? Why can't you just be here again? Be somewhere in the world, anywhere?'

By the time she left the cliffs that evening, she knew she had to get out of there. They could discharge her, move her, anything, as long as she could walk somewhere other than these paths, and breathe air that did not speak of him with every breath.

'Fox, what exactly is going on?'

A few days later, she found herself summoned to stand once more in front of Phoebe Morrison's desk. It was hard to read the sergeant's tone. It was not angry or commanding, just calm and measured, as if she was biding her time.

'What d'you mean, Sergeant?'

'I'm getting consistent complaints about the food. And when I say complaints, the batteries messing in your hut are almost on the point of mutiny. They say the food – if it can be called that – that you're serving them is' – she paused to look down at her notebook, apparently having recorded their expressions of indignation – ' "disgusting, inedible, fit only for the pigs". And so on. The other cooks have assured me that the sudden catastrophic dive in standards is nothing to do with them. Fox, on your watch...' Phoebe Morrison leaned forward to emphasize her words, '... *there was*

297

mustard in the rice pudding! What is the explanation for this?'

Molly looked down at her feet, but not before noticing what she was sure was a flicker of suppressed amusement in the woman's eyes. 'It must have been an accident. I'm sorry, Sergeant.'

'Well, I hope you are. Happily, I'm not the one who has to endure your cooking, but the others are *extremely browned off*. Understandably.' She paused, tapping a pencil on the desk and thinking, before saying slowly, 'Look, Fox, I know you've had a thin time of it recently. Look at me when I'm speaking to you, please. That's better. I haven't just called you here to reprimand you, though obviously this can't go on. There's something else I want to suggest.'

There was another pause. Phoebe Morrison sat back in her chair. 'You know, when you were in basic training, Fox, your performance was very uneven – and that's putting it charitably. In some ways I could see you were trying, that you wanted to fit in. But most of the time you were one of those girls who, to be blunt, looked as if all she was ever going to do in the army was be a pain in the backside. You'll have seen the type – they stay in the army for free bed and breakfast but are in every other way a complete nuisance to everyone. Your performance in basic training did not inspire us to place you in any trade more demanding than general duties.'

Molly listened, blushing shamefully. She knew every word of this was true.

'However, despite your behaviour, I could see you were no fool. I don't suppose you know this, Fox, but when you all did your intelligence tests, you came out in the top handful in that intake.'

'What – *me?*' Molly's head jerked up. She laughed for the first time in days, in sheer astonishment.

'Yes – you. Of course there were the educated girls, Chambers, wasn't it, and the other black-haired one—'

'Win Leighton?'

'Yes, her. Those sort of girls with a mathematical bent can get full marks without too much effort and go off into the more technical side. But you weren't that far behind, Fox. You must have a natural talent for that sort of thing. Some girls score very low indeed, I can assure you.'

Molly felt a bubble of excitement rising in her, the first really positive emotion she'd had for many a day. She was good at something – much better than she'd ever thought! She glowed with the sheer pleasure of being praised by Sergeant Morrison. She'd done nearly as well as Ruth and Win. Could that be possible?

'I s'pose I was always reasonably good at sums,' she said. After all, she'd been the one to help Em catch up, hadn't she?

'Where did you go to school, Fox?'

'Just round the corner from home – in Birmingham.'

'And you left at fourteen?'

'Well – yes,' Molly shrugged. 'Of course.'

Phoebe Morrison stared deeply at her in silence for a full minute.

'How would you like to retrain?' she said suddenly. 'You can be much better occupied than as a C-grade cook – especially one that seems to be trying to poison us all. I'm going to put you forward to retrain in the artillery. Mixed ack-ack. How does that sound?'

Molly knew this was a vote of confidence, quite unexpected, and though not couched as such, a deep act of kindness. And at last she might have a chance to do something more exciting! Her wan face broke into a delighted grin.

'Can I? Really? Oh yes please!'

Phoebe Morrison, smiling faintly, picked up her pen. 'I'll see what I can do. Dismiss!'

Molly turned to go, her heart beating excitedly, but then she heard the sergeant's voice bark her name again. She turned and looked into Phoebe Morrison's handsome face.

'You know, the army can be a very good place for a certain sort of woman – if you work hard and make it your own.'

'Thank you, Sergeant. I'll do my very best.'

'Oh—' Phoebe Morrison got to her feet, as if closing the conversation, but she gave one of her tight smiles back. 'You'd better, Fox. You'd better.'

Homefires

Thirty-Two

April 1942

Em opened the front door, squinting in the spring sunshine. In her arms she held her baby son, Robbie, who was almost three months old.

'Molly – you made it!'

'At last!' Both of them were laughing with happiness at seeing each other again after so many months. 'Oh, and look at the little man – I can't wait to have a hold of him, Em!'

Through in the back room, the two of them gladly looked each other up and down.

'You look so big and strong,' Em said. 'Look at you – all rosy cheeks – as if you've brought a whole lot of fresh air in with you!' A grin spread across her face. 'We're not going to have the redcaps turn up and take you away again this time, are we?'

'No fear!' Molly put her bag down on the chair. 'I've got leave for the weekend – we get away now things are quieter. Now – let me see this little fella.'

She held out her arms and Em handed the little boy over with a proud smile. He had a generous lick of brown hair and an alert, blue-eyed gaze.

'Oh Em – he's beautiful . . .' Molly sank onto a chair by the table. 'He looks ever so like you, yer know.'

'Does he?' asked Em, putting the kettle on, overjoyed to have a chance to show off her baby.

'Hello, Robbie – aren't you a lovely little fella!' Molly drank in the sight of the little boy, stroking his cheek with her finger. He let out a squeak of excitement and pumped his legs, making Molly laugh. Em watched, beaming with delight. She and Molly really were true friends now, she realized. Not like when they were children and Molly had had to beg for her attention. Things had changed – she'd come down a peg or two, and she'd gained a lot of respect for Molly – especially with the awful family she came from. Molly had stood by her through a lot, and they were equals.

'You look ever so well,' Molly said. 'You've filled out a bit.'

'Oh that'll soon go again,' Em laughed, bringing the cups over. 'What with him tripping the light fantastic half the night, bless him! Still – he's the best thing that's ever happened to me.' She loved being a mother. The birth had gone well, come naturally to her, and she was proud of that. She felt as if she had something to hold on to now, Norm and Robbie, her boys. Everything felt right, as if she'd found her place in the world.

'I can see. Suits yer.'

Em's face clouded. 'I just wish Norm could be home and I could stop fretting though. And our mom's not too good – having one of her times. She's in the hospital over at Rubery.'

'I thought she usually went up Northfield?'

'They've got all soldiers over there now.'

'Oh, have they? How is she then?' Molly asked sympathetically.

Em sighed. 'Well – you know. She was all right for a while and then something set her off. I don't know if it was Robbie being born or what but she went right down in herself, like she does. But I suppose she'll get back up again in the end. It's always bad seeing her like that.' She smiled, not wanting to be a misery. 'Here – have some tea.

Em brought two cups and sat down, smiling at the sight of Robbie, who lay contentedly on Molly's lap. It was so good to see Molly, and so much had happened since they last saw each other! The war had moved on – with the bombing of Pearl Harbor and the fall of Singapore, it really was a world war now – and no sign of it ending. The wireless and Mr Churchill's rousing speeches helped to keep them determined, but sometimes it felt as if the shortages and bad news would go on for ever. And with Mom poorly again, even though they knew now she'd get better, it always brought the family down. So it was especially nice to see a familiar face with fresh news.

'Where's everyone else?' Molly asked.

'Dad's gone out somewhere – probably on the hunt for razor blades. You can't find 'em for love nor money at the moment. Sid's doing a shift at work, and I sent the girls shopping for me, so they'll be ages queuing. It can take half the day. Everything's so short – it gets you down, trying to keep everyone fed.'

'It's easier for us,' Molly said. 'That's one thing about the army – you don't have to worry about coupons and where your next meal's coming from – even if what you get's blooming terrible!'

'I shouldn't moan, should I?' Em went on. 'Everyone's in the same boat. At least they've stopped bombing us. And we don't have those Skelton kids round any more – Irene says they're old enough to cope on their own when she's out, poor little things. But I just get so

305

tired sometimes. Anyroad, the others'll be back in a bit, so let's make the most of it. Tell me what you're up to – you're in Wolverhampton then?'

'Near there. I reckon they'll move us again before too long.'

When Molly left the camp on the cliffs, she'd been sent to Oswestry for artillery training, and from there to Anglesey for target practice, the guns firing repeatedly at a coloured drogue towed across the sky by a small aeroplane. Then on to Wolverhampton.

'I still don't know what you do really,' Em admitted. 'I know it's ack-ack, but . . .'

'Well,' Molly sat up straighter, proudly. 'Every battery has a team – the gunners are all blokes, but then there's all the instrument operators for the predictor, height finder, plotter, people on the telephones, the spotters. My lot – we're called the G.L. Girls – gun layers. Radiolocation they call it now as well. We have a transmitter and a receiver with four little screens, see, where we track the planes coming in, find out the height and where they are, and the people on the predictor work out where the plane's going to be and the gunners fire at it. You have to be careful not to jump when the guns go off and you're turning the dials, because your jump will go through to the predictor!'

Em listened, awed. All these things seemed a world away to her. 'That sounds ever so difficult,' she said. 'I couldn't do that.'

'Oh I expect you could.' Molly looked pleased though. She was good at her job, and knew it. 'I had to do an adaptability test to see if I could change trades and I passed that. It's better than flaming cooking, I can tell yer! God it's cold out there in it, though. You should see us, battledress with everything on underneath that you can think of – stockings, long johns, the lot!'

Em listened as Molly chatted on about the work, the fun they had with dances in NAAFI halls, the games and mischief, about the morning she woke up in Anglesey to find a cow looking through her bedroom window. She was full of it all, seemed to be able to talk for ever, the way Em could chatter endlessly about Robbie, given the chance. She couldn't get over how much Molly had changed, especially since last time she had come home, when Em had thought the army might not have Molly back. She seemed different – so healthy and confident and better-spoken even. Even her appearance was altered, her face a little thinner, so that you could see her striking cheekbones clearly.

'Sorry,' Molly said after a while. 'I'm going on a bit, aren't I?'

'That's all right,' Em said, holding her arms out. 'Here – shall I take him? He'll be after another feed soon.'

'He's ever so good,' Molly said fondly.

'He is.' Em took her little son and smiled down at him. 'Aren't you? A happy little soul. Even if your dad's not here to see you.' Her eyes filled for a moment, but she wiped the tears away.

'What's the news of him?'

'He's all right, the last time I heard from him. I don't know where he is – they've posted him abroad somewhere. But he's cheerful enough. And he's in one piece, I think, which is quite something for Norm! He's dying to see Robbie of course.' Talking away happily, Em suddenly became aware of all that she had that Molly did not. No husband or beautiful baby. She leaned forward.

'Are you all right, Molly? It was so terrible what happened, to Tony and everything.'

'Yeah,' Molly said tersely. Em could see that her grief was still close to the surface. 'Well – you know. I keep busy. The army's good for that, all the routine. Helps keep your mind off it. And they're a good crew I'm working with.'

'Anyone special?' Em hinted.

'Oh – no. I'm keeping away from all that. And the bottle. I don't want to get stuck in that. I'm a model soldier!'

'Sounds like it!' Em said, amazed. 'But it suits you.' She saw that Molly seemed to be strong enough to hear what she had to say next. 'Listen, Moll – 'fraid I've got a bit of bad news for you.'

She saw Molly tense. 'What? Bert?'

'Oh no – not him. *He's* doing very nicely thank you by the look of it. I don't s'pose we want to know the ins and outs. He's got the latest blonde bit on his arm; hard-faced little cow she is – called Ada I think, or is it Liza? No – it's about Mr B.'

'Oh, Stanley B?' Molly asked eagerly. 'You know where 'e is?'

'I do now. It took a while. After, you know, that night, they found out he had no family or anyone. They had nowhere else to put him so they took him to the workhouse, up Western Road . . .'

Molly gasped. 'Oh no, not Mr Button. Not the Archway of Tears!' This was the name given in the district to the entrance to the dreaded workhouse. 'Oh God, I wonder how 'e is! I must go and see him . . .' She started to get up as if to leave straight away. Em put her hand on her friend's arm.

'Thing is, Molly, he didn't last long in there. He went down with something and died quite soon after. Must have been the shock of it all, I suppose.'

Molly sank back into the chair, her eyes filling with tears. 'They were so kind to me, Em, both of them. They were like my mom and dad and I wanted to look after 'em – and look what happened. It's all wrong, all of it . . .' She broke down and wept for a few moments.

'I know, Molly,' Em said, her heart wrung at the thought of all the loss Molly had suffered. 'But I s'pose he's better off – you know, going to join her, than being in there on his own.'

'Yes,' Molly wiped her face. 'It's a mercy in a way. But if it wasn't for the war, for that bastard Hitler, they wouldn't have had their house bombed and they'd still be here.' She looked at Em, shamefaced. 'D'you know – our mom was born in there.'

'Where – the workhouse?'

'On her birth certificate it says ninety-something Dudley Road. Ninety-seven it might have been. They didn't put "The Workhouse". Kind of them, I s'pose, not to spell it out. Her mom died having 'er – I don't know if there were any brothers or sisters. I never heard of any.'

Em wasn't sure what to say. The workhouse was always seen as a place of shame and desperation.

Molly groaned. 'Oh, why couldn't that bloody bomb've hit her and Bert instead?'

Em looked shocked for a second, but then both of them were tickled by the sheer badness of what Molly had just said. They burst out laughing, and the sudden sound startled Robbie into screams of alarm.

'Oh, I'm sorry, little man,' Em said, rocking him

against her shoulder. But the two of them just carried on laughing, tears running down their cheeks. Sometimes it seemed the only thing to do.

Molly stayed that night with the Browns, catching up with Joyce and Violet. Bob Brown greeted her warmly after a surprised look, which Em noticed very clearly. There was a time when Bob would not have wanted to give rough, smelly little Molly Fox any houseroom, and now he looked startled by the strong, capable woman who seemed to be emerging more each time they saw her.

Em enjoyed having Molly there, giggling with her and her sisters round the table after tea, telling them stories.

'I wish I could join up,' Violet said. 'It sounds much better than working in the stupid old factory.'

'*I* could,' Joyce said smugly.

'You're only just fifteen,' Em told her.

'So what? I look older 'un that. They'd have me, wouldn't they?'

'That's not fair,' Violet said stormily. 'I want to go in the army!'

'I could though,' Joyce said, sounding excited. 'D'you think I should, Molly?'

Em had a strong pang of anxiety. She dreaded any sort of separation from her family. But she could hardly stop Joyce when she was old enough, could she, if the war was still on then?

'It's up to you, love,' Molly said. 'You'll have to make up your own mind. But you're too young just yet.'

'*I* look sixteen,' Violet was saying, though no one

was listening, since she was only eleven and hadn't even started work yet.

Desperate to change the subject, Em said in a low voice to Molly, 'Are you going to call on your mom this time?'

She saw a disgusted look pass over Molly's face. 'No,' she said. 'I'm not.'

The Viennese
Ballroom

Thirty-Three

Molly spent the next months with her battery, moving from gun site to gun site. They went to Norfolk, then to numerous different sites along the south and east coasts. When the church bells, so long silent, rang out on November 15 to celebrate victory at El Alamein, it was the bells of Leigh-on-Sea that she heard pealing across the gun park. Leigh-on-Sea, where Tony had been supposed to go, and here she was, guiding the guns instead.

Life was stable and busy. Molly immersed herself in army life and tried, apart from occasional letters to Em (whose own were mainly full of news of Robbie's teeth and smiles and sitting up), not to think of anything much else. It was easier to live for the present, not to think about what might happen once the war was over. And as Sergeant Morrison promised, now she had decided to fit in, the army was in many ways a good place to be.

The relationships within the battery were good, and she got on especially well with two girls, Jen, a very sociable girl from Newcastle, and Ann from Leicester, both predictor operators. Every three months they were entitled to ten days' leave. But even though she needed the break as much as anyone else, Molly did not look forward to it coming round. She wanted to stay in the orderly, purposeful army routine and shut out everything else. The thought of life outside now felt like a blast of icy air entering a warm room. After all, what was there for her at home? As Jen was so far from home, she didn't always go back there on leave, even though she missed her family, so once she and Molly had a couple of days away on leave together when the battery was in Norfolk. But mostly they just kept working.

Despite the hardships of army life, the sometimes foul, freezing weather, the long hours and petty discipline, Molly had never felt better. Getting up in the morning, she loved putting on the tough, masculine clothes that some of the others complained so much about, and striding around in battledress and boots, feeling strong and powerful. The routines were second nature to her now and she knew her job back to front. She was fit and well fed. Some days she felt she could take on anything. There were plenty of men about, in the battery and on the gun parks, and she had learned to be friends with some of them and no more than that. Most of them seemed to sense that she had shut down and did not want to know about love relationships. She told them her fiancé had been killed, that she was not over him, which was no lie. Gradually she was finding a new way of living, not hopping from one man to another without thought for what she might really want. And keeping out of all that made her feel free.

By the spring of 1943, Molly's battery had been posted to a gun site outside Reading, one of London's farthest-flung defences. It was a large site, with each group of four Nissen huts arranged end-on round the ablutions hut – an arrangement known as 'spiders'. Life was relatively quiet, since the raids were few and far between, but the routines had to go on, the soldiers' hard-earned skills kept up to date. One of the duties that had to be performed daily concerned the transmitters that were powered by generators which had to be started up; the stand-by team for the first duty shift of the morning had to take down the aerials of the transmitter and receiver, wash and re-grease them, and put them back.

On a freezing March day, Molly was performing this duty with Ann. They had carried out the routine hundreds of times by now, but on this occasion, Ann mentioned that she didn't feel well. Later that day she developed a burning fever, and was soon gravely ill, and this developed into double pneumonia. She had to be rushed to hospital.

'I don't think she'll be coming back in a hurry,' their corporal said. 'We're going to have to move in a replacement.'

A few days later, when the weather had cleared and it was frosty and bright, Molly and Jen were crossing the site after a shift on duty, banging their gloved hands together to try and beat some warmth back into their fingers.

'Here, slow down – I'll do your back,' Jen said. She walked behind Molly, pounding rhythmically on her back, and then Molly did the same for her. It sometimes helped to get a bit warmer. 'God – I thought the spring was s'posed to be here! It feels as bad as January today!'

'I'm dying for a cuppa,' Molly said. 'Come on – let's get over there quick.'

In the distance, a truck had pulled up and there was some activity going on around it. Two ATS emerged from inside and an officer pointed them towards the

Nissen huts behind Molly and Jen. The two women started walking towards them. After a few seconds, Molly focused on them, narrowing her eyes. One was a corporal, but it was the other who seemed somehow familiar and became more so as she drew nearer – the way she walked, and the strands of hair escaping from under her cap, vivid in the morning sun.

'It *can't* be,' Molly said.

'What're you on about?' Jen said. 'Who're they?'

Molly was only certain when they drew right up close. The red hair, the pink, pretty complexion.

'*Cath?*'

The woman turned, recognition turning into an over-joyed grin. 'Oh! *Molly!*'

'What're you . . . ?' Molly became speechless, realizing that she couldn't ask Cath such private questions in front of the others. *What about your baby. What happened?*

'I've come to replace someone on the predictor. There's a girl off sick.'

'Oh yes – Ann. That means you're in our team!' Molly cried, delighted.

'Look,' the corporal said impatiently, 'just come and get signed in – I'll show you your quarters, and then you can chinwag all you like.'

'I'll meet you in the NAAFI,' Molly called as Cath was marched away. 'Come and have a cuppa!'

Molly went with Jen to the NAAFI full of excitement. It was so good to see Cath again! But there were all sorts of questions whirling round in her head. They took their tea to a table, and Jen said, 'I'll get this down me and clear off when she comes, so you can have a catch up.'

'You don't need to go – you'll get along with her all right.'

'I daresay – but I've got a few things to do,' Jen said. 'No offence.'

She downed her tea and was gone even before Cath arrived, leaving Molly to peer at the posters on the NAAFI wall behind her. They were about the Beveridge Report which everyone seemed to be talking about – how they were going to make things better and fairer after the war. Molly sat musing on the few words she could make out, which spelled out the things the powers-that-be proposed to do away with: want, disease, ignorance, squalor and idleness. The words made her think of Iris, then she tried not to think about her. Too late for any improvement in Iris.

'You're in a nice daydream there!' Cath was standing in front of her, smiling, having fetched a cup of tea on her way over, and some bread and margarine, already curling at the edges. 'Did you want another cuppa, Molly?'

'No, I'm all right ta,' Molly said. 'Sit down. It's lovely to see yer. You look ever so well.' Cath seemed even more vividly pretty than before.

Cath stared at her. 'Well, you've changed all right,' she said. 'I never thought you'd make it, to be honest, the way you were in basic training.'

Molly gave a wry smile. 'Yeah, well. I decided I might as well try and fit the bill.' She didn't mention Phoebe Morrison's part in it. 'I thought they'd throw me out too. I ran off once and got brought back by the redcaps and decided to try and pull myself together.' Cath was listening sympathetically, sipping her tea. 'My fella – we were on leave together, down in London, and he was killed by a bomb. UXB. Knocked me aside for a bit.'

'Dear God, well of course it did,' Cath said, her blue eyes softening. After a moment she picked up a slice of the bread and held it up. 'God bless the bread.' She gave a wry smile. 'My granddad used to say that. His father lived through the famine. Never a crumb was to be wasted.'

Molly smiled, watching Cath tuck into the bread. But it wasn't the time for beating about the bush. Both of them had suffered. Despite Cath's cheerful demeanour, Molly could sense it in her.

'What happened, Cath?' she asked softly. 'The babby and everything.'

'Ah, well . . .' Cath took a sip of tea and cradled the mug up close to her face, staring into the distance. Tears welled in her eyes and she wiped them with the heel of her hand. 'I had the baby. I was sent to a home in London. They weren't very nice, but at least it was a roof over my head. I can't go back, see, to Ireland, not with the disgrace of it, and there's too many of us. What would my father do with me turning up with a fatherless child? Anyway, I had her, and I gave her up.' The words came out in a rush. 'My little Bernadette, that's what I call her. She's gone to a new mother, somewhere – I suppose she'll call her something else.' Quivering with the effort of holding in her raw emotion, still so near the surface, Cath looked desperately into Molly's eyes. 'Don't think the worst of me, will you? Please don't! I had no one, and no home to call my own. I just thought, if I can let her go to a better place, a family, and I can get back into the army, well, then maybe I can make something of my life. With her to look after, we'd have both gone under. Sometimes I tell myself I should've done anything to keep her and make a home for her. I'll doubt myself for the rest of my life. But I was frightened, Molly. They said she'd have a good home . . .'

Molly laid her hand over Cath's, aching with sorrow for her. 'I'm sure she will – they're good like that . . .' She had no idea if this was true, but she wanted to be comforting. Cath seemed so much older than before, sadness running through her like a crack in a vase.

'When she'd been gone just a few days, I reapplied to join up. They sent me for training, on the predictors, and I've been round and about ever since. Then a whole lot of things happened – one of our girls fell for a baby as well . . .' She smiled ironically. 'They stood our battery down and split us up to fill in gaps around the place – so here I am.'

'It's ever so nice that you've come,' Molly said. 'You seen anyone else on your travels?'

'From basic? No, except one of those girls from Nottingham, at my first training camp. The mouthy one.'

'They were all mouthy,' Molly laughed. 'Still – so was I, I s'pose.'

Cath soon settled in and became a regular part of the team. Jen, who made friends easily, got along well with her, as Molly had known she would. Molly and Cath were very happy to be back together, and there was a special bond between them, of past times, and of knowing the deep sadness that each of them carried. It was Molly who knew that Cath often cried herself to sleep at night, and she got up to try and comfort her. And it was to Cath that Molly could let out her feelings about Tony.

Spring passed into summer as they worked and socialized together, while the world outside vibrated to them from the wireless and newspapers. Much of the news was sad and awesomely frightening during those spring months. Calamitous numbers of Allied ships were sunk in the Atlantic, the uprising of the Jews in the Warsaw ghetto was violently suppressed in April, and the desert war against Rommel spread across that time. And one day in May, Molly's battery was told that soon it was on the move once again itself. Prepare for transit in two days, the soldiers were told. You're going for practice training – this time at Clacton-on-Sea.

Thirty-Four

As far as the eye could see along the straight east coastline, the artillery had taken over. All day long, from Jaywick to Holland-on-Sea, the bristling rows of guns were at work. There were heavy anti-aircraft guns up to the pier and light Bofors beyond, through Clacton's Butlin's camp. At the end, beyond a small minefield, were the Americans with Browning machine guns, pumping out ammunition at the plane which droned dutifully up and down the coastline dragging its target sleeve behind it. Behind, barrage balloons swayed in the coastal winds, tethered on any available piece of land. The army had commandeered Butlin's, and the town and surrounding area was heaving with army personnel, who had taken over many of the boarding houses and hotels. Some of these old establishments stood forlornly looking out to sea as if hoping for better times.

The ATS were housed in a row of boarding houses in a street guarded by a sentry at one end. When Molly and the others arrived, they all rushed into the house, bagging rooms. Molly and Cath ended up sharing a medium-sized room looking out over the street, with a wrought-iron balcony outside. The house had extraordinarily temperamental plumbing, the pipes coughing and groaning and occasionally, on some apparent whim of their own, producing a gush of hot water. The rest of the time, when the system was less accommodating, they had to boil kettles to wash.

Soon after they arrived, their corporal, a fresh-faced blonde, put her head round the door.

'Settling all right?' she asked. 'Marvellous! Right – tomorrow morning the transport will be here at eight forty-five sharp. Be at the front door on time.'

The weather was set fair and the work began. The old hands in Clacton kept telling them how lucky they were not to have been there during winter, with the biting cold and the east wind scorching their faces. During these balmy months they could get by in much lighter clothing and only one pair of socks. Molly and her team were sent to heavy artillery with a Vickers Predictor, the guns boom-booming in their turn as the plane passed across the sky.

One rather blustery morning as they were all heading for work on the gun park, an ATS came toiling along on a bicycle in the face of the wind, a scarf tied over her hair.

After she'd parked the bicycle, she strode confidently over to them. From a distance, Molly found herself recognizing another familiar face.

'I've been sent to be your spotter today.' It was Ruth's unmistakable, strangulated voice.

Molly turned away, heading for her post. The generators were already running; it was time to get started and she wasn't exactly keen to see Ruth.

The under-occupied Kinnys were being used to help out in the batteries, and Ruth had been allocated to the spotter's chair. This was a canvas swivel chair with movable arms and a headrest. Her job was to sit back in it with a pair of binoculars and record the success rate or otherwise of the gunfire. In the summer this was quite a pleasant job, sitting back in the sun. In the winter it was enough almost to freeze you solid.

They passed the morning working hard, and Molly, conscious of Ruth's presence, worked especially carefully and accurately. The hit rate was high and she was pleased with her morning's work. When it was time to stop for a break, she stepped down, stretching her limbs. Two hours was as much concentration as they could manage at any one time. Ruth was talking to one of the gunners and Molly had set off for a cuppa with Jen and Cath. But a few minutes later, Ruth caught them up on her bike.

'I say – thought I'd say hallo properly,' she called. As they all turned, Molly saw the shock register on Ruth's face. She stopped her bike with a squeak of brakes.

'I say – it's . . .' She searched her mind for Molly's name and clearly could not recall it. 'It's *you*, isn't it? And . . .' Cath's name was even more embarrassing for her to recall.

'Yes,' Molly said with more than a touch of sarcasm. 'It's me all right. Molly. The mouthy one.'

'And I'm Cath. The Irish one,' Cath added, with mischief in her eyes.

Ruth perched half on her bike, the gritty wind teasing at her hair. They could see her mind working . . . *But weren't you the one . . . ?* Everyone in the hut had known Cath was expecting a baby when she left. She looked mortified.

'And this is Jen,' Molly said.

'So – what're you doing here?' Ruth said to Molly, after a nod at Jen. 'Weren't you on general duties at that last camp?'

'I changed,' Molly said. 'I'm a gun layer.' She stood tall, knowing that she looked strong and competent. 'Been doing it a while.'

Gratifyingly, Ruth looked really surprised by this information. 'I say – jolly good,' she said, then looked at Cath. 'And you?'

'I'm on a predictor. You've just been working with us.'

'So I have,' Ruth said heartily. 'Well, well done all of you.'

'You coming for a cuppa?' Molly asked.

'Oh – no thank you. We Kinnys have a hut of our own for making tea. But thank you anyway. See you soon!'

She climbed onto the bike and hurried away.

'I feel as if I ought to bow with gratitude,' Cath said.

Molly snorted with laughter.

'Who the hell was that?' Jen asked.

Molly grinned. 'We were on basic together. She daint half look down her nose at me. Looks as if she's had to think again.'

Jen rolled her eyes. 'I've met a few like that, I can tell you.'

The girls had a lot of fun at Clacton. Although they worked hard, they were not under immense pressure, and the work was repetitive. There was still the normal ATS discipline, like the morning and evening roll call and attempts at PT, but things were quite relaxed. In their breaks, there were plenty of good times to be had around the town, and plenty of people to have them with.

Since Cath's arrival at the camp, Jen, without any offence, had paired up more with another girl called Nora from east London, and the four of them had a great many laughs together. Sometimes, during their time off they managed to get hold of enough bicycles and pedalled off along the coast. They explored the holiday camp, the dried-up swimming pool with its peeling paint, the chalets and mess halls, sand piling against their walls. The golf course was scattered with guns and predictors. They explored the long, straight coast, so unlike the high cliffs and coves they had been used to in Wales. And there were dances and games in the old Viennese Ballroom, which was now the gunners' NAAFI.

One day, once work had finished, Molly and Cath were in their room in the boarding house unwinding. That afternoon they had watched huge clouds massing which had then dumped their fast-falling contents on Clacton, and even though it was summer, they had got very cold, as well as wet. All they wanted to do was relax in the room's warmth, but then Jen came in, combing out her long black hair and bouncing with enthusiasm.

'There's a do over at the NAAFI – we're all invited!'

Cath groaned, curling up tighter on the bed. 'God no! I'm all in, and I want a bath, and the blasted boiler's having one of its turns again.'

'Oh don't say you're not coming!' Jen said. She was always full of life. 'Molly, what about you?'

Molly was lolling on her bed, boots off, with a nice hot cup of tea. 'Oh, I dunno . . .'

'God, you two are a couple of old maids,' Jen fumed. 'D'you not want to get out and have a bit of a giggle?'

'I would if I could be bothered to move,' Molly said sleepily.

Jen came and plonked herself on the edge of Molly's bed, bouncing so that the springs shrieked.

'Come . . .' *bounce, bounce* '. . . on!' *Bounce, bounce.* 'Yer can't just stay in here all night every night! Yer'll go mad and turn grey and all your teeth'll drop out!'

'Oh all right, all right, *stop it!*' Molly sat up, laughing, on the vibrating bed. 'You coming, Cath?'

'I suppose . . .'

'Right – that's settled,' Jen said, leaping up and going triumphantly to the door. 'Be ready in ten minutes.'

Cath groaned. 'Where does she get all her energy?'

Molly leaned up on one elbow. Half seriously she said, 'It's 'cause you and me are old before our time.'

The Viennese Ballroom was a huge, stately affair, with wooden balustrades supporting balconies above the dance floor. Two of its adjoining walls were fitted with floor-to-ceiling mirrors which made it look even bigger. Even though the place was already well filled when they arrived, with a band playing at the far end and smoke and chatter and dancing, the four girls still made a splash when they walked in. Molly and Cath both had striking hair and looks; Jen, though not pretty, gave off a vigorous energy; and Nora was small and sweet-looking with dark hair waving gently round her cheeks.

It had still been raining as they made their way to the Butlin's camp, and as well as damp, all of them were still in uniform, so it was not easy to feel particularly glamorous.

'Look at that!' Cath elbowed Molly. Along the top of one side of the mirror, someone had painted in large letters 'TAKE A LOOK AT YOURSELF. ARE YOU A CREDIT TO YOUR UNIT?'

They eyed themselves in the mirrors, with their heavy, masculine clothing, and laughed, fluffing up their damp hair. They were soon surrounded by male attention. They found somewhere to sit, the men brought beers over and they all took it in turn to dance. Molly, living her careful, sober life now, was careful not to drink too much, or give anyone any encouragement, and for the most part, she and the girls all sat and had a laugh together. But there was one man there that night who she couldn't help noticing. He was a huge, burly fellow with thick, dark hair which, even when shorn into a service haircut, looked as if it was trying to break out and grow powerfully fast. He had a big, fleshy face and a general expression of happy good nature. He came over to them and introduced himself to her as Len Goodliffe and said he came from near Great Yarmouth. Smiling, his wide mouth revealed big square teeth.

'Fancy another drink?' he asked Molly. She could tell he had made a beeline for her. Somehow they were physical equals.

Molly hesitated, then said, 'OK, ta then.' One more wouldn't hurt, she reasoned. The other girls all seemed to be pairing off. Cath was talking half-heartedly to an eager-looking blond lad, Jen was laughing with another and Nora had gone off and was dancing with a lad so tall and gangly that he towered over her.

'Here you go,' Len said, handing her the drink and parking himself on the bench beside her. Molly found herself pleased to have his company. His big, smiling

329

presence was attractive and he was cheerful, and easy to be with. *Be careful*, she told herself.

'So where're you from, Molly?' he asked, holding out a pack of Park Drives.

'Ta—' Molly took one and they both lit up. 'Can't yer tell?' She smiled. 'Most people can spot a Brummie accent fast enough to take the rise out of it!'

'Oh – Birmingham. I got it wrong – thought it might be Liverpool. Shows how much I know!'

He asked questions about her family, in his Norfolk-tinged accent which Molly found quaint and soothing. She gave him a brief, cleaned-up version of her family – yes, she had a mom and dad and two brothers. She suddenly thought of Bert, at which a strange, unexpected shudder went through her which she hoped would not show, but Len said, 'You all right?'

'Yes – course. Just a bit chilly. I'm still drying out.' She switched the conversation to him as soon as possible. 'What about your family?'

Len told her he was the baby of the family: he had a brother and three older sisters. His family were farmers. From the way he talked about them it sounded a loving family. He also, as he soon told Molly, had a fiancée, Sheila, from another farming family, who had stayed at home to work the land. They were planning to marry in a few months, when he would go home on leave.

Molly felt relief wash through her, only slightly tinged with disappointment. She had no need to worry that Len might want to take things further with her – she could relax and enjoy the company of a friendly man, without any other complications.

The evening rushed past very quickly and enjoyably. They swapped stories of their army history. Len let out his big, rumbling laugh when she told him about some of her antics as a cook, cigarette smoke drifting from between his lips as he did so. He told her he was a mechanic, on the permanent staff at Clacton.

'I've always loved cars and engines – ever since I can remember. My mother says my first word was "wheels"!'

Molly laughed. 'Don't s'pose our mom remembers what mine was.'

Len looked surprised. 'Why's that?'

'Oh—' Molly wished she hadn't said it. 'Her memory's not very good, that's all.' *Not to mention the fact that she's drunk as a skunk most of the time and doesn't give a toss what I say.*

She and Len talked all evening amid all the dancing and larking around, almost forgetting about everyone else. She was so relaxed in his company that she found herself telling him about Tony, just the bare facts of what had happened, not going into it all too much because she didn't want to break down and cry.

'Dear God,' Len said, looking at her aghast. 'What a flaming awful thing to happen. I don't know how you'd get over something like that.'

'No,' Molly said wanly. 'Neither do I.'

And she sensed he'd understood that now she could only be alone, and that since he had a fiancée, they could, without confusion, be friends.

'You looked very thick with that big strapping fella,' Cath said as they made their way back to their lodgings that night.

'Len – yeah, he's nice. But before you get excited, he's promised to a girl called Sheila, so don't you go getting the wrong idea! What about that bloke you were with?'

'Oh—' Cath said dismissively. 'He was a terrible stodgy one! D'you know, I don't know what's come over me, but I can't seem to get on with men at all these days. They all seem so young and a waste of time – either that or older and dull as suet pudding.'

'Oh dear,' Molly laughed, 'you are in a bad way. Seems Jen got on all right with her bloke – I ain't seen her for hours!'

'Well, good luck to her,' Cath said tartly. 'I'm more interested in getting into a nice warm bed and getting a good night's sleep!'

Thirty-Five

'Are you walking out with that fella of yours again tonight then?' Jen demanded a couple of weeks later as she and Molly and the others jolted from side to side in the truck to the gun park. 'I should think you'll soon be joined at the hip!'

'I'm not "walking out" with him,' Molly bawled over the rumbling engine. 'Well, not like you mean, anyway.'

Jen looked sceptically at her. 'Looks mighty like it to me.'

'I told you – he's getting married soon! He just wants some company, that's all.'

Even Cath was giving her funny looks. 'Well I hope that Sheila knows what he's up to, that's all.'

'He's not up to anything!' Molly exploded, losing patience. 'For heaven's sake all of yer – leave me alone!'

Len was safe and there was nothing in it, that was what Molly kept telling herself. He had a fiancée – he almost had a wedding date. And nothing had happened – he had not tried anything on, made as if to kiss her, nothing like that. But suddenly, he was everywhere. He seemed to pop up at every opportunity and be very keen to have her company. And she couldn't help being pleased every time she saw his burly frame and amiable face approaching. He was kind, friendly, reassuringly solid and capable, and as there was no threat to her she relaxed into being with him. After all, she would almost certainly have left Clacton within another month, and he would go off and be married. They were just ships passing in the night, so why not enjoy it?

They went to the NAAFI at Butlin's, sometimes with the others, sometimes without. They went for walks and bicycle rides, and then one Sunday after church parade (which they avoided if possible), Len suggested they take a trip to Colchester.

'It's the oldest town in the country, so they say,' he told her. 'I've never been. It'd be nice to go and have a look.'

They spent a warm afternoon looking round the old town, and found a tea room where they could have tea and strawberry tarts – an enormous luxury!

'I've never tried one of these before,' Molly said, gazing at the bright red syrupy tarts. 'My mouth's watering already – I'm drooling worse than a dog!'

Len laughed. 'Oh, my mother grows strawberries, so she makes tarts like this. I bet these aren't as good.' He sank his big teeth into it. 'Close,' he said indistinctly, through a mouthful of pastry.

'You've got a garden then?' Molly said. His life seemed magical, being so utterly different from hers.

'Well, yes.' Len looked surprised at the question. 'It's a farm – there's always plenty of room for things like that. Why – don't you?'

Molly thought of the gloomy yards at the back in Lupin Street and laughed, blushing. 'No. We live right in the middle of Brum. There ain't room for that sort of thing.'

Len was looking at her, seeming puzzled by her laughter. He kept staring, as if he couldn't stop, the tea and cake forgotten, and this made Molly feel self-conscious. She stirred sugar into her tea, avoiding his gaze.

'Tell me about your farm,' she said, to break the silence. 'What's it like?'

Len lit a cigarette and, resting his elbow on the table, happily told her about his home. Watching his face light up as he talked about it, Molly was soon with him in a country world of carrot and potato picking, of dew-drenched summer mornings, hens picking their way across the garden leaving warm eggs for them to collect, the pig called Bertha in a sty at the back, the ducks and dogs.

'The ground's very fertile there see,' Len said with a twinkle in his eye. 'Come the summer, when all the veg crops are coming up, you can see nothing for miles but spuds and carrots and peas and you can hear 'em growing.'

'No – you can't really, can yer?'

'You can,' he said, solemnly.

'What do they sound like?'

'Well – they make a sort of creaking noise, and then, if they grow too fast and they knock into a stone or something, they let out a shriek!' Only then did she notice his lips curling.

'Oh – you're having me on! You cheeky bugger – you can't hear anything. I knew it! You must think I'm a right soft-headed townie! Here – give me one of them to make up!' She picked up his cigarettes and took one, fumbling with the matches. 'It sounds lovely though, where you live. I wish I could live in the country.'

He told her about his dogs then, an old black Labra-dor called Jet, who was really his father's, and a mongrel called Toffee.

'He's mine,' he explained. 'We had him off Sheila's farm when he was a tiny pup. He was always a lovely colour, sort of caramel brown with black brindling in 'im. And he's *fast*. He'll be out round the farm with you all day and it's a job ever to tire 'im out.' He shook his head fondly. 'Ah – 'e's a one. Wish I could have a dog here with me. That's the life – out in the fresh air all day, your dog running along beside you.'

'Sounds lovely,' Molly said wistfully. It was all another world to her. She felt a longing. What would it be like to live that country, fresh-air life?

'I'll have to show you, one day.' Len blew out a mouthful of smoke and suddenly he was gazing at her again, that long look, as if he was drinking her in.

'You got your wedding planned yet then?' she asked, pointedly, because though she didn't want to, she was having to admit to herself that she knew there was a lot in that look. She had sensed over the past few times she had been with Len that he was falling in love with her. At first she told herself she was just being silly, that he was just a sweet bloke who gave you nice smiles. But the fact that he wanted to be with her every spare moment he could, the way he was looking at her – no, it was beginning to seem like more than that.

Her words broke the spell. Len coughed and fiddled with his teacup. 'No – not yet. Sheila's an old-fashioned sort of girl – believes in waiting and all that. There's no hurrying her. She's always saying she wishes we could get married once the war is over, but I told her, it could go on for years yet, the way things are going.'

'Ah well – I s'pect you'll get it sorted out next time you go on leave,' Molly said briskly. She had begun to feel forced to work all the time at keeping things at bay while she was with Len. To prevent his feelings developing – or was it hers as well? She could hardly admit to herself that this gentle giant of a man aroused a lot of tender longing in her, a longing which she had buried since Tony.

She changed the subject and started to tell him about Ruth. She had mentioned her before, meeting Ruth again and the way Ruth was so ill at ease with her.

'I don't know why, but she always looks really frightened of me,' Molly complained. 'She always did, even when we were in basic. Mind you, I had a bit of a big mouth on me then and I've quietened down since . . .'

'*Really?*' Len teased.

'Yes, really!' Molly retorted indignantly. 'I was one of the naughty ones back then, didn't fit in at all. Then things changed. There was this sergeant we had, she helped me out, made me see that army was good for me. But anyroad – Ruth. I saw her again the other day and she came up to me, all stiff, as if she can't move her neck or summat, and she says' – Molly tightened her throat to imitate Ruth's voice – ' "I say – just wanted to mention, Molly, that I'm frightfully impressed by the way you've progressed. I almost didn't recognize you – you've come on in leaps and bounds. Jolly well done!" '

Len roared with laughter at the imitation. 'Does she really speak like that?'

'Yes – as if someone's throttling her!'

'And she's scared of you, you think?'

'I dunno – she seems to be.'

'Well,' he said, twinkling at her. He leaned forward, pushed the cup away and rested his arms on the table. 'That I can understand.'

'Oi you!' Molly pretended to kick him under the table. But he had come up close, intimately, so she sat back to open a wider space between them. They finished their tarts and tea and wound their way back towards the railway station. Molly was thankful to be outside. She knew that the atmosphere had changed between them, as if a line had been crossed in those moments. Fortunately there was plenty outside to distract them. Colchester was a training garrison for troops from many different countries, and they heard snatches of different languages and accents among the servicemen – Australians and Poles, Czechs and Indians in all their varied uniforms – moving to and from the station.

Len stopped near the entrance to the busy railway station, by the wall, to keep out of everyone's way, watching all the coming and going around them with interest. 'I'd like to see more of the world, wouldn't you?'

'Would you want to get posted abroad?' She saw a glimmer of an answer to her problems – he would be gone! And then a pang – she knew how much she would miss him.

'Maybe – that's not how I'd want to see it though, not at war, being pushed around here, there and everywhere.'

'What would you want then?' she joked. 'A cruise?'

'Oh, no! Just – I don't know . . .' He sounded awkward. 'To take off for as long as I wanted and travel about, see the world, all the different places. With – well, with someone special.'

He turned to her, with that look again, and a moment later he had drawn her close into his arms, and was kissing her urgently on the lips.

Thirty-Six

Travelling back in the train from Colchester, Molly and Len were both silent for a long time, neither wanting to admit what had just happened. Molly sat by the window, her face turned away from him, though she was blind to the countryside passing outside. Her thoughts were in turmoil. His kiss, the feeling of being held close to his big, sturdy, farmer's boy body had woken all the longing in Molly which she had locked away since Tony was killed. She had responded – there was no denying that – she hadn't been able to help it. Len was lovely, he was everything she could want, now that she had mourned Tony and time had passed. He was no match for Tony – no one could be – but he made her feel safe and wanted. And the way he looked at her and had kissed her! And God help her, she had kissed him back. But he was engaged, he belonged to someone else. *So why was he messing about with her?*

Anger boiled up in her so suddenly that she didn't care who else heard. The crowded compartment was treated to a dose of her wrath.

'Don't you *dare* ever do that again!' she erupted. 'What the hell d'yer think you're playing at? What about Sheila? Or had you forgotten about her all of a sudden?'

Molly was dimly aware that everyone in the compartment was looking studiedly elsewhere in embarrassment, except for a little freckle-faced girl who stared with blatant curiosity at this unexpected form of entertainment.

Len put his hand on hers as if to quieten her, but she shook him off. 'Don't touch me!

'Molly, please...' He was blushing, speaking in a soothing way, as if to a wayward horse, which did nothing to make Molly feel less annoyed. 'Not here – I can't talk like this in here.'

'All right,' Molly hissed back, glaring at him. 'When we get off then. But you'd better've got your story straight by then.'

The rest of the journey was an agony of bad feeling. By the time they were released into Clacton Station, both of them were weary and miserable. Len drew her to one side amid the busyness around them, his eyes full of emotion.

'We can't go back – not 'til we've had this out.'

'I should bloody think so,' Molly began, but her heart was no longer in a quarrel. 'Look, Len, it's no good. You've got Sheila and you shouldn't be playing about with me – and I should never've let yer.' She looked up at him. 'Let's just call it a day. I thought we could just have a bit of fun together while it lasted, just be friends and that, but it'll never be like that, will it?'

Len seemed lost for words. His eyes searched her face as if he was afraid to speak.

'I just—' He turned away in confusion for a moment, then looked back desperately at her. 'When I'm with you, Sheila seems so far away. Part of a different life. I mean, I love her, I do – but—' He turned back to her. 'I don't know – it's just how it was. Sheila and me were sort of childhood sweethearts. We were always going to

340

get married one day and that was that. Sheila's always just been there, sort of waiting for me. We never thought of anything else, I s'pose. But God help me – I love *you*, girl! I knew it was happening, that it shouldn't be, but I couldn't seem to stop it. You've sort of opened my eyes. Everything's changed and I don't know what to do.'

An ache grew in Molly's chest. Could it be true, that he really loved her? Could she dare to think that that was what he meant, when against her better judgement, she also felt so much for him? Now it was she who could not think what to say.

Len gently laid his hands on her shoulders. 'You're just ... I dunno. I feel different ... You *do* something to me. You're not like anyone else.' He looked towards the roof for a moment as if hoping for inspiration. 'Look, I'm fond of Sheila, course I am – she's a good sort, faithful and kind-hearted. And I feel terrible about her – but it's better to know now, before we get married and everything's settled. Molly, do you – can you – feel anything for me, the way I do for you?'

The ache of longing spread and burned in her.

'God, Len – this is a bit sudden. I haven't let myself think, tried not to – there was always Sheila. But you're lovely. Of course I ... I mean I do, yes ...'

He cut her off, eagerly leaning down to kiss her. When he drew back, she was pulled in even deeper by the look in his eyes.

'You're sure?'

With a feeling of falling she gasped, 'Yes.'

He drew her closer, holding her tightly, and said, 'Molly. My lovely Molly.'

*

341

The telegram arrived two days later, and for the time being took her thoughts away from Len.

19th October 1943

Your Dad died yesterday. Funeral Friday. Sorry.
Em.

Molly stared bewildered at the message. *Your Dad* ... Joe – of course, Joe! Em must have sent the telegram in the certainty that neither Iris nor Bert would bother to let her know. They couldn't in any case, because she hadn't told them where she was.

'Everything all right?' Cath asked gently, seeing the shock on her face. They had come back from the gun park to find the message waiting.

Molly was about to tell her, then thought the better of it. 'Oh – yes. Just a message from my friend.'

Cath frowned. 'Why did she send a telegram? Must be something urgent.'

Molly folded the paper, smiling. 'Oh, she's crazy about her little boy. She wanted to tell me he's walking about now, bless him.'

'That's a lovely thing,' Cath said. Her tone was so wistful that Molly could have bitten her tongue out. Cath's own child would not have been very different in age from Robbie. If only she'd said something else! But she could not have told Cath the truth. Her father, who was not her father in truth, had died. And the tragedy was that it felt as if he had never fully been alive. She did not want to explain any of this.

Upstairs she stood wrapped in a towel, staring at the bath as it filled, agonizingly slowly. The spluttering trickle of tepid water splashed down onto a rusty stain like a giant teardrop in the curve of the bath. Joe was dead. That mild, absent man who had sat vacantly by the hearth for as long as she could remember was no more. That man who sometimes screamed, who cried out and wept in his sleep, a man she had never known when whole and well, but who she had believed to be her father. If only he had truly been her father! Everything she had ever heard about him, when he was young, before the war, pointed to him being intelligent and kindly. He had been able to pick out songs on the piano. She had heard people praise his singing voice. And there had been a piano in their house when she was very small. The brassy gloss of its pedals against the dark wood were what she remembered. But it had been taken away by the Means Test people, since it was deemed that the poor could not be permitted to enjoy music as well as eat. The house had to be picked bare of any assets before they were allowed to fill their bellies. And that was not the only way in which Joe had come down – everyone seemed to agree that he had married beneath him. He'd been an apprentice engineer before the war. Iris, handsome, lively and seductive, had put on her best side for him and he was overwhelmed.

For a moment Molly even pitied Iris. What chance had she stood: her mother dead in the workhouse, William Rathbone for a father, and a shell-shocked wreck for a husband? But her pity did not last long. Even with all that, surely she could have at least have found some grains of kindness for her children? Loathing of Iris's sadistic cruelty and her slovenly neglect outweighed any pity for her.

But for Joe, she found tears running down her cheeks, and was glad that the running water covered the sound of her sobs as she perched on the little stool and let herself weep. Joe had been a good man whose youth and life was stolen. He may not have been her father, but all her life she had lived in close intimacy with his bewildered blue eyes and prematurely bald head, his quivering hands and childlike physical needs. In his way he had been the one benign presence in the house and all that time she had at least believed him to be her father. She mourned him as a daughter and this mourning combined with all her loss and sadness over Tony. She wept from the depths of her.

At last she sat up straight, wiping her eyes. Would she ask for leave to go to his funeral? No – she knew she would not. Joe, the one streak of decency in her family, was gone – only the vile remnant remained. The thought made her so very lonely – they were all she had in the world. For a moment she imagined pouring out the story to Len. How would it feel to lay everything before him, all the things she never said to anyone, every dark corner of her life, and trust him enough to know that he would not turn away in disgust?

Dismissing the thought, she stood up, wearily, to turn off the tap and then drew the towel from round her to step into the bath. How could she ever trust anybody, however kind, with news of a family as foul and shameful as hers? No, none of that could ever be told, not to anyone. It would have to stay locked inside her for ever.

Thirty-Seven

'So – you're not going to tell us you're "just friends" with him now, are yer?' Jen teased. 'Look at you, slapping it on!'

She leaned over Molly's shoulder as Molly made up her eyes. The NAAFI shop had a small supply of Innoxa make-up and the girls had clubbed together for eyeshadow, mascara and lipstick to share for the Hallowe'en dance. Jen had come into Molly and Cath's room for a girls' getting-ready session. They all had to wear uniform, but everyone did their best to prettify it the best they could, making themselves up and pulling their belts in tight.

Molly stuck her tongue out at Jen in the mirror. 'Wouldn't you like to know?'

Jen pulled her sharp features into a gargoyle expression and they both laughed.

'Yeah, I would. Come on – we're supposed to be pals.'

'Ah leave her be,' Cath said from behind them, pulling on her clean uniform shirt. 'You can see she's in love – it's all over her. Oh—' She stood in a self-mocking pose in her shirt and army-issue khaki underwear. 'Don't you just feel the business in these passion-killers? I feel ready for a night of seduction in these all right.'

'Thought you weren't interested in seduction,' Molly said, applying mascara to her lashes.

'No, well I'm not . . .'

'Well you look gorgeous anyway,' Molly said, and of course she did.

'Eh – we'll find out who your mystery lover is,' Jen said. 'It's Hallowe'en! You hold a candle by the mirror and see him looking over your shoulder. Hang on, lovely lassies – I'll get that candle from the kitchen.'

They heard her footsteps clatter down the uncarpeted stairs and she was soon back, holding a lighted candle.

'One at a time now!'

The three of them giggled, taking their turn in front of the mirror as the others held up the candle. Molly watched half seriously as Jen held the candle beside her. In her mind she willed Len to appear, as if she needed confirmation from somewhere beyond her own feelings to tell her she was right about him. She looked into the darkness beyond her shoulder, but nothing appeared. On the other side of her, Jen and Cath peered intently into the glass.

'Can yer see him?' Jen asked.

'No!' Molly wailed in mock dismay.

'Well, how could he not love yer, lass?' Jen gave her a squeeze. 'God I wish I had your hair.' She fingered Molly's thick golden locks. 'You're a stunner. Right, my turn!'

Her dark eyes danced with laughter as they all looked again. Nothing.

'Ah well, someone'll come along sooner or later I s'pose.' Jen was never without a bloke in tow anyway. Then Cath's turn came, her tendrils of hair glowing red in the candlelight, her face wearing an expression of cynical patience.

'Well I wasn't expecting anything.' She shrugged ruefully. 'That's the best way – don't expect much.

Especially when it comes to fellas, that's my way of seeing it.'

'You're a proper cold shower you, aren't yer?' Jen said, rumpling Cath's mop of hair. 'Come on – you never know what the evening will bring. You might end up surprised.'

'Huh,' Cath said.

The girls had been invited to the Hallowe'en dance in the Viennese Ballroom at the Butlin's camp. They had borrowed bicycles to get there, and hurried along, eager to get out of the damp night.

As soon as they pulled up, brakes squeaking, Molly saw Len step out towards them and her heart fluttered like a bird.

'Here's lover boy,' Jen hissed.

'Shut up you!' Molly said. 'See you girls later!'

She was still at a tremulous, disbelieving stage with Len. The sight of him made her feel shaky and excited. Could he really be in love with her? Was it possible that in her lifetime, two men could have loved her and wanted to be with her? All she really knew was that he was obsessed with her and she could not seem to help being sucked into his orbit. To her, that felt like love. Since that afternoon in Colchester they had met as often as they could. The pressure was off, now they had both admitted their feelings for each other, and there had been a few drinks together and walks along the low cliffs, snatched kisses in between looking out over the steel grey sea.

Tonight felt more serious. It was a proper date, and she walked proudly into the ballroom on Len's arm. An army band was playing, and their entrance into the glamorous space felt something like a parade. Molly knew that they were physically well matched – both well-built, strong and good-looking, and they made a handsome pair. She saw others notice them as they walked in, both smiling broadly at each other.

'Let's get a drink,' Len said. She liked the way he took her arm as they moved through the crowd to the NAAFI bar. The music made her want to dance and she was already twisting and swaying as she stood at the bar, looking laughingly at him. Len grinned at her jigging excitement. 'Then we can have a dance, if you like.'

'Thing is,' she confessed. 'I don't really know how to dance – not proper, like. I've never done it.'

Len grinned. 'Nor me, much. We'll just have to make it up. I don't care, so long as I can hold you.'

Molly felt excitement rise in her, the warmth of being wanted and desired.

It was the most romantic evening she could ever remember. Light glinted off the ballroom's long mirrors, which reflected the dancing couples, khaki-clad, glowing cigarette tips, brass buttons, red lipstick. The air was blue with smoke, and the grand space was full of sounds of music, talk and laughter. There were some at the tables round the edge, taking a rest. Someone had made a jack-o'-lantern and it stood on the bar with leering, fiery eyes.

Len led Molly onto the dance floor and showed her how to hold her arms for the dance.

'You *do* know how to do it!' she said indignantly.

'Well, a bit. I did go once or twice with Sheila. She likes a bit of a dance.'

'Oh, *does* she?' She couldn't help speaking tartly. Jealousy flared in her. Before, when she had been trying not to feel anything for Len, she was all consideration for Sheila, but now he claimed he was hers, she didn't want to hear all about their past times together. She wanted to forget that Sheila ever existed – and she wished Len could do the same.

Soon they were having fun, and Molly quickly picked up on the dance steps, the band playing 'Chattanooga Choo Choo' and 'Deep in the Heart of Texas'. It was exhilarating, and they both ended up laughing during each number, trying to keep up and not tread on each other or pull in the wrong direction. Other blokes came up, wanting to dance with her, and Molly went off for a couple, but mostly they stuck together the whole evening. She called hello to Jen, who was dancing with the gunner she had been knocking about with for some time. Cath also seemed to be enjoying herself with her date, a dark-eyed, smiling young man, and Molly was glad to see her chatting to him and looking cheerful.

They did sit out a number every so often to rest and have a drink, but there was not much time for talking, and Molly felt full of energy and excitement and wanted to be up and moving again. It was a night for letting off steam and having fun. She revelled in Len's company, proud to be seen with him, enjoying the admiring looks he kept giving her. But one question kept niggling at the back of her mind. Now that they had agreed they were together, had Len yet told Sheila? He had said he must write as soon as possible, so that Sheila did not go ahead with arrangements for the wedding. Had he done it – or was he holding back? Would he ever really do it, or was he just leading her on? But she tried not to let her doubts get in the way of a happy evening.

After a couple of hours of dancing, laughing and joking, they were both beginning to flag a little.

'I could do with a bit of air,' Len said.

'Me too. My feet're killing me!'

Len took her arm and they went outside. Molly felt the perspiration cooling on her face. She breathed in the salt-tinged night air. The laughter and music faded as the doors closed behind them and Len led her down the side of the tennis courts with their sagging nets, along the sandy path towards the chalets.

'Must be nice, having a holiday here,' she said. Instinctively they spoke in low voices.

'S'pose so,' Len said. 'You don't want to be in one of them in the winter though – they're perishing. You get water freezing on the inside of the walls!'

Molly could hear the low voices and giggles from other couples among the chalets, all having sought out a private spot for a kiss and cuddle. Suddenly, mixed with her longing and desire was the old thread of confusion and dread. Now they were alone like this, how should she behave? How should she feel? She mustn't throw herself at Len, not like in the old days. But she was out of practice – she had been avoiding men for the past two years. She didn't trust herself not to get it all wrong and put him off.

'At last I've got you to myself,' Len said. He stopped beside one of the chalets and listened to check that it was quiet inside. The shape of the chalet loomed behind him, even darker than the sky with its sliver of moon. Len's big, solid hands were very warm as he pulled her towards him. She could smell him, hot, manly. She wanted to be wrapped in his arms, to be kissed and caressed, for her confusion to disappear into him, but the nagging doubt was in the way. She couldn't help herself.

'Have you told her? Sheila? You said you'd write—'

She wanted to speak lightly, but her voice came out sharp with tension.

Len gave a brief sigh. 'Not yet. There's been no time. But I will. I'll do it this week.'

'You promise?' She felt like a child, weak and vulnerable.

'Yes. It's just – well, it's a rotten thing to have to do.'

'Well—' She pulled away, petulantly. 'If what you want is to be with her, then *be* with her. Just don't keep on messing with me!'

'Oh love – Molly, don't!' Len sounded really fed up. She could just see the glister of his eyes in the thin moonlight. 'You know it's not like that. I'm being a coward, I know. It's just it's been so long, and all her family thinking we're getting married, and mine. They're neighbours – it's going to be a shock to everyone. I'm just having to prepare myself. Just don't get all upset, love – I will do it.'

Appeased, she moved back towards him, trying to be understanding, even though what she really wondered was, if he wanted to be with her, why didn't he just get on with it?

'Come here – let's have a cuddle.'

They pressed close, his mouth searching out hers. Molly began to give herself up to the sensation of it, his warm lips, her hands stroking the rough serge of his uniform. They kissed for a long time and she could feel his excitement, his need for her. And she desired him as well, had not reached that dreaded point where she would switch off and go cold.

After a time Len drew back. 'Back there, when we were dancing, it was like the loveliest thing,' he said shyly. 'Just seeing you – knowing I was with you. I can't believe it. You're just gorgeous you are, Molly.'

Molly giggled. 'Well, that's nice.'

He leaned down to kiss her again, eyes glazing with desire. 'I just wish – well, that we could ... well ...' There was a pressure in his voice, words coming out in a rush. 'That we could go further. You won't be here much longer, will you? And then we'll be apart. I mean, Sheila and I never – I mean, she's not that sort of girl, not that I didn't want to ...'

Molly listened to him with rising panic. It was very obvious what he meant, what he was after. She could easily, out of habit, throw herself at him, wind him up until he couldn't resist. But then would he look down on her instead of respecting her the way he did Sheila? And she was afraid of her own reactions. With Tony it had been unsatisfactory, from her point of view at least. She was afraid now that she didn't have it in her to respond to a man the way you were supposed to. Something in her just shut down when things progressed beyond a certain point. And she didn't want him to know that – didn't want to know it herself.

'What makes you think I *am* that sort of girl?' she asked tartly. 'You just think I'm easy and common, do yer? Well I don't know what makes you think that.'

'Oh – no!' Len sounded mortified. 'I don't know why I said that. I just – you're so amazing to me, Molly. You make me feel ...' He was pulling himself together, back to being the old, courteous Len. 'Of course you're not. Just me getting beyond myself. I'm sorry. Let's go back into the dance, shall we?'

'I s'pose so,' she said sulkily. It felt as if he had poured cold water on her. She knew it was the safest thing to go back, but perversely she was now filled with anger and a sense of rejection. She longed stormily for Tony's wiry, urgent need of her, not for this stolid self-control. She needed his desire, to feel able to control him. So he didn't want her now, was that it? She raged inwardly. Why was he being so boring and reining himself in?

Back in the ballroom Len held her apologetically, though it took her several dances to recover her temper. By the time the evening was over, they were back to kissing goodnight tenderly.

'See you tomorrow, love,' Len said softly.

'Night night,' Molly said, giving him her sweetest smile. *My husband-to-be*, she added silently.

As she was drifting off to sleep that night, she imagined the farmhouse where they would live, with the pig, the hens stepping across the backyard laying fresh eggs, the haystacks and carrot crops, the sun always shining and a garden full of flowers and strawberries. She imagined lying naked in Len's arms, his touch, his maleness, his making love to her. Her body stiffened with dread. Longing and despair mingled in her and she welcomed sleep, unable to face her thoughts.

Thirty-Eight

'Molly! Here – hop in!'

The truck was waiting for her at the gun park as they came off their shift a few days later, stiff with cold now the winter was setting in. A mizzling rain was falling.

Len was beaming from the cab. 'Get in with me – I'll take you back.'

'What about us?' Jen shouted, striding up to them. 'Don't we get a lift in the dry as well?'

'Nope, sorry – you'll have to wait for the other transport. This is a military mission!' Len shut the window on Jen's curses, chuckling as Molly clambered up into the cab.

'Cheeky bugger – what're you doing here?'

'Well, we had orders to sort out the anti-freeze for the winter. See, you have to remove the thermostat from the water system, and seal the joiner and then . . .'

'Len – for God's sake, I don't mean what're you doing like that, I mean why are you *here*, now, with me?'

'Oh, I forgot – of course you don't want to go worrying your pretty little head about technical matters,' he teased, dodging as Molly reached over to thump him.

'Technical matters!' she fumed. 'Course, there's nothing technical about what I do, is there!'

'Calm down, little tiger – I thought I'd bring her out for a trial run, and I came here because I've got something to tell you.' He had been about to pull away, but he braked again, suddenly solemn, staring ahead at the khaki figures walking along the road, blurred through the streaming window.

'Well come on – tell me!'

'I've written to Sheila.'

Molly gasped. 'Oh my God – have yer?' Though this was what she wanted, she was also afraid suddenly. It made everything real and very serious.

Len nodded. She could see he was relieved to have done it, but also sad and uncertain. He released the brake and started driving. They drove about half the distance in silence.

'You're wishing you hadn't done it, aren't you?' Molly said eventually. Lately she'd been trying not to say 'ain't'.

'No! Course not. I just feel a bit sorry for her, me backing out on her and nothing turning out how she expected.'

'Well you can go back to her,' Molly said harshly. 'If you feel that sorry for her. I don't s'pose it's too late. You either want her or you want me – you'll have to make your mind up.'

'Don't be like that, Molly.' He sounded wretched.

A moment later he stopped outside her lodging house. A white sheet, hung out to dry, was flapping half-sodden from the balcony railings. For a moment Len looked miserable, then he turned to her with a smile.

'It's you and me now, sweetheart. What d'you think of that?'

Her heart softened, fear and jealousy melting away.

'I think it's the best news ever. You're my fella.' And she snuggled close and kissed him.

Things were sweet after that, for a few days. Len received a letter from Sheila almost by return of post. It was sad, brave and dignified. He showed it to her when they were sitting together in the NAAFI.

> I was always afraid you'd meet someone else, and I suppose now it's happened I shall just have to make the best of it. I'm trying very hard to be brave about it. . . . I always looked up to you, felt you were too good for me in some ways. I know I'll miss you terribly, but I can't help wanting to wish you well . . .

Molly saw tears in Len's eyes as he watched her read the letter, written on pale blue paper, in a looping, careful hand. It made her feel tearful as well.

'She sounds ever so nice,' she said.

'Yeah,' he said, very subdued. 'She is. I thought she might be a bit, well, angrier. She's taken it very well. I'm not proud of hurting her though. And she's buried out there in the country. I hope she'll find someone else in the end.' He stared wanly ahead of him. Molly felt herself shrink inside. She could see his regret, even if he kept telling her he wanted to be with her. And she felt humbled by Sheila's lack of anger or spite, certain that she would not have behaved so nobly if the same thing had happened to her. At the same time she felt very tender towards Len: he had been prepared to do this for her, to give up so much.

'Have you told your mom and dad?'

'Yes,' he said, sighing. 'I haven't heard from them yet though.'

They sat in silence for a moment, both awed by what had happened. *He's all mine now*, Molly thought. Instead of excited, she felt suddenly flat, but she told herself not to be so silly. It was her job to cheer Len up.

'Come on,' she jumped up. 'It's stopped raining. Let's go out for a bit.'

When they were outside, in the blustering wind, Len held her very close and looked deep into her eyes. She could see him wondering if he had done the right thing.

'You won't go and leave me, will you?' he asked.

Tenderly she stroked his cheek. 'Why would I do that?'

The news came very abruptly three days later. Molly, Cath and their battery were being re-posted – this time to Dover. Though they had known it was coming, Molly listened to their sergeant relaying the information, and was shocked to realize that mingled with her dismay at the terrible prospect of being separated from Len was a surge of relief which disturbed her so much that she tried to pretend she had not felt it at all. But the feeling of being trapped had lodged in her ever since she knew about Sheila's letter.

There was no time to see Len and tell him until much later that day. They often met up outside the ballroom, and that was where he was that evening. She hurried up to him and just came out with it.

'We're moving on – the order came this morning. Day after tomorrow.'

His expectant expression fell into one of misery and anxiety.

'The day after tomorrow?' He was rubbing the top of his head as if to make his brain work better. He seemed more uncertain about everything these days.

'Oh Len—' Seeing him, the news suddenly felt unbearable. 'What am I going to do without yer?'

He held her close. 'If only we could get some time to ourselves,' he said. 'Just before you have to go. I can't stand the thought of your leaving. Look—' An idea seemed to come to him. 'I'll see what I can do.'

Whenever she knew they were about to leave a particular site, Molly usually started to feel very attached to it. Knowing that this was their last day but one on the gun site in Clacton brought a sweet preciousness to the work, the place and people. Suddenly she felt very fond of the seaside town on the sweeping east coast, and the ramshackle old house they were staying in. She even gave Ruth a cheerful smile as she saw her go past to spot for another battery. Everything was bathed in the awareness that she was about to lose it and start anew yet again somewhere else.

She worked hard all day, trying not to think about Len, or the horrible unease which filled her whenever she remembered Sheila's letter. Every so often, Len's besotted face would float into her memory, and then the sight of him looking worried and dejected, and she was filled with confusion.

When he met her that evening, though, he looked very cheerful.

'If this is our last proper evening, let's make the most of it,' he said. 'Let's go out on the town, shall we?'

They headed out into Clacton and found a pub popular with service people. It was full to the gunwales and very smoky and noisy, with someone on a penny whistle, songs and screams of laughter, and they had some drinks and joked and chatted with some of the others. After a time, Molly saw Jen come in with her bloke and they waved at each other.

A piano was playing and people were taking turns to get up and do a number. There was a raucous rendering of 'Mairzy Doats and Dozy Doats,' and then a young, fresh-faced ATS sang 'Somewhere in France with You', and several others had tears in their eyes by the time she'd finished. Len looked at her admiringly.

'Are you going to get up and sing?' he asked.

'Not likely!' Molly said. 'I can't sing to save my life – least I don't think so.' She realized that she was not sure if she was any good at singing or not.

'Bet you can – you've got a good strong voice on you. Why don't you give it a go?'

'Don't be silly!' She was blushing now. 'I'm not getting up there, singing. Why don't you sing?'

'I've sung before – in church, when I was young.'

'Have yer? What did you sing?'

'Well, hymns of course. They got me to sing on my own sometimes. I was quite good then – course when my voice broke it all changed.'

Molly stared at him. It was another of those moments when a gulf opened up between them. What did she really know about Len? Her awful feeling of discomfort increased.

'My uncle's a lay preacher, so we go to his church – used to anyway, but then he died.'

'Oh,' Molly said. 'That's nice.' She had no idea what a lay preacher was. For the first time in a long while, she was suddenly filled with the urge to get blindingly drunk.

'Come on—' Len leaned close to her ear. 'Let's go –
I want you to myself.'

She followed him from the pub into the darkness and
the pub's racket receded behind them. A gaggle of
soldiers were talking and laughing across the street and
other couples, some having to prop each other up, were
meandering along the pavement. The sound came of
someone being sick somewhere out of sight.

'Charming,' Len said. 'There's no need for that, is
there?'

'No,' Molly said, glad he could not see into her
memory of the times when she had been in much the
same state, if not worse.

'Let's go and look over the sea. There's enough moon
to see a bit.'

He took her arm, holding her close, as if she was
very precious. She sensed an excitement in him, whereas
she was full of a sense of things not being real, as if she
was distant from everything, or in a dream. The faint
sound of laughter floated from somewhere.

The moon gave just enough light to make out the
edge of the land, where the black sea began. Despite the
buffets of moist wind, the sea itself was fairly calm and
silent below them. It was just possible to make out
where the pier extended out over the water.

'You'll still be looking out at the same water, where
you're going,' Len said, as they stood side by side,
looking out.

'Yes, I s'pose I will,' Molly said.

Len leaned round and kissed her on the lips, then
stayed close, looking into her eyes in the gloom. 'God,
I wish you weren't leaving. My lovely girl.'

These words pierced through Molly. Lovely girl! If

only he knew. The sense of conflict began to grow in her again.

'Have you told your mother and father about me?' he asked fondly.

'My dad's dead.'

It came out abruptly.

'What, and you never told me? How long ago did he die?'

She could hardly tell him the truth, that it had been just two months ago, since she'd never mentioned it before now.

'Some time back,' she said. 'He wasn't very well for a long time. It was the war, and that.'

'You poor girl...' He turned and took her in his arms, holding her close, as if deciding on something. Then, drawing back a little, he looked down at her.

'We must meet each other's folks. Look, I've been thinking a lot over the past day or two. Molly – I need to get things straight, to ask you something...'

Her heart thumped. What did he want to know? God, he barely knew anything about her, and what about when he found out! Imagine Len coming to Birmingham and meeting Iris and Bert, seeing where she came from, after all she'd heard about his wholesome farming life! She knew that was why he was attracted to her, because she was different, pretty and lippy, and drew men like bees. She knew that besotted look in his eyes. She'd seen it so many times before. But what about her real life and family? How would he ever come to terms with that? Why on earth hadn't she told him they were all dead while she was at it? She couldn't gather her wits enough to say anything, so she stood waiting.

'What I'd like to ask, Molly' – he was down on one knee suddenly, so that she was looking into his pale, upturned face – 'is if you'd agree to be my wife.'

Molly stood as if turned to stone. She was filled with complete panic at this reality which had crashed over her, at all it meant. There would be his family to deal with, let alone hers: his would be disappointed that he had chosen this common woman over Sheila, who they'd known since girlhood. Imagine what the wedding would be like! Then there'd be bedrooms where he would expect, even demand, her to give herself to him. But she barely knew him at all! She could never marry him! How could she have even thought it might be possible – her with her drunken mother and the filthy specimens of men she had had around her all her life? And though she longed for it, she just *could not* give herself like that, couldn't tie herself to him, fond of him as she was.

'Molly?' He stood up again, trying to interpret her silence. 'I know it's a bit sudden, but with you going away – and we know we want each other, don't we? Just say you'll be my wife. After all, I've let Sheila go – I need to know you'll be there, that my wife is waiting for me somewhere.'

Words seemed to choke her. It would be so much easier just to do what he wanted and say yes. But in seconds, the whole idea of her being with him, marrying him, had become preposterous. The fantasy dissolved. What the hell had she been thinking of?

'I can't,' she said faintly.

'Molly?'

'This is all a mistake.' She backed away from him until she almost toppled over the low wall of the

362

promenade. 'Oh Len – don't ask me. Not me. I'm not right for you, I'm not right for anybody!'

'What are you talking about?' He sounded lost and utterly baffled.

'I just—' She struggled to find words, holding out her hands to fend him off as he tried to embrace her again. 'I don't know what I've been doing, making you think I could marry you. I'm all wrong. You mustn't think you can marry me. I'm no good for you.'

Len came close. 'What the hell're you going on about? I love you, girl – I can't think about anything else. God, if it wasn't so wrong I'd take you here and now, I want you so much. I've given up Sheila for you – my mother and father are furious with me. That's how much I love you. You can't pull out on me now!'

'You don't want me,' Molly said, speaking low and seriously, trying to get through to him. 'You want to have me, *like that*, you want to take me to bed. Men always do. But you don't want *me* – you don't know anything about me, Len.'

'Well tell me then!' he pleaded. 'I want to know everything about you. But when I ask you, you change the subject. I want to know about your family and your home and, and everything!'

'Len – just believe me. I'm no good.' She was firm now, hard as steel. 'You'll thank me for this one day . . .'

'Don't say that!' He was distraught. 'Molly, what's happened to you?'

'You will. You don't want to get tangled up with me. I'm not much good and my family are terrible. I don't want you to know about them, that's why I've never said. Look, love' – she laid a hand on his shoulder – 'just forget about me. Go back and tell Sheila you're going to marry her. That's what's right. She loves you – no one'd write a letter as nice as she did if she didn't. I wouldn't have done, I can tell yer! Go and say sorry, send her a wire – tell her it was all a mistake.'

He was breaking down, almost weeping now. 'How can you? How could you make me go through all that and then say all these things to me, and turn me down?'

'I thought I could do it,' she said. 'I thought I loved you. But I can't – and I don't.'

Her heart felt squeezed too tight, and she longed to cry and tell him not to leave her, to be with her for ever. But above all there was the relief, the sense of escape. She'd never live as a farmer's wife in a quaint country house with hens pecking across the yard. Deep down she'd always known that, that somehow it would always have been spoilt and it would always have been her fault. But if she'd said any of that to him she knew he would never understand.

'Go on, Len. It's the right thing. Go back, without me. It's been a nice time – but I don't want yer.'

He stood, stunned. Then his face turned ugly. 'You stupid *bitch*,' he snarled. 'You stupid, spiteful bitch – you've messed up everything for me. Everything . . .' He was outraged, lost for words.

'Go and put it right then.' She turned from him. 'And, Len – thanks for the good times.'

And she walked away.

'Molly! You can't just go – not after all this!' She thought he would follow, but she knew, from the way she had spoken, that he had heard that she meant it.

She left him, and moved quickly back to the pub where they had been earlier. By the time she went to bed she wanted to be so drunk that she wouldn't remember anything, or think of anything. Most of all, she didn't want to think of the cold, harsh truth she had discovered in herself: that it would have been the same, in the end, with Tony. That it would be the same with anyone.

Homefires

Thirty-Nine

New Year's Eve 1943

'So come on, Ernie – what're you going to play for us now?'

Dot's sister-in-law, Margarita, a glass of spicy wine in her hand, leaned over and playfully prodded her husband, who was sitting with his accordion across his knees. Ernie turned from sharing a joke with Lou.

'Woman, give me a rest! She's a slave driver!' he appealed to the rest of the room.

They were all crowded into Dot and Lou's cosy front room, a little get-together for New Year's Eve. Em had gone along with Cynthia and Bob, pushing Robbie through the dark streets in his pushchair, and Joyce and Violet had come too. Sam was out with his girlfriend, Connie. Margarita, Lou's sister, a vivacious woman with her long waves of bouncing chestnut hair, was there with Ernie and their grown-up daughter Carolina, whose husband was away in the army. There was Lou's youngest daughter, Clara, and her husband and baby, and two of their elderly neighbours who had been asked to join in the party as well.

'Oh come on, love!' Margarita insisted. 'What's the use of you having the squeeze box here if you won't play it?'

'Give us "Auld Lang Syne"!' Cynthia called to him.

'It's not time for that,' Ernie protested. 'That's for midnight. It's tradition!'

'Well summat then – anything,' Dot insisted.

'Come on, Uncle Ernie,' Clara urged as well.

Ernie, a jolly, round-faced man, took a resigned swig from his glass and set it on the floor by his chair. 'All right then . . .'

He pressed the accordion into a happy jig and immediately everyone's feet were tapping. Em looked round at the faces, pink with drink and the warmth of the room. The two elderly ladies were clearly enjoying the company and music. Cynthia and Bob looked relaxed and Em was happy to see her mom giggling at jokes with Dot. The pair of them were like two girls without a care in the world, and Nancy and Joyce were doing much the same on the floor in the corner. Dot was obviously so happy with Lou, who was a lovely, cheerful man with a big heart like Dot's own, always with room for others in their lives who might need help or a bit of kindness. Clara, who looked very like him with her big, dark eyes, was smiling, watching Ernie's dancing fingers. Violet was parked at Em's feet, a bit left out, so resorted to playing with Robbie as there was no one else her age. But as soon as Ernie had started playing again, Robbie broke away from Violet and toddled straight to him, staring with his mouth open, absolutely rapt. The instrument itself was a lovely thing, creamy mother-of-pearl, and Robbie had been allowed earlier to try pressing the keys while Ernie pumped it to make a sound. Now, hearing the music again, Robbie's eyes stretched wide and he was bouncing and flexing to the music. He had done the same thing every time Ernie played and they all laughed.

'It's like snake charming, ain't it?' Lou said through a cloud of cigarette smoke and wheezing with laughter. 'Now you know what you have to do, Em—' He pointed a stubby finger at the accordion. 'You'll 'ave to get one!'

'Oh look at 'im again, love 'im!' Dot said. 'That's right – you 'ave a dance, darlin'!'

Em smiled fondly at the sight of Robbie getting all the attention. She heard Violet stifle a yawn beside her.

'Why don't you have a dance with 'im?' she suggested.

'No!' Violet squirmed shyly, hiding behind her brown curtain of hair.

'Can I get anyone anything?' Dot asked. 'Cuppa tea?'

Cynthia said she was dying for a cup of tea. 'I'll come and give you a hand,' she said, and she and Dot disappeared, giggling, out the back.

'Why don't you go too, Margarita?' Ernie teased, as if she was a tyrant he needed to get shot of.

'No – I'm staying here to keep an eye on you!'

Dot and Cynthia came back each holding a tray and looking pleased with themselves.

'We've got a little surprise for yer,' Dot said. Everyone looked. Cynthia had the teacups on her tray, but when Dot lowered hers triumphantly, they all saw a lovely creamy block sitting on a plate, and already beginning to turn soft at the edges. Margarita was smiling in expectation.

'Ice cream!' Violet gasped, amid the other oohs and aahs.

'We've all been saving up for it,' Dot said. 'Margarita showed me how to make it. There should be a lick for everyone.'

Making ice cream had long been a traditional living

for the Italians in the area, but had been banned months ago as so much of its luxurious contents was rationed.

There was enough for everyone to have a little square of the delicious treat. Em gave Robbie some of hers as well.

''E can't get enough of it, can 'e?' Dot laughed, seeing the little boy's ecstatic face.

'Thanks, Dot,' Em said. 'It's lovely. Robbie's never tasted it before.'

The ice cream was soon demolished and they drank their tea, but as the evening wore on, Robbie started to get fractious. Em picked him up to cuddle him, but his squalling turned into a full-blown tantrum.

'I think I'd better get back now,' Em said over his screams, struggling to her feet. 'Someone needs his bed.'

'You can put him upstairs for a sleep,' Dot said. 'It'd be a shame not to see the New Year in.'

'No,' Em said. 'I'd better go ... He won't sleep without me settling down with him.'

'You'll spoil him – I've told you!' Cynthia piped up. 'Mollycoddling him like that.'

Em ignored her. Violet scrambled to her feet. 'I'll come with you.'

The others, who were all looking very mellow, said they'd come on later. Em and Violet managed to get a wriggling Robbie into the pushchair and said their farewells and 'Happy New Years', and Dot kissed them goodbye on the doorstep. Robbie quietened down at the feel of the cold air.

'Mind how yer go!' Dot called, waving, then disappeared, not wanting to let the light out. Things were more relaxed now, but they were still expected to keep up the blackout.

The two sisters made their way cautiously through

the darkness as Robbie grizzled himself to sleep under a blanket, his cries dying gradually.

'That's him gone,' Violet said, as he finally sputtered into silence. The two of them laughed.

The streets were ghostly quiet, except for round the pubs, where there were sounds of revelry.

'Nineteen forty-four tomorrow,' Em said. 'It's a funny thought.'

'D'you think the war'll end in nineteen forty-four?' Violet asked.

'Ooh, I don't know. I hope so.' Em found she enjoyed Violet's company nowadays. She was growing up.

'I can hardly remember before it started now. I mean I can, but it seems like . . . well, it was so long ago.'

Em sighed. 'Feels like another life. Not four years – more like twenty!'

The sisters walked carefully, comparing memories of before the war started. As they drew close to home, they slowed down on a corner where there was a pub, to ease the pushchair down the kerb. As they did so, the door burst open and a man and a woman came out, on a gust of shouts and beery air. The man seized the woman's arm and she jerked it away, letting out an angry squeal.

'Gerroff me! Stop pulling me about!' she cried shrilly.

'Well shift then, Aggie. I always 'ave to drag yer along, yer silly cow . . .'

'Don't call me that. You're a bully you are – I hate you when yer like this . . .'

Em and Violet watched as they went on ahead bickering unpleasantly.

'You know who that was, don't you?' Em whispered.

'No – who?'

'That was Bert Fox, Molly's brother.'

'Oh yes.' Violet sounded disgusted. 'He's horrible, he is.'

As they followed, they could hear the same voices raised in argument for a few moments, before Bert and the woman must have moved on too far ahead of them. Em was relieved that Bert hadn't seen her. Whenever they met he always said something rude or suggestive to her. He really was a slimy piece of work.

'Nearly home,' Em said. 'Sorry to miss midnight and everything.'

'I don't care,' Violet said. 'It was boring.'

'They're ever so kind though.'

'Yeah,' Violet agreed through another yawn. 'And that ice cream was beautiful.'

They became aware that they were not alone when an odd little sound came from the entry of a house close by, a noise like a stifled whimper. Em and Violet stopped to listen. Violet gripped Em's hand.

Low whispering followed, and more stifled noises, then a little scream, as if whoever it was had been re-leased.

'Don't! Don't you ever do that to me! Who d'yer think you are, you filthy bastard!'

'Oh shut yer cake'ole, yer stupid bitch! Just stop keeping on, will yer? I've 'ad enough.'

They erupted out onto the pavement this time, him moving away with fast, angry strides, the girl trotting after. Though Em could barely see them, the voices were unmistakable.

'Wait – Bert!' She was half sobbing now, petulant and frightened at once. 'Don't – why d'yer 'ave to be like that?'

Em and Violet shrank back, standing quite still until the pair had disappeared. They walked swiftly into Kenilworth Street and were very glad to be back in the house, where they closed the curtains against the ugly scene and put the light on.

'What d'you think he was doing?' Violet asked, obviously shaken by what they had heard.

Em blushed in confusion as the obvious answer sprang to mind and she didn't feel like explaining it to her little sister. But she knew really that what they'd heard hadn't been canoodling noises. 'I think he had his hand over her mouth,' she admitted, furious that Violet had had to hear any of it.

'It sounded horrible,' Violet said in a small voice.

'Listen, Vi – I dunno what he was doing.' Em said, pushing Robbie along the narrow hall. 'Just don't ever go near him, all right? He's a bad lot.' She looked down at her sleeping son. 'I'd better get this one upstairs.'

Very carefully she lifted Robbie and carried him up to her bed, praying he wouldn't wake. He was very clingy towards her and normally wouldn't settle without her. But tonight he was tired out. She laid him down and sat beside him for a while in the dim glow coming from the stairs, stroking his head adoringly.

'Happy New Year, little man,' she whispered, tears filling her eyes suddenly. 'I wish your dad could be here to see you. I wonder if nineteen forty-four's going to bring him home to us?'

With an ingenuity that had taken Em by surprise, Norm had suggested to her before he left, a code that he could put in his letters to let her know where he was.

'I'll start by making the first letter of every sentence

spell it out, somehow,' he said. 'So if I say something a bit queer to begin with, you'll know what's going on. We're not supposed to let on, see, and they read our letters and cross bits out.'

Sure enough, before Christmas she had received a letter which began as follows:

I hope everyone at home's getting on all right.
Thanks for your letter, love. And for all the news
about our little Robbie. Let's hope he doesn't grow
up too quick as I'm dying to see him! You'll have to
take careful note of everything he does so you can
tell me . . .

She showed Cynthia the letter.
'See, look – I, T, A . . .'
'Oh yes!' Cynthia was amazed. ''E's a clever one – you'd never think it, would you?' She wandered off, smiling. 'I wonder what he'd've said if he was in Timbuktu?'

Knowing where he was made a lot of difference and she paid careful attention to any news about the Italian campaign. It made her think differently about the war. When they were all being bombed it had come very close: they were living the war. Then there had been occasional raids, but now they hadn't had one in months. Though they were left with grievous reminders of the Blitz, the people who were no longer with them, the wreckage of houses, shops and firms, by now the war had come to mean other things. It meant shortages, the endless worry and inconvenience of queuing for groceries, of making do and mending, of sometimes wondering how to spin out the food for the next meal.

It still meant dark streets, restricted lives, and for some, constant anxiety about loved ones who were away.

Em's life revolved around home and her little job with Mr Perry. Sometimes she missed Norm terribly, and felt as if she was stuck, forever a child, in her mom and dad's home, unable to move forward. But it all felt as safe and secure as anything could during a war. Mr Perry was kindness itself, and let her go home if there was any problem, or even bring Robbie into work if necessary. The war became bulletins about huge upheavals; Russia, Italy, the Far East, names which she had never heard before – Smolensk, Anzio, Bougainville – were on the lips of every household, at least for a day or two. It was all so huge, so far away, and for her, now, her real life was centred on one thing – her baby son.

Robbie was seldom out of her thoughts. For almost two years now everything had revolved round him. Watching him grow from a tiny baby into a sweet, toddling child had absorbed her. She could sit watching him for hours, jumping to his every need. Each night, she cuddled up with him in her bed, humming to him and stroking his sweet, fragile body until he fell asleep. He was the first thing she saw on waking every morning – he was her love and her security and she his. Even if she'd wanted to have him sleeping elsewhere, the only space was in with Sid – she was already in a room with Joyce and Violet, who now shared the double bed. And she didn't want it – she would have missed him terribly.

'You're a slave to that child,' Cynthia would say, now and again. 'You want to put him down to sleep and get him used to it, not spend half the evening pandering to him. If you had another babby you wouldn't be able to sit with 'im like that, would you?'

'No,' Em said tartly. 'But I'm not going to have another one at this rate, am I?'

Cynthia had recovered and come home, and of course her being well was a huge relief to them all. But Em resented living under her thumb and being told what to do. 'I don't have to do everything just the way you did, do I?' she'd snap at her sometimes.

Cynthia would clamp her lips together as if to stop a sharp retort from escaping. But something would usually get out, like, 'You're making a milk sop of 'im, that you are. He'll be a proper Mummy's boy.'

These conversations usually ended with Em picking Robbie up and stamping her way up the stairs.

'What's she on about?' she'd mutter in his soft ear. 'Bossing me about. No one knows better than me what's best for you, do they? You're my little man!' As he snuggled him up on her lap she laid her cheek against his soft hair. 'You're my everything,' she whispered. 'What would I do without you?'

She thought about the war, stretching ahead for who knew how long? Those drab, weary days, with her living in dread, like every service wife, of the letter or telegram saying that something bad had happened to Norm, and everything going on just the same, week after week. Sometimes it felt as if it would just go on like this for ever.

It was the end of January, and she had been at work at Mr Perry's all day.

'There we are,' Mr P said, shutting down the awning in front of the shop. 'Another day, another dollar!'

378

Em smiled, as he said the same thing almost every day.

'Tararabit, bab,' Mr P said.

'See you tomorrow.' Em already had her coat and scarf on as it was freezing standing in the shop all day. It was almost dark as she walked home. Keeping her head down, she hurried along towards Kenilworth Street, the bitter wind stinging her cheeks, looking forward to seeing Robbie and to a nice hot cup of tea.

Rounding a corner, however, she looked up only just in time to realize that someone was coming towards her in the gloom, almost colliding with her, and she skipped out of the way. The other person, a woman with what looked like a baby cradled in her arms, gave a startled gasp.

'Sorry!' Em called.

The woman acknowledged her with the barest nod. She was wearing a dark-coloured coat and a hat with the brim pulled right down. Em caught a glimpse of a long, pale face, and a glance from dark eyes that flickered towards her for a second before the woman turned away. She vanished into the evening.

'Well, she was in a rush,' Em muttered.

Something about the face disturbed her. It took a few seconds before it came to her.

'Hang on—' She said it out loud, stopping in the road. 'That was Katie O'Neill!'

Walking on again, she tried to make sense of it. Of course she hadn't realized who it was at first. Why should she? And the woman had seemed in such a tearing hurry. She had been carrying a child – hadn't she? Surely she hadn't imagined that? *She must be married then*, Em thought, with a pang of regret. If the two of them had stayed friends they could be spending

379

time together, their children growing up together. Still, no good crying over spilt milk. She hadn't heard anything about Katie in ages. Had she moved back to the area?

But the more the brief incident came back to her, the more Em realized how odd it had been. If it was her she'd have wanted to stop and show Robbie off to anyone she knew – even Katie. And even stranger had been the hunted look in her eyes.

Reaching home, Em went gratefully inside and straight over to greet Robbie. But over her tea she told Cynthia about her strange encounter.

'They always were a peculiar family,' Cynthia said. 'I never got to know her mom at all – she could be pleasant enough but she was never what you'd call friendly. Never really talked to anyone much. She always seemed to think she was a cut above everyone round here. I've not seen her for quite a while though, not round here. I thought they'd moved on.'

'So did I,' Em said. 'It was just, the way she was just now – I mean, I know we're not friends any more. But even so – it just wasn't normal.'

Cynthia gave a laugh, pushing back her chair. 'Whatever that is! Well – perhaps we'll hear more, sooner or later.'

What is Family?

Forty

February 1944 – St Margaret's Bay

'Hey you two!' Jen's grinning face appeared round the door of Molly and Cath's room. 'Want a cuppa tea?'

'You offering to make it?' Cath asked, surprised.

'Why aye!' There was a glint in her eye.

'Mine's two sugars,' Molly called, adding, 'Ow – bugger it!' as the needle she was using to darn her stocking plunged into her thumb. Again.

'Mine's three!' Cath lay back on the bed, boots kicked off. 'This is the life. What's got into her?' she giggled as Jen disappeared downstairs.

'God knows.' Molly sucked at her thumb, squinting at her dreadful sewing. 'But we might as well make the most of it.'

When the girls had first arrived in Dover, they were appalled at the state of it. The town had been bombed, and shelled from across the channel since the summer of 1940, and the wreckage was terrible. Almost every building they drove past in the city seemed to be damaged to a greater or lesser degree. So they had scarcely been able to believe it when the truck pulled up outside a graceful house on the edge of town, high on the chalk cliffs, and they were told that this was their new billet. They had run round inside, excited as children, bagging beds again in the rooms with a choice of views, across the blue expanse of the Channel, or looking westward along the cliff to the South Foreland lighthouse. There were other service personnel along the road – general duties staff and, as they realized soon after they arrived, a group of Kinnys.

'I've just seen Ruth!' Cath reported on the second day, imitating Ruth's voice with a comical face. 'Oh, hullo girls!'

'What, *again*? Oh, super-dooper!' Molly grinned back.

It felt like a holiday at first. The town was swarming with smartly dressed GIs, with their currency of gum, nylons and sheer novelty. And there were free tours for service people round Dover Castle. But it was not to be a holiday at all. At the end of January, another intense round of bombing on London had begun again, and what soon became known as the 'Little Blitz' also affected Hull, Bristol and South Wales. London, as ever, took the brunt of it, and the batteries all around the east coast were kept busy.

This particular day was an off-duty lull for the girls after intense periods of activity. The previous night there'd been a very heavy raid and they were recovering. Jen, though, seemed to be full of beans.

'She's got some new fella in tow,' Cath said of the surprisingly effervescent Jen, idly waving one leg in the air. 'Some Yank, I bet. God, I wish it'd warm up and we could get out on those cliffs and sunbathe.'

'I've had quite enough of the sodding cliffs,' Molly said. 'I'm surprised the wind hasn't blown our flaming heads off out there.'

'Here we are!' Jen breezed in bearing cups of tea, a tattered-looking newspaper and the post tucked under one arm.

'OK – who is he?' Molly asked. If Jen was treating them to waitress service, there was obviously some new bloke to tell them about.

Jen clanked the cups down on the dressing table. 'Well – his name's Frank . . .'

Cath sat up rolling her eyes. 'I knew it – is he one of them black ones? Oh, letters!'

'No, he's not, he's got hair the colour of corn, for your information.'

'Ooh!' Cath drawled, teasing. 'Ah, hair the colour of corn – how poetic! Has he got eyes the colour of emeralds and muscles like the ripples on the sandy strand?'

'*What*? No! Just shut it, you. His eyes are grey, and he's just nice, if you want to know. And no – no letters for you. One for Molly and a card for Nora. Sorry.'

'S'all right – I'm not expecting any. And ta for the tea, Jen. You're a darlin'.' Cath sat up, tousle-headed, and reached for her cup. They knew she felt very alone in the world, despite her large family back in Ireland, but it was moments like this that seemed to bring it home. There was never any post for her. 'Ooh Molly – is that another begging letter from *himself*?' she asked.

After weeks of silence, Molly had recently received a letter from Len, imploring her to reconsider and go back to him. 'Everything was so hasty. You just panicked and ran away, Molly, and I wonder if you're too proud to admit it. I know I love you like no one else . . . There's only you for me . . .' Hearing from him had been a shock. Not knowing what else to do, she had ignored it, pretending it had not affected her, but of course this was not entirely true.

'No—' Molly peered at the writing. 'It's from Em – my friend from home.' She said this rather proudly.

Even now, it seemed astonishing to her that she had friends. She opened it and began to read, then exclaimed. 'Blimey!'

Cath and Jen were on each side of her instantly. 'What? Tell us!'

'It's just – this girl, both of us were at school with her – proper stuck-up little cow she was . . .' Molly read on incredulously. 'I mean we ain't seen her for *years* – she got some office job and thought she was far too grand for the likes of us . . . She's gone and turned up – with a babby!'

'So what? Jen sounded disappointed. 'People do have them you know.'

'No, but . . .' Molly's eyes were racing down the paper, covered with Em's childish writing. '*Blimey . . .*'

'*What?*' Jen said, exasperated. 'Come on – spill the beans!'

So Molly read out some of what Em had written:

I didn't think much more about it, but then Dot turned up and said she'd seen her as well. She's got lodgings somewhere, wedding ring, the lot, I suppose making out he's away in the forces. But Dot said she found out from someone who knows Mrs O'Neill and seemingly she's disowned Katie because there is no father . . .

'Sounds like our plaster saint Katie O'Neill has gone and had a babby out of wedlock!' Molly crowed.

'Oh sweet Jesus,' Cath breathed.

Molly was immediately ashamed of her glee.

'Sorry, Cath – only this is a hell of a surprise – she was always little miss perfect. Thought she was above everyone.'

'Maybe she was taken advantage of,' Cath said gently.

'Well maybe – but even so – *Katie O'Neill!* You don't know what she was like!'

They moved on to other things: Jen bursting to tell them all about Frank; chores to catch up on; the paper to read. Once they'd finished their tea, Jen went off amid a wave of thank yous and Cath said she was going to coax the plumbing into letting her wash.

Molly sat on her bed, her mind spinning, completely oblivious of the rain banging against the window. Em's news was astonishing and she was very curious about what had happened. She found herself longing to see all the Browns. It was nice the way Em kept in touch. But suppose that had been another letter from Len instead, begging her to see him again, to reconsider? The thought filled her with terribly mixed feelings. She knew that now he was gone, she didn't miss Len, except for the feeling of being flattered that he wanted her, and that he had felt like a safe haven. And she missed having a man to be close to. Being wanted – preferably by someone nice like Len – oh yes, that felt lovely. There was nothing like it. So many of the blokes just bothered her for her looks and assumed, or hoped, she was 'easy'. What she mainly felt now was guilty. Len had broken off his engagement to Sheila, who sounded like a superior person in every way. What he should do was eat humble pie and go back to her! The thought of Len and all that had happened just left her feeling a fool, ashamed of it all and glad to put it behind her. She told herself he was the last thing she wanted to think about. But she still found herself wondering, hoping even . . .

To distract herself she leaned over and reached for the tatty newspaper that Jen had picked up somewhere. It was a two-day-old *Daily Telegraph*.

She laid the paper on her pillow and settled down on her front, shoes off and legs bent up behind her, idly turning the pages as headlines flashed by. News from Russia, the Allies were bombarding a monastery at Cassino, bombs over London. Drowsy again, now she had time to relax, she didn't read the full stories.

It was the name that leapt out of the page, even before the headline, which her eyes raced to next: STRANGLED WOMAN'S BODY FOUND IN BIRMINGHAM CANAL. Then her own surname – her brother's name: 'The suspect, Albert Fox, 24, a local man, appeared at Birmingham Magistrate's Court this morning.'

'Oh my . . .' Her blood was pumping. She sat up, gasping for breath, thankful that no one else was in the room, so that she could try to take this in on her own. 'Oh my God . . . my God!' She got up and moved in agitation about the room. Everything seemed to swim and she had to sit down again, panting. It felt as if something was pressing in on her chest. She had tried to shut Bert, and home, and everything about it out of her mind. He was somewhere else, as if he didn't exist. But now all she could see was her brother's loathsome face and slicked-back hair, feel the cold, metallic barrel of a gun pressed against her neck.

Molly leaned forward, pushing her head down between her knees as bright lights flashed at the corner of her eyes. She should have told somebody about him before, shouldn't she? What should she have done, knowing that her brother was capable of . . . of what? Of lying, cheating, stealing, assaulting – of pulling the trigger on his own sister in cold blood? She should have turned him in months ago. But to grass someone up, turn in your own brother – you just didn't do that . . . She had reasoned herself out of denying the real horror

388

of it all, not wanting to face up to just what a monstrous freak Bert had become.

But now, seeing it here in black newsprint, the terrible message of his actions, it didn't cross her mind for a second that Bert might be innocent. Innocent was something none of them in the Fox family had ever been.

Forty-One

Over the next two days this appalling knowledge burned in Molly's mind.

How can I tell anyone? What am I supposed to do? her thoughts whirled round. *My brother – could he really have done it? Is that monster really my brother . . . ?*

She was in turmoil. Her skin, mostly clear since she had been in the army, erupted now into itchy sores, but nothing would have persuaded her to tell any of the other ATS what had happened. Even with Cath, she had avoided talking about her family, except to dismiss them. As far as she was concerned, she had joined the army to get right away from them, to a place they couldn't reach. She didn't want them invading it. Here she could be someone else and believe better of herself.

But now she was infected by dark, disturbing thoughts. She may have thought she'd got away, but she was fooling herself! The family would always be strung round her like dead rats on a poacher's belt. They were part of who she was, she with her shameful past and frigid relationships. She wasn't a real woman, was she? Not like Em or Cath. Did she really think she was better than Iris and Bert? Wasn't she just another of them, another of the Fox family – dirty and vile?

A hasty note arrived from Em:

So sorry Molly to tell you terrible news. I don't
know if you've heard. Your brother Bert's in
Winson Green. It was that girl of his, Agnes – they
found her in the cut . . .

Her work suffered, concentration becoming almost
impossible. As she sat through the long, cold nights
staring at the location screen, her eyes kept blurring over
and she had to wrench her mind back to the job over
and over again, a bag of nerves in case she made a serious
mistake. Her eczema flared up and she tried to resist the
burning itching on her inner arms, her back, behind her
knees. She even had patches of dermatitis on her face –
something that hadn't happened since she was a child.
On the nights when she wasn't on duty, she lay awake
for hours, scratching, her eyes open, only dozing a little
before dawn and waking pale and irritable, her pyjamas
spotted with blood.

'What's got into you, Mol?' Cath asked on the third
day as they clung on in the transport that took them to
the gun site on the cliffs. It was a grey day, raining again.
'You look really groggy. Has something happened?'

Molly felt so desperate she almost broke down in
tears, but she gulped them away. 'Oh—' She invented
something quickly, though she felt bad lying to Cath.
'It's my mother – she's been taken ill. I'm a bit worried,
that's all . . .'

Cath looked puzzled. 'I didn't know you'd had bad
news. Well, should you not be asking for leave to go
and see her?'

'Well, maybe,' Molly said. She felt a blush rise in her
cheeks.

'After all, she is your mother. You should be by her
side if she's really sick. You never know, do you?'

This little statement, harmlessly made, felt like an accusation. Especially when Molly knew how much Cath missed her own mother. Iris was her flesh and blood – didn't she still have a duty to her, despite everything? She must be distraught over Bert – after all, he had been her favourite, had kept her all this time, and now he was gone. What was Iris going to live on now? Had the police found out what was going on in that house? Even though the reason was not the one she had given to Cath, she started to wonder if she should go home. It was a long time since she had set foot in Birmingham. She found herself longing to see Em, to pour her heart out to someone who knew more of the truth and who understood. And she wasn't doing any good here at the moment – in fact, she was a danger to shipping.

After the shift she went to her CO and requested compassionate leave, which she was given for an overnight stay. The next morning, she was on a train heading north.

Riding on the bus to Nechells, Molly found herself feeling both at home and like a foreigner in her own land. It was all so familiar, people's voices, the good old Brummie accent, the smells and sounds. There were changes of course – the bomb sites, all the marks of the war, but she had seen a lot of those before. She was surprised, though, how much it already felt like somewhere in her past. She was the one who had changed the most.

She couldn't bring herself to walk along Kenilworth Street, not yet, at least, and see the wrecked shell of the Buttons' house again, so she went round another way, all the time aware of people staring at her ATS uniform.

Then she wondered with a horrible lurch inside whether they were staring for another reason. Did they all know who she was – whose sister she was? She was very glad to reach the house, where she could take refuge inside.

Everything seemed quiet at the place in Lupin Street. The front door was open a crack, and Molly could already smell the damp, frowsy smell which her homes had always had. It made her spirits sink even further, made her feel six years old again, taking her back to poverty and cruelty and neglect. She wanted to turn and run away, never to see this place again as long as she lived.

Against her will she pushed the door open further. The stink grew stronger, laced with booze, and she was in the front room with its fancy furnishings – the Welsh dresser and dark leather chairs, the carriage clock alongside a host of other little knick-knacks. Molly looked at it all sourly. All through her childhood they had barely had two sticks of furniture to rub together, and now all this was garnered, or filched somehow, by Bert's criminal doings. She remembered Iris sitting filling the scent bottles in her fancy frock, grotesque and ridiculous, in the murky room upstairs.

Nothing seemed to have been touched. Whatever Iris's part in all the crooked goings-on, she seemed to have got away with it. Had the police been too interested in catching a murderer to worry about Bert's black-market activities? Or had his associates cleared the house at a whiff of trouble? Molly was too disgusted to care. The back room still had its new things in it, but in spite of all these possessions, the place had degenerated into a grim state, as Iris's dwellings always did. It stank of grime and booze, there were greasy plates and overturned beer bottles left on the table, and the floor round the gas stove was ringed with grease and filth. The scullery sink was choked with scum and greasy water, a pile of unwashed plates and pans was jumbled on the floor, and something once white was soaking in a pail. Molly looked round, sickened. How had she lived like this for so long? How had she stood it?

Of Iris there was no sign, but Molly decided to carry on nosing round the house. As she started up the carpeted stairs, she heard the sound of snoring. Typical! Her face creased with contempt. Four in the afternoon, and Iris was still sleeping it off.

The snoring grew louder, and reaching the top of the stairs, Molly realized that it was the sound of not one, but two people. The deep hoggish noise she had heard had been joined by something almost as loud but lighter in tone. She tiptoed to Iris's room and peered round the door.

Under a counterpane hectic with sickly pink flowers lay Iris and a stocky man with a moustache. The room smelt headily of spirits and both of them were so soundly asleep that Molly could have danced a jig in clogs and they wouldn't have noticed.

She moved closer and stood looking down at her mother, squeezed into the three-quarter-sized bed with this strapping bloke in his vest with his chest hair fuzzing out round the neck and armholes. His chin was dark with stubble and his open mouth showed a furred-up tongue. Iris's face was pink and slack, her red nose clashing with the coppery dye in her hair, which was tousled into a mess, almost half an inch of grey showing at the roots. The covers were pulled high over her belly and chest but her shoulders were bare and white as pork fat. One arm lay outside the covers and Molly saw rings on her fingers set with big colourful stones. The hairs on her forearm and a large mole at the top of her left shoulder stood out darkly against her white skin. Anger and revulsion swelled in Molly until she was ready to explode.

'You *stupid*, disgusting old cow,' she hissed. 'You never change do yer? Never do anything – nothing good in yer whole life. You don't care about anyone or anything except pouring booze down yer neck!' She was shaking with anger. What the hell had she bothered coming all the way back here for? Some romantic idea of 'mother' that she had conjured up when she was far away? Of what a mother should be? When had Iris ever shown a single sign that she was a real mother?

As she stared down at this woman, her closest blood relative, with her head so close to this strange man, both of them drunk, both oblivious to anything, for a moment she imagined plunging a knife into her mother's bloated body. Her arm twitched, lips curling at her thoughts. *God, I'll end up in the nick with Bert if I go on like this!*

But by Christ, you've asked for it enough times, she thought. *You wicked, cruel, drunken old whore.* The last shreds of her connection to her family died inside her. After all, what was family? What had she had in the way of relatives who mattered to her? The old man, her foul grandfather, who had sired her, and her broken stand-in father, Joe Fox. Iris had never shown an ounce of maternal feeling. Molly's elder brother Tom had been a pasty, sullen character who had vanished years ago, as soon as he could get out. And there was Bert – rotting in the Green now. The girls with her in the ATS felt more like her family. Standing looking down with loathing at the mother who had brought her into the world, she knew the only thing she could do was to go away and stay away. That was how she would survive. Turn her back on all of it and slam the door.

On a gust of Iris's snores she turned away without a breath of a goodbye and left the house. Her step felt lighter and lighter the further she moved away.

She went to find Em at Mr Perry's shop.

'Someone to see yer!' he called through to the back.

Em came in clutching an armful of cauliflowers. 'Molly!' she almost dropped them in astonishment. 'For heaven's sake, why didn't you tell us you were coming?'

'Sorry,' Molly said. 'Only it was last minute. I daint know either. I got them to give me leave.'

'Very nice uniform,' Mr Perry said admiringly. 'Very nice, I must say. Suits you, wench.'

Em grinned. 'She looks lovely, doesn't she?'

'Ta,' Molly said, blushing with pleasure. She had already pushed Lupin Street far away in her mind.

'You knock off early, Em,' Mr Perry said. 'It's only a quarter of an hour to go.'

Em protested but he insisted, and soon the two of them were walking back to Kenilworth Street together, just as they used to walk to school when they were kids.

'He's ever so kind to me, he is,' Em said. 'You'd never find a better employer.'

'Why's his tongue that funny colour?' Molly asked.

'Oh – it's the pencil he uses for the ration books,' Em laughed. 'The kids get an orange on the ration, and the little monkeys were coming it with him – rubbing out where he'd marked it in their ration books and coming back for another share. So he's had to get an indelible pencil – he licks the end every time to make it work!'

Once again Molly was brought up against the complications of civilian life. For her, food was just laid on and that was that – and at least now she didn't have to cook it herself!

'You've come because of Bert?' Em asked, looking round at her.

'I saw it in the paper, just by chance,' Molly said. There was a pause as they walked on, before she said, 'I don't feel as if he's my brother.'

Em seemed suddenly agitated. 'Thing is, Molly – I feel bad about it. I saw them, him and that Agnes – Aggie he called her – a few weeks back. It was New Year. I was with Violet and Robbie, going home, and he was with her. Vi and me, we heard them – they were in an entry – off Rupert Street I think. We just heard these funny noises, and then they came out, right near us, and went off down the road. It was dark but I knew it was him. The thing was, it sounded . . . Well, he was being horrible to her, hurting her somehow I think . . . I don't know. I can't stop thinking about it – maybe I should've done summat then . . .'

Molly thought again of the cold barrel of the gun against her neck. She was the one who should have done something.

'You couldn't have done anything,' she told Em. 'Bert's a bad 'un through and through. Summat would've happened sooner or later.'

Forty-Two

When they opened the Browns' front door, Molly found herself smiling at the sight that met them. Sid was in the front room playing with Robbie, swinging him up in the air, and Robbie's happy giggles spilled out to the street.

'Go on – up yer go. Yer gunna stand on the roof!' Sid was teasing. 'Shall I throw yer up through the window?'

From the back room came the sound of the wireless, and voices. There was washing everywhere, the air a mixture of steam, soap and cooking.

''Ello – who's this!' Sid suddenly noticed them. 'Oh-oh – it's yer mom, Robbie. Now there'll be trouble!'

Robbie was far too caught up in the game even to notice Em. ''Gain! Do it 'gain!' he shouted, pummelling Sid's chest.

'Oh – 'ello Molly!' Sid said in surprise. 'Almost daint recognize yer there!'

'Hello, son!' Em said to Robbie. 'I've got a little treat for you – you can have the bit of cake they gave me to make up the weight!' But Robbie ignored her and begged Sid again to carry on with the game. 'Well – his uncle's more interesting than my makeweight cake,' Em joked, trying to pretend she didn't mind. 'Come on through, Molly.'

'That you, Em?' The wireless was clicked off in the back room.

'Yeah – I've brought a visitor.' They went through to the back, where Cynthia was at the table, cutting up potatoes.

'Who is it? Oh – hello, Molly love! Back again then?' Cynthia gave a warm smile. She seemed well, Molly thought, and it suited her. Bob was at the table with a paper and Violet was doing sums there too. They looked up and smiled.

'All right, are yer?' Bob said.

'Hello, Mrs Brown, Mr Brown. I've just come home for a couple of days' leave because – well, you know . . . Bert, and everything.'

Cynthia's face fell. 'Oh love – of course. I almost forgot – how could I? What a terrible thing. We couldn't get over it when we heard. I mean, d'you think it might be a mistake, like – that they've got the wrong person?'

Molly shook her head, 'No. I doubt it. He's a nasty piece of work and always has been.'

'Oh,' Cynthia said, looking taken aback at Molly's bald judgement of her brother. 'I see.'

Violet was watching, listening intently, and Molly realized she was thinking of the night she and Em had seen Bert with Agnes. Violet was quite a quiet sort, but she took things in deeply. Molly wondered what the girl thought about it all.

'Here, Em – get yer pal a cuppa tea. You stopping with us tonight?' Cynthia said.

'Well – I don't know . . . Can I?'

'You're all right, love – course you can. We'll squeeze you in. Sid can sleep down here.'

'Oh no!' Sid came in from the front. 'Why's it always me?'

'Oh stop complaining,' his mother said, unsympathetically.

'You'd complain an' all, if you had to sleep on that cowing couch!'

'I'll sleep down 'ere,' Molly said. 'I don't mind.'

'No!' Cynth protested. 'Let this gentleman here give up his bed!'

'No really – I don't mind,' Molly said. 'I can sleep anywhere.'

'There yer go!' Sid said, grinning. 'That's what the army does for yer. And I can sleep safe in my bed!'

Cynthia tutted. 'I don't like having a guest down on the couch . . .'

'It's all right, honestly. Em and I'll probably sit up nattering anyway so that way we shan't keep anyone awake.'

'Well if you're sure, Molly,' Cynthia said. 'Have a seat, anyway . . .' Bob and Violet shuffled round a bit, and Molly sat, warmed by the welcome, thinking how nice it was to be here again, part of the family. Em handed her a cup of tea.

'I'll do a couple of extra spuds,' Cynthia said. 'Anyroad, I don't know when the trial'll be. Did you know 'er – the girl?'

'No,' Molly said. 'There was a girl there last time but her name was Hilda, so far as I remember. Looked a right little madam.'

'They say the girl, Aggie, had no family – was an orphan. It was some pal of hers put them on to your brother, said she'd been hanging about with him a lot . . .'

Molly thought about all the other things Bert had been up to. She wanted to get them off the subject. All she could feel about Bert was shame and revulsion.

'D'you ever see your other brother?' Cynthia was asking. 'What was his name again?'

'Tom – no. Haven't seen 'im in years.' Molly turned to Em. 'How's Norm getting on? You heard from 'im?'

'Yes – just a couple of days ago.' Em's eyes lit up with amusement. 'He wrote me a nice letter – said he had time to write because he was in hospital . . .'

'Oh my God – why? Is 'e all right?'

'He's right as nine pence.' Em giggled fondly. 'It's just typical of Norm. He's in there with a broken leg – somewhere in Italy. He fell off the back of a truck!'

'Oh ain't that just like Norm!' Molly laughed. She had thought Norm was a complete idiot when she first met him – hapless and boring. But she realized he was a nice man really, and his accident-proneness made her feel quite fond of him. After all, when had she been any good at judging men, anyway?

'So how long's he going to be in there?'

'I don't know,' Em chuckled. 'I mean, I'm quite glad in a way – at least he's out of it for a bit – unless they bomb the hospital of course! It's just like Norm!'

Molly enjoyed sitting squeezed round the table with the family that evening as they all ate tea. And as it turned out, she was there for a special announcement.

''Ere – I've got summat to tell you all,' Sid said suddenly. Everyone looked at him.

'Spit it out then, son,' Bob said.

'Well – I've been to see Mr Weston, Con's dad – and asked for her hand in marriage. And 'e said yes.'

'Yeah, but what did *she* say?' Em teased.

'She said yes, *course* she did. I asked her first, daint I?' Sid said heatedly. 'What d'yer take me for?'

'Well – that's lovely, isn't it?' Cynthia said.

Everyone looked at Bob. He put his fork down. 'Well, bugger me. I never thought you'd get round to it, lad.'

Em and Molly stayed down at the table in the back room talking after the rest of the family had turned in. To Molly's surprise, Robbie was still up, and Em settled him down on her lap.

'He'll have to stop down with me,' she said. 'He's used to me getting into bed with him. He'll cry else.'

Seeing her old friend with her baby son snuggling up to her, Molly felt a pang of mixed emotions. It looked so lovely! Would she ever have a baby herself? There was longing – if Tony had lived, would they have had a nice little family, Dymphna the adoring grandmother? But the thought of having her own child filled her with sudden queasy panic. She longed to love and be loved, but she certainly didn't find herself full of maternal feelings. After all, what did she have to give a baby? Would she live in some back street, tied to the house, turning to the bottle for escape like her mother? The thought of it made her want to run away, do anything but that. She envied Em her love for her son, but in those moments she realized she had a horror of being like her.

'You heard anything else about Madam O'Neill?' she asked, reminded by the thought of babies.

'No.' Em stroked Robbie's soft hair. Thoughtfully she said, 'It's funny isn't it – that night I saw her ... I don't know, I couldn't stop thinking about it. She looked so ... bad. Sort of frightened. I don't know what's happened to her, obviously, but I can't help feeling sorry for her.'

'Well, that's nice of yer. I mean, when I think what a little cow she was to you.'

'She was nasty, wasn't she?' Em agreed. 'Hey – there's a few biscuits somewhere.' She got up for the tin and sat down again. 'The thing is, though, she was my pal once. And when you come down to it, Molly – we were only eight years old. We were just kids – and it was her mom made her do it. It's in the past now. And it sounds as if she's had her share of trouble, if what Dot says is true.'

They both speculated for a while on what might have happened to Katie. Who's was the baby? Was she in fact married or not? And why was she back here suddenly – or had she been here all the time? They had lost touch with her and didn't know anything about her life.

They moved on to talk about their own concerns. Molly told Em about life in Dover. As they chatted, she began to itch again. Her skin was always worst in the evening. She struggled not to scratch. It made her feel dirty, like a flea-ridden dog. Inevitably, the conversation soon moved on to Bert.

'It's a relief to be able to talk about it,' Molly said. 'I didn't want to tell any of the girls down there, even my pals. I don't want my family spoiling it for me.'

Em nodded sympathetically.

'Thing is Em . . .' Molly leaned forward. There was one thing she was longing to pour out to her old friend. It was her turn to try and clear her conscience. 'When I was here last time . . . when I got to the house, he was . . . well, it was plain he was up to all sorts. Always has been. I mean, I know he dodged the army. He can put on fits, you know – fake them. And he did it for other blokes as well. They paid him to stand in for the medical – down 'e'd go, one of his turns, and they'd class him as unfit . . .'

Em gasped. 'He never! That's wicked!'

Molly nodded. 'That's Bert. When I got there that night there was all sorts going on – stolen stuff, black market. I don't think there was much he wasn't getting up to. He had all this knock-off perfume, and he and Mom were bottling it . . . And rations – they'd stolen all sorts of stuff. But that's just . . .' She shrugged. 'I dunno. I know it ain't legal, but I wouldn't've turned him in for that. He had mates, a gang of 'em, all in it together. But then . . . I'd had a couple of drinks, you see, that's why – I wasn't clear in the head. He came up behind me, in the front room, and stuck this cold thing in my neck – it was a gun . . .'

Em's mouth fell open, her eyes stretched. 'God, Molly! What did you do?'

'Well nothing – I mean, I sat still. What else could I do? And he never did anything else – just backed off. But after, when my head was clearer . . . I couldn't believe it. It didn't seem real. But I've been worried about it ever since. Should I have turned him in? Then he wouldn't have killed that Agnes.'

'Oh Molly . . .' Em sat back in her chair. She gave a shudder. 'I mean, I know Bert's always been a bully. But you'd never've thought he was capable of *that* . . . But your own brother . . . I mean, it doesn't seem right to turn in your own brother – it's not as if he'd done anything then . . . Agnes was strangled anyway, not shot.'

This bald, terrible statement made them look at each other in silent horror. What else was there to be said?

But Molly felt such a relief, having poured out everything to Em.

'You know,' Em said sweetly. 'With the family you've got, I don't know how you've turned out so nice.'

Molly felt a blush rise through her. She didn't feel nice, not deep down. But she smiled and said, 'Well all I can say is, thank God there's other people about apart from family!'

Forty-Three

As the train eased its way out through the southern suburbs of London the next day, Molly found a place to squat on her bag in the corridor by the door, watching through the rain-streaked windows as the soot-coated buildings give way to countryside. With every mile further from Birmingham and nearer Dover, she felt lighter and freer, as if she had cut her family off from her like an unbearably heavy load. She was floating. It had been wonderful to see Em and let out some of her feelings. It didn't change anything, but it felt like a trouble shared, no longer just whirling round only in her head.

She thought about what she had said to Em last night, those words that had sprung to her lips. Yes, family was something she would have to make out of the people who were prepared to love and care about her. Blood ties were poisonous in her case – they meant not care but cruelty and betrayal. She would have to look elsewhere. Len's face swam into her mind. Len still claimed he loved her and wanted her. Why had she told him she wasn't interested? Didn't she want to be loved by a good, kind man? Why had she panicked like that and hurt him so badly? Now, with a little distance from him, she was overwhelmed with regret. It was all too late now. Why didn't she know what was good for her when she had it?

But when she reached the billet back in Dover, everyone was so pleased to see her that she forgot her regrets for the moment. It was good to be back.

'How's your mother?' they all kept asking, and Molly had quickly to make something up.

The best thing was going into her room and having Cath say, 'Hey there, slacker! You're back then?'

'What's it look like?' Molly retorted, happily.

'Bet you've had a good night's sleep at least. All right for some. They've been shelling the bejaysus out of this place. How's your mother?'

'Oh – she's all right,' Molly said, throwing her bag on the bed. 'She'll live. We're not close, to tell yer the truth.'

'Oh – so she's not on her deathbed then?' Cath pulled on her trousers, tugging at the legs.

Molly sat down, tugging off her shoes. 'No, more's the pity.'

Cath looked shocked for a moment, then creased up with laughter. 'Oh, that's grand – there's not many you can say that to, I'll bet!'

'No,' Molly said. 'Not when we're all so *frightfully* fond of Mummeh!' she added, taking off the accents of some of the posher ATS. 'Hey – d'you want a cuppa? I'm parched.'

'Yes – with lots of sugar. I need all the energy I can get. I've got a feeling it's going to be a busy night. I'll come down with you ... *Oh!*' Cath slapped her hand over her mouth.

'What?'

'I completely forgot! *He* was here, yesterday – looking for you!'

'Who?'

'*Him* – that Len bloke. He was ever so put out that

you weren't here. Oh my Lord – how could I have forgotten?'

Molly's heart was racing. 'But what did he want? Did he say more? Did he leave a note or anything?'

'Yes – well no,' Cath said maddeningly. 'I mean, not in so many words. He went off in a paddy when he found out you weren't here. He didn't leave a note. But he wants you back – it's obvious!'

Len's visit threw Molly into turmoil. Why had he come, suddenly, without any warning? Hadn't she made it clear that she wasn't interested? That they had to break it off? Surely by now he'd gone back to Sheila and made it up, and they'd had their childhood sweetheart wedding in a Norfolk village church strewn with roses, as they had planned all along? But his coming had stirred her up. She'd been so adamant back then that it must not go on. Maybe she'd been too hasty? Len was so decent, so much nicer than most of the men she met.

Sitting at her radiolocation screens that night, once again she had to wrench her mind away from her itchy skin and her own thoughts and keep her eyes fixed on the incoming planes as they crossed the coastline, intent on London. It was a windy night, and she could hear it whistling around the hut. Surely Len would write again? Should she go and try to see him? No – she'd never get more leave ... *Keep your mind on the job!* she ranted inwardly at herself. *Just get through the night.*

That night was one of several involving heavy bombardment inflicted on the south-east of England. The team came off duty freezing cold and stiff, longing for baths and bed and pints of hot tea.

'Winnie says it's "quite like old times again",' Cath

said, quoting the Prime Minister, and yawning as they were driven back to their billet.

'Huh – bet they can do without any more of it in London,' Molly grunted. Mr Churchill's words made the bombing sound almost homely, even if they were meant to be encouraging. 'We could do without it here, come to that.' On top of the raids, the intermittent boom of the shells, aimed at Dover from across the channel, played on the nerves as well.

'Every bomb a broken heart,' Cath said.

As winter faded and warmed into spring, there was a series of such nights. The raids began mostly in the early evening and were over by midnight.

Molly was quite glad to be busy. Len's visit had shaken her. She waited to see if a letter followed, but there was nothing. After a time, the thought of him began to fade into the background again. Her skin gradually cleared up, and life in the army took over once more.

One evening, as they did on many nights when they had free time, a group of them went to the pub. It was the end of March, and the evenings were lightening gradually. All that month, the raids had kept coming and it was good now to get out and have some fun.

They had a number of favourite watering holes in the area. There was one Molly liked especially, a quaint place only a mile or so from the billet, with a crackling fire in the grate and a piano. The place had been heaving with servicemen of a great mix of nationalities, a scattering of WRNS, and of course the ATS girls.

Turns had been taken at the piano, with songs from different countries – mainly sung by the English, Czechs and GIs – and a great sing-song by all. For a while they cleared the floor and those who were in the know showed off their jitterbugging skills.

'Here—' A cheerful-looking English lad leaned over to Molly. 'Let's have a drink, before the bleeding Yanks drink it all!'

'Oh – no ta,' Molly said. If he bought her a drink he'd think he was in there. And she'd had enough.

'D'you wanna dance?' He indicated the gyrating figures behind them.

Molly laughed. 'You don't want to go lifting me off the floor, I can tell yer! Ask Nora over there – she's only a little 'un!' Nora, however, was already on the arm of a GI. The bloke disappeared, grumpily. And so she had fended off yet another approach.

At last the girls spilled out into the dark and windy night, Molly with Cath, Jen and Nora – who had also turned the bloke down – all very merry, arms linked and still singing and laughing. Molly felt outrageously happy. She could go out, have a few drinks and a good time, without the need to drink herself into oblivion – that was progress all right.

'Here, Cath—' She nudged her friend in the ribs, and talked loudly over the buffeting wind. 'You seemed to be getting on all right with that Czech fella – what's 'is name? He fancied you rotten, you could see a mile off.'

'Yeah – 'e did that – no denying it!' Jen nudged her from the other side. 'Come on, Cath – it's time you had a fella!'

'Just shut up about it, you two!' Cath said merrily. 'His name's Tomas, if you must know – but there's nothing in it. We were just passing the time.'

410

'But he's so handsome!' Nora said.

'So you go out with him then!' Cath retorted. 'I've told you – I don't mind a drink with a fella, but I'm not interested in all that' – she put on a drawling tone of mockery – 'courting and falling in love nonsense . . .'

Jen and Nora, who had both spent the evening being chatted up and fondled by two GIs with big lazy smiles, both groaned.

'Oh you're hopeless!'

'Fancy passing up a fella as gorgeous as that! Did you see his hair – lovely thick curls!'

'Well you can't feed a family on pretty curls,' Cath said tartly, and all the others laughed. 'God,' she added, 'I sound just like Sister Anselm at my school back home!'

Soon they were turning along the cliff road towards their billets. Jen started up singing 'Ten Green Bottles', which was about all they were sober enough to cope with in the way of songs. Still with their arms linked, leaning into the wind, they swooped in a line from one side of the road to the other.

'I know!' Molly called out, when they'd still only lost three green bottles from the wall, but it was getting boring, 'How about "Ta-ra-ra Boom-de-ay"?'

This led to more vigorous swooping and giggling.

'Stop!' Nora begged. 'I can't get my breath!'

They paused beside a low wall, perching on it. A few other ATS passed them, all merry as well, and called out to them. It was quiet then, suddenly.

'Let's come back here,' Nora said. 'When the war's over. Let's meet up and have a holiday – when we can go on the beach and swim!'

'You're on!' they all said, though they had no idea if they would and when that might be.

411

'I can't see any stars tonight,' Cath said, looking up. 'Too cloudy.' Sometimes the night sky here was an arch of starlight, but not tonight.

'Listen,' Molly said. 'What was that?'

'What?'

'I thought I heard ... It sounds as if someone's in trouble.'

A muffled sob came from back down the road along which they had just come. They waited, listening. The sounds were very restrained, but there was no doubt, someone was coming and they were very upset. The four of them waited, not sure what to do, and in a few moments, a lone figure appeared out of the darkness. She didn't seem to notice they were there, and made another sound of repressed distress.

'Hey—' Molly whispered to Cath. 'Look – it's Ruth!'

'Go on – you go and see if she's OK,' Cath said hurriedly. 'We'll walk on. Come on, girls.'

'What? Why me?' Molly was protesting, but already the other three were vanishing into the darkness. Ruth was almost upon her, walking with her arms folded tightly, head down, sobs breaking out from her in spite of her attempts to stop them.

'Ruth,' Molly called softly, going over to her. 'Are you all right? It's me – Molly.'

Ruth had stopped, rigid in the middle of the road, horrified that she had been overheard when she thought she was alone. She was the class of girl who had been schooled never to show her emotions.

'I – yes, of course.' Scrabbling in her pocket, she produced a handkerchief. 'Thank you for asking.' She blew her nose very firmly. 'I'm quite all right, only ...' Her voice disintegrated again.

'You don't sound it, love,' Molly said, feeling suddenly motherly and no longer intimidated. 'I don't want to be nosy or anything, but I just heard yer coming. Is everything all right?'

'Well . . .' Ruth stood helplessly and, unable to control her feelings, dissolved into tears again. 'Oh dear me . . . I can't seem to . . .'

'Tell yer what – come over here a minute.' Surprised at herself even as she did it, Molly steered Ruth to the wall. 'Just 'til you calm yerself down. You don't want to go in in that state, do yer?'

'I feel so awful,' Ruth burst out as they perched on the wall. 'I feel such a fool – and so, so – *dirty*!'

Molly was startled. What on earth had happened? She put her hand encouragingly on Ruth's upper arm for a moment.

'Come on, love – it can't be that bad, can it?'

'Well it feels bad to me!' Ruth said explosively. 'I'm not used to all this!'

Another gaggle of chattering ATS were coming along the road, and Ruth paused until they'd passed out of earshot.

'I think that was some of my lot,' she said, more calmly. When she spoke quietly, her voice didn't sound quite so odd. 'The thing is, Molly – I'm not like you. I've had a very sheltered upbringing, all academic and bookish, and I'm not used to men at all. I mean, since the war's started, I've been out with one or two, but nothing very serious . . . And they were never – I mean, something's happened. *Men* have changed, I think.'

'What happened?' Molly asked, gently.

'Well – we went for a drink – one of the pubs a bit further into town. And I met a young man – he seemed very eager, quite flattering actually, for someone like me.' Molly was touched by this frankness. Ruth's pale

413

face stared straight ahead, framed by her black hair. It was true, she was not much of a looker, especially with those rabbity teeth, and there had always been something forbidding and snotty about her. But Molly could see that she wished she wasn't like that.

'He seemed – well, charmed by me. Said his name was Rodney and he's not long been back from Italy – came up through Sicily and everything. And he was all right to look at. I suppose I was just – well, I was pleased to find anyone who was interested . . .' She gave an awkward little shrug.

'Anyway, he'd had quite a lot to drink and he started getting rather amorous, and then he asked if he could walk me home.' Her voice grew stiff with embarrassment. 'Well, as soon as we got outside he was on to me, wanted to kiss me and so forth. So I let him a bit. I wasn't sure what else to do and I sort of wanted him to at first. Well then it all got – he got very insistent. It was horrible. He took my arm and pulled me into an alley – I think between a shop and a house and he was pulling up my skirt and trying to – well, he was so *pushy*. And then I realized . . . he had his – you know – out . . . He wanted to, you know, go all the way . . . So I screamed and made a terrific fuss and I managed to push him off and get away from him.'

'Did 'e chase yer?' Molly asked, worried for her.

'No, well – not far anyway. I suppose he was having to – well his trousers would have fallen down . . .' She stifled a hysterical giggle at this. 'But the worst of it was the things he shouted after me. *Awful.* Words I'd never even heard before. And that I was a tease and a . . . a . . .' She broke down again, sobbing and rocking back and forth. 'I never meant to – I was frightened to death! I didn't know what he was going to do – and he shouldn't

414

have, should he? Not without asking – just *assuming*?' She looked round at Molly, wide-eyed, in honest need of her opinion.

'No,' Molly said. 'He shouldn't. There's some tough 'uns coming back from over there after all they've had to do. But he shouldn't just go on like that. It's not right.'

'It was horrible,' Ruth said. 'The way he looked – his eyes rolling. Oh gosh – is it always like that? I'm so inexperienced, you see.'

As if I'm the one to ask what it's supposed to be like, Molly thought. 'No,' she said reassuringly. 'It's s'posed to be better than that. And it wasn't your fault. He was just out for what he could get – like a lot of 'em.'

Ruth was staring at her with great seriousness. 'Golly,' she said. 'I feel such a fool. I mean, what if I run into him again? It would be mortifying!'

'Don't worry about it,' Molly said. 'He was probably too drunk to remember anything in the morning anyway.'

'Really – d'you think so?'

'Yeah – don't start losing sleep over the likes of 'im.'

'I say, Molly – you know, you really are rather a good sort.'

Molly wanted to feel sarcastic about this remark, but found herself very pleased instead.

'Well – I dunno . . .'

'I mean, when we all started out, basic training and all that, I found you utterly *terrifying*. You know – our backgrounds are so different, and you were so . . .' She grasped for words that didn't sound too insulting.

'Rough?' Molly suggested. 'Loud? Rude?'

'Well – something like that. You were just so *different*.'

Molly thought for a minute. 'Where I come from, it was rough,' she said. She found a frankness rising in her too. 'There's plenty of decent folks there, kindly types. Not everyone's the same. But my family're – well, the dregs. They're vile.'

'Molly! You don't mean that!'

'Yeah – I do.' Her voice was bitter. 'I don't even want to start on telling yer. You wouldn't believe it if I did. The war's been the best thing that's ever happened to me in one way – it's got me away from them. Taught me quite a few things really. Taught me that drowning your sorrows ain't the answer, for a start.'

'Golly,' Ruth said again. She sounded awed, respectful. 'It sounds as if you've really been up against it.' Then she said. 'D'you know – I feel heaps better. Thanks for being so nice, Molly.'

'That's OK.'

'We'd better get back or the other Kinnys'll think I've been kidnapped.'

'Well you nearly were!'

They laughed, walking slowly up the road together.

'I'm glad I got away too,' Ruth said. 'Otherwise I'd have known a whole load of mathematical formulae but not much else.'

'I'd've been in a factory all my life, I s'pose.'

'You're far too intelligent for that,' Ruth said briskly.

'Am I?' Once again Molly found herself enormously flattered.

'Oh yes – stands out a mile. Even when you were at your naughtiest!'

They reached Molly's billet first.

'Well – I can go on from here,' Ruth said.

'You all right on yer own?'

'Oh yes. I'll be fine. Thanks so much, Molly.' Her

voice turned a little gruff. 'You've been such a brick. I think I'll keep out of the way of chaps for a bit from now on. Goodnight!'

With an amused smile, Molly watched her disappear into the darkness. Ruth really wasn't such a bad old stick after all. And was she, Molly, *really* intelligent, like Ruth said? The thought glowed warm in her for a long time.

Forty-Four

By the end of March, the bombing was dying away, though Dover still had to endure the bombardment of shells from Calais. Rumours were starting to circulate that the Germans had yet another weapon up their sleeve, but as yet there was no sign of it. As the weather improved, the ATS girls enjoyed a short time of relative peace in Dover, before being told that it was time to move on again. Their battery was being transferred – back to the east coast.

Molly was not especially pleased.

'I could do without all this boom-boom-boom all the time,' she said to the others. It set everyone's nerves on edge. 'But I like it here.' She liked the house, high on the cliffs, with its beautiful views. And, though she didn't say it to the other girls, there was one new friend she was reluctant to part with – Ruth. From that night when they had talked in the dark, they had discovered a mutual respect and a curiosity about each other's lives. Slowly, awkwardly at first, they had become friends.

'And you do make me laugh, Molly – the things you come out with!' Ruth said. She was gradually lightening up and becoming less stiff, more youthful. Molly found that she could also be quite funny at times.

When the day came to say goodbye, Molly went along to the Kinnys' billet and asked to speak to her. It was a bright day, and Ruth came to the door, squinting in the spring sunshine.

'Just came to say goodbye,' Molly said. 'We're off a bit later. All packed up.'

'Oh dear, what a shame!' Ruth cried. 'I do wish you weren't going! I expect we'll turn up in the same place again – like bad pennies, eh? Listen though, just in case – I'll give you my home address. Come in for a sec—'

Molly stood in the house, one similar to their own billet, as Ruth hastily wrote her address on a scrap of paper.

'What about yours – why don't you give me that?'

Molly shook her head. 'I can't. I don't know where I'll go after.'

'Good gracious! Well, you drop me a line, do, when you've got settled? I'd love to hear from you. I shall be hurt if you don't.'

'All right, I will,' Molly said, meaning it.

There was an awkward moment, then the two women embraced each other.

'Good luck – TTFN,' Ruth said heartily.

Molly smiled. 'TTFN.'

They soon settled into their new billet, just along the coast from Harwich. It felt more like being back at Clacton again, with the low, sweeping east coastline and bracing winds. As the girls were all together still, it didn't take Molly and the others long to settle into a pleasant, if ramshackle billet in the stately little town, or to learn about the Yanks being 'over here' in a big way, and about the German POW camp a few miles away, where the men were trucked out to work on farms.

In between shifts, there was a lot of socializing. Jen

and Nora, who parted from their boyfriends in Dover without undue heartbreak, were soon happily walking out with other GIs. But the Americans were far from being the only foreigners in the area – among the others was a contingent of Dutch soldiers. A group of them were in a pub one evening where the girls were having a night out. Jen and Nora were in a huddle with the two GIs, shrieking with laughter at their jokes, while another huge, gentle character called Hank had sat down beside Molly and was taking great interest in her, and she found she quite liked his company. He was rather sweet, and not pushy, though a little slow on the uptake. He came, he said, from a farming family in Ohio.

'Look at your hands!' Molly exclaimed as she sat beside him. She took hold of one of them, a vast, beefy thing, and he allowed her to hold it up and try one of her own against it. 'They're enormous!'

Hank gave his slow, rumbling laugh, the upper half of his body shaking. Molly was seized by a longing to lie beside him, to feel that immense body greet hers with desire. But she pushed the feeling away. No – no more of that. She knew she had no other feeling for Hank. As she listened to him talk about his family, the farm, the church they attended, and took in the cleanly, good-natured, God-fearing picture he painted of their lives, it all felt familiar – like being with Len, only different. Here was another person who could never imagine her life, her family, who must not be *allowed* to. *Could anyone, ever?* she wondered, with a wrenching sense of despair and loneliness. She dragged her lips into a smile and tried to look amiable as Hank drawled on to her. But suddenly, glancing across the table, her attention to his words faded completely when she saw what was happening opposite them.

Cath was sitting beside a tall, striking-looking man with sharp cheekbones and intensely blue eyes. They were turned towards each other, talking as if there was no one else in the room. Cath's cheeks were rosy, her wild hair springing up in coils, and her expression gentle and intent. She smiled often as they talked. Molly found herself smiling at the sight of her pink-cheeked friend falling in love before her eyes.

Cath was the last one back that night, returning to the billet long after the duty corporal's roll-call at ten o'clock.

'Where is she?' the corporal asked, looking anxious. 'It's not like Cath to be out late.'

'Don't be hard on her, will ye?' Jen pleaded with her. 'She's found herself a fella and it looks serious. One of the Dutch lads.'

'Well I hope she won't be long. I'll have to wait up for her . . .'

When Cath got in, closer to eleven than ten, they were all ready for her. Once she'd signed in with the corporal she was ambushed at the top of the stairs and dragged into the room she shared with Molly amid much giggling.

'OK, OK!' she surrendered, sitting on the bed, the other three all agog. She had a huge smile on her face. 'What d'you want to know?'

'Well everything, you flaming idiot!' Molly said. 'What about his name, who is 'e? What's 'e like?'

'Cath who never ever goes out with men . . .' Jen put in.

'His name's Dirck.'

'Yes – and . . . ?'

'Well go on!'

'He's . . .' Cath breathed in, then let out a delicious sigh. 'He's just so-o-o-o . . . Nice! Gorgeous in fact!'

The others all erupted with delight. 'Ooh, we knew you'd fall for it one of these days!'

Cath looked serious. 'I know, I know – but heaven help me, it feels a bit terrifying, all the same.'

As the spring progressed, the build-up of activity continued. Everyone knew something was going on, but no one knew quite what it would be or when. No trippers were allowed to visit the south or east coastlines. There were all sorts of rumours flying – new, unusual equipment seen concealed in rivers and creeks and woodland glades. There were preparations in airfields, and more and more traffic, all heading for the south coast. But all everyone could do was to watch and wait and wonder.

In May, a grand offensive was launched against the ruined monastery of Monte Cassino in Italy, and on May 18 the Allies captured the monastery. Molly had a note from Em saying that she was hoping and praying Norm wasn't involved. It had been a little while since she had heard from him and she was worried.

Molly passed the spring happily enough. The work was light and there was plenty of social life. She had a few light flings with some of the Americans, who she found different and fun to be with. And she watched as Cath fell more and more deeply in love with her Dutch soldier. Though she felt pangs of sadness and some envy seeing them together, she was very happy for Cath, after all the sad times she'd had. And Dirck, though very tough looking, was kind and easy to be with. Molly found she liked him too.

Late one afternoon, Molly and Cath were hand-washing underclothes in the bathroom, Cath at the basin, Molly with a bucket in the bath. It was still sunny outside and the birds were singing, though inside, the girls were too busy chatting to notice. 'It's nice to see how keen he is on yer,' Molly said. 'You can see it a mile off!'

Cath smiled at her in the mirror. She had blossomed and looked even prettier, her cheeks rosy and a smile lighting her face more easily these days, crinkling the outer corners of her eyes.

'He's lovely,' she said, raising her arm to push her hair out of her face. 'I never thought I'd have the luck to meet someone so nice – and someone who wants to be with me as well. It feels like a miracle, Molly!'

'Well you deserve a miracle,' Molly said, firmly wringing out her stockings. She held them up to the light. 'Damn – another hole! I just hope...' She stopped, realizing that what she had been about to say was not very tactful. *I hope he's as nice as he seems... that he's not a two-timing sod, that he doesn't already have a wife back in Holland...*

'What?' Cath said.

'Just that you'll be able to be together – that you can be happy.' Molly stood up and dried her hands on the roller towel behind the door.

'God, I hope so too.' Cath was standing still, seeming troubled. 'Are you OK, Molly?'

'Course I am!' She was trying to keep her mind on the job at all times, not to think about anything, about the past, about Bert and what he had done, about Len...

'It'll be my turn to find you a bloke now.'

'Oh no – I don't think so! Here – put yours in here

with mine—' She held out the bucket. There was a clothing rack on a pulley in the back room downstairs and they were on their way down to hang their clothes on it, but Jen met them, blocking the way. From her face it was immediately obvious that something was going on. She put her fingers up to her lips urgently and glanced behind her.

'What's up with you?' Molly asked.

'Shhh! Molly ... There's ...' Jen hissed frantically, coming up close. She seemed unusually lost for words. 'There's someone to see you – in the front room. It's *him*.'

Heart pounding, Molly tiptoed to the front and peered inside. A burly, khaki-clad figure was standing with his back to her, one hand holding the net curtain a little to one side, staring out through the front window. There he was, lit by a shaft of the setting sun: so solid, so familiar. Len.

Forty-Five

He heard her steps and, releasing the curtain, turned to face her, his expression nervous, vulnerable. For a few seconds they stood looking at each other. A muddle of feelings rioted inside Molly. Resentment was there, anger: she had told him so clearly she did not want to see him and he had overridden her wishes. There was curiosity. What *was* he doing here, all of a sudden? And there was his familiarity, which made her long simply to walk into his arms, just like old times.

She waited, standing in a stiff, formal way, almost as if she was to be interviewed by an army officer. They were in the communal sitting room the girls shared, amid the tatty boarding-house furniture and smell of stale cigarette smoke.

'Molly?' He walked slowly round the chairs to her, not looking away from her face. His cheeks were pinker, more weathered than she remembered, though his eyes still had the same appealing little-boy look.

'Len. What're you here for?' Molly shifted her weight onto one leg, folding her arms. Her tone was tough. Why had he come, disturbing her heart?

He stopped, with a faded green chair between himself and her, and took his cap off. He gave a little laugh. 'That's what I always love – no soft-soaping with you, is there, Molly? You just come straight out with it.'

She didn't reply. Within her folded arms she clenched her fists.

'You never wrote back. That's why I'm here. I wanted to see you.' He said it so sadly, so appealingly, that she began to soften. After a moment she uncrossed her arms.

'It was no good me writing back.' She shrugged. 'I told yer – there was no point in going on with it and that was that.'

He stepped forward, as if to plunge into a speech, but she held a hand up to stop him. 'How come you're here?'

He looked down, fingering his cap. 'I asked for compassionate leave. Told them there was a tragedy in the family.' He looked up at her, his face tragic to match. 'I had to come. All these months – I left it, I tried to forget about you, Molly. And then when I wrote and you never answered. And I came to find you and you weren't there . . .'

'*I* had a tragedy in the family,' she said dryly. But she was not unmoved by him, the miserable state of him and the fact that he'd come all this way.

'It's taken me a while to be able to get away. They've sent me to Southampton for a bit – all hands on deck sort of thing. It's like a madhouse down there. Everyone says it was a ghost town 'til a few months ago, but now the docks are choc-a-bloc, hardly a bare inch of sea-water, the roads full day and night, tanks, lorries, non-stop. And there's no room anywhere – we're having to sleep in a school . . . They're building up to something big all right . . . But I had to come, somehow. Molly – let's just . . . Look,' he dared to approach, laying his cap on the back of the chair and walking round to her. He put his hands on her shoulders and she didn't resist. 'I know I made a mess of it all. I'm like that – I go too fast. I shouldn't have asked you to marry me, not that quick, when we hadn't spent all that much time together. I just wanted you that bad . . .'

She stood quite still, looking up at him. A truck rumbled past on the road outside.

'Look, Molly – I love you. I want to call you mine, but I don't want to frighten you. I tried to push on too fast, didn't I?'

Already she could feel herself susceptible to him, to the pull of his maleness, his desire and need overcoming her.

'Yeah – I s'pose yer did. But . . .'

The door handle clattered and Nora's face appeared. 'Oh!' she said, startled. 'Sorry – can I just get my . . . ?' She scuttled across the room to retrieve something from the table in the corner, then disappeared. Molly stepped back.

'Look – d'yer want a cuppa tea?'

She went to the kitchen to boil the water. The break gave her time to collect herself. She stood by the simmering kettle, thinking of Cath, her face as she looked at Dirck. *Do I feel that for Len?* Molly thought. *Did I ever?* But she could feel her defences tumbling down. Perhaps she could make do with less. It was so warming to feel wanted and loved. It would be nice to know Len was out there, loving her, even if they were apart.

She took two cups of tea into the front room and they sat down on the battered sofa.

'It was nice of yer to come all this way,' she said, shyly, picking at the frayed arm of the chair. She felt softer towards him now. At that moment it felt truly good to see him, to sit drinking tea with an old friend, now they were in yet another place where the only familiar faces were those of the battery she had arrived with.

'I had to,' he said. 'I've never stopped thinking about you, Molly. I tried to stay away, because of what you said, but my feelings are too strong. I've missed you so much.'

'But . . .' Molly frowned. 'What about Sheila? You should have gone home and married her – she sounded ever such a nice girl.'

'No—' He was shaking his head vigorously and Molly felt a catch of emotion in her. So he really did love her! She had expected him to run straight back to Sheila after she had rejected him, back into the safe certainty of his childhood sweetheart's arms. Molly would be looked back upon as a crazed mistake in a time of turmoil, a young man needing to sow his oats, his head turned by a pretty blonde in the heat of the moment. There would be marriage and then, once the war was over, village and farm life, children, continuing things the way they had always been. But he had rejected that! She was moved, suddenly. Maybe she really had affected him – she hadn't just been a fling.

But Len's face flushed with anger.

'I did go back – after Christmas, when I had some leave. I'd written to her, but she wasn't answering either. I thought it was because she was angry with me for hurting her feelings. You'd expect that, wouldn't you? So I went back to sort things out, to tell her we'd get married after all. When I turned up at the house she looked really put out to see me.'

He tutted, shaking his head.

'Well, she must've been upset, with yer,' Molly said. 'Breaking off the engagement and everything.'

'Upset! She wasn't upset!' Len burst out. 'Turns out

428

she was already set up with someone else and hadn't had the guts to tell me! Some bloody conchie who was working on the next farm. A right pansy, I'll bet you. She didn't want to know about me no more, that was for sure. There was me thinking she was faithful, that she'd be breaking her heart over what had happened, that she'd welcome me back with open arms – and her mum, once they'd got over it. And there they are with this yellow skiver from London with his knees under the table and Sheila saying, "I didn't like to tell you . . ." God, it's a good job I didn't get my hands on that soft bugger I can tell you . . .'

'So what you're telling me is . . .' Rage rose up inside Molly so fast she thought she might explode. She got to her feet and stood towering over him. 'You went back to Sheila, all ready to marry her, and she wouldn't have yer? So then you thought you'd come running back to me . . .' She had sat and listened to him, nearly been taken in. She'd nearly fallen for it – God, she nearly had! What a bloody fool! 'You thought I'd 'ave to do instead, because I'd just be mooning about waiting for yer, without any other thought in my mind. You've got a flaming bloody cheek coming all the way over 'ere when I've already told yer I don't want to know! D'you think you're God's gift or summat and I'll just drop everything for yer?'

'No – but Molly . . .' Len scrambled to his feet, startled by the fierceness of her attack. He looked wretched.

But her anger was boiling like tar. Even as she went for him she knew some of this rage should have been directed at other people – her grandfather, Iris, Bert, the war for taking Tony away from her – but she spewed it all over Len.

'D'you really think I don't have anything else going on in my head? If there's one thing the war's taught me it's that there's more to life – I don't have to spend my time mooning after time-wasters like you and turning myself into a drudge for you and your brats. There are other things to do instead of just running round after some tinpot Hitler of a man! You're all the bloody same, ain't yer? Filthy buggers who take everything you want without a care for anyone else! Well I'm not sodding well having it! I'm not interested in yer – all right? You're not God's gift – you're not irresistible to me any more than you are to Sheila, so go and find some other bloody fool who'll take you on. Go on!' She was yelling now. 'Get out of 'ere. I've got better things to do than sit here listening to you drivelling on, you selfish bastard.'

Len looked completely stunned by the extremity of her outburst. 'But, Molly . . .'

'"But, Molly" be damned!' she roared in an ecstasy of anger. 'Go on – get out, and don't ever bloody come back 'ere again!'

'I've nowhere to go – there won't be a train . . .'

'So sleep at the railway station! I don't care where you go – just get out of my sight!'

But Len sank down on to the sofa again. His face twitched and he looked up at her pathetically, in utter confusion. For a moment she thought he was going to cry. '*Please*, Molly, don't be like this. I don't know what to do. Just be with me . . . I can't live without you, Molly. I never used to be like this, but now I can't think of anything else. Everything was . . .' His face twisted. 'I was all right 'til I met you . . .'

The words pierced into her, but she would not let him see. She managed to speak less harshly. 'It's no good, Len. You've got the wrong idea about me. Just go away – please.'

There was a silence. He drew his gaze from her down to the floor, defeated, and at last stood up slowly and picked up his cap. 'Christ.' He looked at her with revulsion, as if she was a stranger he had just met.

'That's it – *go on*. Door's in the usual place.'

Without turning back he left the room. She heard the front door open and slam, his footsteps along the quiet street. Only then did she realize she was limp and shaking all over.

The next afternoon, the sun was shining and Molly rode against a brisk wind along the cliff overlooking Dovercourt Bay. She had cycled fast, past the Cliff Road Hotel and all the elegant houses, and turned into the village, pushing down as hard as she could on the pedals to relieve her feelings, until her chest was tight and her eyes filled with tears. She stopped, gasping for breath, and wiped her eyes. In front of her was the village church, and she wheeled the bicycle to the gate, propped it up and went in.

To her relief, the graveyard was deserted and she was glad of the sanctuary of a quiet, green place out of the wind. She went and sat at the foot of a tree, from where she could see the church's square tower and the rows of silent, sun-warmed gravestones. The dead seemed to offer company, without comment or judgement, all their loves and mistakes now past and gone. She became aware how quiet it was, so that she could hear bees butting against the flowers and the breeze moving among the leaves. In the distance, someone was striking something, a metallic chink-chink which broke into the silence.

Molly sat with her knees drawn up, her ATS skirt pulled over them. The tears soon came, had been waiting there to be shed since last night, when there were too many people about, the others full of questions when they heard her shouting and Len slamming out of the house. For a few moments she put her hands over her face and gave way to weeping, then wiped her face and sat in the calm shade, wrung out and exhausted. The things she had said to him, much worse than he deserved: she'd been awful! She'd really let rip! But it was his words that echoed in her head. '*I was all right 'til I met you* . . .' She knew she was right to tell him to go, that he had only come back to her as a last resort, and in truth she didn't want him. But if he had never met her, wouldn't he have remained the straightforward, confident boy she had first known? Would Sheila have rushed into the arms of her conscientious objector, or wouldn't they be marrying this spring instead, keeping things the way they ought to have been until she, Molly, came into the situation and poisoned it?

She had felt alone for most of her life, but never more so than now. She was cutting the threads of her life, one by one: home, family, men – for she was not good for them, nor they for her – until what remained? There was Em of course, from a distance. There were friendships, comrades. And there was the army. Without that, she would be floating loose through the world with no one, nothing. It was a love affair in itself.

Soldier Girl

Forty-Six

Molly wrote the date at the top of the sheet of paper, 'July 20th 1944', then seemed unable to write any more. For some time she stared out from her bedroom at the grey sky, then continued: 'Dear Em . . .'

Em seemed so far away now. In her mind she had cut off from Birmingham and almost everything there. But Em was a true friend – she must keep in touch. Who else was there to go back to when the war was over? The thought of the war ending filled her with emptiness and desolation. Where would she go, who could she be if there was not the war to be a part of?

She wrote:

Sorry I've not written and thanks for your postcard. Things keep changing here and it's been very hectic. First of all things went quiet. Then, that day in June, everyone disappeared. It felt ever so queer. We saw it coming, but then again, we didn't. All the Yanks were here and everyone, all the trucks, everything busy – and then they all vanished, just like that. It was a real shock in one way. We all had friends who've gone and are now wondering what happened to them all. Poor Cath is in a terrible state because of course her Dutch boy was part of it and she hasn't heard from him.

She paused. D-Day, June 6th. It had been the strangest time. None of the American boys had breathed a word. Maybe they hadn't known anything to tell. Funny markings had appeared on the roads, trucks parked on them. Then, the sudden silence and emptiness once they'd gone. That night, they'd sat round the wireless, absolutely silent, she and Cath, Jen, Nora and the others, looking at each other with awed faces, drinking in the news of the landings on the Normandy coast. Cath had put her hands over her face, distraught.

'He won't come back – he won't,' she sobbed. She wrung all of their hearts. 'I know it. I knew it was too good to be true!'

Course, we'd hardly recovered from that when the Doodlebugs started coming, the horrible things, so it's all Action Stations again now. I don't suppose it's affecting you all much up there. We're busy enough but I'm glad we're not further south, poor things.

I'm glad you are all OK and Robbie is getting on so well. I hope you've heard from Norm. Any more news of K O'Neill?

This time Molly sat for a while staring at the page, thinking there ought to be more she could say. But she couldn't think of anything and signed off.

12th August 1944

Dear Molly,

I can't even remember the date! Shows what a state I'm in! Not much news really. I've been so busy worrying about Norm that I've hardly been

436

sleeping or taking much notice of anything else. I knew he was in the hospital and then that was that, nothing. I thought the place must've been bombed or something else terrible. It wasn't like Norm to be so quiet. But I had a letter yesterday at last. He's been very poorly, he says, caught something in the hospital. I suppose if you want to stay well you stay out of a hospital! I wish he'd let me know before – even just a line. I feel quite cross with him although I'm so glad he's better.

We're all all right. Sid's getting married next month. Connie's all right. I think we'll get on. Robbie's chattering away – I wish you could see him. I cut his hair this week and he looks a proper little man now, and he's wearing shoes. Frightening how fast they grow up.

I haven't heard any more about Katie O'Neill. Not a thing.

Are you ever going to get any leave? When are you going to come and see us in good old Brum? Come soon!

No other news.

Love for now,

Em. X

Three days after Em's letter arrived, quite early in the morning Molly was still in her room when a scream pierced through the house.

Oh God, she thought, running to the stairs.

Jen was also on her way down. 'Was that Cath? Oh God, that sounds like bad news!'

They saw Cath in the hall by the front door, Nora already beside her. Cath had something pressed to her face, over her nose and mouth, and was making incoherent squealing sounds while Ann clucked beside her. Molly's heart was pounding.

'What's up, Cath – what is it?'

Cath started jumping up and down, pulling the sheet of paper away from her lips and at last managing to choke out the words. 'He's alive! It's from Dirck, my lovely Dirck! He was wounded, but he's alive!'

All of them went to her, and by the time they'd finished hugging and screaming with her, there wasn't a dry eye in the house. The casualties on the days following D-Day had been massive – huge losses among the Dutch alone. But Dirck had survived.

Cath's lovely face was blotchy with tears and lit up with joy. 'Maybe I'm not cursed after all! Maybe he'll make it!'

'Oh Cath – that's fantastic!' Molly cried, and seeing Nora and Jen's watering eyes, she found she wanted to sob with relief, happiness, release of tension and pure joy for Cath. There had been so much grim news all through the summer – at last something good!

'He's alive!' Cath was dancing round the hall now, hysterical with joy, waving the sheet of paper. 'He's alive and I love him so much! Oh thank you, life – thank you!'

Forty-Seven

December 1944

In the past months, the situation in Europe had changed fast. Allied forces had moved across France and into Belgium. Paris, Brussels and Antwerp were wrested from German occupation, but a terrible price had been paid by the Allies at Arnhem. Now, as a bitingly cold winter was setting in, fighting was focused in the Ardennes. Slowly, agonizingly, Europe was being reclaimed.

One morning, made all the more viciously cold by a Siberian wind, Molly and the others were gathered in a requisitioned hall. There was a room full of khaki uniforms, a loud buzz of excitement, and the voices, both male and female, of the gathered ack-ack batteries who were defending the port of Harwich.

Molly leaned round and nudged Jen. 'Anything from Nora?'

'No – I'd tell yer if there was, wouldn't I? She won't've come round yet.'

All of them looked pale from lack of sleep. In the middle of the night, Nora had been overtaken by terrible pains and had been carted off to hospital with appendicitis.

'Poor thing,' Cath said. 'She looked dreadful. And she's missing all this.'

One of the high-ups at the front banged on the table and all fell quiet. Everyone stood to attention as a tall, slim officer, her blonde hair caught up elegantly under her ATS cap, walked in briskly and took up her position before them.

'Stand easy – take a seat!'

Everyone watched, awed. She introduced herself as Chief Commander Lucinda Mossfield. As she spoke, greeting them all and praising them for their work in coastal defence, especially for having faced the new menace of V1 and V2 rockets, her severe expression softened a little.

'As you know, the war is progressing and things are changing. Because of our gains in Europe, we are standing down most ack-ack batteries and transferring personnel to other trades. But we have already sent a number of batteries across to the European mainland. There is still work to be done, and work at which you are now rich in experience.'

She looked round the room. Molly watched her, rapt, in deep admiration. The woman spoke so well, had such command over herself. If only she, Molly, could be like that!

'We are looking, in the first instance, for volunteers. I would like you to consider offering yourself for service overseas, for what we foresee will be the remainder of the war. You will be a new battery under new leadership. We shall need to know quickly, and you must make your decision firmly. The first port of call will almost certainly be Belgium. After that, who knows quite how things will progress? So – think for a moment among yourselves. You can let your Commanding Officer know your decision.' Molly turned instantly to Cath. They met each other's gaze, their eyes shining with such enthusi-

440

asm that there was no need to speak. Oh yes, they were keen all right. They would go – and they would go together.

To their surprise, Jen said she wasn't going to volunteer.

'I don't really want to leave the country,' she said sadly. 'I'm a home bird really and I'm already far enough away from where I come from. My mam's got her hands full and – I don't know. It just doesn't feel right. I'll go into the Pay Corps or something boring like that, back up north. But I'll miss you crazy lassies.' Her eyes filled with tears. 'You'd damn well better come back and get in touch with me – even if I do live way up there!'

Molly and Cath promised fervently that they would. It was a strange, sad time in some ways, with partings and separations. Nora was not well enough to volunteer, and of the little group of them, Cath was the only person going who Molly knew very well. But Cath was her best friend – so what could be better?

Cath was jubilant. 'I'll be nearer to Dirck!' she said. 'I mean, I don't know where he is, but I just feel I'll be closer. And it'll be exciting, going somewhere new.'

Molly felt the same; ready for anything the army could offer her. She, little Molly Fox, was going abroad to a foreign country. When in her life had she ever expected that before?

The members of the new battery were given papers and inoculations and instructions in preparation for their departure just before Christmas. There was already snow on the ground when one morning they were gathered outside, huddled in their greatcoats, for an inspection by their new subaltern.

Molly and Cath stood side by side, toes and fingers frozen, eyes watering in the cutting wind. A car drew up, with an ATS driver at the wheel. Molly glanced at it as their sergeant bawled, 'Attention!'

A second later she was further distracted by it and couldn't help turning her head to look. From the passenger seat someone emerged in a bulky greatcoat, a sturdy, determined figure.

'Fox – eyes front!' The sergeant approached, almost yelling into her face.

But Molly felt excitement and expectation rising in her and had to try to contain a smile that would not stop breaking across her face, however much yelling she came in for. They received the order to be ready for inspection, and their new subaltern proceeded along the rows. She stopped at each of them, looking them over appraisingly. Cath, who had a cough, couldn't help clearing her throat. 'Nasty cough, Private,' she said to her when her turn came. 'Get that seen to.' And then Molly was face to face with Phoebe Morrison.

No words were exchanged, but looking directly into Subaltern Morrison's brown eyes, Molly saw a glimmer first of surprise, then of warmth. And then the senior officer moved on. The smile on Molly's face escaped and spread. Luckily no one was looking.

'Come in – stand easy.'

Subaltern Morrison sent for her the next day, in her office in a graceful requisitioned house. The room looked over the sea, though today it was a murky grey, and the view could not be admired by Molly, who was standing with her back to it. She waited while Phoebe Morrison walked ponderously round behind her desk, then stopped, positioned herself squarely and looked across at her. Her expression was neutral at first, seeming to be weighing things up with professional detachment. She made a small, involuntary movement with her right hand, as if to bring a cigarette up to her lips, but she controlled it. Then she smiled. Molly was startled. She had never seen the woman smile wholeheartedly before: it lit up her face with kindly energy. The smile warmed Molly to the core.

'So, Fox. Here we are again.'

'Yes, Ma'am, so it seems,' Molly said, smiling back.

'I'm glad to see you're still here. The army appears to have suited you.'

'Oh yes!' Molly said enthusiastically. 'It has.'

'Good. I'm glad. It was dashed hard to tell at the beginning how things might turn out.'

They both laughed a little, Molly blushing at the memory of her first ATS weeks.

'It seems that changing trade was a good idea.'

'Yes. Very, thanks.'

'You're an intelligent girl and it appears you have been well able to take responsibility. I have good reports.'

Molly blushed again. 'Thank you.'

'Well I haven't asked you here just for idle chit-chat. I want to give you another fresh start as we go across the water. I'm promoting you, Fox. To Lance Corporal. If that goes well – onwards and upwards! We'll see.'

'*Me?*' Molly burst out, laughing incredulously. 'Why me? Why not . . . ?'

'Because I think you are fit for the job,' Phoebe Morrison said briskly. 'If you have no other questions, that will be all.'

But she was unable to suppress her amusement at

443

Molly's astonished reaction, and with a twinkle in her eyes she held out her hand. Even more amazed, Molly took it, for a handshake over the desk.

'Welcome aboard, Lance Corporal Fox.'

Molly walked back in such a daze that she scarcely noticed the cold wind whipping her cheeks. She stopped, looking out over the steely sea, reflecting equally heavy cloud, but her own spirits could not have been lighter. Soon they would be crossing that stretch of water, she and Cath and her other companions, in the big family that the army had become for her. She could leave home far away, Mom drunk in her bed, Bert rotting in his condemned cell, the past with all its pain and shame. She was becoming someone new, capable, trustworthy, she, little Molly Fox, from the back streets of Birmingham, and she knew there was so much more she could do. She was a soldier girl, that's what she was. She was being given a chance, such a chance. *Onwards and upwards! We'll see.*

Collect the Birmingham set:

Birmingham Rose
Birmingham Friends
Birmingham Blitz

The Times bestseller

BIRMINGHAM ROSE

Life is bleak for Rose Lucas, a spirited, intelligent girl, born into a large family in the slums of pre-war Birmingham. But her friendship with Diana, daughter of a vicar from middle-class Moseley, gives her hope. She learns to aspire to a different kind of existence, vowing never to become a child-bearing drudge like her mother.

Life, however, never follows the way of dreams. After a childhood marked by tragedy, Rose eventually finds and loses the love for which she has strived so hard. From Italy, where she has travelled during the Second World War, she is forced to return to Birmingham and an unhappy marriage, her hopes and illusions shattered.

Finally, after further struggle, she decides to leave the city of her childhood as it rises from the ashes of its bombed devastation. For Rose will not be defeated and she, too, is determined to rise once again above the devastation of her life . . .

BIRMINGHAM FRIENDS

Anna has always been exceptionally close to her mother, Kate. As a child, Anna was captivated by the stories her mother would tell of her childhood in Birmingham with her best friend, Olivia. Olivia and Kate seemed to have a magical friendship. Anna has always regretted that with Olivia's tragic death during the war, she has never been able to meet the woman her mother loved so deeply.

But when Kate dies, she leaves her daughter a final story, one that this time tells the whole truth of her life with Olivia Kemp. As Anna reads, she is shocked to discover how little she really knew about the mother she felt so close to. With Kate's words of caution ringing in her head, she goes in search of the one woman who can answer urgent questions about her mother's life, and about her own . . .

A remarkable, stirring novel, *Birmingham Friends* perfectly captures the complicated intimacy of female relationships.

BIRMINGHAM BLITZ

August 1939. Genie Watkins, a Birmingham kid, would love to have a proper happy family like her Italian friend, Teresa. But Genie hasn't reckoned with the outbreak of war, her already rocky family being split up and the strangely liberating effect it all has on her mother . . .

Narrated in Genie's cheeky, courageous voice, the disasters that follow display her powerful capacity for survival. Under skies darkened by blackout she shares her fears and hopes with Teresa, keeps her spirits up with her nan and glamorous auntie Lil, and tries to hold her family together. And amid it all, she discovers love.

Family life seems set to be destroyed as violently as the city streets around them. But from the rubble come extraordinary surprises, glimpses of hope and, above all, a miraculous human resilience.

WATER GYPSIES

It is 1942, and after a childhood of suffering in Birmingham, Maryann Bartholomew has built a life of happiness and safety with her husband and children, working the canals on their narrowboat. But the back-breaking work and constant childbearing take their toll on Maryann. The tragic loss of her old friend Nancy followed by a further pregnancy lead her to a desperate act which nearly costs her her life.

The walls of her security are broken down further when her husband suffers an accident. To keep the boats working, Maryann is forced to allow Sylvia and Dot, two wartime volunteers, into the privacy of her life. And when she discovers that someone keeps calling for her at Birmingham's Tyseley Wharf, the dark memories of her past begin to overwhelm her. For that someone, who seems to be watching her every move, is becoming more dangerous than even she could imagine . . .

MISS PURDY'S CLASS

In the New Year of 1936, Gwen Purdy, aged twenty-one, leaves her home to become a schoolteacher in a poor area of Birmingham. Her early weeks are an eye-opener: at the school she faces a class of fifty-two children, some of whose homes are among Birmingham's very poorest. One of the teachers, the elderly Lily Drysdale, proves an inspiration, and Gwen begins to understand the appalling hardships endured by the children as she is drawn into their lives.

Joey Phillips, eight years old and man of the house, looks after his dying mother and lives in fear of being sent to the orphanage. When he disappears one day to a life on the streets, Gwen is haunted by his absence.

And there's Lucy Fernandez, an epileptic. Through her, Gwen meets Daniel Fernandez, the eldest brother in another fatherless household. Gwen falls in love and is quickly engaged in his battle to win rights for the working classes. As the International Brigades are mobilized to fight in the Spanish Civil War, Gwen has to accept that Daniel has secrets in his past which she would rather not face up to . . .

FAMILY OF WOMEN

Family of Women is the story of three generations of women:

Bessie – scarred by a childhood of poverty in the slums of Victorian Birmingham and left a young widow with four children; she is a hard, bullying woman who will go to disturbing lengths to keep her family under her thumb.

Violet – one of Bessie's four children – needs to escape, and falls into the arms of a man whose life will be broken by war.

Linda – grows up on a large housing estate in the 1950s with older sister Joyce and her beloved young sister Carol. Intelligent and energetic, she craves education and something more than the life she sees around her. Torn from her longed-for place at the grammar school, she gives up hoping for anything better. It takes a tragic love affair to make her question the limitations of her life and the secrets which haunt her family.

Spanning more than half of the last century, *Family of Women* is a story of one family – and of the joys, struggles and changes in women's lives.

WHERE EARTH MEETS SKY

Beautiful, dark-haired Lily has been abandoned in a Birmingham slum as a tiny child. With few clues as to her identity, she endures a childhood of loneliness and loss. At eighteen she applies for a post as nanny with the family of a Captain Fairford, a soldier in Ambala, north India, and his highly strung wife Susan. Lily is drawn into the emotional life of the Fairford family and adores her charge, two-year-old Cosmo.

When, in 1907, Captain Fairford orders a new Daimler car, it is brought out by a young motor mechanic, Sam Ironside. Sam and Lily fall deeply in love, and it is only later that Lily learns that Sam is married and feels utterly betrayed. When Cosmo is sent home to school, Lily finds another post with a Dr McBride and his invalid wife in a beautiful Himalayan hill station. The place is idyllic, and Lily settles for a quiet life. However, she is unprepared for the pain and misunderstandings that follow, which force her to run from everything she has known . . .

Where Earth Meets Sky takes us from Edwardian England and the British Raj, through the darkness of the Great War to the glamour of Brooklands Race Track in the 1920s. Spanning two continents, it is a story of enduring friendships and two hearts which cannot be kept apart.

CHOCOLATE GIRLS

When Edie marries young to escape her unhappy family home she thinks that life can only get better. At the age of nineteen, she is widowed and, after losing her child from the marriage, she faces the Second World War grieving and lonely. Then one night during the Birmingham Blitz, an infant, mysteriously abandoned during the bombing, is handed into her care. Her lively friend Ruby, meanwhile, doesn't want to be left behind in the wedding stakes and settles for marriage with Frank, a man much changed by war. Finally there's Janet, intelligent, kind-hearted and susceptible to male charm, who is desperately hurt by an affair with a married man, and who assumes she will never love again.

David, the child who steals Edie's heart as she brings him up through a time none of them will ever forget, is the centre of all their lives. And when David is old enough to wonder who he really is, he leads Edie through struggle and heartache to a life and love she would never have dreamed of . . .

A spellbinding saga of three very different women whose lives become entwined by war and their work at the Cadbury's chocolate factory in Bournville – and their love for a child.

THE BELLS OF BOURNVILLE GREEN

Continuing the saga begun in *Chocolate Girls*, this is a story of families whose lives are entwined, of loving and loss ... and of a young girl's search for transforming love.

It is 1962 and pretty seventeen-year-old Greta finds life at home hard. She has no father and loathes her mother's latest boyfriend. She's happiest at work with her friends in Birmingham's Cadbury factory, where she is popular with the boys. When her missing vixen of a sister, Marlene, turns up during the worst winter for decades, Greta decides that she has to get away, and the only escape route is marriage.

However, she soon finds out that life with her old classmate Trevor is not as she'd hoped, and freedom and happiness still elude her. She finds herself out on the streets – pregnant and homeless – until her mother's friends Edie and Anatoli take her in, and provide the safe, secure haven she has never known.

Until, that is, appalling tragedy strikes and shatters not only Greta's world, but also the lives of those around her. Life for all of them will never be the same again ...

A HOPSCOTCH SUMMER

In the impoverished area of Nechells, Birmingham, in the 1930s, young Emma Brown's life is turned upside down when her mother, Cynthia, has another baby. Emma has always been a happy-go-lucky child, content as long as things were all right at home with Mum and Dad, and her brother and sister. But when the baby is born, everything changes. Cynthia doesn't seem able to cope, and even her lifelong friend and neighbour Dot can't seem to get through to her. Cynthia's husband, Bob, tries to do his best, but when he feels he's losing the wife he loves so much he turns to drink. Poor Em can't keep up with looking after the household, and soon it seems that the only thing is for Cynthia to go and stay with her tyrannical elder sister across the city.

Life gets even tougher for Em with her mother away. Plus her best friend ostracizes her, and she's got the Board Man calling at the door about her lack of attendance at school. When Bob stays out later and later, always the worse for wear and gradually falling into the clutches of glamorous widow Flossie Dawson, Em decides it's time to travel across Birmingham and bring her mother home. But the woman she discovers is very different from the mother she remembers . . .

FOR MORE ON

ANNIE MURRAY

sign up to receive our

SAGA WRITER NEWSLETTER

Packed with **features, competitions, authors'
and readers' letters** and **news of exclusive events,**
it's a 'must-read' for every Annie Murray fan!

Simply fill in your details below and tick to confirm that you would
like to receive saga-related news and promotions and return to us at
Pan Macmillan, Saga Newsletter, 20 New Wharf Road, London, N1 9RR.

NAME _____

ADDRESS _____

_____ POSTCODE _____

EMAIL _____

☐ *I would like to receive saga-related news and promotions (please tick)*

*You can unsubscribe at any time in writing or through our website where you can also see
our privacy policy which explains how we will store and use your data.*

Purchase any of these three
ANNIE MURRAY PAPERBACKS
for just
£3.99 EACH*

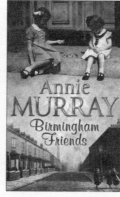
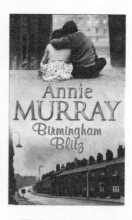

Birmingham Rose   *Birmingham Friends*   *Birmingham Blitz*